I0645347

# SURGE

K.F. BRADSHAW

Surge
By K.F. Bradshaw
Published By
Wishbox Press
Copyright © 2020 by K.F. Bradshaw
ISBN: 978-0-9987518-6-3
First Edition, 2020
Cover by TS95 Studios

All Rights Reserved. This book or any portion thereof may not be reproduced or used in any manner whatsoever without the express written permission of the author except for the use of brief quotations in a book review.

www.kfbradshaw.com

# THE ENCHANTERS TRILOGY

## ENCHANTERS

## CONDUIT

## SURGE

To my wife, who inspired me to write *Enchanters* in the first place. And to all the readers of this series. Your support has meant the world to me and I am so thrilled to present *Surge* to you.

# Chapter 1

# The Resistence

**Damea, 224 2nd Era**
**Azgadar, Azgadaran Empire**

The hollow rattling of dice in a metal cup echoed against the iron bars of the dungeon cells before abruptly ceasing as the pieces were poured onto the table. A long sigh followed.

"Wonderful," the guard muttered before jamming his hand in the black leather satchel that hung from his belt. He pulled out a few bronze coins and tossed them on the table. "Your turn."

His partner for the evening watch chuckled before plucking the coins from the cracked wooden surface. "There, now. No need to be a sore loser."

"The only sore one here is going to be you if you don't hurry up and roll." The guard threw the dice back in the cup and set it down again.

On the far side of the dungeon, cast in the dim, flickering light of a green enchanted lantern was the only occupied cell in the room. The light wavered as the lantern swayed from side to side, casting dark shadows on the occupant inside. Ben Veraun, experienced commander and former general of the Azgadaran Legion sat with his back against the crumbling stone wall, his decorated Legionnaire general's armor replaced with a loose black shirt and pants. His usually cropped dark hair had missed its routine shave and had already begun to grow out since being imprisoned in his cell under the palace.

He rolled his eyes at the guards' exchange. *What a dreary fate for the prisoners down here to have to listen to these two go at it over dice for hours.* He did not consider himself to be the best leader but he had been fair and more importantly, loyal to Empress Ithmeera…unlike these men. *Cowards.*

He gave a long sigh, loud enough for his former subordinates to hear.

The first guard jerked his head in Veraun's direction. "Got something to say, Veraun?"

"As a matter of fact, was just thinking of how disappointed in myself I am for clearly not giving you sorry excuses for Legionnaires enough work to do," Veraun said with a wry smile. "You should consider a new career—you've always been terrible soldiers."

The guard's eyes widened in anger and he started to get up, his armored knee jostling the table. But his partner waved his hand. "Ah, leave him be. He's harmless."

"I assure you I am not," Veraun said.

"Right. You're just *so* dangerous. That must be why you're locked up then. Or," the guard taunted, "is it because you've outgrown your usefulness to Azgadar?"

"Were that the case, I'd be dead. As you can see," Veraun said and climbed to his feet, holding his arms out to demonstrate, "I am not dead."

This time, the guard shot up, knocking the cup over and spilling the dice back onto the table. "You should be!"

Veraun's even voice maintained its coolness. "I am not the one who betrayed the empress."

"No, you just let enchanters bring ruin upon the empire."

Veraun raised an eyebrow. These men were scared, that much was clear. But to parrot the words of the empire's greatest traitor after everything Ithmeera had done for Azgadar was just madness. These soldiers deserved no pity from him. *And they certainly will not receive my mercy when Petra ultimately fails.*

He took a step forward and grabbed the iron bars. "You are weak men," he declared, glaring at the guard. "Your loyalty to Petra will waver, just as it did for Ithmeera. You have no honor and do not deserve to be Legionnaires."

The guard's partner stood up as well and was about to speak when all three paused at a sudden rumbling, which was followed by the unmistakable sound of metal scraping against stone.

"What was that?"

The guard drew his sword. "Don't know. I'll check it out."

Veraun could not hold back a smirk in the dark. He was one of the few in the palace who knew about the secret passage in from the sewers.

An arrow sung through the air and struck the guard's partner in his left shoulder. As he went down moaning, the guard scanned his surroundings, trying to find cover away from the archer hiding in the darkness. Unfortunately, his search was in vain as an armored figure crept up from behind him and wrapped their arms around his neck and face in a death grip, holding him in place as he gasped for air until he finally expired and slumped in his assailant's arms. Another fighter rendered the second guard unconscious before yanking the arrow from his wounded shoulder.

"Tie them up and get me the key," the group's leader, a muscular woman with short black hair and fierce grey eyes ordered as she strode with urgency to Veraun's cell. He recognized her immediately—the guardswoman had stood out during training in the few weeks before the Cataclysm outside the city, besting her fellow Legionnaires and impressing the commanding officers.

"Guardswoman," he greeted, though he was sure his tone betrayed his surprise at her presence and curiosity as to how his rescuers knew of the secret entrance. *Is Elisa with them? If so, then where is the empress?*

"Sir," Guardswoman Taryn answered as the fighter who had taken out the first guard handed her a small metal key. "Just one moment and we'll have you out of here." She inserted the key into the lock and gave it a quick, sharp turn before the mechanism clicked and the door swung open.

"Thank you," Veraun said as he straightened out his clothing. The fighters—he counted at least six of them—gathered behind Taryn before standing at attention. "Now, then. I need a sword. And," he narrowed his eyes at her, "an explanation."

Taryn's intense gaze did not waver. "There will be time for that, sir, but right now we need to get you out of here."

He let out a frustrated huff and pointed past her. "Well, at least tell me who in the world informed you about that door!"

"I did, sir," a familiar, if shaky voice spoke up from the cluster of soldiers.

Veraun tilted his head with interest as Kye stepped forward, standing taller than most of the Legionnaires. At one time, the young man's face had been plastered on posters all over Azgadar, and Veraun could see the effects of the Cataclysm already wearing on him. His short curls had evolved into an unruly blond mop and his face was caked in dirt.

"I told the guardswoman," Kye repeated. "I came back to Azgadar to help. Well, first I was going to meet up with Elisa in Gurdinfield, but I came across the guardswoman near Sadford and I knew I had to help. Other enchanters…" He bit his lip. "I've heard some have been lost already—because of the magic."

*Elisa just couldn't keep her mouth shut, could she?* "How I miss the days when royal secrets used to actually be secret," Veraun grumbled before he had completed processing everything Kye said. For the first time, he noticed the gold ring of the Legion hanging from a chain around Kye's neck. "Wait. Elisa, the empress—you saw them? They're alive?" His annoyance about the secret door being shared was replaced in an instant by a small bubble of hope that maybe, just maybe, his sovereign had survived.

Kye's light brown eyes blazed with excitement as Taryn placed her hand on his shoulder. "Y-yes, sir. I saw them escaping from the sewers just after…it happened. They were going to Gurdinfield to seek help from the queen."

"Queen Lydia? Then there is hope." Veraun pushed past the

Legionnaires and walked to where the guards lay.

Taryn tensed. "Are you certain, sir? Elisa betrayed the empire and—"

"I watched her save Her Majesty's life when Petra attacked." He picked up the first guard's sword and took the sheath as well before sliding the weapon into it. "Elisa is on our side. You will just have to trust me on that."

"Yes, sir," Taryn said, her shoulders relaxing if only for a moment. "What are your orders?"

Veraun looked through the open passage that led into the sewers. "What is the state of the Legion, Guardswoman?"

Once again tense, Taryn answered, though her tone held what Veraun guessed was probably weeks of stress. "We don't know much, sir. Petra controls a sizeable amount. We're still not sure how she was able to convince them to turn against the empress. The ones who refused to betray Her Majesty have either fled or have joined us." She gave her companions a nod of admiration. "We barely escaped the city and have sent in spies for information when we could, but we have lost a few already. Plus, we're too few still and don't have the resources to mount a proper assault to retake the city. But," she said, her voice gaining strength, "we will keep fighting for as long as we draw breath."

Veraun considered her words. He turned to Kye. "Where is your enchanter friend and her Guardian?"

Kye wrung his hands. "Cassie was…tricked by Richard to take all of Damea's magic, sir. Andrea was injured so I took her to Ata in the Western Hills. She's with her mentor—they are working to find Cassie and bring back the magic."

Veraun's memory of Richard was faint, but if the man was truly the one responsible for all this destruction and chaos then there was no question that justice needed to be brought upon him. *But...first we need the empress. And an army.* He looked back at his Legionnaires. Though outnumbered, they were the empire's last hope before the imposter, Petra, brought ruin to a centuries-old dynasty.

"Then we depart for Gurdinfield," he ordered. "If there is any fortune remaining in Damea we will meet the empress and Elisa there." It was a long shot and taking back Azgadar would no doubt require Queen Lydia to meet the obligations of the freshly-signed treaty between the two nations. But it could work. They would have their army and with it, could retake Azgadar. But as Veraun remembered the terror that had struck every citizen in Damea as the sun was blocked out and the skies turned a dead green, he knew even as a non-enchanter it would take more than an army to repair the damage Richard had done.

They would just have to put their faith in Andrea for now. *One thing at a time. First, we save Azgadar and then, Damea.*

# Chapter 2

# Hunted

**Southlands, Gurdinfield**

Elisa squinted as she peered out at Gurdinfield's countryside, the rolling hills disappearing into flat plains. Farther out, patches of forest dotted the Southlands. She knew on a happier morning the tall grasses would have been glowing a brilliant orange from the typically beautiful sunrise. But the greenish-grey skies streaked with the occasional bolt of lightning looming overhead reminded her that these times were anything but happy.

A harsh wind ruffled her copper hair, which had become a greasy tangle of curls since leaving Azgadar. Despite the bit of warmth instilled in the breeze, she shivered. The days had been growing colder and every gust of wind since the cataclysm made the threat of Damea's very life source being drained away a bitter reality.

"Anything?"

Elisa turned to meet the inquisitive green eyes belonging to none other than Ithmeera Cadar, empress of the Azgadaran Empire. "No. Not yet."

"Yet?" Ithmeera tilted her head. "You think they still hunt us?"

"Petra knows you escaped. She's going to keep sending her thugs after us until she has your head. So yes," Elisa said, "I believe they still hunt us. Almost certain of it."

Ithmeera bit her lip. Desperation crept into her voice. "Those 'thugs' are still Legionnaires. *My* Legionnaires."

Elisa returned her gaze to the horizon, scanning everything before her just in case she missed something. She was not in the mood for Ithmeera's denial this morning. "Yes well, *your* Legionnaires have attacked us once already since we left Azgadar. Whatever Petra told them was obviously more than enough to convince them to betray you and form this *New Legion*. Cowards," she spat. But when Ithmeera did not respond, guilt at her own abrasiveness set in. "Come on." She gave a pointed tilt of her head signaling that they continue on their path to the City of Towers, where their ally Queen Lydia, her husband Jacob, and Ithmeera's son Marco were hopefully safe from the chaos that had torn through Damea in the preceding weeks.

"We've been on this path for days," Ithmeera said, drawing her dark green cloak tighter as she trudged behind Elisa in the dirt. "How much farther before we reach my son?"

Elisa's tone softened. "Marco is safe, I promise you." She turned around. "This would be a faster journey had we taken the main road but that will only make it easier for Petra's men to find you."

"Find me? What makes you think they aren't looking for you, too?"

Elisa smirked. "Oh, they'll just kill me. Probably leave my body in some field and take *you* back to Azgadar." When she saw the horrified look on Ithmeera's face she sighed at her tactless words. "We'll be fine as long as we stay off the main road. Probably." She began walking again, with Ithmeera close behind her. "Fimen's Hope is a few days away. We should be safe there."

"I have seen the town on maps. We won't be attacked there?" Ithmeera asked as they reached the summit of another hill.

"I helped defend it not long ago," Elisa explained. "There's a small outpost of Gurdinfielder soldiers there now. They will help us."

"Well then, I hope your outstanding reputation with Queen Lydia has reached the ears of these soldiers."

Elisa bit back a snap to Ithmeera's backhanded remark. In truth, the empress's occasional comments about her service to Gurdinfield were getting tiring. While she had not been welcomed back into the empire's service with open arms, Elisa half-hoped that Ithmeera at the very least saw her as a Legionnaire again. *Perhaps even that is too much to hope for.*

Instead she opted for a more neutral response. "You and me both."

* * *

Late into the evening, the pair sat around a small campfire hidden in one of the clustered patches of trees. Their meager supplies, including Elisa's dagger and two old swords they had found at her house in Sadford, had been cast to the side of the fire, along with an almost empty cooking pot. Although the sky remained a muted green, Elisa could spot a few stars as she gazed up beyond the rising plumes of smoke from the fire. The typical scurrying of small nocturnal animals running over fallen twigs and call of birds from the trees were something Elisa was used to hearing at night out here. But tonight, there was only the crackling of the fire to keep them company. Whether the animals had migrated somewhere else or something darker was at work due to the Cataclysm, Elisa couldn't tell. Truthfully, she wasn't sure if she *wanted* to know. An eeriness hung in the air—Elisa was no poet but if she had to pick one word to describe the savanna tonight, "dying" would have fit perfectly.

"I will never get used to this." Ithmeera's voice broke their prolonged silence. After the sun went down, Ithmeera had struggled to keep up with Elisa, a subtle suggestion that they needed to stop and rest for the night before carrying on to Fimen's Hope in the morning.

A chilled breeze swept through the trees, disrupting the steady flames and causing Elisa to tuck her knees in before wrapping her arms around them. She looked back at Ithmeera, watching as the shadows from the flames danced upon her soft features. "To what?"

Ithmeera gestured around them. "This. Sleeping out here in the wilderness. Being away from the city…and Marco." She looked away, her lower lip quivering.

"I told you he's—"

"I know what you said. You've been saying that since we

left Azgadar." The terseness in Ithmeera's voice gave way to the sadness that settled over them night after night since their escape.

Elisa shrugged. "Because it's true."

"You don't know that."

*All right.* Elisa climbed to her feet and walked the few steps over to the pile of blades in the dirt. Ithmeera watched her with curious eyes. "Take one."

"Excuse me?"

"You heard me," Elisa commanded, surprising herself at her own boldness. "I'm tired of you moping like this every single night. We will get to Marco soon, but we can't do that if Petra's men find us first."

Ithmeera stood up and dusted off the long dark brown dress she'd acquired in Sadford. "Isn't it a bodyguard's job to protect her charge?" she asked.

"I don't recall being reinstated as such," Elisa said dryly, noting Ithmeera's lack of response. She picked up both swords and tested the weight of the one in her right hand before offering it to Ithmeera. "Besides, I can hold off one, maybe two assassins. I can't protect you from ten men."

Ithmeera appeared uneasy as she looked at the sword before grasping the hilt, shifting her weight on her feet slightly as she adjusted to the heaviness of the weapon. "I haven't used one of these in *years*, Elisa."

Elisa let a smile escape. "No time better than the present to get back into it." She held up her sword. "Come on, then."

Ithmeera glanced at her before looking at her own blade and

then back at her. Nervousness entered her tone. "What if I hurt you?"

That got a deep laugh out of Elisa. "You won't. Come on. By the time you swing that sword, Petra's men will already be here."

Ithmeera rolled her eyes and gave a hesitant swing at Elisa, who stepped back with ease, avoiding the blade entirely.

Elisa let the blade fall to her side. "That was rather pathetic."

"*Pathetic?*" Ithmeera's eyebrows went up. "Is that how you speak to all the monarchs you serve or am I the exception?" She rolled her shoulders back. "It's been a while since I held a sword is all. I'm out of practice and…and I didn't want to hurt you on accident."

Elisa leveled with her. "Your Majesty, Kye was more aggressive than you during our sparring. Surely you recall *some* of your Legionnaire training."

"That was Erik's interest, not mine," Ithmeera admitted. "I skipped more lessons than I attended." She shook her head and raised her sword again. "All right, all right. Again, then."

She surprised Elisa when she lunged forward, such that Elisa had to actually block to avoid having her hand cut by the blade, the clang of metal on metal cutting into the quietness of the campsite. She pushed back and parried, hoping Ithmeera would defend herself and was impressed yet again when Ithmeera blocked her attack. She grinned, deciding to go for one more attack, and took a step forward. Unfortunately, Ithmeera's reaction was to step back and as she did so, her boot caught on one of the piles of twigs on the ground and she slipped before falling backwards—arms flailing as the sword fell from her hand.

Elisa reacted immediately. Her hand shot out to grab Ithmeera's and caught it, just keeping her from hitting the ground. "Footwork."

Ithmeera gazed up at her, breathless—the shock apparent on her face from the quick turn of events. "One of the lessons I skipped, apparently." She allowed Elisa to help her to her feet and looked down to where her sword had fallen. "I suppose we can add 'terrible swordswoman' to the list of reasons behind the Legion's mutiny against me," she added with a heavy sigh.

Elisa's lips tightened as she picked up the sword and set it down along with her own near their supplies. Ithmeera had been blaming herself for Petra and the New Legion's actions since their escape and Elisa always felt she never knew the right thing to say. "You did well enough, considering how long it's been since you held a sword."

Ithmeera gave her a dismissive wave as she went to prepare her bed for the night. "I don't need you to try to make me feel better, Elisa." She arranged the blankets so that they looked mostly comfortable before covering herself with the heavier ones. "I'm going to sleep. You may have the first watch. Good night."

Elisa waited until Ithmeera rolled to face away from her before shaking her head in dismay. She had mostly tried to keep Ithmeera's spirits up during their journey, she really had. *What can you say to a woman who has lost her kingdom in a day and whose son is far away in another kingdom to make her feel better?* And it didn't help that Ithmeera found every opportunity to passive-aggressively remind Elisa of her service to Diana after she had fled Azgadar.

She thought, perhaps in naivety, that after returning Erik's sword *and* rescuing Ithmeera when Petra attacked that maybe, just maybe Ithmeera would reinstate her status as a Legionnaire—perhaps even reinstate her as a Royal Guard, even though she had been acting in that capacity ever since they escaped Azgadar together. There had been a few lighthearted moments between them on their journey to the City of Towers so far, even some jokes exchanged, but nothing to indicate that Ithmeera had truly forgiven her for leaving, serving Diana and helping the Guardians, and killing Erik. *I am a fool.*

She considering arranging her own blankets to get comfortable but reconsidered when she realized she was already tired and did not want to accidentally fall asleep. Instead she retook her seat by the fire, her thoughts migrating to Andrea and Kye. She hoped they were all right and that Andrea had recovered from whatever injuries she had sustained from the Cataclysm. But even if she had, Elisa wondered how they were going to fix this.

*One day at a time. Just get to Fimen's Hope.* She grabbed a blanket anyway and threw it around her shoulders before focusing on keeping watch as she tried to not let the silence get to her.

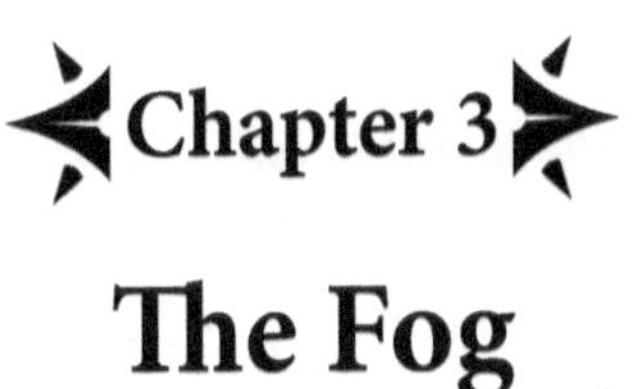

# Chapter 3

# The Fog

**Ata, The Western Hills**

*"Wait for the silence. Then…look for a light."*

*She'd tried to, she really had. But there was only the fog. The same grey fog that had welcomed her for weeks every time she'd tried this. Thicker clouds settled at her knees—they were like smoke, billowing and swirling around her. There was no sound save her own shaky breathing and even that seemed off. It was as though something was trying its hardest to smother any life here and when she pushed against it, it pushed back.*

*Whatever this place was it was lonely. Part of her wished Meredith had never showed it to her but she needed to be here.*

*She needed to find Cassie.*

*"Where are you?" she wondered out loud. She pressed her boot into the ground to test it and found the soil soft. There were no landmarks or structures to be seen so she picked a direction and walked.*

*It must have been hours, or perhaps a few minutes—she could never tell how time passed here—when something appeared… the faintest glimmer of blue light. It was weak and flickered like a dying flame, but it was there.*

*As she slowly approached, she thought she heard…talking? Cassie. It was faint and echoed all around her, the familiar inflections pricking at her ears. But Meredith had told her not to trust everything she heard here. "What you hear may not be happening when you think it is. Sometimes it's a memory. Other times it's a fragment of a memory," Meredith had said. She wanted to trust it though, and gravitated toward the sound hoping to discover a clue or even to take comfort in the fact that it was Cassie's voice she was hearing.*

*The light flickered again before going out. Then there was silence.*

*"No," she pleaded, frantically turning around hoping the light might have simply moved. But there was nothing. "No, no!" She fell to her knees, covering her face with her hands as a strangled cry of anguish escaped her. She had been here every night— waiting in the fog for something, anything that might lead her to Cassie. So many tries, all of them ending in failure. How did Meredith do this without losing her mind?*

*She blinked back tears. "I'm sorry."*

*The light flickered back on.*

*Her eyes went wide when she saw it. She climbed to her feet before stumbling into a run toward it, willing her legs to push her faster before she lost the light again.*

*"…you would just stop for one moment and hear me out—"*

*Richard. His tone was soft, almost soothing. It was hard to match this voice with the same man that forced his own daughter to steal Damea's magic and bring the land to the brink of total destruction. But it was Richard, she had no doubt about it.*

*Her lungs burned from running as she listened. He continued to speak but she could only hear murmuring as the light flickered again—this time far brighter, turning a brilliant white.*

*"...ing bastard! You're insane if you actually think that will work. I don't wa—"*

Cassie! *She had found her! She knew she had to look closer. There had to be a clue—something that would tell her where Richard was keeping Cassie after they'd disappeared from the fields outside Azgadar.*

*"Show me," she whispered, willing her mind and her magic to probe deeper. But just as she did, the light faded once more, shrouding her in darkness again as she felt herself growing weak, her movements sluggish.*

*There was just not enough magic.*

Andrea gasped as the back of her head hit the straw bed behind her. When her eyes opened, she found herself staring at the high rafters of her parents' barn. She heard Kira, her family's horse, give a light snort of acknowledgement. Saturated green rays of sunset crept in through the cracks in the ceiling—they had begun in the morning, which meant she must have been out for *hours*. She blinked a few times to catch her bearings before propping herself up on her elbows. When she felt the presence of someone next to her, she turned her head to the left and found Meredith sitting on her father's favorite work stool. Her mentor's grey-streaked hair was pulled back in a low bun and she sat comfortably in her simple green tunic and dark leggings, not much different from what Andrea was wearing.

"You were there much longer this time," was Meredith's cool, if accurate greeting.

Andrea pushed herself to sit up, even though it felt like she needed twice her own strength to do it. She definitely felt weaker than the prior week. *Maybe I just need to eat something.* "I saw a light."

Meredith was not impressed. "You said that last night."

Andrea shook her head. "It was much brighter this time. I even heard them."

Meredith perked up at that. "You could hear them?"

"Bits and pieces," Andrea clarified. "I'm so close to finding them, Meredith, I *know* I am." She took a deep breath—she knew this was going to be a hard ask. "If I just had a little more magic I could—"

"No."

*Figures.* "Why not?" Andrea protested. "You said you'd help me find them."

Meredith gave her a faint smile, though her small grey eyes were devoid of any pity for Andrea. "And I am. But we agreed when we started: we do it my way or not at all." She stood and offered her hand to Andrea, who sighed before taking it and allowing herself to be pulled up.

"I could find them with more magic," Andrea repeated as she ran her hand through her hair. "Her voice was so clear. It was like I was there with her."

"And Richard?"

Andrea paused. She knew Meredith still did not believe her about Richard's betrayal and the horrible things he had done despite everything she had told her. "He was there, yes. They were arguing."

"About what?"

"I don't know." Andrea rubbed the tiredness from her eyes. Every attempt to find Cassie's projection left her weak and drowsy. She knew she should probably eat something. "I could barely make out what they were saying and then I was pulled away," she said as she wandered over to the filled bucket they had brought outside with them earlier. After splashing some of the cool water on her face, she grimaced when she saw her reflection.

Since the Cataclysm, she had been practicing projection reading with Meredith almost nonstop, only breaking to eat and sleep occasionally. Her normally wavy dark hair fell flat against gaunt cheeks, her hazel eyes bloodshot from the stress of the last few weeks. A scar crossed her right cheek—an injury she had received in the City of Towers when the Azgadaran Legion had invaded Gurdinfield.

She was about to ask Meredith if they should break for dinner before trying again when a sharp pain shot through her right arm. She grabbed it involuntarily and gritted her teeth as nausea overcame her.

"It's time?" Meredith asked quietly.

Andrea made no effort to hide the ache. "It never really stops burning."

"Let me see." Meredith reached out and pulled up the sleeve of Andrea's shirt revealing the purple and black weave of jagged cuts that crawled up her arm and across the right side of her upper body. They were not open wounds but the sickening black with which they pulsed served as a warning to any enchanter who would try to use magic after the Cataclysm. She winced as she let a curious finger touch one of the cuts.

Andrea jerked away. "Don't. Now, my potion, please."

Meredith gave her a disapproving look. "Just a sip." She pulled a small vial from her pocket. About a quarter of the contents remained—a potion Andrea had brewed that was infused with magic. She stared at it and hesitated for longer than Andrea had patience for.

"My potion, Meredith."

Meredith gave the potion one last glance before offering it to Andrea, who practically snatched it from her hands, tore off the cork and quickly drank the rest of it with great relief. She grimaced and leaned against the wall as soon as the liquid slid down her throat—the stuff was foul and nearly made her hurl.

"Thank you," she gasped once the nausea had passed and was replaced by the tingling, almost pleasant feeling the potion left her with. When her arm throbbed again, she looked down and saw the black pulsing had been replaced with a white glow that flowed throughout the complex weave of wounds across her body. While it unnerved her to see magic reacting on her own skin like that, she could not deny the sensation left her wanting more of the potion.

"If I had more, I could see them better. Maybe even find out where they are exactly," she tried again.

Meredith's answer did not change. "Again, no. You only have two potions left. If you go through those on the possibility that you *might* be able to find them, then what?"

"I was so *close*, Meredith! I—"

"And you'll be useless to both Cassie and myself if you die before we can get to them!" Meredith's raised voice swiftly silenced Andrea's protests. She had not seen Meredith this upset since that fateful night of their final experiment to wake Richard in the old manor in the Black Forest.

Sullen from Meredith's scolding, Andrea let her hand wander to the woven threaded bracelet around her right wrist. Just knowing it was from Cassie should have made her ecstatic, but right now it served as a cold reminder of how she had failed her partner.

"We will find them, Andrea. You need to be patient, though. It took me years to master projection readings. You're doing well but you're not there yet," Meredith said, her tone actually bordering on *kind*, which caught Andrea by surprise. "Come. Your mother prepared dinner earlier while you were out." She placed her hand on Andrea's back and began to lead her back to the house.

# Chapter 4

# A Destination

Andrea waited up late into the night until her parents and Meredith had gone to sleep. She grabbed her favorite midnight-blue cloak—a gift Meredith had given her when she'd first left Ata four years earlier—a small traveling satchel, and one of the two remaining potions from her dresser. While Meredith had insisted on holding onto one of the vials during their projection experiments, Andrea kept the other in her room where she could easily access it in the event her injury acted up again.

Taking extra care to be silent as to not wake anyone, she crept out the front door—closing it carefully behind her—and walked to the barn where Kira was. A few minutes later, the horse was saddled and Andrea was riding to her destination: the outskirts of Ata.

She knew the area around the town better than most, given that she spent a great deal of time in her adolescence trying to escape her parents' watchful eyes so she could practice magic.

She held her cloak close to herself as she rode into the clear, cool night—the evening breezes having grown colder over the weeks as fall approached the Western Hills—and passed Bill's inn, a few closed shops, and the stables before leaving the town limits. A small wooded area, the very same one she and Cassie had met Richard in, sat at the top of a low hill directly ahead.

She coaxed Kira into a canter and the two of them headed up the hill. Wind whipped at Andrea's face as the distance between her and Ata grew and for a fleeting moment, she let her mind wander to a happier time when she and Cassie would ride together. She would hold the reins, of course, while Cassie had her arms wrapped around her waist from behind. She knew Cassie's stomach did not sit well when on horseback but to Andrea there was almost nothing better than the two of them riding in comfortable silence with Cassie occasionally leaning on her and holding her tightly as a wonderful reminder that they were *together*.

She sighed as the serene memory of riding to the Western Hills together was replaced by that horrifying moment when Richard forced Cassie to absorb Damea's magic. The terror on Cassie's face, her contorted expression of denial when she saw Andrea trying to use that barrier to save her. The lightning *burning* as it crawled up Andrea's arm and—

She shuddered, snapping out of the trance and finding herself still on Kira—stopped and at the edge of the woods.

She hopped off and took the reins, leading Kira into the cluster of trees and half-wondering if she would run into anyone here. She hoped not. Having Kye with her might have been a nice distraction, but she didn't need distractions right now. *That and he probably would have tried to stop me.* She knew he would have wanted to help her, but Andrea was convinced he had made the right choice when he returned to Azgadar rather than staying in Ata and worrying about her. No, she needed the isolation and silence to focus on the reason she came all the way out here in the middle of the night.

The clearing she found would do fine. She tied Kira to one of the surrounding trees and sat down a few steps away, crushing several already dead leaves beneath her. After flipping open her satchel, she removed the vial she'd brought along and tossed the bag aside.

She eyed the potion and made a silent promise to Cassie before ripping off the cork and drinking the entire vial in a few gulps.

The instant the potion hit her stomach she doubled over, gasping in pain as the vial fell from her hand and hit the forest floor with a muted thud. Her arm throbbed—she sighed with relief as the potent magic seeped into the scars and soothed the ever-present burn. Her vision blurred and her head ached with a pressure so strong she was certain she would pass out.

Then…it was over. Andrea blinked a few times to refocus before realizing she actually felt *normal*. There was no burning, no pressure, and no weakness. Glancing down at her arm she was nearly mesmerized by the bright alternating white and blue glow her scars gave off.

She let out a quiet laugh, probably for the first time since the Cataclysm. She had spent most of her life trying to become an enchanter and she had wound up becoming the enchanted "artifact" herself.

Her eyes closed and she took a deep breath before letting her mind reach for the magic within her. She did her best to clear her mind of any doubts or worries, particularly those concerning what would happen if she failed. *Can't think about that right now. Need to find her first.*

While her abilities did not remotely approach Kye's sheer raw power, Andrea had always prided herself on being an excellent student. Meredith had been doubtful at first about whether she could actually teach Andrea how to read projections. Weeks later, she was able to ease in and out of the realm deep within her mind where she needed to be. In a lighter, less apocalyptic situation, she would have been overjoyed. But not anymore. Reading projections, enchanting, magic—all of it was just a means to an end for Andrea.

Pushing forward in her mind, she could see the fog ahead. *Just a few more steps...*

*She had made it. The grey fog surrounded her as before only this time, she knew where to go. The light appeared almost immediately, already a blinding white. The sluggishness from before was not there as she approached the light with ease that only pure magic could provide her with.*

*The voices came even sooner. She heard Richard first. The usual calm in his voice was missing, though. He sounded frustrated and she couldn't help but take pleasure in that.*

*"...fault. I asked you to do one thing—take the magic—and you couldn't even do that. What am I supposed to do with you?"*

*Bastard. She wished with all of her being she was there with him. With the amount of magic in her, casting a fireball would be so easy...*

*"How about letting me go? Or does that not fit into your crazy 'let's go home but make sure we kill everyone on the way out' plan?" Cassie! She pushed back tears, wanting to laugh with*

*happiness at the fact that Cassie was still fighting Richard and cry at not being able to be with her.*

*Where are you? She pushed further, focusing all of her willpower on the light.* Just a bit more…

*There it was, clear as day. The Black Forest. Of course! Probably Meredith's house—I should have known! She had done it. But they were still talking. She wanted to know what they were saying. And her magic appeared to be holding.* It wouldn't hurt to stay a bit longer, right?

*"The only reason I've put up with this attitude is because I need you. But once we are back in Tarrasha this will not be tolerated. Not that you have a choice anyway."*

*"Right. You had to literally curse me to get me to do what you want. What the hell did my mother see in you?"*

*She wondered the same thing.*

*"Enough. Azgadar has what we need but with that shield it's impossible."*

Shield? What shield? And what do they need from Azgadar?

*"Oh, well. Time to let me go, then," Cassie said.*

*"Go where exactly? You've no home here, Cassie. The only reason these people tolerated you was because you were courting Gurdinfield's Royal Enchanter," Richard sneered. "And, well, I'm afraid you can't rely on her any longer seeing as how she's dead. Her fault though—you did warn her."*

*The rattle of heavy chains and Cassie's ragged shout startled her. Something fell on the ground and shattered, though she couldn't see what. Her heart sank when she realized Cassie must have been bound by those chains.* She thinks I'm dead.

"There, now," Richard said, his tone making that disturbing shift from spiteful to caring. "You'll be happier when we're back home and you can be around people who truly care about you."

"She did care about me. But you wouldn't know anything about that would you?" Cassie snapped.

Richard laughed. It was cold, mirthless, and sent shivers down Andrea's spine. Monster. "Don't be delusional, Cassie. She cared about your abilities. She cared about what you could do for her. There are people who give to this world and people who take from it. Enchanters like Andrea fall into the latter. You and I, though—"

"Don't even try to compare us. I'm nothing like you!"

"Everything I've done, everything I'm doing, I do it for you, Cassie. I want us to be a family again. Now, I must get back to work. There must be a way to get to Azgadar without being detected."

"People are going to find out what you did," Cassie said. "Wait until the Grandmaster finds out you screwed him over and sends his entire army to kill you."

"The Grandmaster...Gurith," Richard breathed.

History was not her expertise but she realized what Richard must have been thinking. Cassie, no...

"Perhaps you take after me more than I give you credit for," Richard said, not bothering to hide the glee in his tone. "I forget even a pit like Gurith once used magic to build its cities."

"W-what do you mean?"

"Not now. I need to get our things in order." A pause. "Better try to get some rest tonight. We leave tomorrow."

*She wanted to yell out at Richard, threaten him, or even let Cassie know she wasn't alone and that Richard was nothing but a traitorous liar. But she knew neither would hear her.*

*Their voices grew muffled and the fog began to swirl around her as the sluggishness set in. The magic was still there but something was pulling her back…*

Andrea's eyes flew open to Meredith's hand clamping down on her shoulder, shaking her from her trance. She inhaled deeply before coughing a few times until her breathing stabilized.

"I've been looking everywhere for you. Your parents have been asking every person in this damn town if they've seen you!" Meredith exclaimed. She held up the empty vial and shook it. "Are you mad? Do you know what you've done?"

"I-I found them," was Andrea's quiet reply.

Meredith glared at her. "You could have doomed this entire mission because you couldn't be patient for once!" She stood up, the morning glow illuminating the clearing and making Andrea realize she had been there all night.

Meredith continued to rant. "I don't know what I was thinking, hoping that you would actually *listen* to me for once and not go off on your own whenever you heard something you didn't agree with!"

Andrea raised her voice to compete with Meredith's. She wasn't about to let her discovery be for naught. "I *found* them. Doesn't that mean anything to you?"

"Of course it does!" Meredith threw up her hands. "But you've only one potion left. If we find them—and that's a big *if*—do you really think you and Cassie are going to ride off together and the magic is just going to fix itself?"

"No, but—"

"Because you don't *think*, Andrea. It's always been about what *you* want right now. Mark my words, this…selfishness is going to get someone killed."

Andrea stood up. She didn't have time for one of Meredith's long lectures. They could deal with talks of consequences later. "Enough! They're going to Gurith, Meredith."

Meredith raised both eyebrows. "You…you heard them again?"

"I did," Andrea said. She tilted her head. "You seemed surprised earlier, too. Should I not be able to hear their voices?"

"It's not normal, no," Meredith confirmed. "But I suppose having the magic within you to draw from might have heightened your sensitivity to projections." She appeared deep in thought. "Gurith, you said?"

"Yes. Richard wanted to go to Azgadar but there's a…a shield in the way. So, he decided on Gurith instead. Said that they used to use magic to build their cities."

Meredith's eyes lit up. "Of course!" She gave a low hum. "If what you've told me so far is true…"

Andrea rolled her eyes. "It's all true, Meredith and I've told you this before. Richard is not who you thought he was."

"…they must be trying to extract magic from structures. In this case, the Shadow Arena." She seemed satisfied with her conclusion. "We're in luck. I happen to know the way."

Andrea recalled her meeting in Gurdinfield with

Grandmaster Balos of Gurith's Merchants' Guild. Balos had seem quite interested in her—more specifically, in her abilities. She hadn't made up her mind on whether she trusted him or not and she did not know what Cassie was referring to when she mentioned Richard betraying the Grandmaster somehow. Still, the Merchants' Guild had an agreement with Gurdinfield, and Andrea could use that to her advantage to find Cassie. "Taking magic from *any* structure will destabilize it," she parroted from her lessons. "If the magic from a building the size of the arena is taken, that would surely destroy part of the city." *Not that Richard would care.* "I know the Grandmaster. I'm not sure I trust him, but if his people's safety is at stake, he might help us."

Meredith did not appear bothered by her warning, and simply gestured toward Kira. "Well, then. We should head out today if we can. But," she said, "you get to be the one to explain to your parents where you were all night."

# Chapter 5

# Loyalties

Master Tobias clutched the crinkled piece of parchment in his hands as he made his way to the throne room. The soles of his boots clicked loudly on the marble floor, the high ceilings carrying the echoes of his hurried steps as he approached the two stone-faced Legionnaires guarding the doors.

"Let me pass," he ordered. "I've urgent news for the steward."

The guard on his left gave him a hard stare. "Her Grace is not to be disturbed. You'll tell us and we can deliver the message."

Tobias stood firm. No matter the state of the empire he would not allow these thugs to order him about. He offered a strained smile. "I'm afraid my news is for the steward's ears only. I'm sure Her Grace has informed you that as head royal enchanter it is my duty to the empire to report on all things magic-related. There are many intricacies that come with that and I would prefer I present her the news personally in case she has any questions only I can answer."

The guard who had refused him entry curled his lip and held his defensive stance. The standoff seemed to last forever until to Tobias's relief, the other guard spoke up in a grumble. "Ah, let him pass. Not like he's got any power left anyway."

The first guard said nothing but moved aside, his hostile gaze unwavering.

"Go in, but make it brief. The steward's not in a good mood today," the second guard said as he opened the door to let Tobias pass.

Still gripping the parchment, Tobias entered the throne room, which to his surprise had still not had its décor changed out despite Petra's promises after she took the throne. The blood-red and gold banners donning the familiar shield and double blade sigil of the Cadar dynasty still hung from the high walls between long, thin windows. The green light creeping in from the darkened skies outside made the usually well-lit, open room feel small and airless. His thoughts drifted to the empress. After the Cataclysm, he'd heard rumors that Ithmeera had escaped in the wake of Petra and the New Legion's mutiny against the crown. He hoped that, wherever she was, she was safe.

He tried to focus on the present, where his attention was most needed and he could actually be useful…well, as useful as an enchanter in a magicless land could be anyway. The empress might have been gone, but he could still help the people of Azgadar.

He approached the white marble steps leading up to the throne and knelt before Petra, the empire's new leader. With her blonde hair pinned back, her petite frame looked even smaller on the throne than usual, and rather than appearing imposing as Ithmeera often did to visitors, Petra just seemed out of place. Her dark eyes glowered at him—it was obvious she barely tolerated his presence in the palace and he knew the day would come when she no longer wanted him around.

He cleared his throat, hoping today was not that day. "Your Grace," he said, announcing himself. "You requested I update you on all matters magic-related. I am here to report…with your permission of course."

Petra eyed him warily before beckoning him with her hand to continue. "Make it quick. I'm in no mood for your posturing, old man."

Tobias faltered before unrolling the parchment with shaky hands. "O-of course. First, there has been…" He swallowed. "One enchanter lost this week. Their possessions have been sent to their family."

Petra seemed unbothered by the news. "Cause of death?"

"She ended her own life when she drew on her own essence to cast a fireball at some of your soldiers in the Market District disturbance a few days ago," Tobias said, trying not to allow the graveness of the news affect his delivery of it. He knew Petra had no love for enchanters—there was no reason she would feel pity for them now especially after the near riot that had occurred in the Market District days earlier.

Petra shook her head in dismay. "A fool. As though we do not have enough to worry about. These enchanters will do anything to get attention, even if it means risking their lives and the lives of those who are trying to protect this city."

"I've received reports that the Market District incident was started by two Legionnaires who were attempting to purchase enchanted artifacts from her shop," Tobias offered. "When the woman in question would not sell to them, they attacked her."

"Ridiculous!" Petra snapped and gave a dismissive wave of her hand. "You may want to reassess your sources, *Master Tobias*. These 'reports' are nothing more than the ramblings of desperate apologists. And selling enchanted artifacts is illegal. Surely you're not that stupid."

It took all of Tobias's will to remain patient. "Of course not, Your Grace. I will look into them."

His answer seemed to satisfy her. "Good. This delusion that we should hand over control of magic to any idiot who can cast a light needs to end." She looked him in the eye. "Do you know why I did not assume the title of 'empress', Tobias?" she asked.

Tobias swallowed at her low but dangerous tone. Ithmeera's moods had always been relatively easy for him to read and predict. Petra, however, was unpredictable, and he never knew if a conversation would end with his dismissal, his imprisonment, or worse. "I-I do not, Your Grace."

Petra smirked. "This empire was once incredibly powerful. But that was before this land and the goodwill of its people were abused by the Cadar dynasty. Enchanters misusing magic are what caused the Starving. Enchanters caused *this*." She pointed at the window closest to them. "The New Legion has no empress or emperor. I was appointed Steward so that I could repair the things that were broken. We will rebuild the Legion to rival what they were in centuries past. And once I'm done, I will step down and the people of Azgadar will finally be allowed to decide their own futures!" Frustration rose in her voice as she stood up. "Your empress nearly caused the downfall of a great nation with her misguided, romantic notions about magic and alliances and let her personal issues cloud her judgement.

*That* is why we are in this situation and why I will not allow enchanters to run around unchecked. And anyone who does not comply with these rules will be subject to imprisonment or death. Is that understood?"

Tobias was silent as her harsh words reverberated throughout the room. He waited a few moments longer before finally bowing his head. "Yes, of course, Your Grace."

A few strands of Petra's hair fell out of place during her outburst. She pushed them behind her ears as she composed herself before speaking again. "Not to worry—we will find Ithmeera soon enough."

"We are…still looking for her, Your Grace?" he asked.

"Of course. I have some of my best searching for her and Elisa as we speak as well as Veraun. But as long as we're on the subject—the shield. What is its status?"

"It's still holding," he said slowly. "I would be remiss if I did not remind you that it was only intended for the direst of emergencies—"

"And would you not call this dire?" Petra demanded.

Tobias tried to ignore the lump in his throat. "I—yes, Your Grace. The shield was designed centuries ago in the event our enemies tried to steal magic from the city. But it also requires magic to power—a great deal of it, and I fear we will run out before we can find whoever did this."

Petra narrowed her eyes at him. "Then I suggest we focus harder on finding whoever did this and quickly. In the meantime, I will require all citizens to donate all enchanted artifacts in their possession. The Legion can see to it. Azgadar must be protected at any cost." She took her seat on the throne once more. "If there's nothing else to discuss, Tobias, you may leave."

Knowing when to hold his tongue, Tobias bowed a final time before turning to leave the room.

"Master Tobias?" Petra called. He turned.

She smiled, and it unnerved him to think she once guarded Marco. "Keep my words in mind," she said. "I expect the coming days will test us all. I would hate to see your experience wasted on old loyalties."

# Chapter 6

# Recruited

"Put the rest of the gear in that pile. We'll sort through it later." Taking charge was something Taryn was no stranger to, but she had not expected her promotion in the Legion to come about quite like this. But here she was—helping General Veraun himself lead a resistance all the way to Gurdinfield on the hope that Queen Lydia would lend them her army to take the empire back.

It certainly wasn't a scenario Taryn had trained for, but she took comfort in the fact that protecting the empire was what she had trained for. *This certainly counts.*

They traveled from dawn to dusk, stopping only to make camp once the sun set. There had been some skirmishes with a few of Petra's New Legion already—traitorous Legionnaires who believed every problem in the empire traced back to enchanters and Ithmeera's handling of the Restoration—but their numbers outside of Azgadar had been small and not much of a challenge to overcome. Many of the citizens on the outskirts were simply afraid, the green skies telling enough to conclude the world was not right. General Veraun's charisma had been invaluable in convincing these people to assist the

Legion with provisions. Even the Legion fort in Sadford, which had fortunately not been corrupted by the New Legion yet, was more than happy to donate soldiers and additional supplies when their general had arrived on their doorstep.

As Taryn observed her soldiers sorting out the supplies, Veraun approached and took a stance beside her. His hair was once again back to its usual cropped length. "It never ceases to amaze me how efficient they are, even if it's just putting up camp."

"They're simply doing what's expected, sir," she replied, noting the daylight beginning to be replaced by the glow of campfires.

He nodded toward the sky. "Going about your daily routine with *that* hanging above you is not easy. You have led them well, Taryn. When this is all over and we are back in Azgadar, there will be opportunities available that require someone with your capabilities."

Taryn's voice caught in her throat. *Opportunities.* She wanted to laugh—joke that in the weeks preceding the mutiny her biggest concern was keeping her recruitment numbers high. Now the top-ranking officer in the Legion was telling her he had career plans for her if they won. *No, once we've won.* "I…appreciate that, sir. I look forward to serving Her Majesty however I can."

He rolled his shoulders back. "We should reach the City of Towers soon if we keep this pace. With luck, the empress will be there to greet us and we can plan our retaking of the capital."

Taryn said nothing at first, her grey eyes following Kye instead. The rather scrawny young man shooed away other

Legionnaires offering assistance as he struggled with an armful of blades while carrying them to the quartermaster on the other side of camp to be sharpened.

"That boy is a mystery, I swear," Veraun said.

"He carries Her Majesty's ring," Taryn answered. "He is eager to prove himself, I think."

Veraun crossed his arms. "I'll say. He scurries from me when I approach, though. Probably thinks I'm going to arrest him."

Taryn raised an eyebrow. "Are the charges true, sir? Did he kill his family?" She watched as Kye finally arrived at the quartermaster's station, covered in sweat, where he practically dumped all the swords at the bewildered quartermaster's feet.

"They are," Veraun said, his fatigue from the day's travels surfacing in his tone. "We believe it was an accident." He sighed. "Such a waste of life. Petra is insane, but she is right about one thing: magic *is* dangerous. I have watched it ruin too many lives to believe otherwise."

"Sir," Taryn began, folding her hands. "If I may ask, the charges against Elisa…?"

He chuckled and rubbed the back of his head. "You are full of questions today, Guardswoman."

"I meant no disrespect," she rushed.

"Of course, I understand. Elisa's situation is…complicated." He paused; his thoughts seemingly distant, as though he was remembering a fond memory. "Even I don't know all the details of it, but Her Majesty trusts her completely. That's all I know." He glanced at her. "What have you heard?"

She chose her words carefully, not wanting the general to

think her a gossip or slanderer of fellow, even former fellow Legionnaires. "That her father had been abusing magic. That her family plotted the empress's death after Lord Philip died and after the two of you were no longer...erm, involved." Saying the words out loud and especially to her commanding officer left her feeling awkward and uncomfortable.

"Ah," was Veraun's simple reply.

Taryn turned to him. "My deepest apologies, sir, I was only repeating what we had been told in the barracks."

But he did not appear bothered by her stammering or her words themselves. "At ease. I lived in the barracks for a long time and I know how rumors spread. It's the worst-kept secret in the Legion that Elisa and I courted, albeit a brief time." He smiled. "We were terrible for each other. I was rising in the ranks and did not have the time necessary to be a proper suitor. She was often at Her Majesty's side whenever there was a special event, which was often. It would have never worked."

Taryn was speechless at how open he was about the situation and let him continue.

"Elisa would probably kill me for telling you this but I discovered her father's addiction when I visited her family's home for dinner. I reported it to General Cadar of course." Veraun's smile faded. "Elisa asked me not to say anything, but I could not forsake my duty, not even for her."

"It would have been treason had you not reported it, sir."

"Yes," he agreed and Taryn could see the conflict in his eyes as he continued. "General Cadar ordered Elisa to arrest her father. When she refused, he ordered her execution. Her father intervened—a fatal error on his part." He shook his head. "Guardswoman, make no mistake: Cadar was my best friend and a part of me will never forgive Elisa for killing him. But… there were other options. There usually are."

"I understand, sir."

"Erik told us Elisa and her father had been planning a coup for some time. He took it upon himself to inform the empress and…and that was that." His jaw tightened. "We cannot go back in time, of course, but there are times I wonder if I would have made the same decision if given a second chance."

"You did your duty, sir," Taryn insisted. But she could not deny a part of her felt sorry for Elisa and her family. Serving the empress in such a personal capacity was a life oath, and Elisa lost everything doing it. "If I may ask, sir, the coup. How was Elisa planning to harm the empress?"

Veraun's pale eyes met hers, the regret in them clear. "There was no plan, Guardswoman." He clapped her on the back, the darkened mood around them lifting immediately. "Now then, why don't we see about some food? You there, boy!" he barked.

When Kye realized Veraun was addressing him, he cringed for a moment before running up to them. Taryn frowned as she took note of the condition of his clothes. The tunic and vest he wore had faded to a dull brown and grey, its original colors unrecognizable. The edges of his sleeves were frayed and dotted with holes. His pants were caked in dried mud and Taryn had to wonder what in the world he was doing that the other Legionnaires were not that left his clothes so dirty.

"Sir," Kye stammered, his lanky form stiff as he stood at attention.

Veraun exchanged an amused glance with Taryn before turning back to Kye. "It is getting late and we should feed these soldiers before we have another mutiny on our hands. Can you assist with that, *Recruit* Kye?"

Kye's eyes brightened and he no longer seemed as afraid, though he still maintained a healthy fear of Veraun when speaking to him. "Of course, sir. I know where the food supplies are."

"Very good," Veraun said. "Speak to the quartermaster and get something out soon. Oh and…" He gestured at the boy's clothing. "Work with the guards—I mean, the captain here and get yourself fitted with a proper uniform and armor. We picked up extras in Sadford I believe…Captain?"

Taryn could only stare at Veraun in shock and it took her a few moments to shake off the initial surprise of being promoted on the spot. "I—of course, sir. Thank you." She took a deep breath and turned to Kye, who seemed equal parts excited and terrified at the prospect of wearing the uniform of the Legionnaire, before placing her hand on his shoulder. "Come, now. Let's get you out of those, well, whatever they once were. Follow me."

"Captain," Veraun called after her. "Give him a blade as well. Make sure he knows how to use it."

When Taryn noticed how wide Kye's eyes grew, she laughed. "Yes, sir."

# Chapter 7

# Forgiveness

**Fimen's Hope, Gurdinfield**

Evening neared when Elisa and Ithmeera finally reached the edge of the woods they had spent the last few days traveling through, but with the sun having been blocked by the dark green clouds, it may as well have been nightfall. From the hill upon which they stood, they could see the village of Fimen's Hope below. Although the surrounding farm structures and crop fields were dark, the town itself was dotted with bright lanterns lighting the dusty streets. The town center—a tall, dark wooden building—loomed over the other structures in the vicinity such as the marketplace stalls and the inn. Houses lined the streets going away from the center.

Elisa lifted her eyebrows in surprise. "The town has grown. There are more houses than were here last time." She turned to Ithmeera. "During the civil war, it was these people who were affected the most when the spoiled nobles couldn't behave themselves."

"I suppose I also count among these 'spoiled nobles,' yes?" Ithmeera asked.

Elisa couldn't tell if she had offended her, and Ithmeera's static expression gave nothing away. "Anyone willing to destroy a town over magic counts among those."

"Don't be so naïve," Ithmeera replied with an exasperated sigh as she looked ahead. "Towns such as this one have gotten caught in the middle of wars all throughout history. It is unfortunate but it is reality. Their role is to ask what they can do to help when their country is in conflict."

"They do not ask for war."

"But they are part of this land and as such they should trust their leaders to protect the land they live on and assist where they can," Ithmeera stated as though she were reciting a well-known fact. "In any case, this town survived the civil war. They seem a resilient people."

Elisa could not tell if she was genuinely impressed or not. "Most Gurdinfielders are."

"You would know better than I." A chilled breeze swept through the trees and Elisa could not decide which was colder: the wind or Ithmeera's tone. But Ithmeera shivered and pulled the hood of her cloak over her hair. "Let's go," she ordered. "I don't feel like freezing to death up here." She pushed forward, and Elisa trailed behind her, wondering how she was going to manage another evening of Ithmeera's unpredictable mood and backhanded remarks.

* * *

*They definitely built more than just houses.* With Ithmeera walking beside her, Elisa found herself gaping at the newly added buildings in town as they made their way to the inn. With the new houses, a new street lined with shops, and a brand-new town center, Fimen's Hope had indeed grown since her last visit. Something still seemed off, however.

"It is as though everyone left," Ithmeera murmured as she let Elisa guide her through the crowds. "Does no one live here?"

Elisa was quiet at first but as she looking around, she could only agree with Ithmeera. Clouds of dusts blew through the town with each cold gust of wind. Only a few people were out and about, but they seemed to avoid eye contact with Elisa as they rushed across the street to their destination. A few children ran around in the street, their playful rhymes with one another sounding forced and haunted. Most of the vending stalls were closed and the ones that were open had long queues of people waiting, their faces all bleak and miserable as they held their baskets. It was as though they did not expect to return home with anything but were willing to try anyway.

She also did not spot a single Gurdinfielder soldier. *Where is everyone?*

"The Cataclysm," she breathed. "It did something to this town."

She brushed all thought of that aside and tried to concentrate instead on getting them safely to the inn—so focused on her goal that she didn't hear the high-pitched voice of one of the children calling her name…and a very familiar voice at that.

*"Lady Elisa!"*

She turned toward the voice just in time to get barreled into by a blur of blonde curls. She steadied herself before looking down at her assailant—who could not have been older than seven or eight—and meeting large brown eyes.

She smiled at the girl whose arms were wrapped around her waist and patted her on the back. "Hello, Amara."

"I *knew* it was you!" Amara squealed. She released Elisa but was so excited she was nearly jumping in place. "I was in the market and when I saw your hair, I recognized you straight away. Have you come to visit me? Is this your friend? What's her name? Are you here to fix the sky?"

Before Elisa could begin to answer the barrage of questions, Ithmeera appeared at her side. "What happened?" But when she noticed Amara, her confusion quickly faded as her lips curved into an amused smile. "Who is this, Elisa?"

"I'm Amara! I'm Lady Elisa's friend. What's your name?"

Ithmeera chuckled at the girl's exuberance and gave Elisa a curious stare before bending down on one knee and holding out her hand. "It is a pleasure to meet you, Amara. I am Ith—" She stopped herself before announcing her name, prompting a relieved sigh from Elisa. They had not discussed hiding Ithmeera's identity prior to entering the town and Elisa was grateful for Ithmeera's quick thinking. "I am Meeri. You have a lovely home."

Amara grabbed Ithmeera's offered hand in excitement and shook it hard. "Thank you! I used to live in another town, but Lady Elisa took me here and then the Fire Lady helped me find a new home because…Mother and Father aren't around anymore." Her eyes cast downward as the brightness in her voice faded.

"Oh…I see," Ithmeera said with a deep nod. She glanced back at Elisa again before looking Amara in the eye. "Well, it was very kind of Lady Elisa to do that. I have a son about your age and I know I would want him to be taken care of should anything happen to me." She patted Amara's hand. "I'm certain your mother and father would be proud of you for being so brave."

A small smile returned to Amara's face. She sniffed. "Thank you, Meeri. I should get home for dinner, though."

"Where do you live now, Amara? Do you want us to take you home?" Elisa asked.

But Amara shook her head and released Ithmeera's hand. "At the end of the street over there. I can make it on my own—it's not far." She pointed at the sky. "Do you know why the sky is green, Lady Elisa? No one will tell me."

Elisa closed her eyes for a moment. She knelt down. "All you need to know is that the Fire Lady and I are going to try to fix it. All right? Now," she said and stood up. "*Meeri* and I should get to the inn." She gave Amara a stern look. "Go straight home, you hear me?"

Amara gave her a final hug and waved at Ithmeera before sprinting away. Elisa kept her focus on the girl to make sure she ran the direction of home as promised before turning to Ithmeera.

"'Meeri?'" she asked quietly as townspeople continued to walk by them.

Ithmeera shrugged. "My father used to call me that."

"Well, thank you for the discretion." Elisa felt a bit guilty for asking as Emperor Nardos' death had been sudden and unexplained, leaving Ithmeera an orphan and in the position to rule at a very young age. "I apologize. I should have thought about how we should conceal your identity earlier."

Ithmeera smoothed out her cloak and dress. "It was nothing. You cannot be expected to think of everything. Come, we should get to this inn. As lovely as sleeping in the dirt is it would be nice to have at least *one* night without a rock poking me in the back."

"Ah," Elisa said, "I can't promise anything."

As they approached the inn, an aging two-story building of dark stone and thick wooden planks, Ithmeera spoke up again. "Who is this 'Fire Lady' the two of you spoke of?"

"That would be Andrea," Elisa explained. "It's a long story." She stepped ahead, off the dirt road and onto the narrow, planked porch of the inn, and grabbed the iron handle of the entrance door to open it for Ithmeera. "Let's hope we can get some answers inside."

Ithmeera removed her hood, allowing her hair to fall past her shoulders, and strode through the open doorway. "Yes. Dinner would be welcome as well."

The inn was unsurprisingly quiet and the warmth from the hearth was a welcome contrast to brisk weather outside. Several of the tables were empty and the murmurings from the occupied ones were low and respectful. A soft glow lit the tavern area as a young, scrawny dark-haired minstrel sang a slow verse on his lute, immediately reminding Elisa of Kye… and their last visit to Fimen's Hope. *I hope he's safe—wherever he is.*

She made eye contact with the innkeeper, who was tending the bar, before turning to Ithmeera. "I will secure a room and food if you can find us a table." When she saw the clueless look on Ithmeera's face she sighed. "Pick an empty table and sit at it while I pay for our room."

"Fine. Make sure it has two beds. I did not share my dirt and I will not share a bed now. Oh, and see what kind of wine they have." Ithmeera did not wait for Elisa to respond before leaving to find a table.

"As you wish, Your Majesty," Elisa said under her breath as she approached the bar, her black boots thudding heavily against the floorboards. She leaned forward against the scratched-up counter and waited while the innkeeper, a tired-looking middle-aged woman, filled a metal tankard for another patron.

"What can I get you tonight, miss?" she said to Elisa once she had finished with the patron. Her grey-streaked dark hair was pulled back into a long braid and her demeanor seemed to give off the same hopelessness as the rest of the town.

Elisa reached into her satchel. "What's on the menu?"

"The hunters have been bringing in deer all week," the innkeeper replied with a weak smile. "It's harvesttime, so normally you'd also have your choice of whatever crop the kitchen is overflowing with but…well, you probably saw we don't have much of a harvest this year."

"What happened here?" Elisa asked.

The innkeeper nodded at the ceiling. "You've seen the sky.

The lightning came down and struck most of our fields. Then came the cold weather. We lost most of the crops in the first week."

*Damn it.* "And the guards from the capital? Where are they?"

"Gone. Left after the second week," the innkeeper replied. "The mayor said he wrote to the queen but hasn't heard back yet."

"I see," Elisa said, and noticed she had captured the attention of some of the other patrons at the bar. She hoped they perhaps recognized her from when she was here with the Guardians and not because of a missive from Petra.

"We haven't gotten much in the way of visitors. Most folk stay inside their homes these days. I'm happy to get you whatever I have left, though. There should be some squash in the kitchen."

"I appreciate it. I'll get two meals," Elisa said. She scanned the tavern and found Ithmeera sitting at a table near the staircase in the corner. "Can you bring it to that table by the stairs? Oh, and a room for two. Just for tonight, please." She figured they would rest tonight and spend the morning recovering and restocking their supplies before moving on toward the City of Towers.

The innkeeper's gaze fixed on Ithmeera for a moment before returning to Elisa. "I've a good vintage from a few harvests ago as well if you and your lady are interested," she offered. "The sky may be green but that doesn't mean folk can't enjoy a romantic evening if they wish it."

Elisa blinked. "Oh. No, no. We're not—I mean, I'll take the wine too, but a room with two beds would be preferable." *Very eloquent. I could give Andrea a run for her money.* The thought dampened her mood even more, when she was once again reminded of the fact of not even knowing whether her friend was alive. She shook the dark thought away. *One crisis at a time.*

"It'll be the third on your right once you're upstairs. I'll have water brought up." The innkeeper did not seem to notice Elisa stumbling over her own words and announced the total due before placing a worn metal key on the counter along with an opened bottle of wine and two empty cups. After she had paid, Elisa stuffed the key in her pocket and grabbed the wine and the cups before heading toward the table in the back.

When Ithmeera saw the wine, the impatient expression she had been wearing most of the day disappeared and was replaced with a relieved sigh. "Finally."

"The food will be out shortly," Elisa grumbled and set the bottle and cups on the table before dropping her pack on the floor and taking her seat across from Ithmeera.

"Excellent. I'm starving." Ithmeera grabbed the wine and filled her cup. "It feels like *months* since I've had wine." She offered the bottle to Elisa, who shook her head.

"I'm fine, thank you," she said and procured her canteen from her bag. She poured the remainder of the water into her cup and resealed the canteen.

"You know, I've never actually stayed the night at an inn before?"

The question actually surprised Elisa. "Really? Never? Not even when you traveled with your father or Alden?"

Ithmeera shook her head. "Never. We always stayed in a guesthouse or someplace similar."

Elisa chuckled. "Your face when I asked you to get us a table makes a bit more sense, now."

Ithmeera took a long sip of her wine, savoring it before answering. "Forgive me if I am not accustomed to walking halfway across Damea. Surely I deserve more credit than you give me. After all, we've made it this far."

"Do I get any credit for keeping you alive?" Elisa asked, nearly enjoying the harmless teasing. She found herself feeling a bit homesick but wasn't sure why.

Ithmeera ignored her question and pointed to the bottle. "Are you certain you don't want any?"

"As I said, I am fine."

The innkeeper arrived carrying a large metal tray and set down two plates of meat and vegetables in front of them. She placed a basket of oven-fresh bread between them and wished them a good meal before taking her leave.

Ithmeera poked at the food with her fork curiously and tried a piece of the meat. "Elisa of Sadford refusing wine," she muttered after the first bite. "What has the world come to?"

"I try not to mix work and drinking. Leads to sloppy decisions otherwise." Elisa took a bite of her own food and found it rather tasty, though she could not determine if it was the food itself that was really so delicious or if she was just relieved to be eating something other than traveling rations.

"Ah, yes, 'work.'" Ithmeera feigned the severity in her voice. "Always a Legionnaire and guard first." She sipped her wine and inspected the bottle's label. "This is actually quite good."

The bubble of homesickness that had built up deflated. *There she goes again.* Perhaps it was the fatigue from traveling all day setting in or just the fact that she was losing her patience with Ithmeera's constant Legionnaire comments, but Elisa's heavy sigh came out much louder than she intended, piquing Ithmeera's interest.

"What? What's wrong? You're sulking again."

"I am fine. Just bothered over the state of this place."

Ithmeera waved her hand. "Nonsense. I said something that upset you. Elisa, I've known you for years. I can tell."

"I just…" Elisa pinched the bridge of her nose. "I don't know why you continue to refer to me as a Legionnaire and your guard when I haven't been either in some time."

"Ah." Ithmeera's playful demeanor vanished as she set her cup down. "Well, last I checked you were still a member of the Legion and I remain your charge," she stated in the stern and confident tone she was renowned for. "You did not resign from your post—not officially anyway—and I did not release you from service. Is any of that incorrect, Elisa?"

*What is she talking about?* The memory of Ithmeera dismissing her in the study in the palace surfaced. *"Go to your queen."* It had been so blunt—*so final.* How could that not have been her discharge from service? "But…when I brought you Erik's sword—"

Ithmeera cut her off. "You are serious? I was *upset*, Elisa. Who wouldn't be after all that has happened?" She leaned back in her chair. "Honestly, I thought you'd be happy I was referring to you as such."

"Why would you think that?" Elisa blurted. The odd look

Ithmeera gave her was telling enough that she should have thought her response through better.

"Because you are an Azgadaran citizen, Elisa, no matter what your dealings with Gurdinfield may have been. You swore a life oath to me when you took up the post of Royal Guard." Ithmeera took another—longer—sip of her wine. "And until *I* release you, there is to be no further discussion about where your loyalties lie. Understand?"

Elisa managed to nod but that did not stop her from cringing inwardly under Ithmeera's powerful gaze. Regardless of what happened with her father and Erik, everything she had done since—abandoning her post, leaving her charge, giving information to Gurdinfield—was considered treason. Ithmeera was right. *Of course she's right.* Where most Legionnaires would have given everything for a second chance, Elisa had taken Ithmeera's graciousness and thrown it back at her. "You're… you're right. I apologize for my careless words."

Ithmeera appeared satisfied with her apology. "Good. Glad that's over with. Now then," she pointed at the wine again, "are you going to have some or do I have to finish the entire bottle on my own? Because I will, you know."

Elisa didn't bother trying to keep a straight face. "Oh, yes, I've been to your parties," she said before finishing the rest of her water in one gulp. She held the cup out. "Fine, then—just a bit."

They ate without speaking for a while, the two of them content letting the minstrel's upbeat chords fill the silence between them. Elisa finished her meal and was impressed with how much she had actually enjoyed it. Ithmeera seemed happy with her food as well, the lines around her furrowed brow having disappeared over the course of the meal—no doubt a result of the both of them finally relaxing for the first time that evening.

After some time, the minstrel finished his final song and most of the patrons had already left for the night. Elisa noticed Ithmeera staring off into space, something she usually did when she was tired, inebriated, or both.

She noted the mostly empty bottle on the table and stood up.

"We should probably get some sleep," she suggested. She grabbed her backpack and put her arms through the straps.

"Hmm?" Ithmeera shook her head and blinked, the fatigue in her eyes obvious. "Oh. Yes…of course." She pushed the chair back and stood up, stumbling slightly.

Out of instinct, Elisa took a gentle grasp of Ithmeera's arm to steady her. "Easy, now," she teased. "We don't want a repeat of the Legionnaire's Ball now, do we?"

Ithmeera allowed Elisa to guide her away from the table and up the stairs. "The Legionnaire…oh, *that* Legionnaire's Ball. Hush, that was what—four years ago?" she protested as they reached the second floor. "I'm *far* more adept at holding my alcohol now. And look!" She gestured at the door to their room once they arrived and Elisa fished for the key in her satchel. "I've reached the room without knocking over a single suit of armor this time."

"Well done," Elisa said with a short laugh, the memory of Ithmeera assailing the decorative armor mannequins arranged specifically for the event after having a bit too much to drink still embedded in her mind. Upon feeling cold metal on her fingers, she pulled the key out of her bag and unlocked the door before giving the knob a quick turn.

As promised, two beds were present—one hugging each wall—though there was barely enough room between them to walk through. An adjacent washroom and a nightstand shared between the beds completed the small but serviceable room.

"Ah, much better than sleeping on the dirt!" Ithmeera breathed as she took a few slightly wobbly steps toward the bed on the left and sat down. "It's not home, but it will suffice."

"I'm glad you approve." Elisa loosened the straps of the backpack around her shoulders and let it fall to the floor with an unceremonious thud. She turned away from Ithmeera to nudge the door shut with her boot and went straight to the task of unbuckling her armor, focusing on her bracers first. "I saw a few shops when we entered town. We can stop there to restock before continuing to the capital. Perhaps see about getting a horse." She dropped the bracers on top of the backpack and went to work on her chest piece.

"Why did you leave?" Ithmeera's voice sounded from behind her, her tone forceful but not accusing.

Elisa turned and instantly saw the hurt in Ithmeera's face. "What?"

"You could have come to me, you know." Ithmeera fidgeted with the comforter of the bed. "You could have told me what happened with your father and Erik. Instead, I had to endure night after night not knowing where you were—if you were even alive." Her voice broke a bit. "Marco asked me for months where his aunt was—when she was coming back and after a while, I no longer had a good excuse to give him."

*Does she really want to have this conversation or has she just had a bit too much to drink tonight?* Elisa wasn't sure which it was or if it was both, but after their exchange at dinner, she decided honesty was the best path for them, despite how uncomfortable it might be. She set the chest piece on the floor, leaving her in a sleeveless undershirt and pants, and sat on the bed across from Ithmeera.

"After Erik…" She let her silence fill in the omission. "I saw his face after it happened, Ithmeera, and I was well aware he'd never liked me. I thought he might try to tell you something that wasn't true."

Ithmeera left the comforter alone and folded her hands together. "You didn't think I would believe you."

Elisa cringed, but she knew Ithmeera deserved the truth. "I was too afraid to take that chance. I am sorry for that." And she meant it.

Ithmeera looked at the floor. "He told me you were planning to kill me. That you wanted to avenge Philip's death by assassinating me."

Elisa bit her lip, remembering Erik's angry words on the battlefield outside the gates of the City of Towers moments before she defeated him in combat. "Did you believe him?"

Ithmeera looked up and for a moment Elisa feared what the answer would be. "No," she said firmly. "Of course not. He was my brother, but no." Her eyes became glossy but she blinked away any incoming tears. "I'm not as naïve as Erik and Alden liked to believe I was. I knew you would never hurt me." She reached across the narrow space between the beds and took Elisa's hands in hers, making Elisa tense up with surprise at the contact. "When you returned to Azgadar, I wanted to believe you came back not just to return Erik's sword, but because I was still important to you." She sniffed and shook her head. "I'm sorry, I don't know what's come over me. Probably the wine again." She moved to withdraw her hands but Elisa gave them a squeeze, holding them in place.

"You are." She took a deep breath, scolding herself for the difficulty she was having in articulating how she felt. "You are the most important person in my life, Ithmeera. You and Marco are the only family I have left. That is why I came back." As she found herself frozen in place by Ithmeera's mesmerizing stare, a strange fluttering took root in her chest. It was foreign to her and there was absolutely nothing rational about it, which both frightened and frustrated her. She tried to ignore it if only to finish saying what she had to say. "And some part of me hoped that if I came back perhaps you might forgive me for leaving." When Ithmeera did not respond, she slowly released her hands and moved on to unfasten her boots.

"On one condition."

Elisa looked up and saw Ithmeera was actually smiling at her. "What?"

"You must promise to return to Azgadar with me when this is over. And stay this time," Ithmeera said. "If you do that, you *might* have my forgiveness."

Knowing it would take more than a smile and a long talk to approach the bond they used to have, Elisa could only agree to the deal, hoping that this would truly be the start of a long healing process for them. "I promise."

# Chapter 8

# The Storm

A clap of thunder shook the room, rousing Elisa from her sleep almost immediately. She had only just sat up in bed, blinking as she tried to regain focus of her surroundings, when another loud bang followed. This time the door rattled on its hinges and the lone candlestick on the nightstand fell over on its side.

"Wh-what? What was that?" The bed next to Elisa gave a sharp creak and even in the dark she could see Ithmeera's figure as she, too, sat up.

Elisa cleared her throat and tried to push away the fog of sleep. "Thunder, I think." She was about to suggest that they go back to sleep when she heard screams from outside the room, possibly downstairs.

Ithmeera heard it as well. "Did you hear that?" Though her voice was still groggy with sleep, the alarm creeping into it made Elisa uneasy.

The room trembled as another rumble rolled through. The screams grew louder. *Something's not right.*

She pushed the covers off and swung her legs over the edge of the bed. "I'll be right back," she told Ithmeera. "Stay here."

Her vision impaired by the darkness, she stumbled over to the door and grasped the handle before pulling it open just enough to poke her head out, the warm light from the hallway spilling into the room. She gasped in surprise when the innkeeper ran by her, yelling for everyone to stay inside before rushing down the stairs. The panic in her voice and the commotion coming from downstairs was enough to convince Elisa she needed to see for herself what was going on.

She turned to Ithmeera, who had pushed her own blankets aside and was sitting on the edge of her bed. "Something is going on," she said and pulled on her boots. "I'm going downstairs and see what it is."

"I'll go with you," Ithmeera declared.

"No. If it's something dangerous I don't want you near it. I'll return shortly."

Ithmeera let out a short huff. "If it is too dangerous for me then it is certainly too dangerous for you and I should be there. I'm coming with you and that's—" A massive boom interrupted her, prompting more screams from below and prompting Elisa to make a quick decision. She grabbed one of the swords.

"Please stay here, Ithmeera," she uttered and left the room before Ithmeera had a chance to protest. After shutting the door behind her, she went to the first floor with haste, avoiding eye contact with a few panicked guests at the base of the stairs who gave her curious stares. The dining room was busy but not with patrons. Most of the people there were huddling together at a table or in a corner of the room. Many of them had young children with them, though Elisa did not see Amara among any of them. One thing was certain—they all wore similar expressions of terror on their faces.

A flash of white light filled the room, blinding her momentarily as the shrill screams of the frightened townspeople rung in her ears.

"Please, everyone, away from the windows. It's just another storm but we must try to stay calm!" The innkeeper's hoarse voice rose above the cries but was drowned out when the thunder hit. A wave of pure energy blasted apart the inn's large front window and shattered countless glasses behind the bar. Elisa barely had time to shield her eyes with her arm before she was thrown to the ground along with several others, her blade falling from her hand and clattering on the floorboards.

Once the shaking stopped, she grabbed her sword and stood, ignoring the dull throb in her side from being knocked down. The front door had swung open and so she walked toward it, watching with rapt fascination as debris flew by the doorway, the howling wind stirring a familiar memory.

It was only when she stepped outside despite the protesting shouts from the innkeeper that Elisa realized this was no ordinary storm. Her jaw dropped in horror as she gazed up, eyes narrowed while the harsh wind stung against her skin.

By the trace amounts of light, she could see that it was just before dawn. But the swirling grey clouds above all too closely resembled the skies above Azgadar when Richard and Cassie had taken the magic from the land: dark, chaotic and then afterwards—dead. Bolts of lightning hurtled down and struck the town's surrounding farmland, the earth-shaking thunder following. Small fires ignited in pockets across the fields.

Richard's actions made no sense. *Why would anyone want*

*this?*

Something brushed against her forehead. Then another. Then again on her arm. It took her a moment to stop staring at the storm to glance down, where a few ashes had fallen on her wrist and forearm. The air grew thin and the wind died down as the ash fell faster and heavier, its presence distracting Elisa from the voice screaming at her from the doorway.

*"Elisa!"* Ithmeera clung to the doorframe. Her presence snapped Elisa out of her trance but not before she was blinded by a brilliant flash of white. A gust of blistering air rushed at her face. A hand wrapped around her wrist...and then she only saw darkness.

* * *

Muffled voices surrounded her. A man, then a woman's—a familiar one at that. Then...nothing again. It wasn't until Elisa felt the coolness of the cloth pressed against her forehead that she was finally able to claw her way out of the dense fog of unconsciousness enveloping her.

She opened her eyes only to be greeted with a pounding headache. She knew she was in a bed, but despite the layers of blankets covering her she shivered. *A headache and a bloody fever. Perfect.* She tried to focus, recollecting the memory of what happened before she'd lost consciousness. There was, or had been a storm. People were taking refuge in the inn for some reason and Elisa had gone downstairs to investigate after telling Ithmeera to stay put until—

*Ithmeera!*

She bolted upright—frantically scanning the room for Ithmeera and her weapon—and a hand came down on her shoulder before trying to push her back down.

"Relax. It's only me."

Elisa ceased her struggling and forced herself to focus, difficult as it was with her head still cloudy. A brief glance ahead told her they were back in their room at the inn. When she saw Ithmeera sitting in a chair next to her, looking no worse for wear, she let out a heavy sigh of relief and lie back onto the pillow again.

"Are you all right? What happened?" she murmured.

A faint smile flickered on Ithmeera's face before worry took over. "I am fine. And you," she said and pressed the wet cloth against Elisa's brow again, "are never to do something that foolish again."

Her concern touched Elisa, leaving her fumbling for words. "I—"

"That was uncontrolled magic," Ithmeera scolded. "Whatever your friend did is probably wreaking havoc on the land's energy. You're lucky to be alive and only with fever."

This time when Elisa tried to sit up, Ithmeera let her. "I did not realize you knew so much about magic." *Or cared so much about whether I was alive or not.*

Ithmeera gave her a strange look. "Because I'm not an enchanter? I run a country whose farms and infrastructure rely on magic, Elisa. Between that and Marco's abilities I've had to learn quite a bit from the royal enchanters." She withdrew the cloth. "The occasional accident would happen in the palace among the newer apprentices. Fevers and burns were common. It will fade soon."

*The lightning.* "Did I—what happened exactly?" Elisa asked, wincing as her temples throbbed again.

"Well, when I arrived downstairs you were outside trying to get struck by lightning," Ithmeera said. She drew her lips back and Elisa could tell she was holding back something.

"That wasn't my intention. And I told you to stay in the room."

"And had I followed your 'orders' who would have pulled you off the street when half a house came barreling down the road after being hit, hm?" Ithmeera challenged and Elisa heard the tremor in her voice this time. "Certainly not those people hiding behind the bar."

*Oh.* "You…saved me?"

Ithmeera scoffed. "Don't look so surprised. What was I supposed to do: leave you out there to die?"

"No of course not, but—I-that is…" Once again, she struggled with her words when she realized she probably offended Ithmeera with her initial surprise.

Ithmeera seemed more amused than anything. "You can say 'thank you' as most people do when they're indebted to someone."

"You're right." Elisa cleared her throat, feeling grateful and foolish at the same time. "Thank you." A dreadful thought occurred to her. "The house that was hit—whose was it? Amara…"

Ithmeera patted Elisa's arm. "Amara is fine; it was not her home. The owners were actually taking refuge here. Apparently, there have been many storms here recently and this inn has withstood them better than most of the houses."

For the first time since waking up, Elisa realized the thunder had stopped. "The storm has passed then?"

"Not so much passed as vanished, but yes."

Elisa took the answer as permission to push the blankets off, despite how terrible she felt. They needed to get to the City of Towers. "Then we should prepare to leave."

Ithmeera's eyebrows went up. "Absolutely not! You need to rest, Elisa."

But Elisa would not hear it. "We need to get to the capital. Diana needs to know about these storms if she doesn't already. Marco is waiting for you. And there still Petra to worry about." She tried to push past the soreness, swinging her legs over the edge of the bed. "Come on, we still need to get supplies." When she saw the worry in Ithmeera's eyes she tried to reassure her with a crooked grin. "Ithmeera, I would be a very poor Legionnaire if I let something like this stop me from getting my charge to her destination." Perhaps it was their conversation the night before or even her brush with death but Elisa found herself wanting to try harder to alleviate Ithmeera's fears as she took her hand, the warmth providing comfort all on its own. "I will be fine."

Ithmeera relented but did not return the smile. "If you're certain."

"The last few weeks I've been anything but certain," Elisa

admitted and withdrew her hand. "We'll make do. Now, where did I put my armor?"

# Chapter 9

# Sea of Serpents

**Gurith, Gurith Coast**

In her travels as Meredith's apprentice, Andrea never saw the city of Gurith. She had been west enough to see the coastal town of Onede, but that was farther north and nowhere near the size of the capital. As they approached the city, a salty ocean breeze surfaced the memory of one of her more exciting trips with Meredith but left a bittersweet longing for the future she wanted with Cassie—one she was not entirely would happen even if they succeeded in stopping Richard. *No, when we stop him.*

A wall of grey and brown stone surrounded the fishing city. It was not as tall or grand as the ones that bastioned the City of Towers or Azgadar, but it looked functional from afar. Andrea could spot two iron gates from where they were—the northern one closest to them and the western one opening at the docks where gulls gathered around the fishermen going about their work, no doubt searching for a stray catch as their next meal.

As Gurith was built upon flat terrain, many of the buildings inside the city were hidden behind the wall, save for a few particularly tall dome-peaked structures and the infamous Shadow Arena. The arena was several times larger than anything else around it—its dark purpose far more imposing than its size. Andrea knew it was one of the greatest income generators for the merchants of Gurith, who would often sponsor matches between desperate rogue enchanters and deserting soldiers before the Restoration. As she watched green-tinted light from the sky play on the choppy grey waters, she wondered how such matches would even be possible with the state of magic as it was, and whether the Merchants' Guild had moved on from them.

"Gurith." Meredith made no effort to hide her disgust for the city as they walked. "This place is a blight upon Damea."

Andrea tilted her head. "Yet you lived here for months."

"True," Meredith conceded. "It is a good place to get lost in. I thought about going back to Darst but…Gurdinfield was my home," she said. A wistful glint in her eyes appeared and faded just as quickly before she pulled her hood over her head, catching the few wisps of her grey-streaked hair getting in her eyes. "I didn't want to be reminded of anything having to do with Richard or my life before." She cleared her throat, taking on her usual, more severe tone. "I should warn you that we are stepping into very dangerous territory, Andrea. 'Order' here is not the same as it is in the empire or the City of Towers. I suggest you keep your identity and your magic to yourself until we know for sure Richard is here."

"Haven't enchanters always been welcome here, though?"

Meredith rolled her eyes. "Don't be foolish. The merchants who run this city will use everything and everyone they can to their advantage if it makes them a profit, especially enchanters who still retain the ability to cast. We cannot afford to make any…rash decisions, understood?" she asked, emphasizing on the word "rash".

*Still trying to control everything. Typical.* "I'm not a child, Meredith," Andrea snapped. "I understand and I don't need to be lectured about how I use magic."

"Is that so?" Meredith stopped and turned to her; an eyebrow raised. "Your potion supply is abysmally low. We don't even know if they are here and we don't have a plan for if they are and we are fortunate enough to find them. Not to mention it seems every time you're left without supervision something terrible happens."

Andrea bit back a denial. "The plan has not changed. We ask Balos if he has seen them," she said, struggling not to let Meredith get under her skin as she proceeded to walk again. "We know Richard betrayed him somehow. We can use that."

"And if you're wrong?"

Andrea whirled on her, shivering as her growing anger pushed magic to her wounds, sending a sharp throb through her arm and up to her shoulder and neck. "I saw Richard force Cassie to absorb all the magic, Meredith! You can believe what you want but the sooner you admit that *maybe* he isn't the man you thought you married the sooner we can get back to saving Damea." She was surprised when Meredith's eyes widened—though whether in surprise or fear she couldn't tell. She grumbled a half-hearted apology before continuing down the dirt road they had spent the last few days traveling on.

They passed through a crowded entry courtyard where

the iron gates awaited—Andrea noting the dozens of beggars huddled in the dark corners of the cracked walls, the base of which were stained from a mix of the salty air and seaweed.

Desperation hung in the air here, though Andrea concluded, not inappropriate at all considering the swirling green clouds above. A few well-dressed Gurithians passed them, many donning the brown and gold scales of the Merchants' Guild on their clothing. Their serpentine mannerisms betrayed their motives as they looked her up and down—no doubt seeing the scars that crept up her neck—as though she were a potential opportunity they wanted to consider pursuing. She drew her cloak closer in an effort to conceal her arm.

"This way. Stay close." Meredith's voice was low and commanding as she pushed through the crowds with methodical movements. Andrea followed, keeping her wits about her in case a confrontation arose. She wouldn't use magic here unless she absolutely had to, and only if it brought her closer to saving Cassie. If someone stood in her way, though, if they tried to stop her…

*No.* The thought appalled her and she wasn't sure why her mind had even gone there. Another sharp pain shot though her arm and she tried not to let it slip through her expression. *I'm not Meredith or Richard. I don't use magic to hurt people.*

*But what if Cassie's life depends on it? What if saving her means someone else has to die?* A small voice flickered in the back of her mind and she recognized it—the beginnings of the deep anger she'd felt in the fog when she saw Cassie's projection.

She glanced over at Meredith, recalling the promise she had made to let Richard explain himself to his wife before any judgements were to be made. She wondered if she'd actually be able to keep such a promise or if her anger would be too overpowering for her to control when she saw him. A part of her hoped it would. A well-placed fireball would do the trick, though it might take longer and would be much…messier. A blow from a barrier to the head would be quick and efficient but Andrea wanted Richard to feel remorse for his actions, for what he had taken away from her—assuming the man was capable of such emotions. Power coursed through the right side of her body and left a trail of pleasant warmth in its wake. It would be so easy.

The warmth withdrew as quickly as it had manifested, leaving her nauseous and with the sudden urge to vomit. *Stop.*

Shocked and disgusted with herself at where her mind went, she shook the thought away and tried to focus on where they were, though the nagging voice remained. *That's not who I am.* They had to get an audience with Balos and quickly.

They escaped the crowds on the other side of the city gates where a long, wide paved road flanked by multi-floored buildings constructed with more of the crumbling stained white stone led to a short flight of brick steps. Smaller cliques of people hurried by them from both directions, most of whom had their heads down and made it obvious they were trying to get to their destination as quickly as possible. Inactive streetlamps lined the street, the long banners hanging down from them promoting or advertising a shop or event. A few city guards were posted on the street's edges, their body language so tense as they gripped sharpened halberds it was clear they were waiting for another disaster. At the top of the steps stood the largest structure in the city save for the massive Shadow Arena in the distance.

"The Merchants' Guild," Meredith said.

Compared to the other buildings, the Merchants' Guild Hall was pristine. Washed white walls accented with gold-painted wooden embellishments framed the three-story building, which stood up on wide ornate pillars. Andrea saw through the façade and thought it looked gaudy but she knew this must be the center of the largest business transactions on the entire Gurith Coast and possibly most of Damea. But judging by the state of disrepair the city was in she guessed the money from these transactions rarely made its way back to the people of Gurith. This was definitely a place where many people looked out for themselves, and in some cases cared not if they had to step on others in the process. Another set of iron bars blocked the entry along with two guards.

"Remember what I said," Meredith cautioned as they ascended to the top of the steps. She remained in front, no doubt attempting to draw attention away from Andrea as they approached the door guards. Clad in chain-linked armor and with halberds at their sides, the two men observed them with suspicious eyes.

"Good day, sirs," Meredith greeted them with a silky tone and a polite smile.

The guards exchanged glances before the taller one, a lean, stern man spoke. "The Hall is closed to unscheduled visitors today. Identify yourself or see yourself back down those stairs."

Meredith's smile did not waver. She offered a bow of her head as she introduced herself, using her name and city of origin—something Andrea was used to her doing before the Restoration particularly when they were within Azgadaran borders. "Meredith of Darst, sir." She gestured to Andrea, who kept her hood on and refused to make eye contact with the inspecting guard. "My ward. We come seeking an audience with the Grandmaster."

The second guard, a bulky man with a trimmed beard, answered her with a harsh bark of a laugh. "The Grandmaster is not granting unannounced audiences. You are not on the list of scheduled visitors today so you will be leaving now." He tightened his grip on the halberd.

Meredith retained her smile but Andrea could see the edges of her mouth twitching. "Sirs, please. I assure you it is a matter of utmost importance."

The first guard took a lengthy step forward, aggression radiating from his armored presence as he stood above Meredith. "You were given an answer. Now, remove yourself from the property before I remove you from it."

Andrea bit her lip. This wasn't working. Meredith had no pull here and with the way things were going they were going to wind up in a jail cell before they could see Balos. An idea came to her—a risky one but they had very few options at this point.

Hoping she wasn't dooming them both, she removed her hood and glared at the guard. "Tell Balos that Andrea of Ata requests the audience." Before Meredith could react, she pulled back her right shirtsleeve and allowed the magic within her to rise to the scars, her jaw tightening from the sensation. White and blue light pulsed from the jagged cuts as both the guards and Meredith gaped at her. "Tell him…I've come to request assistance on behalf of Gurdinfield, per our treaty."

The second guard's hardened eyes bulged in surprise and a bit of fear at the sight of Andrea's injury. He turned to the first, who appeared to be the ranking one of the two and murmured something in the other's ear. Finally, the first directed his attention at Andrea.

"You will be permitted a short audience with the Grandmaster. Any acts of hostility or aggression will be dealt with swiftly and permanently," he said, the end of his sentence coming out in a growl. "Do I make myself clear?"

Anxiety gripped at Andrea's chest but she allowed her anger at Richard to push it down. If she was going to save Cassie, she needed to be strong and that included not being intimidated by a common guard. *Even if that weapon could slice me open in an instant.* She matched his scowl with one of her own. "Just take us to him."

He stared at her for a few long seconds before nodding to the second guard who sighed and uttered, "Follow me." The iron grate behind them groaned as it lifted up, allowing them to pass through and into the guildhall.

Meredith said nothing—the harsh look she gave her was more than enough to tell Andrea she was displeased. Her disapproval mattered little to Andrea, however. After all, her plan had worked.

A wide, open room greeted them—the long brown rug at their feet adorned with repeating gold scales extended the length of the hall. Rows of more guards stood on the left and right between more extravagantly-carved pillars of gold-encrusted stone. Balconies framed with wood railings and occupied by members of the Merchants' Guild overlooked the Grandmaster's seat at the end of the hall. The chair itself was a complex-looking hybrid of wood and stone, the back of it expanding into a huge wooden carving proudly displaying the Gurithian symbol. It was all just overdone to Andrea.

She wondered what Cassie might say about Gurith if she were there with them now. *Probably that they're worried visitors might forget where they are if they don't put the damn gold and scales on* everything.

Thinking about Cassie reasserted her focus on the chair and the man who sat in it. With dark-skin, amber eyes that seemed to match the overabundance of gold in the hall, and an easy, kind smile, Grandmaster Balos was a well-dressed, handsome man whose presence gravitated the attention of a room. When he recognized Andrea, he stood, the low ponytail of his jet-black hair remaining stationary. With all the grace of a diplomat with years of experience, he greeted her with an elegant bow.

"Enchanter Andrea. Welcome to Gurith." He spread his arms, gesturing to the grand hall around them. "Welcome to my home. I admit I did not expect you to consider my offer, though it could not have come at a more fortuitous time."

Bowing herself, Andrea drew on what little diplomatic training she'd had while serving as Royal Enchanter of Gurdinfield. "Grandmaster. I thank you for receiving us on such short notice." She rose, meeting his curious gaze. "I am here on behalf of Queen Lydia." It was a lie, one she did not like telling, but she hoped Diana would understand given the circumstances. "I have come with an offer of aid…as well as a request for one."

"An offer *and* a request." Balos took his seat. "I see. The queen has sent you to make good on our treaty, then? I don't suppose this has anything to do with the strange times we face now on the Coast?" A servant approached from his right side with a tray atop which sat a single glass of wine. "Can I offer you a drink?" he asked her as he took the wine.

"No thank you. And to answer your first question, yes."

He gestured at Meredith, the glass of wine in his hand. "And who might your lovely companion be?"

In a bow rivaling any Andrea had seen in a royal court, Meredith answered him with a mannerism only someone who had been raised as nobility could have. "Meredith of Darst, Grandmaster. I am an old friend of Andrea's and have sworn myself to assist her in her travels here."

Balos leaned back in his chair. "And what might this great cause be exactly that requires two capable women to pursue it? And why would Her Majesty send you as her liaison?"

Out of instinct, Andrea looked to Meredith for guidance. When her mentor's expression said nothing, she decided to try a more direct approach. "We seek an enchanter by the name of Richard, Grandmaster. We recently learned of his plans to travel here. He is being…accompanied by a woman about my age." She left out the part about Richard being behind the Cataclysm. There was a tension in the hall that left her feeling uncertain about whether she could trust Balos. The man was a little too opportunistic for her liking.

At the mention of Richard's name, Balos' calm manner

faded and was replaced with a hardened glare. "I am familiar with the man. Not many break a deal with the Guild, let alone the Grandmaster himself." He took a sip of his wine. "Most who have do not survive long enough to tell the tale in any case. Your interest in Richard is curious, I must say."

Meredith cut in. "You know where he is, don't you?"

Balos extended a suspicious glance in her direction. "In Gurith, information is as valuable as any other good, my lady. It is a rare day when the Merchants' Guild gives away something for free."

*The fate of the world is at stake and he's trying to cut a deal?* Andrea knew she shouldn't be surprised given the Guild's reputation, but some part of her had hoped that he would just honor the treaty he'd made with Diana, even if their alliance was mostly related to matters of trade. "Your city is in danger, Grandmaster. If you don't help us, people could be hurt, possibly die!" she blurted, her exclamation reverberating in the long hall.

A deathly silence settled over them. Chainmail clinked and metal plates shifted as the guards who lined the sides of the room closed in by a step. To her left, Meredith let out a sharp breath.

Balos' cold stare twisted. "Are you threatening me in my own hall, Enchanter Andrea?"

Meredith stepped in before Andrea could explain herself. "Forgive her rudeness, Grandmaster. It has been a harrowing trip and Enchanter Andrea obviously needs to *rest*." She shot Andrea a warning glance to *not* interrupt as she continued. "The man is my husband, Grandmaster. We have been seeking him for some time."

It took all of Andrea's willpower to not tell Meredith what she thought of her right then. She did not need to rest; she needed to stop Richard and save Cassie. She needed for people like Balos to cooperate. "We believe he may try to siphon magic from the Shadow Arena."

His sight fixed on Andrea, Balos' shoulders gave the slightest slump. His guards backed up in response. The hall had calmed. "I see," he said. "And do you have any evidence to support your claim?"

This time waiting for Meredith to give her an approving nod, Andrea answered him while making more of an effort to remain as courteous as possible. "None that we can show you, Grandmaster. But we would like to assist you in apprehending him."

Balos pointed at the ceiling. "You've seen the sky and have heard the stories about enchanters no longer being able to cast without devastating side effects. Do you mean to tell me this man has the ability to manipulate magic without these consequences?" He lowered his hand. "And if that is the case, what good are you to stop him? Being an enchanter yourself, I imagine you have little desire to suffer the same fate as many of the others have."

Andrea frowned. Was he toying with her? Surely someone had informed him of her display at the door. "I have retained my casting abilities," she explained before conjuring a small ball of white light in the opened palm of her hand, inciting gasps and whispers from others in the hall. "As for Richard, he has the means to achieve his goal. We mu—" she stopped herself before she accidentally made another comment that could put them both in a prison cell. "I wish to aid Gurith in this matter, Grandmaster."

"How noble of you," Balos said with a light chuckle. He took another sip of his wine. "All right. It is true—it was reported to me earlier that this man, Richard, was seen entering the city with the woman you've described. I seek them both and have sent my agents into the city to search for them. It is curious he would dare show his face here in Gurith, especially after what he did."

Eager at the chance to get more information, Andrea carefully pressed him. "How so?"

He shook his head, obviously displeased with the memory he was recounting. "He came to me some time ago offering a deal. He actually mentioned you by name."

*What?* Andrea was stunned by the news, but she remained silent as he continued.

"He asked me for the use of a few of my guards for a task of his and promised me that he would send you back to me when the task was complete." He shrugged. "The Guild coordinates contracts such as this often so I figured it was a routine transaction."

"Why would he promise you Andrea?" Meredith asked, though Andrea knew the answer.

An unsettling grin appeared on Balos' face. "Most likely he was trying to appeal to our members who deal in matters of entertainment and tourism. Many would pay a great deal to see a royal enchanter in the arena."

*So* that's *what he's after.* "I am not a gladiator, Grandmaster, and I had no knowledge of this deal he brokered with you," she said with firm conviction, though if Andrea were being honest with herself, she wasn't sure whether to be offended or flattered by the notion that she might participate in one of the infamous Shadow Arena matches.

Balos laughed. "Of course. My apologies, I meant no disrespect, Enchanter Andrea. I was led to believe Richard had spoken with you about the exchange and that you had agreed to the arrangement." The pleasant smile had returned. "In any case, even if there is some truth to what you say, the Shadow Arena is the most heavily guarded spot in the city today."

Andrea exchanged a worried look with Meredith. "And why is that?"

Balos seemed genuinely surprised. "Why, the Grandmaster's Tournament begins this afternoon and goes on for the remainder of the month. Did you not see the banners all over the city?"

*A tournament.* That meant there would be people present in the arena when Richard executed his plan! "Grandmaster, please," she begged. "If Richard succeeds the Shadow Arena will be destroyed. If people are in it when it happens…"

Balos just shook his head. "I will not delay the tournament and turn an already frightened city upside-down to search for one man who may be a danger. My guards can handle it, Enchanter Andrea."

"But—"

He interrupted her. "Many people's livelihoods rely on this

tournament, Enchanter. Surely you can understand that."

"He *will* be there, Grandmaster," Andrea insisted.

Balos sighed and for a moment it seemed as though he might give in. "The problem does not seem to be *if*, Enchanter Andrea, but *when*. Without that there is just too much at stake here to simply shut down the arena and the tournament."

Meredith, who had remained relatively quiet save a handful of interjections, asked, "What if we could guarantee a time he would show?" She looked at Andrea. "He was looking for me, yes? What if we could draw him in by announcing my name in the tournament? The entire city would hear, yes?"

The idea seemed to pique Balos' curiosity. "Draw him into the arena where the guards could apprehend him? Interesting, but I will not have the tournament paused for one man. And," he added, "I would not risk your personal safety. You do not have the look of a fighter and unless you can also cast…?"

Meredith shook her head. "I cannot, Grandmaster."

*Wait.* The strands of a plan came together in Andrea's mind— perhaps this was what Meredith was going for all along? "You don't need to pause it," she said. "*I* will fight in the tournament."

The air in the room shifted as all eyes fell on her. The guildmembers above murmured among themselves. Meredith spun to face her with bewildered grey eyes. *Perhaps not.*

"You would?" The last word came out with barely contained excitement as Balos set his glass down on the arm of his chair. "That…changes things." He rubbed his chin in thought. "Yes, I think that will definitely change things. An enchanter who can still cast, especially one with your reputation," he said and

Andrea could practically see the prospect of money in his eyes. "This could work."

"Grandmaster," Meredith said, "respectfully, I must object. Enchanter Andrea has had a long journey. I'm certain she is merely tired and as such she is prone to making irrational decisions." She shot Andrea a harsh glance on the word "irrational". "In any event, if she were to be announced as a combatant, there is no reason to believe he would make an appearance. If anything, I would think he would try to avoid her."

Andrea wished she knew how to use magic to silence Meredith but she hoped Balos would support her after she announced the second part of her plan. "Of course he would. That is why I'm going to be competing under your name, Meredith."

Meredith's jaw dropped. "That is *not*—"

But Balos put his hand up, silencing the room. "Enough. It is decided. The tournament will proceed this afternoon as planned. Enchanter Andrea, you will be allowed to compete under your companion's name. When you are announced and Richard appears, you are to assist my guards in apprehending him." He made a hand signal to the merchants above him and a few began furiously scribbling on the pieces of parchment they had in their possession. "I caution you, however, that you are willfully putting yourself in harm's way. There will be no quarter given to you, Enchanter Andrea, for the games must appear as authentic as possible. Do we understand each other?"

*If Richard or the magic doesn't kill me then the tournament surely will. Wonderful.* "I understand."

He stood and clasped his hands together, the smack of them sending an echo in the otherwise silent hall. "Wonderful! Then our business, it seems, is concluded for now." He motioned to the guard who had brought them in and had been waiting patiently. "Please see our friends out."

"Thank you, Grandmaster." Andrea and Meredith spoke in unison as they bowed.

Balos flashed them a brilliant smile. "Of course. Meredith of Darst, you will be granted prime seating for the event. And Andrea," he said, his amber eyes carrying a hungry glint that made Andrea feel like she had already been thrown into the arena, "I especially look forward to seeing your performance."

# Chapter 10

# Breaking Point

"Foolish girl! Volunteering to fight in the arena, what were you thinking? Inconsiderate, immature, reckless—must I go on?"

Andrea quickened her step as Meredith practically chased her upon leaving the Merchants' Guild. "I don't have time for one of your lectures, Meredith," she said as they clattered down the brick steps and proceeded down the city's main road in the direction of the Shadow Arena.

"You will *make* time for them! Andrea!" Meredith called after her as she ducked into an alley that seemed to be a shortcut. White-hot pain lanced through her arm and shoulder as she was suddenly yanked backwards. Whirling around, she saw Meredith's slim fingers wrapped around her wrist.

"Let. *Go*," she ordered, enunciating each word in a growl she didn't recognize as her own voice at first.

Meredith's grip did not loosen. "You are not in your right mind."

"I'm fine!"

"No!" Meredith fired back, her hand shaking with anger

as she ignored the curious onlookers that passed them. "You are not 'fine'. You are drunk on these potions you've been consuming. Flagrant displays of magic, lashing out at everyone, starving for your next drink of that foul concoction—you may be able to cast still, Andrea, but you have grown addicted to this power!"

Andrea scoffed. "That's ridiculous. And I'm starting to think I'm the only one of us who actually cares about saving Damea, which by the way, wouldn't need saving if it weren't for *your* bloody husband! Now," she said as she tried to free herself from Meredith's grip, "let me go."

But Meredith would not relent. "No! We will find Richard, but this reckless plan of yours is not the way. You are out of control, Andrea."

The nagging voice from earlier returned as an itch in Andrea's arm, pricking like dozens of needles searching for the first stitch and growing into a raging burn that seared the right half of her body. "I've told you—I'm fine! Now let go!"

"I will not!" Meredith pleaded. "Listen to yourself, Andrea! What would Cassie say if she saw you like this? If she saw how far you had fallen?"

White and blue light peeked through Andrea's clothes as she pushed back with her arm and let out a cry of rage, sending Meredith stumbling back several steps.

Panting as the burning ebbed, Andrea pushed back the horrific reality of what she had done to offer a thinly-veiled threat instead. "Never mention her name to me again."

Meredith held up a hand as she caught her bearings.

"Andrea…"

But Andrea just adjusted her shirt and cloak before regarding Meredith with an icy glare. "I am going to the arena, Meredith. Follow me or don't. Just don't get in my way." She turned on her heel and strode out of the alley, now more than ever determined to succeed in her plan to find Richard and Cassie.

She would keep her promise to Meredith to spare him if she could. But if Richard did not cooperate, she would not hesitate to end him with the hottest fireball she could conjure.

∗ ∗ ∗

The sky over Gurith shifted, the grey clouds thickening and the green muting as late afternoon approached. Lines of people, mostly of the mercantile and nobility classes, gathered around iron-gated entrances lining the edges of the elliptical Shadow Arena. White stone rose up several stories from the streets—the tallest structure in the city by far and the only one of magical construction. Within, layers of stacked seating made up the bulk of the stadium and framed the central ring, where the dirt-covered fighting pit itself was situated.

The gates lifted and the spectators began pouring into the arena and methodically finding their seats, some of which had cost a great deal—the profits of which would go directly to the Merchants' Guild and funding future tournaments.

*Balos was right about the guards.* Clutching the now-crumpled piece of parchment the guildhall guard had handed her when she left, Andrea noted the postings of guards at every entrance. More were probably inside where they would no doubt be watching for all manner of cheating, exploitation, and most importantly, Richard.

They would not be there to protect her, though—she knew this as she handed the parchment to the gamemaster standing behind a podium at the main entrance. A thin, woman with a birdlike face, she glanced at the parchment, grimacing at its wrinkled condition, before turning her attention to Andrea.

"The Grandmaster sent word ahead that you would be arriving, Enchanter…" She checked the parchment again before addressing her. "Meredith. As the rules go you are responsible for supplying your own weapons and armor should you require it. Any injuries, up to and including death, which occur while in arena combat are your fault and your fault alone. There are three matches today and you will be fighting in the final one."

*Remain calm.* She could do this. She *had* to do this. "How do the fights work?"

The gamemaster scribbled something in her ledger. "Each fight has a ranked combatant who will compete against a group of challengers," she explained, not bothering to look at her she made her pen strokes. "If you win, you will be granted a rank increase and will compete against more difficult opponents in future rounds."

Andrea didn't need to ask what happened if the combatant lost.

The gamemaster looked up from the ledger. "Any other questions?" she asked, though the terseness in her voice did not seem to encourage more. When Andrea told her she had none, the gamemaster directed her to a wooden platform that would take her down into the arena's understructure where the combatants were housed until it was their turn to fight.

A helmed guard waited for her on the rickety platform as she approached. Once she had stepped on, he threw a metal lever next to him. A harsh grinding of metal against metal filled the air as the platform began to descend.

Even with his face hidden beneath the metal plating of his helmet, Andrea could still hear scorn in the guard's voice as they slowly dropped into the depths under the arena.

"You're the enchanter." When she said nothing, he continued. "I hear you're up against a bunch of Legionnaire deserters. This particular bunch hates enchanters and magic, too."

She opted not to meet his gaze. "Thanks for your concern, but I'll be fine."

The guard gave a dark laugh. "For Damea's sake, I hope they tear you apart within the first minute. It's people like you who are the reason for the sky turning green."

Andrea stiffened but said nothing as she tried not to show any reaction to his taunt.

They reached the understructure, a dank cave-like space that spanned the length of the arena. The chants of the impatient crowds above were a dull rumble down here, the old wooden pillars holding up the ring above vibrating as they shouted for the matches to begin. As she stepped off the platform and onto the soft dirt, she could see there were several other moving platforms around the cave that ascended to the fighting ring.

"You'll be the third one so you'll go to that one," the guard said and pointed at the platform directly ahead, where another guard stood beside it, waiting for her. He didn't wait for her to respond before pushing the lever, the platform shifting and rising back up to the entrance, leaving Andrea to fend for herself in the understructure.

The room shook again, the cries above a sure sign the first match had begun. She moved toward her assigned platform, trying to push down the panic and rising doubts that had plagued her since her argument with Meredith in the alley earlier. Shocked and ashamed at her own behavior—she had *struck* her mentor—she wondered if some part of what Meredith had said to her held any truth. *If I hadn't bottled that magic, I'd be dead now. Damea would be as good as dead. It is up to me to stop this.*

She didn't know what had befallen Gurdinfield and hoped Diana and Jacob were safe. Kye had briefed her on the mutiny in Azgadar as well as telling her Elisa and Ithmeera were on their way to the City of Towers. But Gurdinfield was too far to help her in Gurith and even if she could contact Diana, it would take at least a week before any help would arrive. And with Meredith afraid to make the hard choices that *needed* to be made…no, she was on her own.

The first match ended with a cut off scream that could be heard all the way down, sending a shiver through her spine. As the crowds stomped and yelled, she closed her eyes in an attempt to block out the noise. *I can do this!*

The second match began and as she stood in front of the platform, she suddenly realized that she had left her last potion with Meredith. Clenching her fists, she drew upon the supply of pure magic within her, letting herself feel the familiar burning for only a moment. She still had a decent supply; it would have to be enough. Perhaps after she saved Cassie, she would find Meredith and use the final potion while she found a way to restore magic to the land again.

The understructure shook again as the second match ended. A foul stench coated in smoke permeated the air. As her mind ran through the possibilities of what happened, her stomach lurched and for a moment she thought she might throw up.

The guard next to her platform beckoned her with a chainmail-covered arm. "You're next, enchanter. Let's go."

She inhaled deeply, trying with all her might to focus her mind on the magic within her. She would need to draw from it as efficiently as possible if she wanted to survive against these former Legionnaires. She did not want to kill them though, which only made her task more challenging. Everything she did would require precise control. Moreover, she would need to conserve enough magic to apprehend Richard when he inevitably appeared.

She stepped forward, the low rumble of the awaiting crowd above shaking the platform, and nodded to the guard.

He pushed the lever.

# Chapter 11

# Gladiator

"…Meredith of Darst, Former Royal Enchanter of Gurdinfield!"

Ears ringing from the cacophony of cries from the spectators, Andrea had to shield her eyes for a moment as they adjusted from the darkness of the understructure to the dim, green light of the fighting ring as the platform came to a jolting stop, the base locking with a low click.

She took in her surroundings, trying to analyze the ring and what she might be able to use to her advantage. A lump in her throat quickly formed when she saw no less than ten mostly armored men and women closing in on her from several paces away. Some wore more armor than others, but all were armed with either a sword, an axe, or in one case, a massive spiked club. A few still wore the armor of the Legion, though most wore a mismatch of leather and metal pieces that looked worse for wear. The club-wielder, a man in a leather vest and baring muscular scarred arms, appeared to be their leader as the others formed around him. They surrounded her as they slowly approached—the hatred they held for her clear in their eyes and faces even from where she stood.

They wanted to kill her. But she had already come too far to let a bunch of deserters get in the way of her finding Richard and saving Cassie.

The first attack came from a woman wielding a sword, who yelled out as she put all of her strength behind the blow.

The focus Andrea had been struggling to achieve in the understructure snapped into place as a brilliant white translucent barrier came up around her, stopping the blade just before it sliced into her. The force of the barrier mirrored the force of the sword back onto the woman, the impact sending her flying backwards and into another Legionnaire.

"Die, enchanter!" an axe-wielding man cried from behind Andrea as he swung down on her head, the metal edge whistling as it cut through the air.

Whirling on him, Andrea let the magic bubble up to her arms and hissed in pain as she threw the barrier at him. He flipped backwards before smashing face-first on the dirt and rolling.

The arena shuddered as the crowd let out a collective roar that rippled throughout the fighting ring and sent Andrea's heart racing.

Her blood on fire, she cast another barrier and had just caught her breath when she turned back in time to see the fist of another deserter coming at her. The barrier caught it, but the collision made her stumble and the shield flickered if only for a moment.

She heard the low whoosh of the club before it hit the weakened barrier. The spikes punctured it and she threw her body to the ground to avoid it, crying out when she felt cold metal tear through her cloak and rip into her right shoulder before she hit the dirt.

*Get up.* The pain was overwhelming. What in the world had she been thinking? She was in absolutely *no* way prepared for this.

The leader stepped forward, a cruel grin exposing gaps in his mouth where teeth used to be as he prepared to attack.

She *had* to get up. If not for her own survival, then for Cassie's.

Adrenaline rushed from the wound and ignited the magic within her further as she rolled out of reach of the club-wielder. She climbed to her feet as her shield was bolstered by the power that now pulsed on the right side of her body. She coughed up some of the dirt she'd inhaled when she fell.

"I don't want to kill you," she warned, wincing as she tried to ignore the thin rivulets of blood that ran down her shoulder and stained her shirtsleeve. "But I will if I have to."

The leader's eyebrows went up in mild surprise as the Legionnaires around him laughed. "Trying to talk your way ou—"

The fireball hit him in the arm that held the club, the flames immediately eating away at his skin. He let out a howl and dropped his weapon before falling to his knees, rolling on the ground in a frantic attempt to snuff out the fire.

Watching the contempt on the Legionnaires' faces turn to hesitation and in some, fear, Andrea maintained her barrier with one hand while she conjured a second fireball with the other.

A rush of air flooded the ring, throwing all the Legionnaires back several paces where they were pinned by translucent barriers not unlike her own. A hush fell over the crowd and Andrea's breath hitched when she turned around.

In a blue collared shirt and clean dark pants tucked into boots, he could have been another of Gurith's merchants or perhaps a diplomat from Gurdinfield. His neatly styled blond hair blended into a short, trimmed beard, complementing blue eyes. He was not a short man, but she knew her father was larger and stronger and would probably try to tear him apart if he had the chance.

He smiled at her in greeting, which made her despise him even more—if that were possible. "Hello, Andrea."

It took every ounce of willpower for her to not throw the fireball at him. "Where is Cassie?" she demanded. But when a familiar, faint voice called out her name, Andrea shivered as her heart sank, a coil of cold dread wrapping around her.

She stood a few paces behind Richard, slightly hunched over and wearing the traveling shirt and pants she'd worn on their last day in Azgadar—both of which were filthy and frayed at the edges. Her blondish-brown hair was pulled back into a loose, messy ponytail, the once shaven sides now partially grown out and falling at the sides and in front of her dirt-streaked face. Around her neck she bore a long scar that ran along her collarbone and beneath her shirt.

But it wasn't until Andrea saw her eyes that she wanted to cry. Once a bright blue that rivaled the clearest of days in the Western Hills, the irises were replaced with an unnatural blue glow, and the area around her eyes was tense with pain.

The burning in Andrea's shoulder worsened as the adrenaline began to wane. *What has he done to her?* "Cassie!" she cried out.

The haunting expression Cassie wore did not change but the break in her voice made Andrea desperately want to go to her. "Y-you're alive."

How long had she thought Andrea dead? Had she mourned her? Had Richard just watched with the cold, calculating observation Andrea had seen him display in the past? The stacking possibilities only added to the sorrow she felt when she saw her strong, free-spirited partner now reduced to a shade of her former self. "I'm…I'm here, Cassie! I'm going to take you home, all right?"

Where were the Grandmaster's promised guards? She scanned the arena, finding the answer to her question at the edges where a cluster of Gurithian fighters had also been held in place by Richard's spell. *How did he do that?*

"You will not be taking anyone anywhere," Richard cut in, waving his hand. "Curious that you would use Meredith's name to lure me here. A clever trick, but I already had plans to come here." He gestured to the stands around them. "A shame these people have no idea what is coming. But I don't expect much from a cesspool like Gurith." He noticed her bleeding shoulder and clicked his tongue. "That wound looks painful. Almost as painful as the one you received in Azgadar but not quite, I am guessing? Magically-caused injuries tend to pack a bit more of a punch," he added. "You should go home, Andrea, while you still have your life."

The flame hovering over Andrea's palm flared, its orange

glow illuminating a small radius around them. "Release her or I promise I *will* kill you."

Richard sighed. "I see we're going to have a problem. Had I known you survived perhaps I would have planned this differently."

"Meredith is here in Gurith," Andrea said, trying a different approach. "She believes you are not a threat. There is still time for you to prove that to her."

"Andrea," Cassie whimpered. "Get out of here. You *have* to—please!"

But Andrea responded by pouring more magic into the barrier and flame. "No. I'm going to save you, Cassie, and then we're going to go home. I promise."

"I *am* interested in how you figured out we would be here," Richard continued, not seeming to notice the exchange between Andrea and Cassie. "I suppose you could have guessed, but…"

"Did you not hear me? Meredith is here, Richard. She's been looking for you." Andrea glanced at the crowd, who appeared to be watching with rapt fascination. *They think this is part of the game.* She wanted to warn them but she couldn't let her guard down in front of Richard. Not if she hoped to save Cassie.

His lips curled into a cold sneer. "Stupid girl. You think invoking my wife's name will somehow convince me to put everything on hold? No." He crossed his arms. "I'm going to give you one chance, Andrea, and just the one. Leave and do not interfere with my plans again."

"I'm not leaving without Cassie."

He nodded, his expression softening for a moment. "Very

well." Uncrossing his arms, he began turning toward Cassie. Andrea struck.

The barrier she had been holding warbled as it flew towards Richard's chest, her aim true as she held her breath—waiting for the impact to send him careening into the dirt.

But just as the shield was about to hit Richard, the magic suddenly slowed and halted, inches from his body, before dissipating.

She barely had enough time to process what had happened before a powerful force of magic collided with her, sending a shock through her injured side and emitting a loud crack that rattled her very essence. She fell hard on her back, the wind knocked out of her, and gasped for air.

"No!" Cassie yelled. "Stop, *please!* I-I'll do whatever you want."

Rolling onto her stomach, Andrea groaned as she tried to push herself up. She froze when she was met by Richard's boots as he stood above her.

"Interesting," he mused and for a brief second Andrea could see a tether of faded light manifest between him and Cassie before it vanished just as quickly. "You can still cast yet you do not appear to be trying to draw from the land. Which means you must be drawing it from somewhere else…perhaps yourself?"

She let out a few more deep coughs, her throat rough from the dust she'd inhaled. In the distance, the once consistent blast of cheering from the crowd had dulled to a collective murmur. "Why are you doing this?" She felt once more for the magic and recalled her tactic with the Legionnaire. Perhaps if she got him talking…

Richard shook his head, amused. "Because I wish to go home, Andrea. And since you so effectively destroyed my machine, this is the only way I can gather enough magic to replicate the conditions necessary for portal generation."

"We can find another way, though!" The muscles in her back and arm tensed as the energy returned. *Almost there.* "Meredith will help, too—I'm certain of it. You don't have to—"

Cassie's cries rung in her ears as she was once again thrown through the air like a rag doll. She hit the dirt with an audible thump and rolled, her concentration broken and any casting preparation canceled.

"That was unwise," Richard said as she pushed herself up so she was on her knees. "Do you think I am stupid? That I couldn't sense what you were doing?" He let out a harsh laugh. "You've managed to store pure magic in you! A fool move considering you don't have Cassie's abilities—you'll expire once it's gone if the magic itself doesn't kill you outright. Although…" He rubbed his beard as curiosity returned to his tone.

"We are done here, Cassie," he called back to her, not taking his eyes off Andrea. "Take whatever magic she's keeping in her and then absorb the arena's."

Cassie took a few shambling steps toward Richard, her face contorted in horror. "No! I-I won't do it!" Her head jerked and she fell to her knees.

"Stop it! Leave her alone!" With every fiber in her being aching, Andrea tried to tap into the diminished adrenaline if only to will her body to stand again.

His patience finally gone, Richard spun to roughly grab Cassie by her collar and pulled her off the ground. Malice poured into his voice as he shook her. "I tire of your backtalking. You *will* take the magic or I will have you kill her yourself and I will make you do it slowly. Do we understand each other?"

The field went quiet and in her weakened state Andrea blocked out even the noises from the crowd in the stands. "Cassie," she croaked. "Please, you have to fight it. I know you can!"

"I've *tried!*" Cassie's face was wet with tears as she squeezed her eyes shut, her boots scraping through the dirt as she approached. "I-I can't—that necklace, Andrea…it gave him control!" She pulled back a bit and immediately jerked again, crying out in obvious pain. "You can stop him! Andrea, you can…get the magic back. You have to…" Another step. "You *have* to kill me, Andrea. It's the only way!"

*Never.* She wouldn't do it. Not even for all the magic in Damea. "I-I can't do that, Cassie. I won't. There has to be another way!" She clutched her arm as it gave another spasm, the pain shooting up to her neck and spreading across her right side. The fights with the Legionnaires and Richard had depleted a considerable portion of her resources. Even if Cassie didn't take her magic, she would have run out soon regardless.

She hung her head, the crushing weight of her failure eating away at her as Cassie stood in front of her with trembling hands. This couldn't be how it ended for them. It wasn't fair that someone as awful and evil as Richard got to have his way while the woman she loved suffered like this. While she and the rest of Damea suffered.

Eyebrows arched, the illumination in her eyes so intense that for a moment they were all Andrea could see, Cassie sniffed and closed her right hand.

"I'm so sorry," she whispered.

Andrea gasped as *something* wrapped itself around the store of magic she had been pulling from. It was foreign and powerful, a deep, raw magic she didn't know could even exist in Damea. It convulsed, squeezing so hard she felt something within her snap. Pain exploded in her skull and she screamed as the vision in her right eye burned and blurred before going dark.

She thought she heard Cassie sobbing, begging for forgiveness but it sounded far away as she collapsed again, moaning, her own harsh breath loud in her ears as her skin and hair were peppered with the white flakes of ash that now fell from above. There was other screaming, though not hers, as she tried to take in what was happening through her remaining good eye.

Cassie stumbled to the center of the arena and extended her hands again. She let out an anguished cry before translucent wisps of power began pulling into her arms from the edges of the arena.

The earth rumbled beneath them, the gravel bouncing as the stone walls of the structure began to crack. Spectators trampled over each other in a desperate attempt to escape the stands as the magic holding the Shadow Arena together started to destabilize. Andrea tried to call out to Cassie, but her voice wouldn't work. The magic in her was gone as she tried to crawl to her partner. *Have to stop this. Have to save her.* But she fell again, the constant debilitating pain too much for her—the last thing she remembered was the sensation of arms under her back before the world went dark.

# Chapter 12

# Safe

**City of Towers, Gurdinfield**

Lydia Diana Taylor leaned against the wooden balcony railing of the royal suite she shared with her husband, Jacob, looking out at the cobblestone main road that wound downhill through the City of Towers, the capital city of the Kingdom of Gurdinfield. Choked, filtered green sunlight managed to break through the thick swirling clouds that had covered the city for weeks. Blue, white, and gold banners donning the lion and towers of Gurdinfield's crest hung from the stone walls of the palace, the thick fabric flapping in the occasional gusts of wind.

She watched with admiration as Gurdinfielders made their way from home to work and the destinations in between despite the eerie sight hovering over them. They were a hardy people used to war and unrest, having only been out of a civil war for the better part of a year, and she was proud to be called their queen.

A bell tolled, coming from the Sky Tower, the tallest of the three great white towers that were the city's namesake.

*Someone comes?* She knew that bell as she peered on the horizon, where sprawling grasslands gave way to the forest line of the Gurdin Woods in the distance. Her long dark hair, gathered in a single braid, slipped down her shoulder and fell to her side as she leaned forward even further to get a better look, the fabric of her dark grey tunic bunching against the balcony's edge.

Two riders on one horse approached. The copper shade gleaming off one of them betrayed one of the riders' identity.

"Elisa!" she breathed, pushing away from the railing as she rushed back into her bedroom before swinging the thick wooden door open and bolting down the stairs. Posted in the great hall and leading out into the palace courtyard were Guardians, legendary protectors of House Taylor turned rebels turned protectors once more. They stood at attention as she flew past them and nearly collided with her husband Jacob as he stepped through the open double doors. A big man sporting green eyes and his usual shaggy blond cut, he stepped aside with agility rivaling the best Guardian sword masters, being one himself.

"What's the rush?" he called, his jovial mannerisms always seeming to find a way into his tone, cataclysm or not. "Who is here?"

"It's Elisa!" Diana yelled back as she kept focus on the path in front of her. "Get the others and meet me at the gates!"

✳ ✳ ✳

They did not have to go far to meet Elisa. The gates, long since repaired after the great battle that held off the Azgadaran Legion in its last attempt to conquer Gurdinfield, had been raised by the Guardians at the base of the city, many of whom recognized Elisa and Ithmeera when they saw them approaching.

Diana stood at the gates of the palace, watching as they rode up the hill—the clatter of the horse's hooves alerting the citizens in the street, who watched with bewildered expressions as the Empress of the Azgadaran Empire rode into the city unannounced.

Behind Diana stood her entourage, which included Jacob of course as well as her grey-haired adoptive father, Alexander Telman, and two of her closest companions, Victor and Roe. "I believe I see the empress with her."

Victor, a tall, auburn-haired fighter with a long pale face gave her a querying glance. "The empress's come here? Times are stranger than I thought, Your Majesty."

"She's come for her son." Jacob concluded. He turned to the huge, dark-skinned man beside him. "Roe, where is Marco?"

Roe gave a nod of his bald head. "He is in his quarters, sir. Shall I go get him?"

Diana answered before Jacob could. "Do it, please," she said as the riders approached. "Hopefully, we'll be able to get some answers at last."

"Perhaps they know of the scouts we sent," Alexander added.

Diana sighed, her gaze flickering to the sky for a moment. "I hope so."

Upon reaching the summit, Elisa brought the horse to a

stop before swinging her leg over and dismounting. Turning, she offered her hand to Ithmeera and assisted her in climbing down. Both looked exhausted, as though they hadn't slept very much in the last few days at least. Elisa's black leather armor was torn in several places and the bottom of Ithmeera's cloak and dress were coated in mud.

Elisa took a few steps toward them and bowed. "Your Majesty. Your Highness." Ithmeera followed suit, and Diana found herself blinking in temporary disbelief that Empress Ithmeera Cadar was in her home, *bowing* to her.

Diana rushed forward. "Welcome to Gurdinfield. Please, come in, come in." She pointed at the open double doors of the palace, indicating for everyone to go inside. The others followed once she entered along with Elisa and Ithmeera.

"My son," Ithmeera spoke, the urgency in her voice masked with thin composure as they approached the great hall. "Please, Lydia, I must know if he's all right. The magic…"

Diana's hand went to her shoulder. "Marco is fine. We've been supervising him, making sure he does not try to use magic. Roe just went to fetch him from his quarters, actually. He should be here shortly."

As though on cue, a small, frightened voice sounded in the vast space of the great hall. Standing beside Roe was a boy of eight. Dark curls fell in front of light brown eyes, eyes he had inherited from Philip, his late father. "Mother?"

Crossing her arms, Diana's throat tightened as she watched Ithmeera rush across the room and gather Marco in her arms—tears of joy and relief rolling down her cheeks. Jacob called Victor and Roe to the nearby war room as Alexander announced he would be checking on the palace supplies before joining them later. Elisa remained next to Diana as the two of them observed the heartfelt reunion between the empress and her son.

"What happened, Elisa?" she demanded, her voice low so only Elisa could hear. "We sent scouts to Azgadar after the sky went dark and they never returned. Enchanters in the city have been injured or killed by the Cataclysm. And where are Andrea and Cassie? Where is Kye?"

Elisa bit her lip. "Petra is the leader of the New Legion. She led a mutiny against Ithmeera and turned the Legionnaires in the palace against us. We barely escaped with our lives."

Diana thought she heard wrong at first. *Petra?* Her lady-in-waiting?"

"The very same," Elisa said with a grim nod. "She sent soldiers after us when she discovered we had survived. We had to take the long way here, through Fimen's Hope, to avoid them." Her eyes widened. "The storms. We saw them in Fimen's Hope. They nearly destroyed the town and neighboring fields. Have they hit the city yet?"

"No. We sent a rider to Fimen's Hope but haven't heard back." Diana closed her eyes. *If Azgadar has fallen...* It would fall to her and Gurdinfield to help fix this—she knew that much. "And...Andrea?" She watched as Elisa rubbed bloodshot eyes, the tiredness in them even more apparent now that they were indoors.

"I do not know. She and Cassie found her old mentor's husband, Richard, while they were in the Western Hills. Somehow, he managed to take Cassie under his control and forced her to use her power to absorb the land's magic." Elisa let out a long breath. "It happened right outside Azgadar and Andrea was badly injured when I last saw her. It was…terrible." She cleared her throat—it was clear whatever had happened had shaken her up. "Kye took her to Ata to find an enchanter who could help her."

Diana patted her friend's back. "It's going to be all right, Elisa." Her attention was redirected to the woman in front of her. Ithmeera walked toward the pair, holding her son by the hand.

"Thank you…for keeping him safe," she said, gratitude emanating from both the relief in her glossy eyes and her words. "I would like to take him to his room and talk to him for a bit, if that is all right? I shall join you both after."

"Of course," Diana replied, making sure to give Marco a friendly smile. Elisa nodded and bowed her head but remained quiet.

Once Ithmeera and Marco had left the hall, Diana turned to Elisa again. "Where is Cassie?"

Elisa gave a helpless shrug. "I do not know. Kye says when Richard disappeared, he took Cassie with him. They could be anywhere."

Diana gestured for them to move into the war room, a small round room framed with bookshelves and small tables. A larger table upon which sat an unrolled piece of canvas—a map of Damea—was the centerpiece of the room. Jacob, Victor, and Roe waited for them on the other side of the table—Victor sitting while Jacob and Roe stood.

"We have new information," Diana announced. "Ithmeera's lady-in-waiting, Petra, is responsible for the New Legion and the coup in Azgadar."

Jacob's brow furrowed. "A coup? How—"

"She had the time and the means to plan it well. She was close to Ithmeera and took advantage of the growing tension in the city," Elisa answered, not bothering to hide the anger behind her words.

Diana waited for her to finish before she continued. "There is more. Richard, a man we know as the husband of Andrea's former mentor, is responsible for the Cataclysm. He has Cassie."

Victor's jaw dropped as Roe's scarred face contorted in grief. "Against her will?" he boomed.

When Diana nodded, Jacob slammed his fist on the table, making everyone in the room jump. "This is my fault. I should have had her train longer before taking on her own charge!"

"It is no one's fault, love." Diana tried to soothe him, but what could she say when the news they received only grew grimmer? "But…Andrea was injured—badly. Kye took her back to Ata to get help from an enchanter there."

Heavy silence fell upon the room and remained until Alexander entered. Diana and the others updated him on the state of things and had just finished when Ithmeera, too, arrived.

"How is Marco?" Elisa asked. Diana watched as the two exchanged glances of something unsaid but known among the both of them. She wondered what had transpired between them in the weeks since she and the Guardians had left Azgadar with

Marco.

"He is fine. And more importantly, safe." Faded green eyes met Diana's as Ithmeera thanked her again.

"It is no trouble. We are allies, now, Your Majesty. Gurdinfield stands with Azgadar." She turned to the map on the table. "It appears we have two problems here. We don't know where Richard and Cassie are, but more importantly, we can't find them while holed up here. This man is a threat to all of Damea. We need every available body searching for him." She looked at Ithmeera. "We need the largest army in the land. We need the Legion, Your Majesty."

Elisa, who had been leaning back against one of the bookshelves, perked up. "The Legion has been taken over by fanatics."

"Surely some remain loyal to the empress," Jacob said and Diana took a moment to admire her husband's stubborn streak and the ability to see the positive in everything.

Ithmeera clasped her arm with the opposite hand and sighed. "If there are, they were most likely arrested or killed. General Veraun…lost his life defending me. Too many have died already, Lydia. I am not certain I can give you what you ask."

Victor stood up, speaking out of turn despite the company around him. "Why not take back Azgadar, then? Stick a nice sword through that idiot who stole your throne, Your Majesty."

No one spoke for a moment.

But Jacob's face soon lit up at the idea. He turned to Diana. "Victor's right. Gurdinfield's armies are strong, Diana, stronger than ever."

Elisa shot him an incredulous look. "And you would… what? Send your army into the heart of the Azgadaran Empire against the Le—sorry, the New Legion? These are no ordinary Legionnaires, Jacob. They are motivated by hate and that drivel Petra has fed them. They will do anything to see Ithmeera dead."

Jacob pinched the bridge of his nose in frustration. "I would not suggest sending Her Majesty to the front lines to battle the New Legion herself, Elisa," he explained, extending a hand toward Ithmeera.

"But you would risk the lives of your own men?" Elisa said. "With all due respect, Jacob, that sounds equally foolhardy. Surely we can come up with a better plan than breaking down the front door."

With tensions rising in the room, Diana knew she had to put a stop to it. They were already in dire times—there was no need to add arguments among friends to the list. "Enough!" she ordered, her tone much sharper than she was accustomed to using even as queen. When Elisa and Jacob both ceased their bickering, she continued. "We are in troubled times, friends. We must remain united or we are no better than those who have taken our way of life from us. Ithmeera," she said, surprising herself when she addressed the empress by her first name. "Azgadar is your home. Per our alliance Gurdinfield is honor-bound to help you take it back. But I will not march an army into Azgadaran borders without your blessing."

With all eyes on her, Ithmeera's gaze landed on Elisa before focusing on Diana as she swallowed. "Even if we somehow manage to take down Petra and take back the city, there is no guarantee the old Legion will be there. This is not what you want to hear, but I need to consider my son." She did not have the confident, unbreakable aura of the empress Diana had met in Azgadar, but that of a frightened, desperate woman.

Elisa jumped in before Diana could answer. *"Abandon Azgadar? Ithmeera…we cannot just give up, now. Marco is safe and—"*

Ithmeera's head snapped to where Elisa stood, where she treated her to a punishing glare, her heightened voice raising well past the point where others in the palace might not hear her. "He is safe *in spite of* my actions, not because!"

"This is not your fault."

"Yes, Elisa, it is!"

The shock of her outburst sent hushed discomfort through the war room. Diana watched as Alexander and Jacob looked away out of respect. Victor appeared frustrated, no doubt at the lack of action they were taking and Roe stiffened in the most formal Guardian stance Diana had ever seen him take.

She observed Elisa. If her friend was shaken by Ithmeera yelling at her, she was trying hard not to show it.

*So we find another way. We always do.* "It is fine. We will continue to come up with ideas until we find one that works. In the meantime, Your Majesty, you and Marco are welcome to remain in the City of Towers for as long as you like."

With drawn lips, as though she struggled to contain her frustration, Ithmeera offered a stiff bow. "Your hospitality and aid are appreciated, Lydia," she said in a broken voice. "Perhaps I could be shown to where I'll be staying in the meantime? I…

think better when I am not so tired, especially after traveling."

"I will show the empress to her quarters." Alexander's offer was accompanied by a kind smile. When Diana nodded her approval, he extended his arm in the direction of the hall. "Please, Your Majesty, right this way."

"Victor, Roe," Jacob said once Ithmeera had left with Alexander, "get a head count of our current forces in the city. I want to know exactly what we're working with should we decide to mount an assault on Azgadar."

"Do you really think she'll change her mind?" Diana asked after the men had given their affirmative responses and also departed.

Jacob shrugged. "I don't know. She seems desperate, but she's also right. We have no guarantee the Legion will be in a position to help us even if we successfully retake the city."

"She's being a fool," Elisa muttered.

Diana sighed. "Elisa, I understand you're upset, but if this is what the empress wishes I cannot go against that."

"Then I will leave and find this Richard myself. Or…I'll head to the Western Hills and get Andrea." She let out a frustrated noise. "We need an enchanter if there is to be any hope of fixing this."

Jacob raised an eyebrow. "And where would you look?"

"We don't even know if Andrea is alive and none of our enchanters can cast without being injured or killed," Diana added.

Elisa thrust a hand toward the window. "Look at the sky, Your Majesty! You may have not seen the storms, but I have and they will destroy Damea if we do not stop them."

Diana was beginning to lose her patience. "I understand your frustration, Elisa, but make no mistake—I know very well what it is we face. Now, I don't know what all happened on your trip here with the empress, but you both look like you can barely stand. I suggest you take some time to rest as well."

"But—"

She didn't let Elisa finish. "That is all I will say for now, Elisa. Your quarters should be just as you left them." She took Jacob's arm and began to lead him out of the war room. "We will speak again on this later. You have my word."

# Chapter 13

# The Shield

*The magic pulled at her, urging her to use it. A fireball here, a barrier there…it did not take much before the village itself was on fire. Hot flakes of burning ash surrounded her, swirling about like a shield of their own as she passed burning buildings, ignoring the panicked cries and shouts from the people trapped within. The streaks on her arm pulsed to the rhythm of her heartbeat, the blue and white energy pricking at the surface of her skin and giving her far more than she needed. But she would not turn away what was offered. Not when so much was at stake.*

*Then she saw him.*

*His back was facing her and he was hunched over in the center of the square, as though cradling something in his hands. She couldn't make him out entirely, but something deep within told her it was him—and now he was helpless against her.*

*"You are out of control!" A familiar voice but one she did not care to remember. She had a job to do.*

*She closed in on him, hand raised as a scorching fireball appeared in her palm. Smoldering embers crackled in the collapsing structures around them as she called out to him. She didn't remember using the words, but something reassured her they had been said.*

*He stood upright, no longer hunched over, before turning around with agonizing slowness.*

*No.*

*He was gone and in his place stood Cassie. Her hair wild and unkempt, she grinned with unsettling glowing eyes as she extended a clenched fist to Andrea and opened her palm where the metal necklace sat atop raised, burned skin.*

*No!*

*"I'm so sorry."*

*The burning in her right eye returned and she screamed.*

✶ ✶ ✶

Jolting awake, Andrea did not recognize Meredith's face when she saw it hovering over hers at first. Instinct kicked in and her arms shot out to push her assailant back only to be caught by strong grips as Meredith held her down.

"It is only me! Calm yourself." The stern voice was recognizable enough to make Andrea freeze. She let out a shuddering breath and attempted to regain her awareness. Blinking away the strange, fleeting dream she quickly identified the telltale sounds of the forest. She was lying on soft grass, her head propped up on a rolled-up blanket in the middle of a clearing, though in what forest in Damea she couldn't tell right away. Her torn cloak and bloodied shirt had been removed, leaving her in an undershirt where she noted the heavy bandages wrapped around her upper arm and shoulder.

The weakness that made her entire body feel like she had been thrown down a mountain was still there, as was the low burning sensation in her arm. To her relief though, the vision in her right eye was partially restored, if blurry. She recalled her battle in the arena and with Richard, before Cassie…

*Before she—*

Panic began rising in her as she feared the worst. How many people had been injured or killed when the Shadow Arena fell? Was Cassie all right? Where had they gone and what was Richard's plan now? Did he have enough magic to open a portal home?

Meredith shook her head and released her arms before picking up the damp rag that had been dropped during the struggle moments earlier. "I suppose you're having violent dreams now, too?" She pressed the cloth against Andrea's forehead, the coolness a welcome if brief reprieve from the constant heat her wounds continued to generate. "It would not surprise me considering your behavior lately."

"Meredith? How did you—where are we?"

Meredith withdrew the cloth and helped her sit up. "The Western Hills, a few days southwest of Azgadar. Hold this, I must inspect your shoulder wound."

The Western Hills? She noted the light brown horse tied to a nearby tree as he munched on the long grass. "Where did you get him?"

"The stables near the arena," Meredith said. "The saddle looks quite expensive so I imagine whatever noble or merchant owned him before has another just like him back home. Now, hold this."

That would mean they had been traveling for some time. She took the rag from Meredith and held it above her brow as she fished for memories of the lost time and came up empty. "Gurith…what happened? Where's Cassie?"

Meredith began slowly unwrapping the top layer of bandages on Andrea's shoulder. "Gone, both of them. The Shadow Arena was destroyed, as were many of the surrounding buildings. I saw much of your confrontation with Richard." She peeled away the last of the outer bandage and set to inspecting the wound. "I tried to go to you in the ring, but after what happened to the guards sent out to apprehend him, the Grandmaster would not allow it. I saw them both walk out of the arena before I could reach you."

Andrea let out a sigh of relief. "You saw what he did?"

"I did." Seeming satisfied with what she saw, Meredith proceeded to rewrap the bandages. "It'll scar, of course. Perhaps you will not be so eager to give up enchanting to become a gladiator in the future."

"Meredith…"

"What is it I'm supposed to say, Andrea?" The bitterness in Meredith's tone did little to mask the sadness in her weary grey eyes. "I saw what everyone else did. But the man I knew would never do this."

Even after all that had happened, Andrea had to fight down the urge to comfort her mentor. "Perhaps you don't know him as well as you think you did." She hissed as the slight pressure

Meredith's hands put on the wound stung. "Careful!" It dawned on her that despite Cassie taking her magic she could still sense the liquid magic hovering beneath her skin, ready to be drawn on when she needed it. At first, she wondered if perhaps Cassie had not taken it all.

But the nightmarish memory of the magic being ripped from her was still fresh, which left only one other possibility. "You gave me the last potion, didn't you?"

"Only half of it," Meredith said. "But yes. You were feverish and fading quickly. I had no choice." She gave her a disapproving look. "Had you simply been patient we could have found another way, one that perhaps didn't involve you going into that ring and—"

"And what would you have suggested instead?" Andrea snapped, the anger blazing through her making her head spin and the scars on her arm pulse with light. Meredith slipped an arm behind her back to hold her up.

"Calm down," she said. "And to answer your question: I cannot say for certain. But…what's done is done, I suppose." A clap of thunder sounded and both turned their gazes to the sky.

Through the tree cover Andrea could see it was still the same unsettling green, only the clouds were moving much faster than they had been and periodic flashes of lightning streaked overhead, not dissimilar to what she had seen when Richard had first made Cassie absorb the magic.

Meredith's lips parted as she stared at the impending storm. "We are running out of time."

"What do you mean?"

"The land is destabilizing, Andrea." Withdrawing her arm after confirming Andrea could sit up on her own again, Meredith retreated to a nearby knapsack, which she opened and pulled a canteen from. "During the Starving, the magic was being slowly siphoned away from the land and into that machine you claim Richard built."

Andrea rolled her eyes. "Enough already, Meredith. He *did* build it and you know it."

Meredith glared at her but continued anyway as she handed Andrea the canteen and took a seat on the grass next to her. "Drink. My point is that had that machine been allowed to drain Damea of its magic completely, we would have most likely seen a slower process of what is happening now. But now…" She gave a visible shudder. "When you cast a fireball or a barrier, you must draw on the magic that exists around you and change it. The magic is then released back into the land. Here," she said, pointing at the sky, "it is just gone. There is nothing for the land to take back."

Another distant boom, much deeper this time, as though Andrea could feel it in the earth itself. She took a long drink of water, nearly emptying the canteen before taking a breath. "That's why everything feels so…disconnected. The magic is what keeps the land balanced?"

Meredith eyebrows went up. "Remember the storm? That night, when we brought Cassie here?"

*How could I forget?* "Yes. You said that magic comes from nature."

But Meredith just shook her head. "Magic *is* nature, Andrea. They are one and the same and cannot exist without each other."

Andrea took another sip of water before closing the canteen. Knowing the world was going to end was all well and good but useless if she couldn't stop it. She wanted to laugh and cry at the same time—why did it have to be *her?* The weight that had been on her shoulders since waking up in Ata after the Cataclysm grew heavier. And with her final potion halfway gone, she wagered she had one last chance to stop Richard. *And save Cassie.*

Cassie's plea still rang in her mind. *"You have to kill me, Andrea. It's the only way!"* That wasn't the solution—that *couldn't* be the solution. Andrea knew she would die before entertaining such a notion.

She was exhausted and the constant pain and stress she'd been under for weeks was wearing on her. Her shoulders slumped as she buried her face in her hands, whispering, "I don't know what to do."

Meredith placed an unexpected hand on her shoulder. "We will figure this out. But we must consider our next move carefully, Andrea. There is…one other thing we must consider."

Andrea sighed. "I don't know if there's anything that can make this any worse than what it already is but go ahead," she said with a wave of her hand.

"It's about the magic and…enchanters," Meredith began, though slowly, as though she were choosing her words carefully. "Even if we find Richard and Cassie, there is still the matter of returning the magic."

Andrea didn't see the issue. "Cassie and I already had plans to redistribute it. That was our mission before…" Her voice threatened to break, but she pushed herself to finish. "Before all of this happened."

"Yes, but it's not just the magic distribution you need to take into account," Meredith said. "Andrea, you don't feel it because you are still drawing from those potions, but the connection all other enchanters have with the land is severed, corrupted. It is too dangerous for any enchanter to draw on magic normally." She swallowed and pointed at Andrea's scarred arm. "That is why *that* happened."

"I think I'm well aware of what happens, Meredith."

Her biting comment did not appear to faze Meredith. "There is no guarantee that returning the magic to the land will repair that connection. You recall I hesitated to destroy that machine in Rhyad?"

Andrea remembered. "Yes, you were worried Richard's body was too attuned to the levels of magic during the Starving and that he would not survive when the magic was released."

Meredith gave a solemn nod. "Imagine that but far, far worse. And not just for one man this time, but for all enchanters."

Dread pooled in Andrea as the nausea from earlier returned. Kye. Marco. Jheran. *All those enchanters…dead because of me. Because I failed to see what Richard really was.* "But…you don't know for sure, right? You were wrong about Richard not being able to adjust and you could be wrong about this."

Meredith's expression remained unchanged. "I could be. I hope I am. But I've studied magic my entire life, Andrea. But you're right—I cannot be certain." She glanced up again. "Sometimes I wonder what it was like in the First Era. No Starving, no struggle for magic between nations, no sickness for enchanters." She gave a quiet laugh as a longing note entered her voice—one Andrea hadn't heard her use in years. "At the Enchanters' Academy, they taught us about enchanters in the First Era—how they were far more powerful than the ones of today. They knew how to more efficiently harness the land's energy. And they were not feared for it."

Andrea smiled, the first time she had remembered doing so in weeks. "You miss it. The academy."

Meredith's eyes lit up. "I do. Oh, you would have loved it, Andrea. Knowledge to be found in every classroom, every book, and every lesson! And the enchanters who taught there were wonderfully talented. Perhaps if things had been different, I might have become a teacher there." She sighed and they fell into a quietness that could have been almost peaceful had it not been for the consistent thunder claps that passed over them.

"I could try to find them again—use their projection just like last time," Andrea suggested.

"No." With the reminiscing over, Meredith's answer was firm. "You are on your last potion and we cannot risk you going near Cassie so unprepared again. We need a plan. Did they say where they were going?"

"Only that he wanted to open a portal and go home. For all we know, he's already done that and it's…it's over." *What if she's already gone?* Not for the first time since they had left Ata, Andrea wished she were back in her bedroom with Cassie in the City of Towers.

Meredith gave her a curious look. "He has not, I can tell you that for sure." She pointed at the bracelet around Andrea's wrist. "Do you know how the magic in that works?"

Andrea shook her head. She remembered the warmth of the magic that had flowed up her arm and throughout her body when she had slipped the threads over her hand, but she had not given much thought to the specifics of it. No one had ever told her and she never asked.

"A weaver enchants the bracelet. When you put it on that magic binds to you, becomes a part of you. Your partner will receive a bracelet at the ceremony and the magic from theirs and yours will bind," Meredith said, holding up her own wrist to show her bracelet. "For as long as you both breathe and wear the bracelet you will always know they are alive. And I know Richard still wears his."

A bubble of hope formed. "That means he doesn't have enough magic to create a portal. What if..." She reached for the memories of the projection where she had heard the conversation between Richard and Cassie. "He said Cassie didn't absorb enough magic the first time. What if the Shadow Arena wasn't enough? Where else would he get magic from?"

Then it came to her. It was the one part of her eavesdrop she did not understand, but knowing what she knew now, it seemed clearer. "Azgadar! When I was listening to their projection, Richard mentioned Azgadar! Something about a shield. He was frustrated because he couldn't get past it."

"A shield?" Realization flickered on Meredith's face. "I have vaguely heard of this." She climbed to her feet and it wasn't long before she was soon pacing across their small campsite. "The Azgadaran Palace. More specifically the spire itself. It was built using massive amounts of magic. That's why it's so tall, though"—she gave a quiet laugh—"that could also just be typical Azgadaran arrogance."

Incredulous at the fact that Meredith was actually making jokes right now, Andrea pressed for more information. "What exactly does this shield do?"

"It was only touched on during my studies at the academy, but it was designed to prevent any enchanters from absorbing magic from the spire, as such an act would surely destroy the tower and the palace with it," Meredith said. "The level of destruction in Azgadar would be similar to what happened in Gurith, though probably worse."

Despite the constant ache in her body, Andrea managed to straighten up. Richard needed the magic in the spire to create the portal, assuming creating a portal was even possible. That Azgadar was under Petra's rule and occupied by the hostile New Legion added a layer of complexity, but still, the idea she had been forming earlier became clearer. "Could the shield be disabled? From the outside?"

Meredith stopped pacing to look at her. "Hmm. Possibly? It would involve a level of force that neither of us have, however. It was designed to withstand an invasion. What are you thinking?"

It was risky, but what other choice did they have? "What if we could give Richard what he needed: access to Azgadar and the spire?"

Meredith blinked, her brow wrinkling in doubt. "And why in the world would we do that? What good would it do, other than guaranteeing the bulk of the land's remaining magic being absorbed and possibly accelerating *this?*" She gestured at the sky.

"We could set a trap."

"Another one? After what happened last time? Aside from this plan being just as foolish as your first, Andrea, you would need an army to disable that shield. Not to mention the city itself is crawling with these new Legionnaires your friend spoke of. We are just two enchanters. And I even less of one as I cannot use magic."

*Yes, an army!* Kye had to have reached Gurdinfield by now, perhaps Elisa and Ithmeera had as well. And if the empress was there, she might know a way to disable the shield. "I wouldn't be alone this time. We need the Guardians! We have to get to the City of Towers, Meredith. I need to speak with Diana."

"You are in no condition to travel across Damea and—" Meredith started, but Andrea refused to hear it, her voice escalating into a breaking cry as she pleaded with her mentor.

"Please! Meredith, I…" The streaks on her arm began to pulse again, the light emitted from them fading and brightening with each throb of pain. "You couldn't see her. What he—what he did to her." She sniffed but quickly composed herself before she would allow herself to cry. She refused. *Not while Cassie's still out there, under the control of that monster. She's probably so scared right now.* "I brought Cassie here and it's my fault this happened. I know the dangers, I know the risks, but this isn't about me. I promised her I would save her, Meredith, and I will, even if…if I don't make it." She reached out to Meredith with her right hand, the threaded bracelet hanging from her wrist. "Please…*help* me fix this!"

Meredith said nothing at first—only stared back at Andrea with a blend of concern and, to Andrea's surprise, sympathy.

"I spent decades trying to bring my husband back, Andrea. I know what desperation feels like. I know what it means to do anything for someone you love, even if it means someone else will pay that price." She took a step toward her. "There is no guarantee what you propose will work," she said, "and even if it does, enchanters everywhere might still die. Are you willing to risk that? Could you live with yourself afterward?"

Could she? It was not too long ago that Andrea wanted nothing more than to find Damea's lost magic. She wanted to help people, particularly enchanters who risked falling ill whenever they drew upon the scarce magic. She'd had the illness—she knew what it was like, watching the world fading around her as she felt her life essence literally slip away. But seeing Cassie like that—the unsettling glow in her eyes, the way her face contorted in fear and pain as she was forced to do things Andrea could not have imagined even in her worst nightmares—made Andrea wonder if she had gotten it all wrong.

Her father's parting words to her before she left Ata nearly four years ago resonated with her. What if enchanters *were* the problem? Would not having any enchanters be so terrible? What if they were never meant to use magic?

*Stop.*

She shook her head as the racing thoughts became a swirl of questions and confusion. She would save Cassie, but she would not become a murderer doing it.

She shook her hand at Meredith, emphasizing her demand. "I'll do what must be done to save her, Meredith. As for the enchanters, I won't give up on them. I can't say more than that."

The faint lines around Meredith's grey eyes tightened. She closed the distance between them and took Andrea's hand. "Then we must make haste to Gurdinfield." Her gaze turned toward the sky again. "And hope there is still time to stop this."

# Chapter 14

# Changed

"Damn it all!" Richard's yell was immediately followed by a loud crash as a table was flipped, the glass vials atop it shattering as they crashed to the floor and a whirlwind of papers flying through the air before settling in the spreading puddle.

At the edge of the room in the abandoned house Richard had found on the outskirts of Sadford, sitting on the floor away from the upside-down table and knocked over shelving, was Cassie. Her arms around tucked in knees, she let out a cold laugh at the sight of Richard's latest tantrum. "Has anyone ever told you that you have an anger management issue?"

Richard whirled on her, panting with exertion and the remaining adrenaline of his outburst. Damp strands of his blond hair fell in front of dark-circled eyes and his beard was longer and untrimmed. "You." He took long strides across the room before grabbing one of the chains restraining her and yanked her to her feet, ignoring the yelp she let out. "I am *this* close," he growled, demonstrating with his thumb and forefinger, "to making you do something you will truly regret. You should be grateful I did not have you just kill Andrea. How in the world did Serena put up with you for so long?"

Cassie's response was to spit in his face. Richard reeled back in shock before treating her to a swift backhanded slap. White streaks slashed through her vision as she was sent to her knees.

He chuckled as he wiped his face. "You can hate me as much as you want, Cassie. The simple truth is that I'm not going anywhere and neither are you unless I say so."

She looked up at him, a faint wheeze escaping each breath, and wiped the smear of blood that trickled from the corner of her mouth. "You're right," she gasped. "You're not going anywhere. Even with all that magic, you still can't open a portal." She laughed again in spite of the pain in her already bruising face. "You're lucky I'm wearing these chains. Andrea had the decency not to kill you, but I won't be so nice."

Richard rolled his eyes and walked back to the flipped table and broken equipment. "You speak as though you're convinced you're getting out of those." He met her eyes with glaring blue ones of his own. "I will find a way to disable the shield in Azgadar and when I do, we are going home. And if Andrea interferes with my work again," he said, his lips curling in disgust, "then the last thing you will do before we go home is use that wonderful ability of yours to take her life. How fitting would it be, since she brought you here, if the last bit of magic to send you home were to be from her death." He laughed to himself and set to picking up his mess. "It's almost poetic."

Clenching her fists so hard her nails bit into her palms, Cassie shut her eyes in an effort to block out his voice. Every fiber of her wanted nothing more than to break through the chains so that she could rip him apart, father or not. But she had been trying for weeks to break them and no matter how hard she tugged and pulled against the iron shackles, she just wasn't strong enough. *Couldn't even stop myself from hurting Andrea—how would I be able to break a few stupid chains?* Tears sprang to her eyes and the bleak hopelessness she had been fighting on and off set in once more.

The events of Gurith were mostly a blur in her memory, particularly after Richard had ordered her to steal the magic from the Shadow Arena. But the earth-shaking rumble and the panicked cries of the spectators trying to get to safety as the structure broke apart were memories she would never forget. A shiver ran down her spine as Andrea's scream of agony rose up louder among the others and she doubled over. *That wasn't you. It was Richard.*

Out of instinct she opened and closed her hand, wincing when her nails parted from the skin they'd pierced. Even now she still felt the pure energy from the magic she had taken from Andrea pulsing within her, brighter and stronger than what she took from the arena despite it being less. She knew from experience how painful magic extraction was, being the subject of Meredith's early experiment when she'd first arrived in Damea as well as when she had strengthened Kye's abilities at the City of Towers. But whatever Andrea had done to herself to counter the effects of the Cataclysm clearly had made the process more torturous.

The urge to throw up surfaced again. *You did that. You hurt her.* Did it matter who gave the order? *I should have fought harder.* She wanted to kick herself—none of this would have happened if she had just refused to let her guard down around Richard in the first place! Even if she saw Andrea again, she wondered if her partner would ever be able to forgive her. *Not to mention the rest of Damea.* Cassie was far from an expert on magic, but she knew her and Richard's actions had caused a great deal of damage across the land. Even if Andrea did somehow forgive her, would their friends? *Should they?*

She lifted her head to glance out the window—the only one in the small house, which gathering from the stacks of supplies lining the walls and the small cot in one of the corners Cassie surmised was used mostly for storage and possibly for guests. Upon arriving, Richard had left to go into town for supplies. The people of Sadford clearly had no idea who they were dealing with as he returned later that afternoon with boxes of vials, rolls of parchment, and other supplies Cassie figured were for his continued attempts to discover a way to disable the shield around Azgadar's spire.

Richard rarely spoke to her most of the time, opting instead to mutter to himself as he performed experiment after experiment, scribbling down the results of each and occasionally chuckling or, more recently, swearing and breaking something. She could see his patience was fraying, but while any sane person would have given up once they saw the damage they were inflicting on others, Richard's failures seemed to embolden him.

Through the window she could see the peaks of the low buildings in Sadford as muted green clouds passed over them. That she had caused this—all this *destruction*—was something Cassie still could not come to terms with. Magic was something she didn't even believe existed until little more than a year ago, and now here she was holding nearly all of it. The sensation of having so much energy coursing through her had been overwhelming at first—every nerve in her body thrummed with it and, more often than not, she teetered on the edge of nausea. The fury she held for what Richard had done only made it worse.

She missed Andrea so much it hurt in ways she did not know were possible. Seeing her alive had given her hope, though, and Cassie could only continue to hope that in the end Andrea would find her again. *And forgive me.*

✶ ✶ ✶

The stone walls of Elisa's dimly-lit quarters shook with each wave of thunder that crashed into the city, rattling the iron knobs of the furniture and sending the shadows from the candlelight into a flurry of movement. Grey beams of light peeked in through thick blue drapes, the afternoon still young but deceiving as it had been since the Cataclysm.

She sat on the large, made bed, playing with her long dagger as she flipped the blade over her fingers in a fluid motion, breaking every so often to run her thumb along the ornate metal embossing of the silver handle. It was a habit she had picked up in her second year as a Legionnaire. The long sword was the iconic weapon of choice for the Legion, of course, but she had gained an interest in knife play after seeing some of the older Legionnaires in her company using them in sport. Legionnaire training also included gaining proficiency in a number of weapons in addition to the sword and Elisa had wanted to learn them all. Anything that would make her a better soldier was worth learning, especially after she was named a Royal Guard to Ithmeera.

She stopped flipping the dagger as another clap of thunder quickened her heartbeat. *Another life.*

"Elisa?" A familiar voice called her from the open doorway. She turned, her chest tightening when she saw Ithmeera standing there. The last thing she wanted was to be yelled at again.

She still stood, however. After all, Ithmeera was still her empress. "How can I help, Your Majesty?"

Ithmeera put a hand on her hip, the long dark blue gown—something she had no doubt received from Diana—not something Elisa was used to seeing her wear, but it fitted her nicely all the same. "Honestly, it never gets less strange when you do that."

It took all of Elisa's willpower to not sigh. *I can't say anything right, apparently.* "I'm simply addressing you as you are." She cracked a small grin. "Or would you prefer I use your childhood nickname?" That seemed to get a smile in response, which warmed the room a bit.

"'Ithmeera' is fine and will do for now," Ithmeera said and stepped into the room, observing it while running her hand along the worn surfaces of the dressers and side tables. "This place is so different from the palace. Everything feels so…so…"

"Cold?" Elisa suggested. "I am always cold here. It's as though they forgot to put in more hearths when they were building the place."

Ithmeera smirked. "My quarters have a fireplace. It's quite

nice. You should come see it." She nodded at the dagger Elisa still held. "When you're done brooding in the dark and prepping for your next assassination, of course."

Elisa snorted. Ithmeera often found the strangest times to jest and when she did her jokes veered from silly to dark in a matter of seconds. "I don't know if you're trying to make me jealous or are actually inviting me to an evening of deep conversation and riveting gossip."

Ithmeera's brilliant green eyes seemed to sparkle in the orange glow of the candlelight. "Perhaps both?" she quipped and Elisa noted for the first time how rested she appeared. Indeed, she had also been able to relax a bit since arriving in the City of Towers, an army of Guardians ready to defend them if necessary. Diana's hospitality had been a welcome change to trekking across Damea and sleeping on hard dirt and lumpy mattresses.

"Ah, well in that case…" *In that case…what?* Her conversations with Ithmeera had certainly become more amicable since that night in Fimen's Hope, some of them even turning into friendly teases as each often brought up memories of the past. But there was something else there, something Elisa could not begin to describe or recall when it began. Perhaps it had always been there—whatever *it* was. Or perhaps not.

She knew they would never go back to how they used to be. Too much had changed—*they* had changed. But Elisa couldn't deny that whatever drew her to Ithmeera now was new and different, and without question more powerful than whatever had drawn her to the empress before.

Once again frustrated at her inability to explain her own

feelings to herself, she opted to sheath her dagger and reiterate her concerns to Ithmeera. "It's been days. Do you really intend to stay here forever?"

Ithmeera's eyes widened, as though she had not seriously thought Elisa might ask her that question. "Back to questioning my decisions, then? Marco is safe. That is all I care about right now." She glanced at the covered windows. "Marching into Azgadar with Gurdinfield's army behind me—can you imagine how that might look to a city that has already thrown out its ruler?"

Elisa shook her head. "Azgadar did not throw you out. You were betrayed."

But Ithmeera held up a hand to silence her. "I did not come here to discuss this, Elisa. I came to apologize."

Apologize? That certainly wasn't something Elisa expected, least of all from Ithmeera Cadar. "You've nothing to apologize for."

Ithmeera turned to face her, which made things even more difficult as Elisa had found it an increasing struggle to maintain eye contact with her. "In Lydia's war room, when I yelled at you. I was angry at—well I have been angry at many things but mostly at myself lately. I should not have yelled." She took a deep breath before continuing. "You escorted me from Azgadar and are the reason I am with Marco again. I am…glad you are in my life still, Elisa." Her eyes cast downward as she looked away.

"I was only doing my duty." Elisa wanted to kick herself for her stilted answer, but it was the first thing that presented in her mind. How were they to mend their friendship if she kept sounding like a first-year Legionnaire recruit every time they spoke?

"Oh." Ithmeera's answer carried a hint of disappointment, which made Elisa wonder if perhaps she had said the wrong thing again. "Yes, well, that was all I wished to discuss. I did speak with Lydia earlier and she wished to meet with both of us later to—" She froze, as did Elisa when a low, booming horn blared from outside the palace.

Elisa knew that horn. It sounded once more, sending her heart into a pounding rhythm. "The Legion comes!"

Ithmeera gasped and ran to the window. "Did Petra send the whole army after us?" she exclaimed as she pulled back the curtains. Her tone jumped from fearful to disbelief to elated in seconds. "What in—it can't be!"

"What?" Elisa stood behind her, trying to get a better look.

In the grasslands outside the city gates, underneath the brewing stormy green skies a small army of Legionnaires approached. Some wore armor while others were in civilian clothing but still carried weapons. Leading them was a man whose face Elisa could not make out from this distance, but she knew from the way he marched exactly who he was. "Ben," she whispered. And just behind him walked a thin young man. He wore the uniform of the Legion and carried a sword, but Elisa knew his blond mop of curly hair anywhere. "Kye." Then to an already-grinning Ithmeera, "They're alive! And Kye is with them!"

She was stunned when Ithmeera burst into joyous laughter and threw her arms around her neck, bringing the two of them into a tight embrace.

"They're alive!" Ithmeera's soft echo of relief was the best thing Elisa had heard in days. She returned the embrace when Ithmeera did not let go, stirring up the confusing thoughts from earlier all over again. But when Ithmeera began to pull away she found herself reluctant to release her—instead holding onto her for just a moment longer than necessary before withdrawing just as quickly. She hoped her prolonged clinginess had not been noticed, but luck was not on her side as she caught the crooked smile Ithmeera was giving her. *Fool! Holding on to the empress like…like—*

She cleared her throat. "We should inform Lydia and go meet them," she said, relieved when Ithmeera simply agreed before the two hurried out of the room to meet the Legion at the gates of the city.

✳ ✳ ✳

By the time Elisa and the others made it down the main road on horseback and to the city gates, swirling green clouds connected by sporadic bolts of lightning had already begun converging over the surrounding grasslands as it headed in the direction of the City of Towers. Even to the north, she could see similar clouds settling over the distant mountains of Rhyad, the coldest region of Damea and one Elisa had no desire to step foot into again.

*Not good.* She knew they had a finite amount of time before the storm began as she remembered seeing similar clouds in Fimen's Hope. "Your Majesty!" she called to Diana, who rode next to Jacob several paces ahead. "We must be quick—there is a storm coming!" She watched Diana glance up before calling back in the affirmative and ordering the Guardians who rode beside them including Victor and Roe to start moving people into their homes.

Sitting behind her in the saddle, Ithmeera's quiet, awed voice broke through the harshening winds that picked up as they rode down the hill. "It's just like the one in Fimen's Hope," she said, mirroring Elisa's thoughts from earlier. "That lightning will set the city ablaze."

"We will figure it out. Right now, let's see to the Legion." Elisa tried to sound reassuring, but the darkening sky above worried her, too. Houses had been tossed about like ragdolls and entire crop fields had been set on fire in Fimen's Hope. How much damage would the storm wreak here?

At the gates, Ithmeera hardly waited for Elisa to bring them to a stop before she dismounted and raced to the waiting, exhausted Legionnaires led by General Veraun. Elisa had to admit it was odd to see Veraun's normally cropped hair longer, but she was amused that he had been determined to keep his face shaven. To Veraun's right stood Guardswoman Taryn, a Legionnaire Elisa had only interacted with briefly but was fairly certain was not a fan of hers based on a message Cassie had passed on to her weeks earlier in Azgadar. But Taryn's straight-faced expression said nothing about her personal feelings toward Elisa. The fact that she stood on Veraun's right was of interest, however, as a typical guardswoman would normally never be honored with such a position. *Perhaps she was promoted?*

"General!" Ithmeera ran straight for Veraun, who despite his haggard appearance managed a graceful bow.

His stoic expression and formal manners could not mask the relief in his voice, though. "Your Majesty. It is…good to see you safe." He gestured to the Legionnaires behind him. "Please accept my deepest apologies for the delay in our getting here. We made a point of stopping at several Legion forts to collect recruits and supplies and—" He was cut off with an abrupt grunt as Ithmeera stunned everyone by throwing her arms around him.

Elisa shook her head, though she allowed a smile to escape. A few Legionnaires let out quiet laughs while others applauded and cheered praise for their empress.

Ithmeera pulled away, a slight blush having risen to her cheeks. "Apologies, General," she said, beaming at him. "It's just…I don't believe I've ever felt more relieved than I have right now."

If Veraun was uncomfortable, he did not show it. "Ahem… well, we are here for you to command, Your Majesty. Azgadar is unfortunately under New Legion occupation."

Elisa watched Ithmeera's jaw clench and her eyebrows arch up, her voice heavy with guilt as she acknowledged Veraun's report. "A-and their numbers, General? What are we dealing with there?"

Veraun wavered for a moment. "It's hard to know for sure, Your Majesty. Based on the information provided to me by Captain Taryn here," he said while nodding toward Taryn, "the New Legion has a number of ringleaders that have taken the city through force and fear."

"Then you have my thanks, Captain. You have done well—all of you have," Ithmeera declared, prompting a collective bow from the soldiers. She turned back to Elisa, catching her worried expression before returning to the Legionnaires. "Is the young man Kye with you, General?" she asked.

Something that passed for an amused grin flashed on Veraun's face. "He is, Your Majesty." He cleared his throat before calling for Kye in a deep bark. "Recruit Kye!"

Elisa stepped forward, watching with eager interest as a blond curly head made its way through the ranks and laughing when she heard the clang of metal on metal followed by a rush of apologies. Moments later, Kye emerged from the cluster of soldiers to take his place next to Veraun, who regarded him with a tilted head.

"The empress wishes to speak to you, Recruit Kye," he told him.

Elisa swore he had grown even taller since she last saw him weeks earlier. Ithmeera's gold ring still hung around his neck, mostly hidden behind the black and red chainmail fastened to his chest and shoulders. Leather and metal-plated bracers covered his wrists and the trademark sword of the Legion hung from his belt. The suit was not custom-made however, and despite Kye's height, it still looked a bit big for him. But as Elisa remembered, it had for her as well.

Kye bowed, the metal rings of his armor clinking as their shifting weight made him stumble a bit. "Your Majesty," he said just as Elisa arrived to stand next to Ithmeera. "I have returned from Ata as promised."

"He was instrumental in my rescue, in fact," Veraun added.

"I believe he had been previously briefed on the secret entrance to the dungeons." He shot Elisa a knowing glance, and to her added shock, he *winked*. "Perhaps it is a good thing it was not so secret after all."

Ithmeera's smile did not fade. "Rise, Recruit Kye. You have performed admirably. But where is Enchanter Andrea?"

Light-brown eyes widened, darting from the empress to Elisa and then back again. "She was…not fully recovered when I left. But her old mentor, Meredith, arrived in Ata after we did. They told me to find you while they looked for a way to find Cassie and stop Richard."

Elisa wanted to say something to Kye—yell at him, embrace him, let him know how relieved she was that he was all right. But then a brilliant light flashed across the city, startling nearly all who had gathered at the gates as lightning pummeled the grasslands, sparking a fire in the dry brush.

Still on horseback, Diana, who had been hanging back with Jacob while Ithmeera spoke to the Legion, called out from behind Elisa. "My friends, we should continue this conversation inside the city walls." She pointed at the clouds over the grasslands as thunder rolled through the land. "That storm will be here soon!"

"My men are working on getting people back to their homes," Jacob said. "We need to get everyone inside—board up the windows and secure what we can. Can you help us, General?"

Veraun snapped to the task, the air of celebration vanishing as he issued orders for the Legionnaires to head into the city and help the city militia prepare for the storm.

# Chapter 15

# Elisa of Sadford

Elisa turned to Ithmeera just as the sky lit up in another flash of green and white. "We need to get you inside. Come on." She assisted Ithmeera in getting onto their horse before climbing up into the saddle herself. They began to make their way back up the cobblestone road, passing by clusters of the city's citizens and the guards who were rushing to get them back into their houses.

The hairs on the back of Elisa's neck stood up as they rode, the hot static discharge from the storm escalating as it settled directly over the city. Pandemonium broke out as many of the citizens began panicking at the site of the phenomenon spinning wildly over them, their frightened screams and the powerful winds ringing at her ears as the memories of the disaster in Fimen's Hope replayed in her head.

"Where is Lydia?!" Ithmeera shouted over the wind, her concern sending a spike of panic through Elisa's chest.

*One thing at a time. Need to get her to safety first.* "We're almost there!"

"But—"

Roof shingles and a few large wooden boards ripped from the tops of a few houses and blew within a few paces of them. Elisa managed to steer clear of them, but it was only a matter of time before their luck ran out. She needed to focus. "I will find her, Ithmeera! But we need to get you back to Marco!"

Not arguing for once, Ithmeera tightened her grip around Elisa's waist as they crested the hill—avoiding more debris and fragments of buildings along the way until they finally approached the palace entrance where Victor and Alexander waited for them.

Alexander waved at them. "Inside, Your Majesty!"

Elisa dismounted and helped Ithmeera down. "Where is Diana?"

"Saw her with the captain just a moment ago!" Shielding his eyes with one hand, Victor squinted as he peered down the hill. "What the—someone's in the field still!"

She spun around to see for herself—her heart sinking when she recognized the familiar mop of curls. *No.* "That *fool!*"

"Is that Kye? What is he doing?" Ithmeera gasped. "Is he mad?"

"He's going to get himself killed is what he's doing." Elisa reached out to mount her horse again when Ithmeera's hand shot out and wrapped around her wrist, pulling her back hard.

"Where are you going?!"

"I need to go get him." She nodded toward Alexander and Victor. "Go with them and get to Marco. I will join you after."

Another bolt of lightning crackled above and hurtled down, striking one of the larger warehouses in the city and setting it ablaze in an instantaneous explosion. Chunks of debris and splintered wood were sent flying in all directions, prompting new screams as more people ran through the streets in a frantic effort to find shelter.

Their horse let out a cry and reared back as Alexander repeated his calls from the palace entrance. "We need to get inside!"

Elisa tugged Ithmeera's arm. "Let me go," she said. "I will be right back!"

But Ithmeera's grip did not let up as she met Elisa's eyes with frightened green ones of her own. "Elisa, no!" Her shout was barely audible over the winds and the sound of wood rending from stone. "It's too dangerous. I-I forbid it!"

Elisa bit her lip. Her empress had just given her a direct order, but she had just gotten Kye back safe and sound and she couldn't risk losing him. Not after everything they had been through. "I need to go to him, Ithmeera. Please, he is my responsibility." *No...not quite.* "He is...family to me."

"And are Marco and I not?" Ithmeera's face was red now—her eyes wet as her fingers dug into Elisa's wrist. "You said you would come back to Azgadar with me—you *promised!*"

"And I will!" Elisa yelled back, the adrenaline running through her veins driving her to throw all formalities away. She swallowed, the struggle to compose herself nearly impossible as she fought to steady her voice. "I will come back, Ithmeera. I swear it."

The stones beneath their feet shuddered, a sign that, if Elisa's memory served, the storm was growing stronger.

"Please!" What had once been a demand had now turned to a plea as tears streamed down Ithmeera's face, twisting Elisa's heart in ways she never knew were possible.

Making a quick decision, she pulled Ithmeera close, crashing their lips together for no more than a second before pushing her back with enough force to break a stunned Ithmeera's grip on her. "Get her inside, *now!*" she shouted at Alexander and Victor, climbing on her horse and spurring it into a canter as she began to race back down the hill.

She thought she heard someone screaming her name, possibly Ithmeera, but she blocked it out and focused every bit of concentration on the road in front of her. Leaves and bits of debris flew past her and into her, one piece cutting into the corner of her lower lip despite her keeping her head low.

What was Kye doing? Why would he put himself in danger intentionally like this? These questions ran through Elisa's mind among others as she flew past Guardians, Legionnaires, and citizens ducking into whatever shelter they could find to escape the raging storm, the brunt of which was descending on the city now in the form of more lightning strikes and cyclonic forces.

*Must…go…faster!*

As the gates loomed in her field of vision, a thought crossed her mind and she realized she knew what Kye was trying to do—what he had been trying to do since they met that night in Azgadar.

*No!* At the base of the city she dismounted her horse before taking off on foot to meet Kye in the fields beyond the gates, ignoring the guards' warning calls as her sprinting legs carried her under the stone arch and into the grasslands.

Away from the buildings and the screaming, everything was much quieter as she stumbled to a stop, her boots kicking up dirt around her. A light dusting of white ash fell from the sky like snow. The winds were not as strong, though the air had a certain emptiness about it—similar to the moment of calm Elisa had experienced in Fimen's Hope before the peak of the storm had come roaring down on her.

A few steps away stood Kye. Ash peppering his hair and piling onto his armored shoulders, he remained motionless as he gazed up. Amidst the swirling clouds, the sky remained green, broken by jagged branches of light that threatened to strike them both.

"Kye!" she called to him—her feet fused to the ground as her blood ran cold with fear. "Kye, you must come back to the city!"

Kye turned slightly to face her, his expression displaying nothing but calm despite the peril surrounding them. "Elisa?" He blinked, as though in disbelief. "You should go back, Elisa. I can stop this."

Elisa shook her head slowly. "No, Kye! You cannot use magic here—"

"I *can!*" His sudden shout hushed her. "Andrea showed me how...I-I can use a barrier to stop the lightning from hitting the city."

*He chooses* now *to play the hero?* She wanted to go to him but feared any quick movement to interfere might push him to do something irreversible. "Magic is broken, Kye! If you try to cast a barrier here it will kill you!"

He glared at her, his face going a deep shade of red. "I *have* to try, Elisa! I did what you asked! I brought Andrea to Ata. I kept my promise!" He raised his hands. "If I don't try here, what is left for me to do?"

"No!" Tears sprang to her eyes. How could she convince him? "You are not done yet, Kye! You are a Legionnaire now and you have a duty you have sworn yourself to—"

"I *murdered* my family!" he screamed, his hands falling back to his sides. "I murdered those Legionnaires in battle and I am n-not worthy to be one of them. This is who I am, Elisa! I-I've hurt too many people. The least I can do is help the people here. If that means I die, so be it!" He raised his hands again as another bolt of lightning struck the grasslands, the impact rattling Elisa so hard she nearly collapsed. Something ignited nearby as hot air blew in her face, the shallow cut on her face stinging.

There was perhaps, one thing she had not considered. But was it enough to get through to him? "Kye," she said, pushing the frustration out of her voice in a desperate effort to reach him. "Kye, I lied to you!"

Kye's hands dropped. His lips parted. "W-what?"

She took a step toward him as the nausea and the heat gradually wore her down. "Back in Azgadar, at your family's home…I lied to you. About why I continue to risk my life for Ithmeera. Why I keep going back to her."

Eyebrows arched, Kye's hands trembled at his sides. "Why, then?"

Elisa tried to swallow back her tears, but it was too late as a few spilled over and rolled down her cheeks. "Because I am in love with her, Kye. And…and nothing would give me more happiness than to go back to Azgadar and be with her for the rest of my days." The tightness in her chest, the guilt, all of the frustrating feelings she could not decipher—they all came undone in her admission to him. How could she not have seen it before? How long had she felt this way? Did Ithmeera feel the same way?

The answers to these questions never came, only more tears. "I left her, Kye!" she choked. "She asked me to stay, but I told her I had to go to you."

Another crash of thunder ripped through the grasslands as Kye stared at her with bewildered shock on his face. "Why… why would you do that?!"

Elisa took another step forward. "Because you are also my family, Kye. And I will not leave you behind." She offered him her hand. "Please. Come back with me. We will figure this out together."

Kye took another longing look at the sky, a look that lasted an eternity to Elisa before she watched his shoulders slump. He faced her, eyes glossed over, before rushing at her and taking her into a fierce hold.

"I'm sorry!" he sobbed as he clutched her shirt. "I just want this to be over!"

She sniffed but did not bother to hold back her own tears anymore. "It will be," she soothed. "It will be and then, Kye… then we will go home."

He sighed. "Promise?"

"I promise."

In a sudden roar, the heat around them magnified as the fire from the earlier strikes scorched through the dry grass, surrounding them with a tall ring of flames and blocking them from returning to the city gates.

Elisa's hand shot to her belt before she realized she did not have her canteen or any other water supply with her. "Damn it," she hissed as the flames inched closer. "I'm not going to be able to keep that promise for very long if we burn to death."

Kye stood with his back to hers. "I've got water! Here!" He ripped his own canteen from his belt and tore off the top before hurling the liquid at the blaze. Steam shot up from the ground but was quickly replaced with more flames.

Panic wiped Elisa's adrenaline as she looked toward the city, where she could see some of the Gurdinfield guards waving at her and others heading their way. *Too far. They'll never make it here in time.* "It burns too hot. We need more water!"

Kye shook out the now empty canteen. "That's all there is!" he moaned. The flames crept closer—Elisa noting the thinning gap of dirt and grass was all that was keeping them from being engulfed in an instant. She needed to find them another exit and fast.

Before she could make any decisions, a shiver ran through her as the air around them cooled in seconds. The wall of flames vaporized into towering columns of steam that dissipated, the remnants blown away by the now frigid gusts that had replaced the hot winds.

Hooves trampled past them and kicked up clumps of dirt as

a shimmering light emitted from one of the horse's riders came up around them.

"Go!" a familiar-sounding voice rang out above the howling winds. "Get to the city!"

In an instant, Elisa recognized the disembodied voice: Andrea. *It can't be!* With the immediate danger abated but the storm still raging above them, though, there was no time for confirmation. Not needing to be told twice, Elisa grabbed Kye's hand and the two took off running for the gates, the shield around them maintaining as Andrea and the other rider stayed within range. Lightning still coursed above them but fortunately did not strike again, even as they crossed the threshold into the city where Elisa's horse was still waiting for them. As they rode back to the palace, Elisa could see the damage the storm had already inflicted on the city—many of the larger buildings had suffered roof cave-ins and the road was littered with debris. And it wasn't over yet.

"Andrea!" Kye cried once they reached the summit. Elisa saw Diana and Jacob waiting at the doors for them—both wearing expressions of worry and exhaustion but uninjured save a few scrapes to her great relief. All were rushed inside and the doors barred behind them, the worst of the storm over as the people of the City of Towers held their breath and waited for the rest to pass.

# Chapter 16

# War Room

An eerie dark-green cover blanketed Gurdinfield soon after all had retreated into the palace as night fell. Servants rushed about the throne room ferrying bandages and pitchers of water to the citizens, Guardians, and Legionnaires who had been injured while out in the storm.

In the dining hall, Elisa along with Diana, Jacob, Ithmeera, Andrea, and Meredith had gathered around the table. Veraun stood at attention behind Ithmeera with Kye next to him. Candles had been lit, but the room still felt darker than Elisa ever remembered it.

A servant offered Diana a wet cloth for the shallow cuts on her hand, but she declined it, asking them instead to bring it to one of the citizens who had taken refuge in the throne room. Jacob sat next to her, leaning on his hand propped up by an elbow, his shaggy hair and face coated in dirt and ash.

On the bench across from them sat Andrea and Meredith. While Meredith looked more or less as tired as anyone who had traveled across Damea while hardly stopping might, it was Andrea whose appearance sent a cold chill down Elisa's spine. Her white blouse, while it had been washed, was stained with blood on the right sleeve. Her cloak was torn at the shoulder—Elisa surmised, probably from whatever had caused the bloodstain. But creeping up her neck and down her right arm were dark, purple and black tendrils, almost like open wounds, some of which stopped at the bottom of her cheek. Also noticeable was her right eye, the white of which was almost entirely bloodshot.

Had Richard done this to her? Had she tried to use magic? There were a number of questions Elisa wanted to ask, but Andrea didn't seem the least bit interested in answering questions yet. After they returned, she had asked Diana for her help, to which Diana had suggested they gather in the dining hall.

Ithmeera had not uttered a word to Elisa so far. Upon her return, they had made brief eye contact but said nothing to each other before following the others into the room.

"Andrea," Diana said, her voice low and gentle. "Are you sure you would not rather sleep first? You look exhausted. We should get you a change of clothing as well." She turned to Meredith. "Is there nothing that can be done to help her injuries?"

"I'm afraid not, or at least nothing that any of us can do," Meredith said. "She needs magic. She is drawing from the magic of those potions she created—the ones she created here in fact."

Elisa vaguely recalled mention of such potions when Andrea and Cassie were packing for their trip to the Western Hills. Her thoughts gravitated to her father. After Philip died, he had isolated himself in their home, buying enchanted artifacts on the Azgadaran black market and absorbing their magic, a distraction to cope with the loss of his son.

The desperation behind Andrea's intense gaze were almost a mirror image of what Elisa saw in her father's when she discovered his habit. This was not the same young woman she had parted ways with in Azgadar.

Andrea jerked her head up. "I'm fine. Can we please get to the reason we're here?"

Meredith put a hand on her shoulder, though Andrea flinched when she made contact, prompting worried glances from the rest of the table. "They are only trying to help, Andrea."

Andrea's response was to run her hands through her already disheveled hair, something Elisa had noticed she did whenever she was stressed. "I know—I'm sorry." She looked up, her attention directed at Diana and Ithmeera. "Your Majesties, Richard is…he's Cassie's father. He and Cassie are not from Damea. It's a long story, but he's trying to take all of Damea's magic so that he can return home with her. He doesn't care who he hurts or kills along the way, and he is…forcing Cassie to take magic from the land and from magically-built structures."

"The storms we are experiencing are a side effect of this," Meredith added. "They will get worse."

Ithmeera leaned forward. "Where is this man, now?"

"We don't know." The rough, broken croak in Andrea's voice was unlike anything Elisa had heard from her before. "We think he might have been staying at Meredith's home in the Black Forest but after Gurith…"

"He has command over Cassie's abilities and has not hesitated to use them," Meredith finished. "I would not recommend trying to confront him there."

"And he is your husband?" Jacob demanded, his brow furrowed in disbelief. "You mean to tell us you had no idea what his plans were?"

"Jacob." Diana warning was accompanied by her hand settling on his arm. "We were not there. We don't know all of the circumstances here."

But Meredith offered a faint smile to them both. "Thank you, Your Majesty, but your husband is correct—I had no idea what Richard was planning or where he was from until Andrea told me. To be honest," she said, her grey eyes turning downward, "I still find it hard to believe, despite having seen the…atrocities he committed firsthand. But Andrea has an idea that I believe is worth hearing out, if Your Majesties are willing."

Ithmeera sat up before folding her hands in her lap. "I am listening, though I cannot guarantee anything."

"As am I." Diana nodded as all eyes were on Andrea, waiting for her to share this proposal.

Andrea inhaled. "The spire. He wants to go after the palace in Azgadar and take its magic. But he can't. There is some kind of shield that has been put up around it."

Recognition crossed Ithmeera's tired features. Her gaze flickered to Elisa before she spoke to the rest of them. "Petra must have enabled it. The shield is powered by Azgadar's magic stores and was designed to protect the palace during an attack. These stores are enchanted objects hidden at the base of one of the city walls."

"Can it be disabled from the outside?" Andrea asked. Behind

Ithmeera, Elisa saw Veraun's eyebrows shoot up as Ithmeera leaned back to look at him. "General?"

He cleared his throat, his expression one of clear surprise that he was being asked such a question whose answer was typically kept secret in the empire's ranks. "A well-placed ranged attack to take out the southeastern outer wall might disturb the stores, Your Majesty. With minimal casualties of course." He placed his hands behind his back, his chest puffing out somewhat. "Though I will say it would require a great deal of force and precise aim."

"What would be your plan once the shield went down?" Speaking out of turn in the presence of not one but two rulers was not something Elisa had planned on doing, but she was just as invested in finding out what Andrea was thinking as any of them.

"Richard believes the spire has enough magic to help him open a portal. Despite what he did in Gurith, he still remains in Damea." Even through Andrea's exhaustion Elisa could still detect the determination she was accustomed to hearing from her, however desperate her plan sounded. "Azgadar *will* be his next target. If we can lure him there with the promise of magic, he will come. And we can be ready for him."

"This is the same man who destroyed the Shadow Arena with a single command," Diana said. "Andrea, you know I trust you, but you are risking an entire city on the chance you'll be able to stop him." She looked at the others. "If this shield is all that protects Azgadar from him, perhaps we should find another way."

A harsh bang reverberated within the room as Andrea's fists

collided with the table. "Are you not listening? This *is* the only way! If we don't stop him now he will find a way himself, that is if Damea does not collapse upon itself first." She gestured at the exit. "You saw the sky—the storms. They will just get worse until there is nothing left, Diana!"

Seeing the dumbfounded expression on Diana's face after having been yelled at by her own royal enchanter as well as the frightened look on Kye's, Elisa decided to intervene before things got out of hand. "Calm down. What you're proposing is risky and dangerous, Andrea, and we'd be fools to not at least question this plan," she said. "You are asking us to leave Azgadar vulnerable—"

"Just long enough to get Richard into the city," Andrea clarified.

Ithmeera shook her head. "The city is designed to defend itself from any invasion." Guilt showed on her face—not for the first time that day. "Petra will know every possible defensive and offensive advantage. Not to mention Azgadar is under New Legion occupation. You cannot just waltz into the city and wait for this man! We are dealing with multiple enemies here."

A low hum came from Jacob's direction. "While I'd never normally suggest this, Gurdinfield can certainly provide ample force and the precision necessary to accomplish this," he said. "And perhaps I speak out of turn, but I believe your Legionnaires know Azgadar better than anyone, Your Majesty."

Diana's dark eyes grew wide as she gaped at her husband. "You are serious!"

Veraun responded before Jacob could. "We possess only a fraction of the Legion, but we could provide support. Captain

Taryn and her fighters could retake the city while I assist you and your fighters at the wall, Your Highness."

Diana and Ithmeera each held in silence on opposite ends of the table until Diana finally spoke again. "And what about Richard himself?"

"I can go with the captain," Andrea said. "We can stop him together. You'll need an enchanter to...to redistribute the magic once Richard is handled. Meredith and I can help Cassie." Something on the edge of her voice made Elisa uneasy, as though she were holding back something. She brushed it aside. *The girl is tired. Who wouldn't be after what she's been through?*

All eyes were on Ithmeera now.

Diana bowed her head. "It is your city, Your Majesty." She took Jacob's hand. "Gurdinfield is ready to march on my command, but this is your call."

Elisa held her breath as she watched Ithmeera bring her hands to her mouth while she considered the options. She hated seeing Ithmeera in distress like this—the mutiny had been bad enough as had running halfway across Damea not knowing if her son was safe or not. But now the fate of the land would be determined by whether she was willing to invade her own home and put her own people at risk while at the same time confronting Petra, the woman who had already taken so much away from her.

"I assume we have one opportunity to attempt this?" she asked, receiving nods and affirmations from everyone. She addressed Veraun. "Petra will see us coming. She will be ready for us."

Veraun nodded as his mouth twitched upward. "I am counting on it, Your Majesty. The Legion stands ready to retake the capital on your order."

"Elisa?"

Realizing Ithmeera was asking her opinion on the matter, Elisa chose her words carefully. "If what we've heard is true and the storms will only get worse, then I believe we must do whatever we can to stop them, Your Majesties." She looked Ithmeera in the eye. "Before there is no Azgadar left for us to take back."

Ithmeera stood up, the others following suit. "Then we will march. We leave at first light." She took in a sharp breath. "As for Marco, I wish for him to accompany us and then be taken to a location away from danger, General."

Veraun bowed, though Elisa could see lines of concern etched in his forehead and around his eyes. "As you would have it, Your Majesty. The Legion fort in Sadford is still safe. Recruit Kye will escort Prince Marco there once we close in on Azgadar."

Ithmeera thanked Kye, who answered with a bow of his own, before turning to Andrea. "I suggest you get some rest, Enchanter Andrea. Much of this plan depends on your abilities. I would hate to see us fail because you did not get enough sleep." She bowed to Diana before taking her leave.

"I will see that the Guardians and other fighters are prepared for tomorrow," Jacob said and Veraun echoed his words but for the Legion as he excused himself as well, with Kye on his heels, leaving Elisa alone with Diana, Andrea, and Meredith.

"Elisa, you should get that wound looked at," Diana said, gesturing at her own lip. "And then you should rest yourself. Azgadar will be a few days journey, especially since not all of us will be on horseback."

Elisa bowed. "Of course, Your Majesty." She nodded to Andrea and Meredith. "Thank you for your timely assistance this afternoon."

A familiar smile spread across Andrea's face, easing Elisa's worries about her friend if only by a little. "I wasn't about to let you and Kye burn to death, Elisa."

"That is a relief to hear. Goodnight, all." With a final bow to Diana, Elisa retreated from the dining hall and turned the nearby corner to head to her quarters. A damp cloth and a bucket of water would be next on her list, if only so that her face did not wind up looking like she'd taken a dive face-first into one of the empire's farming machines. As she climbed the stairs to the second floor, she knew she wasn't particularly tired—the adrenaline from her near-death experience with Kye kept her alert for now. She thought perhaps she should speak with Ithmeera about their exchange outside the palace earlier, but just thinking about how angry and betrayed Ithmeera had looked before she left made Elisa shudder. How could she possibly face her now?

That Elisa had also *kissed* her seemed to have made everything worse. Had she gone completely mad? Had the lack of magic in Damea affected her judgement somehow? *Pushing people away and messing up what few relationships I have left. My expertise, I suppose.* She had not expected to admit so much to Kye, but she knew he would not say a word to Ithmeera.

Another shudder ran through her as she realized how close she had been to losing him, too.

She passed a few empty rooms on both sides of the long corridor of bedrooms, the palace having once housed the entire Taylor family rather than just Diana, Jacob, and a handful of visitors along with the staff. Most of the doors were open to prevent the air from growing stale in them, their interiors dark. One open room on her right emitted a flickering glow, however, and a small voice called to her as she passed it.

She stopped, recalling that this was Marco's room, and took a step back to peek her head in. Her nephew was in bed under several fur blankets, a book in his hands, though Elisa could not see the script on the front cover from where she stood.

Marco stared back at her with familiar eyes. The tightness returned to Elisa's chest as, for the first time in a long time, she could see how much he resembled Philip. His eyes were the same of course—kind and thoughtful—but even his expression he took from his father—straight-lipped while also slightly turning up at the corners, as though he knew something others did not.

"What is it, Marco?" She had not spoken more than a few words to him since arriving in the City of Towers, preferring to hang back in order to allow Ithmeera more time with him. She knew she had been away for what amounted to quite a long time for a boy his age, and she feared he would no longer remember her as the aunt who ran with him around the palace gardens or read to him at night while his mother was in a late meeting and his father was away on a trip, but instead as little more than a stranger with a familiar face.

"Is Mother upset?" he asked, letting the book fall into his lap—a few pages turning back. As Elisa walked over to the bed, she recognized the book as a collection of children's stories she had grown up with, her own Gurdinfielder mother having read them to her. She noted from the script on the pages that this particular story told the tale of a wolf who found himself separated from his pack. As these stories usually went, he traveled across all of Damea, meeting new friends—most of whom were, of course, not wolves—and defeating a terrible monster before finally finding his pack in the end.

She sat on the edge of the bed, the mattress dipping slightly as she sighed. "I think she is just worried. She wants to make sure it will be safe for you to go home soon."

Marco tilted his head and smiled. "We're going home tomorrow, right?"

Elisa nodded. She did not want to lie to him, but at this hour she saw no use in scaring him with the full truth. "We are going to try. But we need to make sure the city is ready for you and your mother, too. Queen Lydia and Enchanter Andrea are going to help with that."

He seemed satisfied with her answer. His next question, however, was a little tougher. "Are you coming home with us, Elisa?"

"I…" Of course she was—she had promised Ithmeera hadn't she? *Yes.* Regardless of her feelings or what had happened earlier that day, she had promised Ithmeera she would go back to Azgadar with her. "Yes, of course I am." She reached for the open book, taking care not to bend or tear any of the pages, and closed it before setting it down on the nightstand.

"Now, it is late and you should sleep." She rearranged the furs so that they were adequately covering him. "You will need your energy, especially if we're to travel all the way to Azgadar. You are getting too old for me to carry you on my shoulders."

Marco detected the tease in her voice—he always could—and giggled before lying back on the pillows, his eyes fluttering before finally closing.

Elisa bit her lip and stroked the top of his head gently. As she stood up to blow out the candles, she felt the presence of someone watching her and turned. Ithmeera stood in the open doorway, pensive and quiet as she gave a small tilt of her head—a sign Elisa should follow her.

# Chapter 17

# Firelight

Ithmeera's quarters were at the end of the corridor—spacious with a great stone fireplace that had been lit earlier in the evening and still burned, and decorated with far more wardrobes, chests, and dressers than Elisa thought necessary, even for a visiting ruler. Even the bed was larger than hers—the bedposts taller and the mattress covered with enough blankets for someone to survive a winter in Rhyad. The long curtains had been partially drawn and Elisa could see the occasional bolt of lightning streak across the night sky, a soft rumble following. Unlike the storm in Fimen's Hope, which had vanished quite suddenly, this storm was taking hours to disappear. She wondered what Meredith had meant exactly when she advised that they would get worse.

"Close the door."

Not questioning the simple order, Elisa turned and pushed the heavy iron studded door shut. Turning back around, she saw Ithmeera had already let her hair loose for the evening, the faint glow of the fire reflecting off her dark curls as she stood by the fireplace, her attention drawn toward the window.

Her voice soft, Ithmeera spoke first. "Thank you for easing his worries. He's missed you so." Elisa thought she saw her hesitate, as though she had wanted to say something more. Instead Ithmeera nodded at the view before them. A foggy mist had settled over the City of Towers. The lanterns outside of homes and shops had long been snuffed for the evening, although the streetlamps remained burning. "It's so quiet tonight. Perhaps it's just me."

"It's not just you," Elisa said, and made the few steps across the rug-covered floor to stand at Ithmeera's side. "I used to feel that way whenever I was deployed to the outskirts—almost always the night before some skirmish with bandits."

Ithmeera took a deep breath. "Growing up, I always dreamed of one day staying here, in the City of Towers, as a guest of the new king or queen. Gurdinfield: finally reunited." She shook her head. "I was even naïve enough in these dreams to believe I had something to do with stopping the civil war. History, it seems, has an interesting sense of humor."

A faint smile crossed Elisa's face. "The empire's influence was certainly noticed here."

"You mean when it stormed the gates of the capital city?" Frustration heightened in Ithmeera's tone. "I wanted to bring peace and prosperity to the empire. And what did I do instead?" She gestured at the window. "I brought *war*, Elisa. I brought war and fear a-and death." Her voice lowered. "My legacy to the empire will be its destruction."

Elisa reached out and placed a hand on Ithmeera's arm, letting her thumb gently brush against the soft material of her dress. "You've done no such thing."

But Ithmeera jerked her arm away. "How can you say that? You were here when the Legion invaded, when Erik—" She paused to compose herself before continuing. "You nearly died, Elisa, and had you I might as well have been named your executioner."

Elisa let a quiet laugh escape, despite how obviously upset Ithmeera was. "Now you're being a tad dramatic. You made the calls you thought were best at the advice of those you trusted."

"If I had just stopped for one minute to consider the consequences—if I had not listened to Alden and Petra and even Erik—"

"We'd be in some other crisis. I'm certain of it," Elisa said.

Ithmeera threw up her arms. "Well, look no further. The sky is green and my capital is under enemy occupation. My son is an exile of his own kingdom." She sighed. "No *competent* ruler would have let this happen. Perhaps…perhaps the people need an empress who can make the right decisions."

"That would be you. Azgadar is yours by birthright. You've done much for the country and its people love you," Elisa argued. "And you need to stop blaming yourself for the treachery of others."

"I chose Petra to be Marco's bodyguard. How is this not my fault?"

"Even an empress makes mistakes. No matter what people would choose to believe otherwise." Elisa wasn't sure what exactly she was trying to convince Ithmeera of, but she knew for certain she could not allow her to lose hope. *Not now.* "The people of Azgadar are loyal to you and any true Legionnaire would gladly lay down their life for you. Ben, Taryn, Kye, and all of the Legionnaires who will accompany us tomorrow— they are all willing to fight for you, Ithmeera, because to them you *are* the empire."

Ithmeera contemplated in silence as she gazed out the window, her thumb and finger resting on her chin and bottom lip. "And what about you, Elisa?" She turned to face her, thrusting an accusatory finger in her face. "You swear a life oath, run away, make promises, and then you disobey direct orders from your empress. Why?" she demanded. "Why lie to Marco about coming home with us? Why—" Her voice broke. "Why kiss me before galloping off to throw your life away if you aren't really going to come back? Do we really mean so little to you that you would toy with us like that?"

Elisa faltered. "I-I wasn't lying—"

But Ithmeera cut her off. "Do *I* really mean that little to you, Elisa?"

"No!" Elisa cried. She swallowed, wishing with every fiber of her being that her heart would stop twisting itself into the tight coils that seemed to be preventing her from putting together a coherent sentence. "Ithmeera, I didn't kiss you because I wasn't coming back. I kissed you because I *love* you and…and I can no longer ignore what I feel for you. But…you are my charge and I refuse to bring any more shame on this family simply because I can't control my feelings."

*There it is.* The coils in Elisa's chest unwound but now felt exposed and inflamed. The truth was out as she offered up everything she had—everything she was to Ithmeera. And regardless of how Ithmeera felt about her, there would be no going back after this.

She had never actually considered what Ithmeera's reaction might be, generally having been more worried about the inappropriateness of the situation than anything. If she, a disgraced guard, could not keep her own feelings for the empress in check then how was she to protect her?

A single tear rolled down her cheek. She looked away, concentrating as hard as she could on the swirls of patterns in the large floor rug—until she felt Ithmeera's soft hand cup her cheek before gently pushing her to meet her gaze.

"Elisa," Ithmeera said softly. "I see the guilt you carry—I always have. Guilt over your father, Philip, Erik…me." She moved closer. "You don't always have to face the entire world alone." She smiled. "No matter how good at it you've become."

Elisa trembled once she realized just how close Ithmeera was standing to her. "You don't understand," she whispered, refusing to look Ithmeera in the eye. "I left my post—I left my *charge*, Ithmeera. Even if we succeed, even if we restore order—don't you see? There is no place in Azgadar for me anymore." She closed her eyes, her breath hitching when she felt Ithmeera's thumb brush away another stray tear—her confident tone tearing Elisa from her trance.

"Yes, there is. With me."

Before Elisa could finish processing Ithmeera's words, soft lips pressed against hers. Her eyes flew open as she realized Ithmeera had both hands on her face and was kissing her. Out of instinct she could not understand, Elisa wrapped her arms around Ithmeera's waist and pulled her closer with unsteady hands, kissing her back and shuddering when Ithmeera's fingers began running through her short hair. Relief lifted from her as the ache in her chest healed and warmed, replaced by something entirely new. There was no more guilt, no more reservations. It was freeing and terrifying and wonderful all at once.

She let herself be lost to the overwhelming sensations when Ithmeera pressed harder into her lips in just the precise spot where she'd been hit by stray debris earlier, coercing a quiet yelp from her as the wound on her bottom lip shot out a sharp pain to the rest of her face.

Ithmeera froze, eyes searching until they focused on the culprit behind their interruption. "Here, let me see."

"It's nothing."

"You're *bleeding*," Ithmeera said with a raised eyebrow. She reached out, her fingers brushing against Elisa's freckled skin near the small wound. Something in Elisa's chest fluttered, though it was not enough to make her ignore the ache in her face.

She chuckled. "Ithmeera, this is not the first time I've been hit in the face and it certainly won't be the last. I've received worse in bar fights."

"Bar fights! As though that's something one should brag about," Ithmeera muttered. "Always an answer for everything with you. Now, hold still." She procured a white handkerchief from her pocket and used it to wipe the blood from Elisa's lip. Once she finished her inspection, she gave a low hum and set the cloth on the nearby end table. "Well, it will definitely bruise. Perhaps you'll think twice before running into the next storm, but given your history with them, I doubt it. And…" She moved in again, her warm hands settling on the small of Elisa's back.

"I love you, too. You are stubborn and sulky and you always have to be right, even when you're not. But," she said softly, "you are also the bravest, most kind-hearted person I've ever known." She looked down, a nervous smile appearing on her face. *Ithmeera Cadar is* nervous *about something?* "After everything that has happened, I cannot imagine a life without you. I want..." Her eyes were filled with something Elisa had never seen directed at *her* before. "I want this, Elisa. I want *us*."

Elisa's hold on Ithmeera tightened. "As do I," she said. "But in case you've forgotten: you are the empress of the Azgadaran Empire and I, well...I think at this point there are rats in the palace that rank higher in the nobility than me."

Ithmeera wrinkled her nose. "Nonsense! There are no rats in the palace."

"You obviously have not spent enough time in your dungeon. Trust me, they're there."

"Then getting rid of them will be among the first orders of business when we return. That is..." Ithmeera looked at her with hopeful eyes. "You will come back with me, right? When this is all over?"

"I promised I would. Though I must admit, *this*," Elisa said, giving a short nod down at their arrangement, "isn't exactly proper etiquette for a Legionnaire, let alone a disgraced one. The people still think I had plans to kill you, Ithmeera. I cannot—"

Ithmeera silenced her with a brief kiss. "I will see to that. I will see to all of it, Elisa, I swear to you." Her face lit up. "Oh! I nearly forgot." She pulled away, much to Elisa's disapproval, and went to the corner of the room just to the left of the fireplace. A dark, familiar silhouette Elisa had not noticed before stood upright, leaning on the grey masonry of the hearth. When Ithmeera reached for it, a glint of gold came off the top of it as it passed near the firelight.

Elisa's lips parted in disbelief as she recognized it.

Ithmeera held the sheathed Legionnaire sword with both hands. Even in her private quarters with just the two of them in the room she emanated the grace and poise she was famous across Damea for, and Elisa could not fathom how this was the same woman she had been kissing moments earlier.

Ithmeera smiled. "I had Ben bring me this after the storm. Yours was lost, but I trust you still remember how to use one of these?"

Elisa stumbled over her words. "Ithmeera, I am not worthy of—"

"You will not finish that sentence, Elisa of Sadford," Ithmeera ordered, though her smile remained. "I cannot retake Azgadar if my guard does not have her sword. Now, kneel so that I can give you this."

Swallowing, Elisa dropped to one knee. Having done this once before, she knew the words Ithmeera might speak before she said them as though it was still that overcast day years ago when she knelt on the cracked stone steps outside the palace to swear her life oath to the empress.

Ithmeera kept her hold on the sword, allowing it to hover just above Elisa's head. "Elisa of Sadford, I have witnessed your deeds in service to the empire and its allies and I commend you for them. I ask you: will you renew your oath to protect our empire, its crown, and its allies until you are released or no longer draw breath?" She bent slightly, presenting the sword to Elisa.

The words were different—it wasn't often Legionnaire oaths included the empire's allies. Serving in the Legion was a promise to the empire first. But Elisa knew Ithmeera had done this for her, even though she had no obligation to. "I will."

She lifted her arms and carefully took the sword from Ithmeera, waves of awe and gratitude washing over her as her fingers gripped the ornate sheath.

When Ithmeera commanded her to rise she did, appreciating the weight and balance of the blade as she gripped it in both hands. "Thank you." She stared at the sword in amazement, her face growing sore from grinning so hard. "I-I don't know what to say but…thank you."

Ithmeera's hand went to her wrist, her fingers digging into Elisa's shirtsleeve. Looking up, Elisa froze when she saw the deep fear in Ithmeera's illuminated tear-filled eyes. "What is it?" She propped the sword against the table and rushed to take Ithmeera's hands again. "Please tell me?"

Ithmeera sniffed as she blinked a few times. "We march tomorrow," she whispered. "And I cannot think of anything more terrifying than losing you so soon after finding you again."

Letting out a long exhale, Elisa pulled Ithmeera close and pressed her lips against her forehead. "I made a promise to you and Marco, and I intend to keep it." Tilting her head, she reached a hand up to stroke Ithmeera's cheek. "We *will* take back our home, Ithmeera. And you will not lose me, as I am never leaving you again."

Though Ithmeera's breaths eventually evened out, the tears had still not stopped when she grabbed Elisa's collar and leaned in to take her into another long, slow kiss.

As they held each other near the fireplace, Elisa pushed down the final remnants of paralyzing guilt she had been holding in since running away from Azgadar and forsaking her oath. Her breaths grew shallow when she felt purposeful, confident hands wander down her back and pull at the fabric of her shirt. She finally let herself sink into Ithmeera's embrace, having never felt more at peace.

# Chapter 18

# Last Rest

"You did not tell them the whole truth."

Andrea shrugged as she pulled back the blankets on the bed she and Cassie shared. "It wouldn't have helped ease anyone's mind to know that all enchanters might be dead when this is over."

Hands on her hips, Meredith let out an audible sigh as she observed the room. "You do not think the empress deserves to know her son's life may be in peril? Or your friend, Kye?"

"I think it doesn't matter because there's nothing I or anyone else can do about it right now," Andrea said, stacking the pillows that had been shuffled around from her bedmaking. When she finished, she glanced down at her shirtsleeve and grimaced. "I should change. Fetch me a shirt from the top drawer of that chest behind you, please."

Meredith turned and found the dark wood chest of drawers Andrea was referring to, and opened the top drawer as instructed where several clean, folded shirts had been placed one on top of the other. Picking another white one from the top of the stack, she lifted it out before tossing it back to Andrea. "Quite an impressive space you have here. The queen seems generous to her friends."

"She is generous to everyone." Andrea's arm gave a deep throb as she pulled off the bloodstained blouse. She tried not to look at the streaks on her body as she threw on the new shirt. All they did was serve as a reminder that she had not yet saved Cassie, if anything the fact that they had grown darker only emphasized the fact that she had failed in her latest attempt to stop Richard. "My lab is near the throne room. I spent more time there than here to be honest."

Meredith gave the dresser drawer a gentle push to roll it back into place. "I don't suppose you saved any more of the bottled magic there?"

"No," Andrea said with a sigh. "All I might have are some ingredients left but without magic they're useless." Sitting on the bed, she realized just how big it actually was with only one person sleeping in it and was immediately reminded of how much she missed Cassie. Looking down, she noticed the rug Cassie had spilt soup on had been replaced with a different one. Her hand went to her bracelet as her eyes burned—the tears she had been pushing back for weeks threatening to spill over. She was exhausted, her arm still hurt, and she was tired of sleeping alone.

Meredith must have guessed what she was thinking because her hands dropped to her sides and where she once appeared to be on the verge of lecturing Andrea again, her expression softened instead. Hope lined the fringes of her words. "We… don't know for certain if enchanters are at risk at all. After all, you recovered in Rhyad, as did Richard."

Andrea said nothing—she didn't know what she could say.

Everything at this point was speculation other than the very real battle they would be heading toward in the morning. The entire plan hinged on the combined Legion and Guardian armies successfully taking out the shield and Richard taking the offered bait. And after what had transpired in the Shadow Arena, Andrea wasn't entirely confident she could defeat him in combat. She would have fighters to help her, but unless they could surprise Richard, it was unlikely they would be of any use considering how easily he had disabled the arena combatants. And then there was Cassie. If Richard forced her to use her powers against them…

She shivered as a haze settled over her, making her eyelids feel much heavier than they had hours earlier. *Maybe I just need to sleep.* The last several days had been some of the most physically and mentally taxing she had experienced in recent memory, and while she hoped her plan would work, the uncertainty of it all brought with it a constant nausea, though that could have just been a sign she needed more magic. "My potion—"

"I will give you the last of the potion in the morning," Meredith said firmly. "You should try to rest." She reached for the door handle and hesitated. "I will be next door should you require anything. Good night, Andrea." She finally stepped out, closing the door behind her with a soft click and leaving Andrea alone in the huge bedroom.

After snuffing out the remaining candles, Andrea settled under the covers but struggled to get comfortable. The room felt cold and unwelcoming, as though it wasn't really her room anymore. The space beside her where she'd normally reach for

Cassie's hand was empty, the cool fabric a stark contrast to the warmth she was used to.

She moved over to Cassie's side where she rested her head on the pillow there and swallowed in an effort to once again fight back the urge to cry. *Find her first. Save her.* The events of earlier—the storm, riding into the City of Towers, saving Elisa and Kye, proposing a massive effort that would likely result in people being hurt or killed—ran through her mind over and over again until fatigue finally won out, and she drifted to sleep at last.

* * *

When Ithmeera opened her eyes, the room was still quite dark. A chill hung in the air—the fire having long since gone out although the few candles that had been lit still burned. Having long been an early riser, being greeted by a dark room in the morning was nothing new to her.

She shifted, turning over to face the door. The sheets, though nothing comparable to the ones on her bed in her palace, were surprisingly soft. A blissful warmth came over her as she recollected how the other half of her bed came to be occupied during the night.

Elisa was awake. Sitting on the edge of the bed facing away from Ithmeera she had used some of the fur blankets to cover herself, leaving her mid-back and up bare. Ithmeera wondered if she had stayed up all night or had woken up even earlier. *Most likely the former.* For as long as she'd known Elisa, she knew that despite all of her regimented Legionnaire training, given the chance, the woman would sleep all day.

Her bliss gave way to worry, though, as they would be leaving the City of Towers soon. "Elisa? Did you sleep at all?"

Elisa's freckled shoulders hunched. "I closed my eyes for a while but no, not really," she said, the calm, natural lowness of her voice soothing Ithmeera despite not receiving the answer she had hoped for.

"Why not?" Holding the furs close as to not allow any precious heat to escape, she quietly moved behind Elisa—her hands sliding underneath the blankets to hold her from behind. She placed a kiss on Elisa's shoulder before resting her head comfortably on it. "Are you all right?"

Elisa tilted her head to rest against Ithmeera's, the seized muscles in her back and shoulders untensing and relaxing. She took some time to answer, as Ithmeera recalled she often did when something important was on her mind. "You want the truth?"

The worry over possible lack of sleep compounded with the dreading concern that Elisa perhaps had regrets. Ithmeera moved back a bit, though she kept her hands around Elisa's midriff. "Of course I do. After everything you said last night it would do neither of us any good to keep secrets."

"Apologies, I meant—I'm not very good at sincerity at times." Elisa leaned back, allowing more of her weight fall against Ithmeera, who was more than content to accept it. "Particularly when I am nervous."

A lazy smile spread across Ithmeera's face as she found herself wanting to confess her love all over again. *Did it really take me this long to realize it?* How different would their lives have been had either of them admitted their feelings earlier? "I've known you for quite some time now, Elisa. You can tell me anything."

But Elisa still held back. "I am…worried my words will scare you."

Ithmeera chuckled. "You are welcome to try, but I fear you will find I am difficult to frighten."

Elisa sighed and closed her eyes briefly. "You asked me if I'm all right. Ithmeera, I…I don't think there has ever been a time where I've been happier than I am now. And yet," she said, her teeth coming down on her lower lip, "I suppose some irrational part of me is afraid if I fall asleep that I shall wake up and this all will have been a dream. I would be lying if I said I was not worried about what will happen once we return to Azgadar, assuming we win."

"What will happen is we will go home," Ithmeera said. She brushed her lips across the back of Elisa's neck. "You will return to Azgadar a hero. And of course, I will have your things moved to the palace, wherever they may be. There is plenty of space in my quarters."

Elisa stiffened. "I had…figured I might be able to reclaim my old bedroom. I did not want to assume you would—"

"I do not court lightly, Elisa—you of all people should know this. You will be disappointed if you hoped I would hide you or us from the people." She was resolute in her words but said them with just enough lightness in them that she was satisfied when Elisa let out a soft laugh.

"If you are certain," she said.

Ithmeera raised an eyebrow. "I meant every word I said

last night." She kissed her again. "Besides, my bed is far more comfortable than yours."

Elisa grinned, another quiet laugh escaping her and ushering a wave of joy that swept through Ithmeera. "This is true. All right," she said. "No hiding, I promise. But it may take the people some time to get used to me again."

"Let me handle that. And to address your earlier concern, this is no dream and you really should have gotten some sleep." Ithmeera moved her hands a bit, freezing when her fingertips ran over a long, raised scar on Elisa's side.

Elisa's breath cut short. "Petra," was her explanation.

"I'm sorry." Not for the first time Ithmeera wished she could be put in a room with Petra. A sword would not even be required—she would gladly pummel the traitor with her bare hands if necessary.

Elisa shrugged. "I should have been faster. I did not anticipate her to be as quick as she was. I suppose it makes sense that she was, given she had to guard Marco." She paused, giving thought to something for a moment. "Speaking of, what do we tell him?"

After feeling so powerless for the last few weeks it felt so good for Ithmeera to be able to alleviate Elisa's concerns. "The truth: that his mother is in love with a remarkable woman. He adores you and will be happy for us. You needn't worry." The faintest signs of dawn crept through the heavy drapes, casting a sliver of grey light across the bed. "It is almost time to go. We should probably get ready." She moved to withdraw her hands when Elisa stopped her.

"You should stay. You and Marco would be safe here in case something went wrong," she said. "Ben and Diana can handle this, Ithmeera. There is no reason for you to risk your own life."

Ithmeera partially agreed with her—Ben and Diana could very well handle the assault on Azgadar. But that was beside the point. "I will not ask others to risk their lives like this if I am not willing to do it myself." She squeezed Elisa one more time before pulling away. "I'm going and I will not accept any more arguments about it."

Elisa did not argue, but the pleasant mood between them earlier was gone—replaced with the same somberness that had brought Ithmeera to tears the night before. Pushing the blankets off, she quickly dressed and grabbed her boots before sitting on the bed again.

"You are upset with me."

Elisa pulled on the right boot before getting to work on the buckles. "You are the empress. I do not get to be upset with you." The sullen undertone Ithmeera had heard from her countless times returned. "Even when I think you are being foolish."

"Tell me." Ithmeera snaked her arms around Elisa again, stopping her mid-buckle. "What kind of empress would I be if I did not fight for my own home? Would that not be a better reason to be upset, if I were to hide in another kingdom while those loyal to the empire fought for me?" She pressed her lips against the side of Elisa's neck, and smirked when she received a sharp inhale in return. "And let's not forget: I shall have my Royal Guard there to protect me. So you see, there is no need to be so concerned."

"Your confidence is appreciated, but I cannot take on an entire army, Ithmeera." Elisa turned her head just enough to kiss Ithmeera on the lips. "But if this is what you desire then I will be at your side." She kissed her again—slower this time—

leaving Ithmeera dazed and stirring up the memories of what had transpired between them only hours earlier.

Much to her protest, Elisa finally had to pull away and Ithmeera couldn't help but take pleasure in the guilty look on her face, not to mention the faintest dusting of pink in her upper cheeks. "I…should probably see about getting some new armor," she said, her voice raspier than usual. "Perhaps Ben and the rest of them brought extras in their supplies." After glancing at the window, she stole one last kiss and returned to the buckles on her boot. "You should get ready."

"I will." Ithmeera breathed deeply and leaned against Elisa's back. She savored their closeness for just a bit longer, desperately hoping this would not be the last time.

# Return to Azgadar

**Azgadar, Azgadaran Empire**

Afternoon waned over the outer fields of Azgadar as the remaining patches of daylight fought to break through the thick, green cloud cover that suffocated the city and its surrounding hills.

Within the high, tan clay and stone walls stood the Azgadaran Palace, and around it, a luminous field that hummed and crackled as it fed from the rapidly depleting stores of magic—stores which had been gathered centuries ago and kept over generations in the event an army from a foreign nation tried to invade Azgadar.

Today, the invaders arrived. From the east, the joined armies of Azgadar's loyal Legionnaires and Gurdinfield's Guardians—having set out from the City of Towers only days prior—now crested the low, dry hills. Their combined forces spanned long enough to surround the city and far enough back that from the spire they surely would have appeared a significant threat. On the left, clad in the red and black chainmail and armed with the trademark sword and shield of the empire marched the Legionnaires, with General Veraun leading them at the front on horseback. Jacob led the sword and spear-wielding Guardians on the right, most of whom were wearing the blue, white, and gold uniform of Gurdinfield under leather and plated armor. Between the marching soldiers, others rolled massive carts upon which sat heavy catapults—their solution to taking out the magic shield around the spire.

Next to Veraun, outfitted in her own Legionnaire attire, rode Ithmeera. As the city loomed in the distance, she shifted in her saddle—not for the first time as she was not accustomed to wearing armor. It was regulation Legionnaire mail armor; had the situation been different, she might have been wearing the more embellished armor the Cadar rulers traditionally wore into battle.

Elisa, who rode between her and Diana, took notice of her discomfort before muttering her own complaint. "When this is over, I request that you dismiss whoever came up with this chest piece design. It is atrociously unbalanced compared to the old one. And it itches." She gave Ithmeera a long-suffering look to which Ithmeera just smiled as she took in the rather impressive sight of Elisa in full Legionnaire armor again, the swords and shield emblem of the empire blazing proudly on her chest. From her belt on her left hung the sword Ithmeera had gifted her, its golden hilt catching the faintest of the thin beams of light cast down from the sky. On the other side of her waist hung her dagger, having allowed Kye to keep her other one. The once wild copper strands Ithmeera recalled with fondness running her hands through the night before leaving Gurdinfield had been braided, the ends hanging just above the sturdy round shield strapped to her back.

"Are you certain it's not just because you've forgotten how to wear actual armor, Lady Elisa?" Victor called out from behind them, eliciting a few chuckles from the other soldiers.

Sparing a short laugh herself, Ithmeera was grateful for the brief respite as she directed her attention to the city. "General, can we expect Petra to utilize all of the defenses? Even the magic-based ones?"

"It is difficult to say for certain, Your Majesty, but I would not count it out," Veraun replied. "However, I do not recall our stockpile of those being very high. Perhaps three or four existed at most before the New Legion took over."

"Magic-based? Like the explosive the Legion used on the gate in the City of Towers?" Andrea, who rode on the back of the horse she shared with Meredith, had barely spoken more than a few words the entire trip. The marks that webbed across her arm had darkened since leaving Gurdinfield, and Ithmeera could only assume they had done the same on the rest of her body where she was afflicted. In fact, even after ordering the girl to get rest Ithmeera thought she appeared even more tired than she had in the days preceding. She recalled Meredith giving her something to drink before they left the City of Towers— Andrea had turned a slight tinge of green after, gasping and holding her arm. Ithmeera suspected the drink had been one of the liquid magic concoctions Meredith had spoken of earlier. She couldn't imagine the awful things the stuff might do to a person when ingested, but she was not about to interrogate two enchanters on the matter.

"Yes," Veraun said. "You are familiar with those, Enchanter Andrea?"

Elisa answered for her, her tone dark. "One of them nearly killed her." Veraun nodded his acknowledgement and the

Guardians—particularly Jacob, Victor, and Roe—focused their gazes elsewhere as the mood among them all sobered.

*Erik must have used it to try to breach the city.* She remembered the royal enchanters working on the weapon years before she had sent the Legion to take the City of Towers. But with the unstable state of magic in the land, there was no telling how the explosives might behave if fired. Out of the corner of her eye, she caught Lydia, no, *Diana*—she always had to correct herself as she remembered the woman went by her middle name— glancing back at Andrea from her place in front of the other Guardians, her dark eyes filled with concern.

Elisa ended up leaning over to murmur to Diana, though Ithmeera was just in earshot of it that she could hear. "She will be fine."

Diana bit her lip. "I just wish there was more I could do to help her."

"The best thing we can do is make sure that shield goes down." Elisa straightened up and rolled her shoulders back. "We will have to leave the rest to her and trust that she and Meredith know what they're doing."

Diana responded with an unassured sigh before turning her head to inspect the sprawling army behind her. Ithmeera noticed Veraun performing a similar inspection of the Legion. She noted Captain Taryn riding a few rows back, her grey eyes narrowed and alert as she fired out maintaining orders to her subordinates. Not for the first time, Ithmeera searched for Kye and Marco, only to be reminded that they had left the company a day earlier and headed to Sadford's Legion fort where they would remain until a messenger could be sent to inform them Azgadar had been retaken.

She swallowed hard, remembering her son's worried expression when she had attempted to mask her fear with a faint smile and kissed him on the head—letting him know she would see him soon. But of course, Marco was too smart for her words to be convincing. He had argued at first, demanding she and Elisa accompany him and Kye. When his tears came, Ithmeera had to practically tear herself away so that she would not lose her composure in front of him. Elisa had been more steady-voiced than she had, and ultimately had been the one to see them off when Veraun approached with information on their upcoming assault.

"They have fighters covering the southeastern wall," Jacob announced, the others peering ahead. Sure enough, ranks of Legionnaires had formed in front of their target wall. A glance up toward the battlements confirmed Ithmeera's suspicion that Petra would have ordered the activation of the city's defenses. *If she deploys the explosives this could be a disaster.* Had she a group of enchanters at her disposal, she would simply have ordered them to cast a barrier over the fighters. But only Andrea had the ability to cast and, according to Meredith, she needed to save her magic for once they were inside the city.

"The sentries must have finally spotted us. Your Majesty," Veraun addressed her, "we will be within striking range soon."

"Ready the catapults the moment we are in striking distance, General," Ithmeera ordered. "Do *not* engage those fighters, am I clear?" They were still too far away for her to try to seek out Petra among them, but Ithmeera could feel her former lady-in-waiting's eyes watching her all the same.

Veraun's response was swift. "By your order, Your Majesty." He signaled for the Legion to quicken their pace and Jacob issued a similar order for the Guardians as the city grew larger.

"They will have the explosives." Elisa seemed to read her mind. "Ithmeera, a single one of those can rip through an iron gate. With magic unstable—if Petra deploys those…"

"I am well aware, Elisa. We will keep our distance until the wall has been struck down and the shield disabled."

Bright green eyes flashed with determination at her. "The moment I see them I am getting you out of here."

With the city nearly in striking distance, Ithmeera did not feel up to arguing this point, turning her attention to Diana instead. "Lydia, are your men ready? Veraun can direct the catapults, but we will need your Guardians to defend them in the event those fighters charge us."

The Guardians directly behind Diana shouted their support. Ithmeera's eyebrows went up in surprise—she would never understand the lack of discipline Gurdinfield's armies seemed to have. But what they lacked in formalities they certainly made up for in bravado and loyalty, something she certainly couldn't say the same for when it came to the Legion.

Diana just grinned and Ithmeera had to remind herself that the woman was a former rebel fighter herself. "We are ready, Your Majesty. We stand ready to take back Azgadar with you." Her declaration was followed by more cheers. "Andrea, Meredith— you two hold back until Veraun gives the word for the captain to escort you to the city. Not a moment sooner."

Meredith's answer was accompanied by a short bow of her head. "We will remain with you until the order is given, Your Majesty." Andrea said nothing, her eyes focused hard on the spire ahead.

A distant thunder sounded in the distance before rolling under the earth beneath them. Ithmeera shivered as the hairs on the back of her neck lifted—a hot wind passing across the fields and prompting Legionnaires and Guardians alike to turn their gazes upward.

"Not now," Elisa breathed, her brow furrowed with worry.

"We have time!" Meredith called. "We may want to act soon, however, Your Majesties."

Ithmeera brought her horse to an easing stop and held up her hand to command the others to do the same as her ears were met with a rush of chain links clinking and heavy leather boots shifting in the dirt.

Azgadar stood a short ride away from them, a beacon in the darkening day as clouds of muted grey and dead green slowly began their telltale spin, gravitating around the towering palace. Small balls of fire hovered over the wall—archers with lit arrows no doubt—and the fighters standing between them and the wall stood vigilant, though they had not yet drawn their weapons.

She closed her eyes and breathed deeply, the static in the air clinging to her as though the very land was suffocating. They had one chance at this. Whatever happened today would determine the fate of not only Azgadar but all of Damea.

Opening her eyes, she smiled as she took in the view. She refused to remain an exile any longer.

"Ben," she said. "On my order, take out that shield." At his acknowledgement, she spurred her horse forward a bit, turning to face the combined armies and drawing her sword.

"Legionnaires!" she shouted, the adrenaline of being able

to address them loud and clear already setting her blood on fire. "Guardians! We stand here no longer as enemies, but as allies fighting side-by-side for our home. You fight not just for the Azgadaran Empire or Gurdinfield, but for all of Damea." She found Elisa in the crowd—her fiery gaze matching that of Veraun's, Diana's, Jacob's, and all the others, bolstering her confidence as she continued. "We will take down that shield and bring order to the chaos these traitors have unleashed upon us. We will take back our land and soon, our sky." She held up her sword, her final piece joined by another roll of thunder. "I fight for all of Damea today! Do you stand with me?"

The booming roar from both armies rattled Ithmeera's very being and rung in her ears as many of the fighters held up their swords as well, their war cries rolling over the hills and echoing across the field.

Her heart pounding, she took her place by Veraun and Elisa again. *"Now, Ben!"*

Veraun gave a shout as his arm shot up, the creaking of the catapults at high tension filling the air moments before his arm came down and a hail of massive boulders rained down on the Azgadaran wall. The impacts blasted through the hardened clay and stone, sending chunks of it and the Legionnaires posted in the battlements flying through the air.

"Jacob!" Diana barked. In an instant, Jacob's arm was also up as the Guardian-controlled catapults prepared to unleash their own might on the wall. Ithmeera held her breath as he waited just long enough for the smoke to clear out from the wall to ensure a clear shot. Then his arm, too, came down ushering a second wave of the huge stones soaring through the air at breakneck speeds—crashing through the exposed wall.

A low warble sounded from deep within the city and Ithmeera watched in nervous anticipation as the shield gave an angry pulse before exploding in all directions—the magic fading as it stretched out and disappeared into the air.

*"The shield is down!"* she screamed and was joined by a chorus of cheers from the Legionnaires and Guardians as she watched the remains of the crumbling wall break off in smaller pieces, the smoke rising from within the city. The panicked shouts of the New Legion were audible now. "General, have the Legion assemble at the gate so we can—" Her voice trailed as the air around them fell into a deathly stillness and a pit of dread settled in her stomach. The sky darkened considerably as evening fell, giving her a clear view of the roaring orange and blue mass of rippling magic hurled from the adjacent wall… followed by another. They scorched the sky as they headed directly at the armies.

Ithmeera's mouth went dry. That Petra would deploy the explosives in Damea's unstable state meant one thing for certain. *She truly* is *mad.* "F-fall back," she whispered, not realizing at first that no one could hear her.

Elisa must have seen her hesitate. She elbowed Veraun before yelling to the others. "Fall back! Fall back, *now!*"

Panic ensued as Veraun and Diana also began shouting for the armies to fall back, but it wasn't soon enough. The first explosive smashed into the ground just next to the Legionnaires in a blazing impact that threw dozens of screaming fighters into the air. The second hit a cluster of Guardians near the middle of the group, killing several of them instantly and sending the survivors and surrounding soldiers running for their lives.

"Fall back to the camp! Fall back!" Jacob repeated, his voice all but drowned out by the dozens of beating hooves on the dirt as Legionnaires and Guardians fought to escape the firestorm.

A paralyzing shock gripped Ithmeera. She watched in horror as the second explosive tore itself apart with an ear-splitting noise that left her nauseated. A chunk of fire broke off from the secondary explosion, headed straight for Diana—who had been thrown from her horse.

Ithmeera wanted to move, to push Diana out of the way. But she was too slow—too far to be able to react as time seemed to slow down. She watched helplessly as terror crossed Jacob's features, the realization that he had strayed too far from his wife.

"Diana!" Victor moved like lightning as his long strides took him within enough reach of Diana to push her out of the way with powerful arms—an instant before the fire warped around him and reduced him to ashes in the blink of an eye.

Amidst Jacob and Roe's wails of denial, two more explosives hit several paces away from the front line, spurring Ithmeera's horse into a panic before it threw her off. She cried out as she fell on her back, the hard dirt knocking the breath from her and her horse bolting out of reach.

She let out a frightened whimper as the bright light from the exploded magic singed her hair and burned spots in her vision, obstructing her view of the field as she desperately tried to crawl away from the immediate danger.

A warm, armored hand grasped hers, the strong arm behind it pulling her up to scrabble up onto Elisa's horse.

"I've got you!" Elisa gasped. "Come on, we need to go!"

Ithmeera ducked her head, squeezing her eyes shut while

Elisa used her body to shield her as they galloped away from the raining fire. Dizziness overtook her as her mind spun and the nausea returned—the reverberating cries of Legionnaires and Guardians rushing to escape the inferno the last thing she registered before being dragged into darkness.

# Chapter 20

# Blame

The sky lit up—bright as day for an instant before Damea was blanketed in darkness once more. With dusk nearing, Richard quickened his movements as he hoisted the now full bucket of water from the well.

The abandoned house on the outer edges of the small town of Sadford had suited him well enough for his experiments. He had packed very little from Meredith's house in the Black Forest, and only needed a table and his research notes to make do. And Cassie, of course. He was glad he remembered to take the shackles with them, particularly since Cassie's tantrums had grown worse as of late. He had some concern one of their distant neighbors might hear her yells, but he was willing to risk it. After all, it was necessary for him to be within range of the spire to truly understand how the shield worked so he could work on disabling it. If only those insufferable enchanter-hating New Legion weren't standing in his way—then he would have been free to investigate the shield as he pleased.

*She will come around once we get home.* He admitted he could have handled the situation with Andrea a bit differently, but after she had called to him under the guise of Meredith and then *attacked* him, he had not been feeling particularly merciful. Surely their relationship had been no more than a brief dalliance and Cassie would get past it eventually.

As he carried the bucket back to the house, the sky flickered again—a brighter white than the distant lightning strikes had been. Turning to meet the source of the light, he saw the spire in the distance and his heart leapt in his chest at the sight of Azgadar's shield exploding.

Had something broken it? His answer came quickly—even from Sadford the flaming balls of magic were visible as they were thrown to the fields outside the city walls. Azgadar was being attacked and its invaders had disabled the shield.

Hardly believing his good fortune, Richard dropped the bucket, the water that spilled onto the threshold suddenly yesterday's problem, and hurried inside to fetch Cassie and pack their things.

✶ ✶ ✶

Andrea leaned forward on the small cot, her elbows resting on the blue fabric of the cloak folded on her lap as she observed Elisa tending to a rather nasty burn on Ithmeera's left arm. When the two had made it back to the camp on the far eastern outskirts of Azgadar, Ithmeera had been unconscious for the first few minutes, prompting elevated concern and in some— like the normally composed General Veraun—full on panic until Elisa had to tell them all to go away so she could tend to the empress's wound.

Ithmeera had been too close to the explosive—not that anyone could be far enough away from them were it up to Andrea—and according to Meredith's muttering after they had retreated, it was nothing short of a miracle that she had survived the blast.

"Ah!" Ithmeera yelped in pain, yanking her injured arm back from Elisa, who held a damp cloth in one hand and a bottle in the other. "Would it kill you to be at least a little gentler?"

"I am." Elisa's face displayed no humor, in fact Andrea could not remember the last time she had seen her friend this worried. "I'm sorry, just—please try not to move. I know it's painful."

Ithmeera hung her head as she held out her arm again. "It is fine. Just get it over with." She blinked a few times and winced. "My head still spins."

"A side effect," Andrea spoke up, trying to be somewhat helpful. "Enchanted objects behave unpredictably here. It should fade soon."

Elisa paused to give her a curious look. "Has it for you?"

"No. But it's not the same thing." She stood up and threw the cloak around herself, her white shirt visible under the large tear on the right shoulder, before fastening it. "I'm going to go check on Diana."

"Andrea." She felt Elisa's low warning in her chest. "She is in shock and the rest in mourning. We should leave them be."

Andrea knew she would never forget the expression on Diana's face as she watched Victor crumble into ash on the battlefield after he'd saved her from the explosive. How she had shifted from disbelief to denial in mere seconds, the awful scream she had let out as Jacob practically carried her off the field. "She is my friend, too, Elisa, and I knew Victor well," she said, keeping her voice as gentle as she could. "Please tell Meredith where I went if she comes by." She bowed to Ithmeera. "Your Majesty."

She took quick steps across the somber encampment, passing by Legionnaires and Guardians, their faces coated in sweat and soot and many of whom were nursing minor cuts and burns of their own or huddled away where they could mourn for their lost friends in peace. A few turned their heads at her, their eyes bloodshot from exhaustion, crying, or both. Smoke rose from the small campfires dotting the encampment, but the scent paled in comparison to the strong burnt odor of magic from the explosives that still permeated the air. A thin line of fighters surrounded the area in the event the New Legion advanced on them. Fortunately, they had not.

Andrea had only been in one other battle—at the City of Towers when the Legion had tried to siege the city to take Gurdinfield's magic—and while she had no desire to repeat the horrible experience, her plan to save Cassie and stop Richard was in movement. She knew it was only a matter of time before Richard arrived to take Azgadar's magic. And she would be ready for him. She had to be for Cassie's sake.

The added complexity of how the magic would be redistributed to the land without putting enchanters at risk was something she had not given much more thought to. Meredith had no answers other than to warn that the fate of all enchanters was potentially in Andrea's hands assuming they could successfully apprehend Richard this time. She had continued to hold back from telling Ithmeera or Kye about the risk. It was certainly not Andrea's finest moment, but she had a feeling Ithmeera would never have gone along with her plan had she known it might put Marco in danger. *But we're all already in danger!* Until Richard was stopped, everyone was at risk. Every death, every building that crumbled, every life the storms took—it was all because of him.

No, this had to end. Richard needed to be stopped or all of Damea would fall.

When she reached Diana's large tent, one of the double dark blue flaps opened and Roe stepped out. So tall was he that he had to bend down to clear the top of the entrance. When he saw Andrea he stood there, blocking the way as he towered over her. "I am glad to see you safe, Enchanter Andrea." Guilt set in upon seeing the long tear stains on his cheeks. Victor was dead in part because of her plan.

She didn't know what to say to him. What could you say to someone after they had just lost their closest friend? She settled on simple yet sincere. "I'm so sorry, Roe."

He gave her a sad smile and patted her shoulder. "He was a Guardian to the very end, Andrea. He'll not be forgotten." He sniffed before withdrawing his arm and brushed past her, stumbling a bit in his grief as he walked away.

Her throat constricted, she paused before opening the flap and stepped into the tent where she found Diana, resting on the large cot and Jacob sitting on a short wooden stool next to her. Diana's face and hair were covered in ash and her eyes were closed—the tension on her face evident enough that Andrea could see it was not a peaceful sleep. Jacob's large hand was on her head, his fingers gently stroking her dark hair as he looked upon her with tired, worried eyes.

He must have sensed Andrea's presence and turned to meet her. "Andrea." No longer the jovial man she knew, his voice was hollow. "I…I have no words."

Andrea took a tentative step forward, a soft crunch coming from her boot as it pressed down on the dirt. "Is she injured?"

"No," he said, his gaze returning to Diana. "But I know Diana. She will never forgive herself for this."

"It wasn't her fault."

Jacob's shoulders shook. It was heartbreaking to see the strongest man in Gurdinfield falling apart like this. "No. It was mine. I was too far away. I should have been better, should have been faster." He let out a trembling sigh. "I lost one of my best friends today, Andrea." He bit his lip, holding back tears. "H-he was there and then he was gone. Just like that. And…" He spoke in short bursts, his body tense as though he might shatter at a moment's notice. "I nearly lost my wife. And Cassie." Guilt-ridden eyes met hers. "I am sorry I was not there to protect her, Andrea. I should have been more vigilant with her training. Perhaps—"

Andrea stopped him, surprising herself at her interruption of someone who by all accounts was considered royalty. But the last thing she wanted was for him to blame himself for what happened. "Richard is cunning and resourceful, Jacob. There was no way we could have foreseen this. Trust me," she said, "I've done my fair share of blaming, mostly myself. But we'll get her back. And we'll stop him." She nodded, trying to convince herself of her own words. "We have to."

"Yes," he said, though his voice still broke. "Forgive me. I-I would like to be alone with Diana for a while. Please let the empress know we will be ready to reconvene later this evening." He swallowed. "We can…we can sort out our next move then."

"Of course, Your Highness. I will do that right away." With a final bow, she made sure to remain as quiet as she could while leaving the tent as to not wake Diana before heading back to the spot where Elisa had been tending to Ithmeera's wounds.

# Chapter 21

# Full Circle

With night having finally fallen over Azgadar, the leaders of the alliance gathered around a table outside Ithmeera's tent to discuss their next strategy. Flashes had streaked across the cloudy skies all evening—the coming storm growing more intense by the hour. A hastily drawn map of Azgadar on parchment had been rolled out on the old, chipped wooden surface, its edges torn. A lit lantern hanging on a post outside the tent along with the glow of the surrounding campfires cast shadows on the faces of all who had assembled there.

Elisa pressed her palms to the table and leaned forward. Across from her, arms folded over her chest stood Ithmeera, who so far had remained quiet and allowed Veraun to speak for the most part. Her arm, treated and bandaged, appeared to be giving her less discomfort than it had earlier, but Elisa could sense the heavy guilt and grief from her—she knew Ithmeera felt responsible for their losses and subsequent retreat.

"...to breach the Market District, here." Veraun tapped an armored finger on the area of the map representing the busiest district of Azgadar. "The shield appears to be disabled still. If Captain Taryn and her fighters can secure the outer steps of the palace and get Enchanter Andrea to the spire, we can move in with a larger force and disable the New Legion tonight."

Next to Veraun, Jacob studied the map closely—rubbing his beard while exchanging the occasional worried glance with Diana. "Can we be certain there are no more of those explosives before we even attempt to approach the city? We cannot take another attack like that."

"There were very few of them when I left Azgadar," Veraun said, though his hesitant tone betrayed his uncertainty. "Unless Petra and the royal enchanters have discovered a way to create more of them with the state of magic as it is, it is doubtful."

"The farms." While quiet, Ithmeera's voice seemed to rise above the others and the surrounding sounds of the camp. "If she took magic from the infrastructure powering our farms, she might have enough to make them."

Diana gave a dismayed shake of her head. "When you've already pulled an entire city into chaos, what do a few farms matter?"

"Petra has committed mutiny, treason, and murder, not to mention she tried to kill you." Elisa's attention went to Ithmeera. "She seems to hold a deep hatred for enchanters, but I would not put it past her to use them and the city's magic to create more weapons and then blame it on the enchanters when it all comes back to her."

"We might have to take that chance," Veraun said. He pointed to the area of the map bordering the city boundaries. "We can have our remaining Legionnaires stay outside the walls in case she takes the fight to the field," Veraun said. "If your Guardians can reinforce them—"

"They will," Diana said. She rubbed her eyes, and Elisa could see the redness in them still. "But I have concerns about attempting to take the city at night. We are still recovering from earlier. The Guardians are exhausted—surely, we could use some sleep. Why not launch at dawn?"

"If we wait, we will lose any advantage of cover at night," Veraun said.

"No. I will not attack the city in the dead of night while its citizens are asleep," Ithmeera insisted. "No doubt they're already frightened out of their minds."

Elisa sighed. They were moving too slow, and for all they knew, Petra was mounting an assault on their camp as they spoke. They needed to stop wasting time. "They are frightened because a traitor sits on the throne. Your Majesty, the sooner we do this, the sooner Petra pays for her crimes."

"Ithmeera is right. We also don't even know their numbers, not truly," Diana pointed out. "Fighting within city walls is not the same as engaging them on a field, Elisa."

"You think I don't know that?!" Elisa hadn't intended to lose her temper, especially not with Diana, but between their losses that day combined with their inability to agree on a strategy her patience had been thinned.

"*Elisa,*" Jacob warned.

Diana stiffened before narrowing her eyes at Elisa. "I think you have allowed your hatred for this woman to cloud your judgement and push you to make rash decisions you would not have made otherwise."

"My home—*our* home," Elisa exclaimed, gesturing at her

and Ithmeera, "has been taken over by a fanatic. I am trying to get it back! Now, I am sorry about Victor, but surely you can relate to that, Your Majesty."

Diana's eyes widened. "Of *course* I can! But you saw what happened back there, Elisa. It was chaos! Gurdinfield will stand with Azgadar, but if I can prevent the pointless deaths of my fighters, I will."

Fed up with arguing, Elisa threw up her hands. "All of these deaths are pointless. This…inaction is pointless!" She felt a hand touch her shoulder and tensed before realizing it was Ithmeera's. She turned to see pleading green eyes staring back at her.

"Elisa, I appreciate what you are trying to do." Somehow in all this, Ithmeera had managed to remain calm and Elisa couldn't understand why. "But she is right. We need to give our fighters the chance to recover before sending them back out there."

Veraun glanced at the two of them nervously before taking a deep breath and pushed away from the table. "Right, then. Your Majesty, with your leave, I will inform the Legion that we will attempt to retake the city at dawn."

Chewing her lower lip in frustration, Elisa made no effort to hide her disappointment when Ithmeera gave Veraun her approval. He gave Elisa a curt nod and bowed to Ithmeera and Diana before departing, leaving the rest of them in a stony silence.

The air around them tense and awkward, Jacob cleared his throat. "Perhaps it might be a good idea for all of us to get some rest."

"I agree." Diana rolled up the map before picking it up. "The Guardians will be ready to leave at dawn as well. Goodnight, Your Majesty. Elisa," she said, her tone edging on sadness before she and Jacob left as well.

Alone at the table together, Ithmeera did not wait to speak as she took one of Elisa's hands. "I see raising your voice is not just something you do to your empress but to queens as well." An eyebrow went up, a teasing smile playing on her lips. "Do I need to be jealous?"

Elisa rolled her eyes. Was Ithmeera really trying to jest with her right now? "I thought you wanted to go home."

"I do," Ithmeera said. She squeezed her hand and Elisa had fight the urge to kiss her. "I do and that you are so dedicated to helping us get home means the world to me. But Lydia is right, my love. You know she is."

*My love.* Heat spread to Elisa's face as she was reminded of their night together in Gurdinfield. "I…yes. I know. I should apologize to her. Especially after what happened to Victor. That was out of line."

"You should. Perhaps once this is over, I will see about hiring a tutor to refresh your manners on how to properly address royalty."

"Very funny," Elisa said, taking Ithmeera's other hand and facing her. "I am sorry for losing my temper. I just want to see Petra dead." She sighed. "I can't help thinking about everything you said—about going home, telling the people what really happened with my father, about…us. I'm just afraid that the longer we wait, the less chance we have of, well, having any of that."

If Ithmeera had any reservations about publicly announcing their relationship before they returned to Azgadar, they were cast aside as she leaned in to brush her lips against Elisa's. The kiss was brief, and as she pulled away a shy smile had already formed on her face. "Who would have thought Elisa of Sadford was such a romantic?"

Elisa took a shallow breath. "I am no such thing," she declared when she found her words again. "I just want that woman gone so I don't have to sleep in the dirt anymore."

Ithmeera laughed. "I agree completely, though I suppose I would not be averse to sharing my dirt this time."

Taking comfort in how close they stood, Elisa's hands went to rest on Ithmeera's hips as she nuzzled her cheek. "I almost lost you today," she whispered.

"But you didn't and I am fine," Ithmeera replied in a tone equally as hushed. "My Royal Guard made certain of that." She gave one of Elisa's hands a gentle tug. "Come. Even broody Legionnaires need to sleep on the eve of battle."

"I do not brood."

"Of course you don't," Ithmeera said as she led them away from the table and back to their tent.

* * *

As night passed over Azgadar, the Legion and Guardians settled in to get what hours of sleep they could before it was time to execute their plan to breach Azgadar's gates and retake the city. The fields surrounding the capital were mostly quiet, but as Andrea sat under the awning of the tent she and Meredith shared, the haunting moan of the winds and the growing static charge in the air served as a sign the storm was picking up. She watched the clouds above the city swirl faster as they converged over the top of the Azgadaran Palace, the last bastion of magic in Damea.

Leaning back against a short stack of burlap sacks carrying supplies the armies had brought with them, she winced as an all too familiar sharp pain shot through her arm. She had taken the last of the potion before they left Gurdinfield, and while it had alleviated the worst of the burning it had not soothed it completely.

She looked down at her arm, her shirtsleeve pulled up just enough that she could see the purplish-black streaks that crawled up under her shirt and to her shoulder. They had definitely darkened since the last time she looked at them. The vision in her right eye was still mostly blurred and she wondered what would happen to her even if they figured out a way to get Damea's magic back. Would the scars remain? Would she die anyway, having run out of the potion? The Restoration had reversed the effects of the magic sickness she'd contracted in Rhyad but this?

She had been cut off from Damea's magic for so long— perhaps Meredith was right and she would be one of the many enchanter casualties when this was all over. A bittersweet victory, but if it meant Cassie would be safe…if it meant Richard would be stopped from destroying everything…

She craned her neck back, resting the back of her head on the top of the sacks and let out a loud exhale, tensing when

Meredith's voice tore her from her thoughts.

Leather boots stepped softly on the ground next to her and stopped. "Have you slept at all, Andrea?"

She sat up. "No. I don't think I could if I tried."

Meredith hummed her acknowledgement and knelt down to take a seat on the dirt next to her. "Neither can I." She looked ahead, grey-streaked hair blowing past her face. "It's so strange. I remember a time when I would avoid Azgadar whenever possible. Now we're risking our lives trying to get in."

"Not alone, though."

"No," Meredith replied. "Not alone." Her eyes turned downward to Andrea's arm. "How are they?"

Andrea gave a half-hearted shrug. "Still the same. They might get worse soon. I can never tell how long the potion will last, but it will run out quicker once I start using magic." When Meredith did not respond they settled into a comfortable silence. It reminded Andrea a bit of when she lived in Meredith's mansion, studying as an apprentice under her. There had been times when the two would go for days without speaking more than a few words at meals—both consumed by either an experiment or in Andrea's case, studying and research.

Meredith's hand went to the bracelet on her own wrist, her fingers running over the colored threads as she spoke. "I have watched you closely since we began traveling together again, Andrea. It is…remarkable what you've endured. And despite all that has happened, you've kept going." She looked up, admiration in her eyes. "You remind me of myself when I was your age. Smart, determined, but more importantly, willing to do what is necessary to save the person you love."

Andrea scoffed. "I am not you, Meredith. I don't hold people hostage or…or torture them. And I certainly don't fall in love with mass murderers." She shook her head, avoiding Meredith's gaze. "I don't know what in the world would compel you to compare us when we are nothing alike."

Any confidence on Meredith's face crumbled away as the lines around her eyes tightened. "You're right to some degree. I would be lying if I said I did not feel partly responsible for Richard's actions."

"That's one way of putting it," Andrea grumbled. "You've never seemed to feel bad about it before."

Meredith's eyebrows arched as her voice broke. "He is my husband, Andrea! I made a promise to him that I would do everything I could to save him after he fell ill. But I could not have foreseen this. You need to stop blaming me for what Richard's done and focus on what's important right now, which is stopping him."

"I know!" Andrea cried. She buried her face in shaking hands. "I know. Even if everything goes according to plan, even if we do stop him—I still don't know how we're going to fix the damage he's done. Or…" Her eyes pricked and she found herself having to push back tears again as she looked up. "Or if I'll even get to be with Cassie after." An arm reached around her shoulders and she did not pull away.

"You will. And we will figure this out." Andrea had never known Meredith to be a particularly doting woman, so she was stunned when she felt her mentor lean into her. "I have known you for a few years now, Andrea, and if there is anything I can be certain of, it is that you've never given up. Not once. Even on the most foolish endeavors you have set out on." She chuckled, making Andrea let out a sharp laugh as well before the sadness from earlier crept back.

"I miss her so much. We were supposed to leave Gurdinfield together after I gave up enchanting and…" She held up her wrist to observe the bracelet before dropping it and shook her head. "It seems like a dream, now. Just…a silly dream. You're right Meredith," she said. "This isn't your fault. It's mine. I should have never left Ata."

Meredith withdrew her arm. "Well, we cannot change the past. And you give yourself too little credit." She smiled. "You have become a skilled enchanter, Andrea, and while we have had our differences, I could not have asked for a better apprentice."

Andrea couldn't help but grin with pride. Praise from Meredith was rare enough, particularly when it came to enchanting, but hearing this from her mentor was satisfying in a way that being Royal Enchanter of Gurdinfield had never been. "Thank you. You were—have been a good teacher. I… regret that I did not get to finish my training with you."

Meredith shot her an incredulous look. "You are the Royal Enchanter of Gurdinfield and have the ears of the most powerful people in Damea. There is nothing more I could teach you that you don't already know."

"Funny. I sometimes felt like my promotion wasn't truly earned," Andrea admitted. "Diana asked me to be her royal enchanter, but in many ways I just felt…underqualified. Like an apprentice who didn't know what she was doing and was just lucky to be alive after Rhyad."

"You think you were 'just lucky'?" Meredith said. "Your accomplishments were the result of many things, luck of which was not one of them." She laughed again. "You know me well enough to know I don't believe in chance, only in the combinations of events and how we react to them." She clicked her tongue before climbing to her feet. "But if it will help you accept the obvious, *Enchanter* Andrea, you stopped being merely an apprentice a long time ago." After straightening her clothing, she glanced out at the city again, where the first rays of dawn fought to break through the clouds. "I am going to check in with Captain Taryn to see if she requires anything from us before we make our move. I would suggest you try to get some rest, but I don't suppose you would listen to me."

"Probably not."

Meredith tilted her head, perhaps out of concern, but did not press the matter. "As you wish. In that case, I—"

A great explosion in the distance froze both of them, turning Azgadar into a massive ball of light as deep thrum rippled across the fields. A strong gust of wind collided with the tent, ripping the fabric back and making the anchored posts creak in protest.

Scrambling to her feet, Andrea pushed aside the dark hair that had blown into her face and shielded her eyes from the blast. The light dimmed, and Azgadar stood as it had only now the shouts of the New Legion and citizens alike carried in the breeze.

"He's here," she whispered.

Meredith's mouth was parted in fear as she pointed at the fresh bolts of lightning above the spire. "We need to get to the city quickly. Come, we must get the others!"

# Chapter 22

# Second Assault

"Captain!" Roe yelled over the strengthening storm as he rushed along the front lines of Legion and Guardian fighters where he eventually reached Jacob and the other leaders who were all on foot as they once again closed the distance between them and Azgadar. Standing at attention, he reported his findings—panting as sweat ran down his face. "More of the New Legion have gathered outside the destroyed wall. At least twice what we saw yesterday."

"What about the gate?" Elisa asked. She glanced back to check on Andrea and Meredith, who shared one horse as they stood next to Captain Taryn and a group of Legionnaire riders, ready to make a run to the city. The rest of the fighters were on foot as they eagerly waited for the order to charge the New Legion to be given.

"Torn to pieces. This Richard must have used something powerful to break through it. But that's not all." Roe faced Ithmeera. "Petra leads them, Your Majesty."

Ithmeera's face hardened and for the first time since departing Gurdinfield Elisa could see the anger for Petra she'd been holding back. "So...she's not going to hide inside the palace any longer while we invade Azgadar." She clenched her fists before looking at Diana. "I say we end this, here and now."

"We stand by you, Ithmeera. Jacob," Diana ordered, "prepare everyone to charge on the empress's order."

Elisa waited for the two men to leave to rally the rest of the Guardians before clearing her throat. "Your Majesty," she said, tensing when Diana's attention shifted to her. When she felt Ithmeera's watchful gaze on her as well, she closed her eyes and tried her hardest to focus on what she wanted to say. "I was… out of line with how I spoke to you last night. You have been a good friend to me and I apologize. And…" She bit her lip. "I am truly sorry about Victor. He was a good man."

Diana placed a hand on Elisa's shoulder. "Elisa," she said warmly. "I will always be your friend, though I understand why you were frustrated. And I will do whatever I can to get you both home, I promise."

Letting out a sigh of relief, Elisa bowed her head. "Thank you, Your Majesty."

Diana's expression quickly turned to amusement as she rolled her eyes. "Elisa, we are friends. At this point, it's just 'Diana.'"

"Of course, Your Majesty." Elisa gave her a wry grin before she reached behind for the round shield bearing the Azgadaran emblem on her back and equipped it over her left hand. "These are heavier than I remember." Out of the corner of her eye she caught Ithmeera's frown. "What?"

"Just," Ithmeera pleaded quietly. "Be careful." She looked out at the sprawling army of New Legion fighters, only a small dirt field separating them. "Petra is out there. I imagine it won't be long before she comes for me."

"I will be fine. Would she not send her traitorous Legionnaires instead of risking her own neck?"

Ithmeera shook her head. "No. This is personal for her. She will come for me. I know it."

"She will not go near you." Elisa moved to draw her sword but froze when Ithmeera's hand came down on hers, their eyes drawing to each other one last time before they charged.

"Elisa…"

"We *will* win, Ithmeera. And then we'll go home." Her pulse quickened when she saw the barely-restrained fear on Ithmeera's face, and she wanted more than anything to make it disappear. She leaned in—murmuring words meant only for her. "I love you."

"And I you." Ithmeera's hand fell to her own blade. "General, are we ready?" she called.

"We are, Your Majesty," Veraun said. "The enchanters are ready as well. Once we charge, Captain Taryn will escort them into the city."

With both armies acknowledging their preparedness for the next assault on the city, Elisa finally drew her sword and looked out at the enemy ahead. Rows upon rows of New Legionnaires, armed with swords and shields themselves, blocked the crumbling stone wall. With the distance mostly closed between the armies save a small patch of field, Elisa could now spot Petra at the front and center.

She adjusted her grips on her own sword and shield before

inhaling deeply, quieting any and all thoughts unrelated to the battle ahead. If they were to have a chance at emerging victorious, she needed to be focused.

"Whatever happens," she heard Ithmeera say to Diana, "I am glad we are here together. You and your Guardians have my deepest gratitude."

"We are honored to assist." Diana finally drew her own weapon and the numerous Guardians behind her followed suit, their blades glinting off the dying rays of green light that stretched over Azgadar. "When you are ready, Your Majesty."

The tension in the static-charged air thick, Elisa held her breath as Ithmeera lifted her sword, a slow hush coming down over the combined armies until all that remained were the gusts of wind battering her ears and the fierce words Ithmeera uttered in a harsh whisper. "Time to go home."

Her sword sang through the air as the blade swung down, sending the horde of roaring fighters rushing forth in a blur of red, black, and blue.

* * *

The powerful yells of the charging fighters sent Andrea's heart pounding as she and Meredith galloped on a horse alongside Captain Taryn and a few dozen Legionnaires toward the warped front gates of Azgadar. Four fighters flanked them, their objective to ensure that they were protected from any stray arrows that might be fired in their direction. Wind whipped at her face, the discord of the nearby battle ringing in her ears as she reinforced her hold around Meredith's waist.

"Stay close!" Somehow Taryn managed to elevate her voice over the cacophony around them. The thundering of their horses' hooves amplified as they departed the fields and rode onto the hard-packed dusty path leading up to where the iron gates had been replaced by a frame of melted, warped metal— grey smoke drifting from the edges.

The streets of Azgadar were enveloped in chaos, the noise of it all making Andrea's head spin and her chest seize in fear when she saw the disaster before them. Fires had broken out in many of the squat, brown buildings—mostly shops but some homes as well. Crumbled stone and misshapen metal littered the ground, a result, Andrea knew, of the raw power Richard had at his disposal thanks to Cassie. Citizens cried out as they ran through the streets, some rushing their families to safety while others stayed behind, trying to put out the flames. New Legionnaires yelled for order and mustered in the square nearest to the gates upon spotting Taryn and the others.

Taryn wasted no time. "Into the city, now!" she shouted, her sword out—the other Legionnaires yelled their affirmation in the form of battle cries as they charged the New Legion.

It took all of Andrea's willpower not to shut her eyes tight as metal clashed with metal—the sharp, cut off cries and moans of the first casualties assaulting her ears. Several were knocked from their mounts but many more attacked with rapid and precise slashes and thrusts of their swords as Legionnaires who had trained together since recruitment now fought each other to the death.

A New Legionnaire came at Taryn and, in a fluid movement,

she stepped to the side with ease before running her own blade through him. "There are too many of them! Get to the tower. I will send backup if I can," she ordered. *"Go!"*

Meredith veered them to the right, taking them away from the thick of battle. A few New Legion fighters saw them and moved to cut down their horse, but Taryn's men intervened, their blades barely missing the horse's flank as they pushed through what had become a bloodbath in the streets.

"Down this street!" Andrea yelled as they passed the trail of destruction Richard had left in his wake. She gasped when air rushed just past her ear, the arrow just missing her.

Meredith must have seen it, too. "We need a barrier, now, or we'll never make it!"

Without hesitation, Andrea concentrated on pulling the magic from deep within her and hissed when it surfaced through her scars. The familiar white and blue glow illuminated the streets ahead of them, the barrier manifesting in a ripple of white, translucent energy as it came up around them. The pain took her by surprise at first, sharper and nearly instantaneous this time. She figured it could be the storm—judging by the furious vortex forming above them the magic was far more unstable than anywhere else they had been. "Hurry! I can't... hold it for long!"

The barrier gave a precarious flicker but held up as arrows continued to hail down on them until Meredith was able to get them out of range of the New Legionnaires by taking them through the more crowded areas of the city and down the streets that forked off from the main road.

"We should be safe for the moment," Meredith panted and

Andrea dropped the barrier before they both dismounted in a small alley, the spire just within reach as they peered around the corner. "I don't see Richard or Cassie."

Trying not to focus too much on the sounds of the battle that still raged in the main square, Andrea poked her head around the edge of the alley wall, the surrounding area barely visible through the thick smoke that wafted through the streets. "They're here. I know it." Several paces away, the cracked steps leading up to the Azgadaran Palace were occupied by a group of vigilant New Legionnaires.

She winced again, her hand going to her arm as the burning from earlier returned with a vengeance and spread from her injured side to her chest.

Meredith noticed right away. "Already? You've barely used any magic."

"I…I don't know," Andrea breathed. "It's like somehow *more* was taken than usual when I cast that barrier." She gasped as another wave of pain rolled through her. "I don't—there's not much left."

Lightning flashed—Meredith's grey eyes becoming as bright as the rough waters of Gurith on a clear day—and the ground gave a sudden, deep rumble, knocking stone and plaster off the sides of the buildings and walls, including the corridor where they hid.

Meredith's jaw clenched, her hand falling to the knife on her belt. "Without the Legion, I am unsure how we can succeed here, Andrea. Richard—"

"We still have time," Andrea insisted, scanning for any sign of Richard and Cassie. "Cassie needed to be in the Shadow Arena to absorb the magic there." She pointed at the tower. "They'll probably need to be at least on those steps to do the same here."

"Wait." Meredith silenced her with a raised hand, her eyes narrowed on the steps where the New Legionnaires stood with their weapons at the ready. From the spiraling smoke nearest to the steps, two dark figures faded into view.

Andrea didn't have to look closer to recognize one of them. *Cassie.*

Her face was strained and tired, as though she hadn't slept in days. A faded bruise had spread near her lower lip and her eyes, while still a burning blue, were ringed with dark circles. She walked with a limp; her steps staggered as Richard dragged her roughly by her wrist.

The fighters of the New Legion tensed the moment they saw Richard. One of them, an officer by the decorations on his armor, barked at them. "You! Back away from the steps, citizen."

Richard just smirked and took another pointed step towards the palace, his eyes tilted up and toward the top of the spire.

The officer's eyes widened as he growled his order again. "I order you to stop and return to your home or you *will* be arrested!"

But the sneer on Richard's face remained, and as Andrea watched him open his right hand, she knew exactly what he was going to do before his fingers closed over his palm. He and Cassie were gone.

Meredith gasped as Andrea closed her eyes and took a shaky

breath. She knew where they had gone.

"Wha—where did they go?" The officer began throwing out orders to his scrambling subordinates to search the premises and calling for reinforcements. "I want a full search of the palace! We have a rogue enchanter on the loose! Now!"

"H-how is that possible?" Meredith's voice was small and frail as she stared in utter disbelief at the spot where Richard and Cassie had been standing only seconds earlier.

"He's using Cassie's magic," Andrea said. "He's done this once before." She pointed at the tower. "They're at the top."

"The top?" Meredith spluttered. "But if Cassie takes the magic from the palace it will surely crumble."

*Enough.* Andrea was far past fed up with Meredith's constant refusal to see the truth. "Meredith, when will you see that he doesn't care what happens to anyone else? He will take the rest of Damea's magic here and will disappear just as he did now if we don't stop him. It's up to us." She grabbed Meredith's wrist, forcing her mentor to look her in the eye. "You *know* I'm right, Meredith! I know you do!"

Her forehead creased in deep distress, Meredith's lips parted as her eyes wavered from the tower to Andrea before her gaze settled on Andrea's scarred wrist and the bracelet that hung from it. Another quake shook the earth as a harsh gust of wind howled across the city, the frightened screams of Azgadar's citizens louder than ever as more of them scurried through the ruined district.

Andrea pulled her hand back, making the decision to abandon Meredith and get to the spire on her own when

Meredith reached for the bracelet. Desperation clung to her voice. "You will need to be swift."

Andrea blinked. "What?"

Meredith tugged hard at the bracelet again. "This still has magic in it as does mine. I will use it to get you past the guards, but you *must* get yourself to the top."

Bewildered by both Meredith's sudden change of heart, her actual suggestion took longer than it should have to sink in as Andrea realized in horror what she was saying. "N-no."

Meredith fired back with tear-filled eyes. "You don't have a choice, Andrea! As difficult as it is to admit this, you are right. It *is* up to us."

*No.* There had to be another way. "Meredith, there's no way there is enough magic for that."

But Meredith could only offer her a faint smile—forced confidence. "I was trained by the best minds of eastern Damea. I can handle a few guards."

"Meredith, no! I can't—I can't face him alone!" Before she could protest any further, a quiet gasp escaped her as the whisper of warmth the magic from the bracelet Cassie had given her was gently drawn away.

Meredith's voice calmed her enough to listen to her words of reassurance. "You can and you must." She drew the magic from her own bracelet, a tear falling down her cheek before she took Andrea's hands in hers. "We all must face our choices eventually and it is long past time I faced mine. Look around." She gestured with her eyes at their crumbling surroundings. "I could not live knowing I helped cause this if I did not try as hard as I could to stop it. I cannot go up there with you, Andrea, but I can give you a chance to stop this…this madness." Her shoulders rose and fell and she let out a trembling breath, as though a great weight had been lifted from her.

She released a speechless Andrea's hands and took in the sight of the battle-ready fighters on the steps ahead before looking back. "I will clear a path. When you see an opening, go."

"Meredith…" Another flash of lightning.

But Meredith's smile widened and for the briefest moment, Andrea only saw the determined, brilliant enchanter she had met at the inn in Ata. "You never gave up on Cassie. Thank you…for not giving up on me, either."

Her heart torn over letting her mentor face the New Legionnaires alone and getting to the top of the spire to stop Richard, Andrea watched, her chest tight with grief as Meredith left the alley, her steps brisk. A blue glow sparked and surrounded her hands as she charged the guards.

# Chapter 23

# To the Death

Sharp pieces of dead grass and sand peppered Elisa's face, the unforgiving winds blowing whatever debris they could find as the massive electrical storm settled over Azgadar and the blood-soaked battlefield outside the walls.

Metal gleamed out of the corner of her eye as a sword thrust out at her, the New Legion fighter delivering all of his weight behind the attack. But Elisa had seen him coming long before he moved in—her heavy shield went up, blocking the blade before she rammed into the man with all of her strength. He lost his grip on the sword, gasping for air as the wind was knocked from him, and barely had time to cry for help from his fellow Legionnaires when Elisa knocked him to the ground and finished him off with her own blade. Another New Legionnaire tried to cut her down from behind, but she could hear and feel the heavy thud of his armored boots and easily dodged the blow. Spinning around, she bashed the side of his helmet with her shield, absorbing the rattle of solid armor as it rippled up her arm, and kicked him in the gut with a yell before running her sword through him.

A third fighter swung her own shield down at Elisa's wrist to disarm her. But she only needed to step back for the woman to miss and then a few more fluid steps to end the confrontation. Battle was a dance to any worthy Legionnaire and Elisa knew she was one of the best. Most of these fighters were either inexperienced or impatient and at the end of the day, she was simply faster.

Sweat dripped from her brow as she turned to check on Ithmeera, who had just impressively taken down a New Legion fighter of her own. When Ithmeera withdrew her sword she looked up, meeting Elisa's gaze. Curled strands of her dark, pulled back hair had come undone and her face was caked in dust from the storm. A fire burned in her deep green eyes—the rage in them something Elisa had only heard in Ithmeera's voice but never seen like this.

Diana and Jacob were nowhere to be seen—Elisa thought she had heard them move to bolster the Guardians attempting to break through the lines of New Legionnaires closest to the wall, but she couldn't be certain. Once the armies had clashed pandemonium had taken over, with Veraun several paces away commanding his men and fighting right alongside them. Under Petra's command, the New Legionnaires were relentless and spared no quarter against their former comrades. Bodies littered the field from both sides and Elisa had to fight down every urge to take Ithmeera into the city to help Taryn and Andrea. The two sides appeared evenly matched and she had a feeling what happened inside those walls would determine the outcome of this fight. Until then, though, they had to keep up the pressure on Petra.

She darted to Ithmeera, noting how winded she was as she

held her side. "Are you all right? Are you injured?" To her great relief, Ithmeera shook her head, though she still panted with effort as she spoke.

"I am fine! We should regroup with Ben." She scanned the battlefield. "Where is he?"

Elisa searched for Veraun's figure in the crowds of soldiers. "I saw him moments ago. Come, we should—"

*"Elisa!"*

White light and stars masked her vision as she was knocked to the ground, Ithmeera's shocked cry ringing in her ear. Running on fear and adrenaline, she spit out the dirt she'd inhaled and willed her arms to push herself up, looking up just in time to see Petra—in full armor and wielding a sharpened Legionnaire's blade—turn a hardened predatory gaze to a stumbling Ithmeera. *No!*

She had to get up. She *had* to.

Fingers closing tight around the metal handle of the shield, Elisa willed her body to push past the pain and climbed to her feet, sword in hand, before making the long, rapid strides she needed to get to Ithmeera before Petra. Putting all her strength into her movements, she leapt to close the distance and shoved Ithmeera out of the way, taking the full brunt of Petra's swing on her shield. The force behind the blow was extraordinary and Elisa gritted her teeth as her body endured the painful reverberation of it. Staring into Petra's cold eyes, she gasped upon seeing the yellow illumination that ringed the darkness in her irises.

"You feel that, Elisa? Do you see what pure magic can do for the Legion?" Petra crowed as she pushed Elisa back with her sword. "What it can do for Azgadar?"

"You—you consumed magic?" Elisa poured all of her hatred for Petra into the glare she shot back. "You bloody hypocrite. After all that talk about enchanters—"

Petra shoved her away, the strength behind unexpected and more than anything Elisa would have guessed could come from her as she staggered back a few steps. "Enchanters were bringing ruin upon us, Elisa. I have brought *power* back to the empire. Soon we will be just as the empire of old was without the need to beg other countries for magic or pointless alliances. And no one—not you, not Gurdinfield, not even your failed empress will stop us from achieving what we were *meant* to be!" She tensed and held up her sword, her dueling stance one Elisa had seen and practiced countless times over the years. The scrape of metal on metal was all she could focus on as their blades crashed against one another.

Elisa's eyes followed the aggressive death spiral of Petra's sword as she dodged or blocked every swing—the attacks so fast she was unable to get a strike in herself as the two of them danced deftly across the field. Her ribs burned from being knocked down and she struggled to keep her breathing steady as Petra continued her overwhelming assault, ending a multi-swing strike with a mighty two-handed downward blow.

She saw it coming. It was only for a fraction of a second, but that was all Elisa needed to move left and ram her shield into Petra's side, knocking her off balance and leaving her gasping for air. She jumped back, pushing her body off the ground quicker than what should have been possible for any ordinary

Legionnaire fighter. But Elisa knew Petra's abilities had all been enhanced by the magic she'd consumed.

She held up her sword to drive it through Petra's chest and lunged, the roar she let out amplifying the power of her attack as she prepared to end this—once and for all.

At first, she wasn't sure what happened, but one moment Petra was in front of her, clutching her side and vulnerable, the next she was a blur and Elisa's surprised cry was cut off as an armored hand collided with her jaw, then another over her eye, before a final one came down on her wrist. Her shocked hand opened and the shield dropped. Drawing her dagger out of instinct, she tried to compensate for her missed blocks, but then Petra's boot came under hers and Elisa saw the green, stormy clouds sailing above her as she was thrown on her back. Her sword and dagger both flew out of reach as Petra caught the falling shield and yelled out her rage—bringing down all of her fury as the heavy shield smashed into Elisa's right knee.

Elisa's back arched and she let out a piercing scream, unbearable pain flooding her leg as she was rendered immobile.

Petra tossed the shield to the side and stood over her, eyes wide with excitement as a low chuckle escaped through her lips. "Weak," she spat. "That's what you are, Elisa. That's what your father and brother were, too." She reached for Elisa's bloodied face with the blunt edge of her sword, letting the metal drag along her bruising skin for a few seconds before withdrawing. "I want to *savor* this. Being able to finally purge the empire of your blood is something I've wanted for some time. You will—" She grunted, her feet shuffling in the dirt as she fought to throw off Ithmeera, who had jumped onto her back with Elisa's fallen dagger in hand. But Ithmeera refused to relent as she lifted her hand and brought the knife down with force, crying out as the blade pierced skin and sunk into the bottom of Petra's neck.

Petra let out a stunned choke before her eyes rolled back and she fell backwards, taking Ithmeera with her as the two of them crashed into the dirt. Her body gave a subtle twitch before she lay still.

The intense pain in her leg as well as the rest of her body still consuming her, Elisa's breaths came quick and shallow as she watched out of the corner of her eye while Ithmeera shoved Petra off her, rolling the traitorous guard onto her stomach. One of her ragged breaths came out as a sigh of relief and she let her head fall back onto the dirt again—Ithmeera was all right and Petra was dead. They had beaten her.

*"Elisa!"* Ithmeera cried, scrabbling through the dirt on her knees to reach Elisa's side. "I'm here!" Her hand closed around Elisa's as she inspected the damage Petra had done. "Stay with me." She sniffed, covering her mouth with her other hand and even in her weakened state Elisa had the urge to brush away the tears that streamed down her face. "Oh…that monster! Here." Elisa whimpered at the loss of warmth in her hand before she found herself being propped up.

Ithmeera held her tightly in her arms, her voice a soothing distraction from the battle that still raged around them. "I have you, my love. It's going to be all right."

Elisa could only groan in response. Her head throbbed, each time sending a wave of dizziness through her. Wetness dripped down the side of her face—whether it was sweat, blood, or both she couldn't tell. Her ribs were certainly bruised if not broken and she couldn't move her leg without wanting to scream. Certain she would pass out soon, she tried to say something, anything to Ithmeera while she still could. How sorry she was for everything. How much she loved her. "Ith-Ithmeera, you—"

But Ithmeera hushed her. "Don't talk," she begged, stroking stray copper hairs from Elisa's bloodied brow. "We need to get you healing, just…just stay with me." She held Elisa close, her pleas becoming a whisper. "Please stay with me."

She tensed when the ground gave another tremble and they both looked up at the spire in the distance where the storm spun around the pinnacle of the tower as though attempting to consume the very structure itself. Even with her limited field of view, Elisa could see the frightened expressions of the soldiers on both sides as many stopped mid-fight to gaze up in horror at the phenomenon that, if left unchecked, would surely destroy Azgadar.

And if Richard was there, the end of Damea would not be far behind.

# Chapter 24

# Enchanters

Lightning seared across the darkening sky, the thunder following shaking the land angrily. Andrea clung to the chipped stonework of the stairwell as the wind howled with such force it threatened to rip her from the tower.

She'd watched Meredith attack the unsuspecting guards at the palace entrance, their eyes going wide with fear when an experienced enchanter had launched an array of fire and lightning at their feet. As they were occupied with Meredith, Andrea had slipped by and into the tower, the inside of it surprisingly empty save a few frightened servants and royal enchanters, before heading up the long flight of stairs that would carry her to the top.

The burning in her arm had dulled but so had most of the feeling she had in it. The rest of her body throbbed as though she were covered in painful bruises. She knew it was a side effect of the remaining magic in her running out. She forced herself to put one foot in front of the other, climbing one agonizing step at a time, and used the interior wall of the spire to guide herself as the vision in her right eye became little more than a blurry mess.

Screaming. It was rough, as though it had been going on for hours instead of minutes. Andrea's heart leapt to her throat. *Cassie.* She was at the top with Richard—Andrea knew it. *Just a few more steps.* She raised her left hand, preparing to attack Richard with everything she had. There were no rules, no promises to Meredith that she cared to honor—just the oath she had made to herself. She would save Cassie and end Richard. And with her own magic dwindling, Andrea knew this was her last chance. Moreover, she knew even if she made it to them in time and stopped Richard that she would probably die. But if it meant seeing Cassie one last time, safe, then it was worth it.

Barely keeping her balance, she climbed the final step and walked out onto the spire platform. The hair on the back of her neck stood up, the air around her clearly charged with wildly unstable magic. She thought she could hear the cries of battle in the fields far below, but even at their loudest they competed with the roar of the swirling vortex above. Damea's final moment.

Cassie stood in the center of the platform, her eyes flaring beacons of stormy blue as her hands outstretched to the sky above. Her clothing was torn and caked in dirt. Tears streamed down her face, which was contorted in a horrifying blend of terror and pain. It took all the remaining willpower Andrea had to swallow back the fear and sorrow that ate at her to see the woman she loved like this, and to focus instead on the man standing a few steps away, near the edge of the platform. Richard had his arms extended, palms out as he appeared to carefully control Cassie in how she absorbed the magic.

A series of thunderclaps rattled the tower. Andrea felt the

reverberation in her bones.

"Let her go, Richard!" she yelled over Cassie's cries and conjured a fireball in her hand, the hottest she'd ever made. "Let her go and maybe you'll still walk away from this alive."

Narrowed blue eyes focused on her as Richard was distracted for only a moment before renewing his concentration on the task at hand. "Still alive?" he spat. "You are stubborn, aren't you?"

"A-Andrea?" Cassie whimpered, struggling to turn her head.

"I'm here, Cassie." Andrea sucked in a deep breath to keep her voice as even as she could. Her chest burned. She turned again to Richard. "Last chance, Richard. Let her go."

If Richard was worried, he did not show it. Rather, he gave a mirthless laugh. "You're a fool if you think you have any pull here, girl. In just a few minutes, I'll have all the magic I require to open a portal. Then I will take my daughter and return home at last."

Andrea's injured arm spasmed—she clenched her jaw as the fireball blazed above her palm. *No more.*

"I wouldn't do that if I were you." Richard's warning dripped with condescension. "Attack me again and I *will* have her kill you."

Cassie let out a strangled cry but somehow managed to lock eyes with her. "Andrea, *please.* He-he'll do it. Get…out of here!"

But Andrea stood her ground. "No. I made a promise, Cassie and I intend to keep it. I'm not leaving you. No matter what."

Her stomach suddenly lurched and before she realized what had happened, she was flying through the air, the harsh winds whipping against her face as she inhaled the nauseating but telltale burned out scent of dissipating magic—the fireball evaporating into nothing as it was pulled into the vortex. She grunted upon colliding with the stonework of the platform and rolled. After finally coming to a stop, she gritted her teeth and immediately tried to push past the pain as she climbed to her feet. Her left ankle and wrist pulsed in pain.

Cassie's screams shook her, fueling the pure rage Andrea had pent up since Gurith.

"You just don't learn, do you?" Richard taunted as he approached her before slinging a brilliant barrier at her. This time Andrea was ready and she reacted quickly enough to block it with one of her own. Her head swooned for a moment, but she managed to recover enough to send a new fireball his way. It grazed his arm, the flames burning through his shirt immediately and engulfing his forearm. He roared in agony and set to putting out the flames with a counter spell.

Andrea did not let up. With everything she had left in her she flung barrier after fireball after barrier, screaming out her anger at him for everything he had done—for everything he had put them through. Her head buzzed and her breathing grew shallow and strained—she was losing energy fast and she knew it. She *had* to take him down before she collapsed. She had to.

But Richard just crooked an icy smile at her before raising his hand toward Cassie. A new barrier appeared around him, stronger and brighter than the one before. Her attacks bounced off it harmlessly before he raised his hands and hurled the shield at her with such force the air around them crackled.

The world exploded around Andrea in a flash of blinding white light as she found herself once again violently thrown to the ground—stars burned into her vision, ears ringing. Her throat raw from screaming, a raspy breath escaped her as she tried to get up. But the combination of weakness and her injuries sent her to her knees—rivulets of sweat running down her face—she panted as she struggled to conjure something, *anything* that might help. But nothing came. Her magic was drained. She looked down, registering the heavy steps of Richard approaching her but not reacting to them. The bracelet around her scarred wrist fluttered in the wind, equally drained and useless. Somewhere far below she could barely hear the sounds of battle. More fighting. More death. None of this would matter.

It was done. She had failed.

"And now, you never will."

She refused to meet Richard's gaze as he stood over her, ignoring the arrogant parting words that came out of his mouth. Instead Andrea turned her attention toward Cassie, who could only stare back with the glowing blue orbs that had taken over the eyes Andrea loved so much.

Her vision worsened, not from the magic, but from the tears that welled up and spilled onto her cheeks. Her chest heaved as she began to cry for the first time in weeks.

"Cassie," she sobbed, hoping Cassie could hear her above the storm. "I'm sorry. I'm *so* sorry!"

"I...*ah!*" Cassie jerked in pain, the remaining magic rushing into her faster now.

"Cassie, enough!" Richard ordered. "You will end her *now*. Then we finish this!"

"*NO!*" Cassie shouted, her voice raw. Despite the fight she gave, she took a step toward Andrea, her boot dragging against the platform. "I'm going to…hold on for as long as I can, Andrea!"

"Cassie!" Andrea shivered as Cassie took another step forward, her hand extending slowly. "I'm sorry I brought you here. I'm sorry for *everything!*"

"Don't!" Another step. "You gave me the best…year of my life. I—*argh!*" Another cry. "I-I love you, okay? I always will!" With a yell of denial, her hand closed.

"*Now,* Cassie!" Richard bellowed.

Andrea's eyes shut, the tears still escaping as she wrapped her arms around herself. The familiar life-draining tendrils of Cassie's raw power wrapped around her essence. Fear spiked in her, but it was dulled by the sheer lack of energy left in her body. A final whisper was all she managed to get out.

"I'm sorry."

A blast of air ripped her from her almost peaceful state as Cassie screamed again, only this time she was joined by Richard as well. Andrea opened her eyes and gasped when she saw a growing blotch of red pooled in the front of Richard's shirt. With bewildered wide eyes he croaked, "Meredith?!" before those same eyes rolled into the back of his head. He gave a final heavy sigh before he collapsed on the stone in front of Andrea. A shaking Meredith stood behind him, her eyes wide and her lips parted and trembling. A bloody dagger fell from her hand.

"Forgive me," she mouthed.

Before she could say anything, Andrea froze as the air gave a loud *crack* and a white ribbon materialized above Richard and struck Meredith. In the center of the platform, Cassie hissed as her head snapped up to face Meredith, who stiffened and clutched her chest in alarm.

"T-the magic, I—it's so much!" Her grey eyes were wide with surprise and…Andrea could swear she saw awe and wonder in them. But when she started to shake and her face twisted in pain, Andrea knew something was wrong.

"Meredith!" She tried to push herself up and failed, each attempt resulting in her crashing to the ground again.

"I-I can't control it, Andrea! You…you *have* to finish this. You must!" Meredith choked out a final breath before falling. Andrea watched in shock as the light left her mentor's eyes before she crumpled on the stones next to Richard's body.

Just as quickly as it had happened the first time, the pulsing ribbon of light—the very lifeline of Damea itself—wafted for a moment before slamming into Andrea's chest, knocking her on her back and leaving her breathless.

Cassie's cry of horror reached her ears. *"No! Andrea!"*

And then the world seemed to stop.

# Chapter 25

# The Strands

Bars of white light flew past Andrea like hundreds of shooting stars as she stood, motionless—unwavering.

At first, she was frightened, but the fear evaporated when she realized she had fully regained the vision in her right eye as well as the feeling in her right arm. She brought her hand to her face and as her shirtsleeve slipped down her wrist, she could see the scars had disappeared.

Peering through the veil of stars racing past her, Andrea spotted something even more curious—a strange webbing of countless colors connecting in a mural of shapes that could have been from the clear night skies of Ata. *What is this?* She wasn't certain if she'd asked that aloud. Regardless, someone answered.

*"Between."*

Andrea couldn't decide if she had heard the voice or if it had been in her head. She decided to answer. "Between what?"

*"Everything."*

The voice was familiar. Andrea *knew* that voice. "Cassie?"

The lights flew by faster, now, the bars beginning to blur together.

*"You have to make it right."*

She turned around, seeing if perhaps Cassie was somewhere in this "room" with her. But she was alone. "How are you— where are you?"

A pause. *"That's impossible."*

What was she talking about? Nothing made sense here. Where was the spire? And the storm? And Cassie and…Richard. *Meredith.* There had been all that noise, all that pain, and then everything had just ceased to be.

*The magic.* Somehow, she had connected with all the magic Cassie had absorbed. *All the magic in Damea.* Or very nearly.

Something pulled at her, as though a string had been tied to her chest and tugged from within. The bars of light shifted. If she focused on them hard enough, Andrea thought she might be able to navigate in this "between" as Cassie called it though she still had no idea what it actually was.

*"You'll see it soon. Then…then you'll know."*

Andrea blinked and shook her head. "Know what? Cassie? How do I get to you?"

Cassie did not answer. But as soon as Andrea asked, the lights sped up noticeably and continued to as the tugging grew stronger. Her chest burned, but it was different than what she had experienced on the spire. Still, the pressure was so intense she was sure her heart would be ripped from her chest.

Finally, the lights blurred so tightly the air around her became engulfed in white light. Moments passed as she shielded her eyes until the light abated.

And then she was somewhere else.

The room was small and cluttered—tiny cracks scattered upon the bare walls. Pale, yellow light spilled in from the few windows around her. An old, round table with three chairs had been shoved into one corner—a bowl containing a few pieces of odd-looking fruit sat atop it. Papers piled haphazardly covered what little counter space there was of what appeared to be a very strange looking kitchen. A metal tea kettle sat on what could have been an oven, though it was unlike any oven Andrea had ever seen. A tall block structure with a black handle secured to its front took up a large portion of the kitchen. More papers had been pinned to it by means Andrea could not decipher.

The kitchen opened up into a living room that was hardly any bigger. A dark green couch lined one of the four walls, its fabric worn and frayed at the edges. Other pieces of furniture, mostly tables and bookshelves in poor condition, were placed around the room and held a variety of objects from books to things Andrea could not give names to.

Directly across from where she stood was a windowed door leading out to what seemed to be a very tiny garden. The few other windows in the house were open, the air coming in thick and carrying the heavy scent of smoke and an unpleasant mix of other scents she wasn't familiar with. Wherever this was, it wasn't home.

*Unless…*

A silver glint caught the corner of her eye. She turned and there, on a low, rickety end table was a small painting that could only be described as the most lifelike she'd ever seen, framed in silver. Depicted were two people—a young, blonde girl with a rather familiar roguish grin and an older dark-haired, olive-skinned woman with a regal face and a knowing smile. She reached for the frame, holding it in shaking hands as she studied it.

Realization hit Andrea nearly as strong as the magic had. This *was* home. Only, she had arrived much, *much* later.

She was in Tarrasha. This was Cassie's home. And the woman in the painting was Serena.

"Who are you?" A thick Azgadaran accent startled her and she nearly dropped the frame.

The woman—the very same one from the painting—stood in front of the door, wearing a long yellow skirt and a black blouse, her dark eyes wide and angry. "How did you get in?" She reached to her left and pulled out some sort of staff from a bucket on the floor before shaking it at Andrea. "Leave my house at once before I call the authorities!"

Andrea held up her hands in surrender, though she still held on to the painting. "Wait!" she stammered. "Please, I'm…" What was she going to say? *"Hello! I'm your daughter's betrothed and I thought I'd stop by for some tea before heading back to my own world, which by the way is ending as we speak. Nice to meet you!"* She nearly laughed at her own thought when she realized Cassie probably would have encouraged her to say something so ridiculous. The scowling woman a few steps away quickly discouraged her from doing so, however.

She decided to start over. "I know your daughter." *No, that's probably not right either.*

Serena jabbed the clothed staff in Andrea's direction. "My daughter? I've heard enough—you stay away from her, you hear me?!" She began advancing on her.

"Your Highness, please!" Andrea rushed.  "My name is Andrea. I'm from Ata! I mean you no harm!" Having no desire to even attempt to use magic in this land, she put up her hands to cover her head and squeezed her eyes shut. But the staff never came down.

"Ata?" The anger in her voice was gone, though the shakiness remained.

Slowly opening her eyes, Andrea lowered her hands before placing the frame back on the table. "Yes. I'm from—"

The staff fell at Serena's side. Her face crumpled as she sighed. "You're from there aren't you? How did you find me? What do you want?"

Andrea wasn't sure how to respond. Why *was* she here? Cassie had somehow brought her here but for what purpose? Was she to convince Serena to come back with her? *How is she even still alive?* Cassie had told her Serena had died when she was only fifteen of an unknown illness. "Damea is in danger. Richard, he—"

Serena's eyes flashed with anger. "*Richard?*" She took a moment to breathe deeply before gesturing at the table. "Sit. I'll put some tea on."

Knowing this was probably her only path forward, Andrea took a seat in one of the wobbly chairs at the table while Serena began preparing the tea, carrying on a conversation as though it were completely normal for an enchanter from another *time* to visit. "Black all right then? I don't know what you're used to, but I hope this will do. Andrea, was it?"

"Erm, yes," Andrea said hesitantly. "And black is fine, thank you."

"And from Ata," Serena mused as she set a fire underneath the kettle. "Farmers, most of them. Do they still put on those festivals in the summer?"

"They do. The fall as well."

"Lovely. Probably one of the few things I still miss about… well, you know." She turned to Andrea and leaned forward on the counter.

Andrea could only stare at the woman and wasn't sure whether she should be shocked or awed by her. *This* was the fabled missing heir of the Azgadaran Empire? The woman who could control *armies* with magic was now serving her tea in this tiny house? "Your Highness—"

Serena waved her hand. "Please. Just Serena. I haven't been that…other person in years."

"Serena. I don't understand. How are you, well, here?" Andrea gestured at the walls around them.

The woman actually smiled this time. "Ah, I see the story didn't make its way across Damea. How the heir to the greatest throne in the land left to pursue a life of adventure instead."

"Richard was from here. He took you back?"

"That he did," Serena answered with a nod. "He asked for my help in bringing magic back to this land. As you can see, that didn't turn out quite as planned." She opened up a cupboard above and to her right and procured two small white cups. "You're an enchanter?"

This was taking too long. Things were still chaos in Damea. She had to figure out what Cassie needed from her here and then find a way back. Everything and everyone was depending on her. "Serena, please, if you could just—"

The tea kettle let out a shrill whistle as steam puffed from the spout.

"There's nothing you can say or do to get me to return as long as that man is alive," Serena said with a tone that was both polite and firm, telling of someone raised in diplomacy. With the turn of a knob she extinguished the flame and began the task of pouring the tea. "We may not have much, but I am far happier here with my daughter than I ever was in Damea."

"Richard is dead," Andrea said slowly. "And so is the rest of Damea if I don't get back there."

That made Serena look up—both of her dark eyebrows raised. "Dead? I don't understand." She picked up the cups and carefully walked to the table before setting them down and taking a seat herself. "Start at the beginning."

And Andrea did. Between tentative sips of the odd-tasting tea she told Serena everything from her apprenticeship with Meredith to meeting Cassie, destroying Richard's machine in Rhyad, and finally how Richard used Cassie to absorb Damea's magic in a failed attempt to return to Tarrasha. She left out most of her relationship with Cassie. It didn't seem relevant at this point and she honestly wasn't sure how to bring up how the two of them got together to Cassie's mother.

When she finished, Serena was quiet for a long moment. Her

face was a few shades paler than it had been when she burst out in anger, slamming her fist on the table. "That horrid necklace! I never should have left it."

Andrea's jaw dropped. "You *knew* what it would do? How could you leave something like that behind?!"

"You don't know me," Serena said with a scowl, "and you are in my house so I'll not have you sitting there judging me for my actions, which you have no history of." She regained her composure, though it took a lengthy moment and Andrea could see where Cassie had inherited her temper from.

"I had that necklace created when I was still in Azgadar," Serena continued. "It was designed to give us an edge, turn the tide of battle if necessary. It was *not* designed for someone to control another with it. Certainly not anything I would want my daughter wearing." She rubbed her eyes and sighed. "I thought I'd hid it well, but Richard was always finding new ways to use old artifacts. And Cassie…she's really there now?"

Andrea cringed at having to answer when the truth was so awful, but she was committed at this point. "I think so. I'm not sure what it is I'm supposed to do here, but I think it might be to bring you back. I can't—I don't think I can control the magic, Serena. I'm not strong enough."

Serena scoffed. "Nonsense. From all you've told me, you are strong enough and more. And the very fact that you are sitting in front of me right now is living proof. But," she said with hesitation. "I cannot return with you, Andrea."

Andrea panicked. "But you have to! Damea is dying—*your* land is dying and I can't do this alone."

The familiar rattle of a door opening alerted them both.

"Quickly," Serena hissed. "Hide in the other room. Go!"

Without protest, Andrea bolted from the table and ducked behind a wall on the far side of the living room bordering a narrow corridor, no doubt leading to the bedrooms, just as she heard the door slam shut and a vaguely familiar voice call out.

"Cassie!" she heard Serena exclaim. "You're home early."

Something heavy fell to the floor. "Just for a minute. I'm going to Jess's after."

A pause. "Again? You were there nearly all weekend, Cassie. Did you get any studying done at all?"

"I got some!" Even her tone was so familiar. "Jess already took the same class last year and she said she'd help me."

"So long as this 'help' doesn't involve me finding you on the other side of town again," Serena said, her voice far sterner than it had been earlier.

"That was *one* time!" Cassie protested. "Okay, twice, but both times were an accident—we really did get off at the wrong stop!"

A sigh. "Perhaps exercising a bit more focus in the future then, hmm?"

"I *know*, Mother, I know."

Another pause. "I have a lesson tonight. You'll be home before six?"

Cassie let out a long exhale. "Yes."

Andrea couldn't help herself and peeked her head around the corner, where she could make out the back of Cassie's head and nearly gasped at the sight of her partner *here,* when she knew for a fact the Cassie she knew was back in Damea.

Her hair was around the same length it had been when they'd first met, the sides grown out of course, and she was a bit shorter. Andrea watched as Cassie stood there in front of Serena with very much the same mannerisms she now had as an adult. Serena smiled with such fondness Andrea felt her chest tighten.

"You are growing too fast," she said, placing a hand on Cassie's cheek.

Cassie gave a short laugh. "You always say that." She reached into the bag she had dropped on the floor earlier and pulled out a thick book. "Can I go now? Please?"

Serena sighed again. A shadow crossed her face, revealing a burden Andrea hadn't seen before but suspected had something to do with what she was about to share before Cassie had arrived.

"Mother? Is…is everything all right?" Cassie asked.

Serena cleared her throat and a faint smile quickly replaced the heaviness that had been there. "Of course, dear. Just a bit tired is all." She planted a kiss on Cassie's forehead. "Tell Jess I said hello, yes?"

"I will. See you tonight!" Andrea watched with fascination as Cassie bolted out the door, leaving a pensive-looking Serena staring after her.

She turned the corner and emerged from her hiding spot, eventually taking a spot standing next to the other woman. The two stood there for a moment, listening to the sounds of the world outside, neither one of them saying a word.

Serena finally broke the silence as she turned to her, a proud smile on her face. "My subjects used to call me the greatest enchanter Damea had ever seen, Andrea. Once I held the future of Damea in the palm of my hand. Entire armies knelt before me, other nations practically begged to be our vassals as I conquered them one by one, both in the throne room and on the battlefield. I was destined to rule the world. But," she said, the smile fading, "none of that mattered after Cassie was born. I'd promised Richard I would help him restore magic to his world—this world. He'd somehow managed to come to Damea through a portal he created himself. He showed me this world—showed me the possibilities we could have together if I helped him save it. But I was young, impatient, naïve. After she was born, when I realized what siphoning magic from Damea would do to the land, I knew that wasn't the legacy I wanted to leave for her."

Andrea said nothing and waited for her to continue.

"I wanted to return to Azgadar and take up the mantle of empress again. I wanted for Cassie to inherit the empire but only after I had made it a peaceful one." Her face darkened. "Richard did not care about any of that. He accused me of betraying him and threatened to take Cassie and leave me behind. I knew even with my power as an enchanter that as long as he was alive, he would find a way to carry his threat through. And…I could not bring myself to murder my daughter's father. So, I did the only thing I could."

Andrea's lips parted in surprise. "You…you brought Cassie here. You stranded Richard in Damea. In the past."

"And now Cassie is paying the price for my ignorance." Serena's voice was tight, as though she were on the verge of tears. "Andrea, this machine Richard built—it is similar to a design of a weapon my country had produced but on a much larger scale."

*So Azgadar controlled a vast army and tried to take magic from other nations centuries before the Cadars ever took power.* Andrea was not exactly surprised by the revelation as Ithmeera had told her a similar story. The two dynasties' methods of conquest were certainly different, however.

Serena took a deep breath, as though formulating her next words with extra care. "I believe that the machine is what eventually ended Damea as you know it."

"But Damea is still there!" Andrea exclaimed, her frustration climbing.

Serena didn't seem surprised by that. In fact, her eyes lit up with something that resembled realization. "The machine was destroyed, Andrea." She paused and stared at Andrea with a knowing smile, as though waiting for an answer she already knew.

*The machine was destroyed. Cassie and Meredith destroyed it and the magic—*

"We stopped Damea from ending in Rhyad," she said, the events of past turning over and over in her mind as she struggled to figure out what Serena was trying to tell her. "But then why are we *here*? How come Tarrasha is like this?"

Serena extended her hand, motioning for them to move to the living room. "Richard and I spent years studying magic and its effects on the world, Andrea." She sat on the worn couch and offered Andrea the space next to her. "Magic in my time was more than just a way to power a farm or a machine. We believed it was the single constant that connected everything. Richard even theorized that there were other worlds, perhaps even other versions of our worlds that were the result of magic interacting in new and unexpected ways."

Andrea struggled to follow. "What does that have to do with Richard's machine?"

"Tarrasha exists as it does *because* of the machine, Andrea. But you and Cassie stopped it and—ah, yes!" Serena concluded, her voice raising with obvious excitement. "That must have changed everything." When she saw Andrea's confused expression, she held up her pointer finger.

"One moment. I believe I can explain this better with a demonstration." She left the couch and went to open a drawer on a nearby end table. After rummaging through the drawer muttering under her breath for a few seconds, she returned with a cord of red yarn, which she held up between both hands and continued.

"Imagine a thread. A single strand connecting Damea and Tarrasha. They are one and the same, but one has happened *because* of events in the other. There is one course, one future. Now, if something were to happen to alter that course," she said, gently plucking one of the smaller threads and pulling it apart from the main cord.

Andrea's eyes went wide as she understood at last. "Cassie did that. Or rather, bringing Cassie to Damea did that!"

Serena gestured around them. "I have tried to give Cassie a

future here because a future in a dying Damea seemed so much worse. But you," she pointed at Andrea, "you have somehow created a new strand! A strand where Damea does not collapse on itself in a few hundred years."

Andrea could not see how this was a good thing. "Serena," she began, "everything Cassie has endured, the reason she suffers now is because *I* brought her to Damea."

Serena seemed to read her mind. "You found a way here so you think you might find a way to stop yourself from bringing Cassie to Damea? Don't you see, Andrea? *You* can give my daughter the future I couldn't. Everything you've done, everything that has happened so far *must* occur as it did. Your world's existence depends on Cassie going to Damea."

She couldn't. Meredith's torture, Rhyad, all the pain and fighting and death that had happened because Andrea had brought Cassie to Damea—if she could prevent it all, why shouldn't she? *Damea would die, but Tarrasha would be born. Cassie would never know me. We would never meet and never...*

But Cassie would be safe. "I can save her, Serena!"

"Please, Andrea!" Serena begged, taking Andrea's hands in hers. "Because of you and Cassie, your world stands a chance at surviving. I..." Her eyes were glossy with tears now. "If saving Damea is to be my daughter's destiny, if it gives her a chance at a better future than this, I ask that you not take that from her."

"She could still die! She's already been through too much," Andrea fired back and tore her hands away. "No. I won't decide that for her."

"If it were Cassie making this decision what would she say?"

Serena thrust a finger at the threaded bracelet hanging from Andrea's wrist. "You *know* her, Andrea! You have not told me everything, but I can see it clear as day." She lowered her hand. "Tell me. What would she say?"

A shaky silence passed between them.

"She…she would want it," Andrea whispered. "But I won't let her die."

A single tear rolled down Serena's cheek. "Then you must ensure she does not. Her life and the lives of everyone in Damea hang in the balance, Andrea."

"Then why can't *you* come back and help me?"

"Because." Serena rolled up her sleeves and took Andrea's hands once more. "You will need every ounce of magic you can get. Before I left Damea, I wanted to be as prepared as I could. Before I went through the portal, I took what I needed."

A surge of power crawled up Andrea's wrists and made its way to her arms until finally settling in her chest. "You can absorb magic! Like Cassie!"

"You cannot?" At Andrea's shake of her head, Serena clicked her tongue, disappointed. "Ah. It seems some of the art was lost over the years. I imagine that is why Cassie's abilities seem unique to you."

"Could Richard…?"

Serena seemed offended at the thought. "Goodness, no. I tried to teach him what I could and while he did pick up some things, he never understood that enchanting takes years of study and practice to master. Always wanted a faster solution to everything." Her face twisted in disdain at that. "I began studying magic when I was a very young child, as was tradition in my family."

Andrea blinked a few times as she tried to make sense of everything. "What will happen to you?" she asked in a small voice.

If Serena was upset, she did not show it. "My body has become attuned to the magic I brought with me. I should have a few months at most." She began the transfer of energy. "It is enough time to…to make arrangements."

Andrea wanted to cry again. Serena's death would be her fault. How could possibly tell Cassie, if she didn't already know? She was reminded of Cassie's voice, speaking to her in that strange void she had traveled through. Could Cassie see what was happening now?

She let out a soft gasp as the bulk of the energy passed into her, joining with the massive energy store already within her. When it was over, Serena released her hands with a strangled breath and slumped forward. Andrea immediately caught her.

"Cassie will never forgive me."

Serena patted her hand. "She will. As long as you tell her the truth, she will." She gently grasped the bracelet between her thumb and forefinger. "Tell me about this."

Andrea looked down and couldn't help but laugh despite everything that had happened. "She got it for me. Before Richard—before it happened." She took a deep breath and smiled fondly at the sight of the green, blue, and red threads around her wrist. "I found it later. We haven't actually talked about it yet."

Serena chuckled and shook her head. "That sounds like my daughter. She's never really been one for talking things out."

Andrea smiled, a warmth spreading from her chest and then outward. It was a welcome change from the constant burning the magic had done over the last several weeks. She froze when Serena's dark eyes met hers, the laughter gone but the intense gaze Andrea recognized in Cassie there.

"You love her."

She did not require even a moment's pause to answer. "More than anything."

Serena leaned back, that intense gaze leaving her eyes as she let out a long sigh. "Good. That is all I wished to know. I am… grateful I was able to meet you, Andrea." She glanced at the nearby window. The light was beginning to change color and fade as the day grew long. "I have some matters to attend to before Cassie gets home. And you have a land to save if I'm not mistaken."

"You are certain you can't come with me?" Andrea tried.

Serena turned to face her again. "I suspect if I return with you there is no telling what could happen. My presence there could have dire consequences and could possibly destroy both our worlds, or perhaps even all of them. I am not willing to risk that. But if you could, there is one thing I ask that you do for me."

Andrea bit her lip, both out of fear for what she would return to as well as what Serena might ask of her. She nodded.

"Please tell Cassie the truth. All of it," Serena said, and for the first time Andrea could see the distress in her face, the knowledge that she would die and leave Cassie alone already beginning to weigh on her. "And tell her I love her."

Something pulled at Andrea from within. It was familiar—the door Andrea had somehow used to get here would be opening again to take her away and back to Damea. Back to the spire where Richard and Meredith lie dead and she dying. She used the arm of the couch to brace herself while she stood up. "I will," she promised. "And Serena…thank you. For everything."

The fire in Serena's eyes from earlier returned. "Go," she commanded. "After all, you have a world to save."

The tugging intensified, and without further warning it tore Andrea away from the room, from the house and from Tarrasha. A flash of light and she was once again flying in the tunnel of light.

She tried to focus on returning to where she came from—picturing the spire in Azgadar in her mind at first but the familiar force nudged her just enough to make her want to look up.

That was when she saw it.

Around her was a great barrier, a shimmering transparent wall that served as her window through which she saw colorful beams streaking across the void. Each one connected to another, some merging into another color while others branched off into new tree with an equally complex weave of combinations following. *The strands!*

For a time that felt infinite and brief at the same time Andrea saw Damea, Tarrasha, and all of their permutations and possibilities. She saw her friends in most if not all of them, though there were some where it was only her and some where she never existed at all. The light dimmed as the strands diverged from one focal point. Infinite futures split from the focal point, the magic fading away in all of them.

Another nudge, this time toward two strands in particular. Damea—*her* Damea—and Tarrasha. They stood close but were not quite touching—the walls between them too thick for anything to get through.

A storm. It settled firmly over one of the strands, the rain beating down on the forest below. Lightning streaked across the sky as two women worked to set up the machinery for their next experiment. One of them was no more than a year younger than her, but it had felt like an era had passed since that fateful night in the Black Forest with Meredith.

*Why am I here?* The answer came to her as quickly as the question had.

She focused her attention to the other strand, the other world in which there was no storm, only an alien city—covered in smoke and dark save the glow of lights coming from the metal and glass structures that grazed the sky. Another young woman walked home—her hands stuffed in her pockets. Her loneliness emanated from the barrier surrounding the world—Andrea's heart breaking when she felt it, too. She could see along the strand how much the woman had endured, how she had lost her mother over the span of months, how she had been taken in by her closest friend only to lose her to an accident, and then how she was finally cast out onto the streets to fend for herself. It was a cold, harsh world.

The storm had not moved, though. *Nothing will happen... unless—*

She heard the excited shouts from the first world where the two enchanters were ready to begin their experiment and re-called the magic she had received from Serena. It was barely enough, but she could *just* push the strands close enough that the fates of the enchanters and the young woman were now tied. As the storm spread into the second world, she used the remaining power from Serena and poured it into the strand connecting both young women.

Something clicked for Andrea as she now understood what she had done. Cassie's arrival in Damea had not been an acci-dent nor had her powers.

*This is where it happened.* Andrea had altered the strand here. She had given Cassie the magic they would later use to find their way to Rhyad. *All of this was connected.* She recalled the ease with which Cassie learned how to absorb energy in Richard's lesson and it came to her. Cassie *was* an enchanter; she always had been. But she had the abilities of enchanters who lived hundreds of years ago—the practice of absorbing and retaining magic, which had long since been forgotten.

Serena had been the most powerful enchanter in history. And even through the barrier, Andrea could sense Cassie was even stronger.

*"Did you always know?"* A familiar voice broke her concen-tration and sent her spiraling back into the tunnel of light. It was quiet and sad but not accusatory.

"No."

A final tug.

"I'm sorry."

There was no answer as the lights sped up and pulled together.

281

# Chapter 26

# Tethered

The raw magical energy and the pain from her injuries slammed into Andrea with such force she gasped, writhing on the ground as she struggled to get air back in her lungs.

*"Andrea!"* She could just make out Cassie's yell over the storm that circled overhead. Lightning and debris riddled the clouds swirling in the dark maelstrom above. Memories of the fields of Azgadar surfaced. But things were different this time. Everything had changed, especially her.

*Finish it!*

Tethered to Cassie, Andrea reached for the magic, finding strength she didn't know she had and rolled over to push herself up—gritting her teeth as the scars on her arm began pulsing so bright that the blue and white light pierced the fabric of her shirt and burned spots into her vision.

When she finally climbed to her feet, she found herself only a few steps away from Cassie, who was holding her side. She was beginning to tire, the strain of the magic and the multiple severed connections no doubt taking a toll on her physically. Her eyes still burned that fiery blue, but around them the desperation had slightly worn away, replaced with the faintest glimmer of hope.

"You have to stop it, Andrea!" she pleaded. "Please—I don't think I can keep going like this for much longer."

*How to stop it, though?* The pieces were in place, but Andrea still didn't know what to do with the power. If she released the magic, countless enchanters would die. But holding on to it would surely kill Cassie.

"I-I don't know how!"

Cassie fell to her knees. "You *do.* I know you do!"

The world began to spin as the surge of power threatened to consume Andrea on the spot. Enchanters had used magic for generations—but the severed connection made it impossible to reverse what had been done. And if *nothing* was done, then Damea would decay until the storm destroyed everything and everyone that was left.

She froze. *The storm.*

*"Magic* is *nature, Andrea. They are one and the same and cannot exist without each other."* Meredith's words echoed in her mind—her final lesson.

The spire shook as a rumble, louder and deeper than any she had felt before rippled across the land, toppling some structures and half the armies below. But it wasn't finished.

The storm quieted, if only for a moment, as though taking a deep breath. The rumble returned, a massive force in the earth barreling toward the city.

"You have to do it now!" Cassie screamed. "You *have* to!"

It was less than a second, but in that final moment, Andrea

knew exactly what had to be done.

She needed only to look inward for the focus she needed. There was no storm or battle. It was just her and Cassie and Damea's magic tethered between the two of them. Extending her right hand for the power and control she needed, she began siphoning the energy through their connection.

A deafening boom rocked the spire—the energy exploding out into the twisting sky before plunging back down to feed the earth itself. She watched as Cassie threw her head back and closed her eyes as the magic begin leaving her.

The clouds above began to part and the lightning gradually ceased as she poured all of the magic back into Damea, restoring the equilibrium the land depended on to survive.

Her knees buckled as she fought to keep her balance. *Just a bit more.* The pressure behind her injured eye returned with a vengeance. Her arm throbbed and she yelled out in agony, the reality setting in that she would not survive this. She glanced over at Cassie. Their journey had taken them across Damea and beyond, everything they had done and endured leading up to *this*.

She wanted to hold onto their connection for just a moment longer. Before it was all over.

*"I wish it hadn't come to this."*

She could sense Cassie's surprise. *"Why?"*

*"I really wanted to marry you."*

Cassie's laugh warmed her. *"You will. But you have to not die. You have that perfect record of not dying to live up to."*

*"Cassie..."*

*"Plus, I never got to ask you. So, you have to wait for that too, because I want to do it properly."*

A burst of magic knocked Andrea off balance, bringing her to her knees. The ringing in her ears swelled to a rattling thunder. *Almost.*

Cassie's voice somehow managed to break through the noise. *"Hang on, we're almost there, Andrea."*

She smiled and did not try to fight the tears that came. She regretted not having time to tell Cassie everything about Serena, but she could tell her how she felt one last time with everything she had. *"I love you."*

The remaining pulses of magic left her, faint streams of light that trickled down the stonework of the spire before finally being absorbed by the land.

The edges of her vision darkened as she fought with everything left in her to look at Cassie one last time. The weight of everything she'd been through over the past few weeks lifted from her shoulders as she took in the sight of Cassie's eyes. The unnatural glow from the magic was gone—all that remained was the blue Andrea knew so well.

She watched Cassie's eyebrows arch up as relief crossed her face, followed by surprise.

Her vision darkened completely before she fell back against the stone again.

✶ ✶ ✶

A warm breeze ruffled Ithmeera's hair—the thick blended scents of metal and smoke assaulting her nostrils. She groaned when her face pressed against the cold chain links of Elisa's armor. Lifting her head, she was greeted with a blue sky, clear save a few puffy clouds that floated lazily over the land.

She gasped. The storm was gone! She craned her neck just enough to see Azgadar—the walls around it cracked and crumbling in some places but the spire still standing. Smoke rose up from inside the city. *Andrea did it.*

Her attention was directed downward, where she still held a barely-conscious Elisa in her arms. Her face swollen and bloodied in several places, Elisa could only look up with hooded eyes as her breaths came in pained, ragged pants.

"Ith-Ithmeera? Are you—"

"I'm fine." Adjusting her hold to pull Elisa closer, Ithmeera took another scan of the battlefield. Her heart sank when she saw the dozens of dead Legionnaires—both New Legion and otherwise—and Guardians littered across the field. Many survivors were walking around, their gazes toward the sky, while others remained sitting or kneeling on the ground, either tending to the dead or to their wounds. To her right, no more than a few steps away lay Petra, facedown with her arms extended, the dry yellow grass beneath smeared with blood from where Ithmeera had stabbed her with the dagger.

Ithmeera closed her eyes and breathed deeply. It was over.

Memories of their battle with Petra came back to her in a rush. Elisa's face, particularly around her eyes, was swollen and already showing signs of bruising and she sported a long cut across the top of her forehead.

Ithmeera tore her eyes away from Elisa's face and took in the rest of her injuries. "Your leg!"

Elisa let out a shaky breath before leaning into her. "I-I've had worse. Actually," she coughed, "perhaps not."

"Come. We need to find Lydia and the others," Ithmeera said as she worked to get both of them to their feet, Elisa leaning on her for support. The rings and plates of their armor clinked together as they collided. In the distance, she could see General Veraun acknowledge her, the relief on his face obvious as his men were rounding up the surrendered New Legion soldiers, most of whom appeared to be cooperating fully.

She took a moment to settle. They had won. With Petra dead, the New Legion was broken. Ithmeera still wasn't certain what had occurred on the spire, but she took the color of the sky as a good sign there would be a future for Damea.

"Your Majesty! Elisa!" Jacob's deep voice and heavy steps behind them cut through the quiet. Keeping Elisa steady, she turned slightly to face him. While covered in a light coating of dust and mud, he appeared uninjured.

Upon seeing Elisa's state, he took a stance beside them and extended his arm. "Here, let me help."

"What of Andrea and Cassie?" Elisa's voice was heavy with fear and Ithmeera stiffened when she felt Elisa grip her wrist.

Jacob's eyes cast downward and he sighed. "I sent Guardians to the city to find them, but we won't know until they return."

"And the others?" Ithmeera asked.

"Diana is fine. Most of the Guardians made it through."

Even with Jacob's support, Elisa struggled to hold herself

up, her sharp cry of pain bringing tears to Ithmeera's eyes. "We need to get her aid quickly," she urged. "Can you carry her?"

Elisa let out a deep cough. "I…will not…be carried."

"Hush, my love. Jacob?"

With ease, Jacob lifted Elisa—who did not protest—off the ground to carry her. "If you'll follow me, Your Majesty," he said, "we've got a spot set up for healing not far from here."

Taking another long look at her damaged home, Ithmeera sighed and motioned with her hand, allowing Jacob to lead her across the field where Lydia and the Guardians awaited them.

# Chapter 27

# Healing

Andrea let out a soft sigh as she leaned back against one of several plush pillows propped up behind her back, her gaze wandering to the drawn curtains of her bedroom in the Azgadaran Palace where she was relieved to note the blue in the sky outside. A brief cough escaped her, the latest of several since she had woken up minutes earlier with a severely parched throat, and she reached for the cup of water on the nightstand next to her.

Ithmeera of all people had been at her bedside when Andrea had awoken. Dressed in a deep green dress, hair loose and all but barely covering a faint scar above her brow, the empress had not had the look of someone who had just fought in a days-long battle for her homeland. But then Ithmeera had informed her that she had been unconscious for a little over a week, inciting immediate worry in Andrea before she asked where Cassie was. Ithmeera had given her a warm smile and told her she was fine—that all of her friends were fine—and that she had sent Cassie to the kitchen to get herself something to eat, muttering something about being unsurprised at Cassie's stubbornness given the new information that she was, in fact, of Azgadaran descent. Adding to Andrea's relief was the news that the cities and farms of Azgadar were still lit and powered by Damea's restored magic, though enchanters—all of them safe and well after the battle—were discovering they could no longer touch it.

With her vision in her right eye now completely restored, she took in the room around her again, the extravagant décor and luxurious fabrics draped across the windows and her own bedspread contrasting starkly to the nightmare she had lived for weeks and was now finally over. Her focus turned downward at the clean white blouse her torn, dirty shirt had been exchanged for. Her left wrist, wrapped in bandages, had been placed in a splint. But it wasn't until she looked at her right wrist that Andrea felt the corners of her mouth turn up.

The feeling in it had returned, though it was still not to its full strength. The scars remained. But they were no longer that sickening black, but a hazy grey instead.

After setting the cup down, Andrea's attention returned to the small, open box that sat on the comforter covering her lap. In it, set in a dark red velvet cushion, was a gold ring, a gift from Ithmeera accompanied by an offer to remain in Azgadar and lead the former royal enchanters in a quest for knowledge to better understand the changes Damea's magic had undergone.

The nightmare had become her greatest dream. An offer to lead the royal enchanters of Azgadar from the empress herself! There would be no more enchanting for Andrea, but she could continue her research, learn how magic worked in the world all over again. But after nearly losing everyone and everything she loved to magic, was that what she really wanted?

Shortly after extending her offer and promising a visit from the others the next morning, Ithmeera had departed, leaving Andrea to process everything that had happened. She took in another deep breath, relishing the absence of the constant burning in her chest she had endured for so long. *We did it. It's over.*

The creak of floorboards depressing drew her attention to the open doorway where Cassie stood; her eyes wide in disbelief. Her hair had been trimmed and the sides shaved, the dirt washed away from it and her skin. Wearing a brand-new tan buttoned shirt and dark pants, she carried a tray holding various samples of dishes Andrea recognized by the scent during their last visit to the palace.

Silence descended upon them, the air between them heavy with everything that had happened. It was Andrea who broke it first.

"Did you bring enough for both of us?" she found herself joking, barely able to contain her joy at seeing Cassie again, alive and well and not under the control of anyone but herself. Everything they had fought so hard for could finally happen now. At least, Andrea hoped it could. There was still so much they needed to talk about.

After shutting the door behind her with her foot, eyes shimmering, Cassie closed the distance between them in a few steps before setting the tray down on the bedside table. Without a word, she threw her arms around Andrea's neck and collapsed on the bed, her head resting on Andrea's chest as her cries came out in deep breaths and choked sobs.

It didn't take long before Andrea lost her composure as well. She wrapped her arms around Cassie in an unrelenting hold and cried harder than she ever remembered, overwhelmed with grief and happiness all at the same time. They remained like that for some time, the light flooding the room shifting in color as their sobs became occasional sniffs between silence, until finally they both succumbed to sleep, the tray of food forgotten.

* * *

When she opened her eyes again, Andrea thought at first that they had slept the rest of the day and evening away, but the lit candles in the room and the remains of the sunset told her nightfall had not yet come. It also told her that someone had been in the room while she and Cassie slept. She couldn't bring herself to care though, privacy or not. Her eyes dried out from crying, she looked down at Cassie's sleeping form and reached out to gently stroke the blonde hair.

"...Andrea?"

"I'm here," Andrea murmured. "I'm here, Cassie."

With a grumble, Cassie shifted her body so that she was lying beside Andrea on the bed, her head resting on the adjacent pillow so they faced each other. "You're here."

"Yes." Andrea hummed a soft laugh. "And so are you."

"Then...it's over? For real?" Cassie swallowed. "Because I thought...I really thought that was it, Andrea. I thought you had...that you'd—"

Andrea leaned over and softly pressed her lips to Cassie's, the first kiss they'd shared since that fateful day in Azgadar before the Cataclysm. Cassie eagerly returned the kiss, her hand coming to rest on the back of Andrea's neck before bringing them closer together. Grabbing the front of Cassie's shirt and clinging to it, Andrea deepened the kiss as it went from soft to desperate in seconds. She never wanted it to end, never wanted to be apart from Cassie for as long as she lived.

Unfortunately, she still needed to breathe, and when they reluctantly pulled away from each other, Cassie stared back at her with dazed eyes and a crooked smile. "I thought the whole dramatic interruption kiss was my thing," she said, spurring both of them into giggles, with Andrea not being able to recall the last time she had laughed so hard.

It took a few minutes, but they eventually calmed down, Cassie's breaths slowing gradually until she looked away. "I'm sorry about Meredith."

*Meredith. Without her would any of this have happened?* "When I first told her about Richard, she didn't believe me. I think...I think she still struggled to at the end, but she saved me. I suppose she saved all of us." She scooted closed to Cassie. "Speaking of Richard, what he did was unforgiveable but—"

"Yeah," Cassie cut her off, showing zero signs of remorse. "It was. And he deserved what happened to him. I don't care if he was my father. But that place where you went after. My...my mother. Did that really happen?"

The transfer of Cassie's tether. Being wrapped in more magic than Andrea thought possible before seeing the white light that took her to Tarrasha and then to the strands where she had touched the fate of two worlds. "It did. I saw...everything, Cassie. And your mother, she..." She struggled to finish, chewing her bottom lip as she closed her eyes, the tears she was certain she'd cried out earlier threatening to return. How could she admit to Cassie that she had been personally responsible for her mother's death?

"Hey." Cassie planted a single kiss on her forehead. "It's okay. I know."

Andrea thought she'd heard wrong. "You do? How?"

"While you were there, I couldn't see you. But I knew I was connected to you somehow. And I guess," she sighed, "I guess I felt it. And after Richard told me who she was I had a feeling maybe…" She shrugged as her smile returned. "We both know my family isn't exactly what you'd call 'normal.' But you know what I think about being normal anyway."

"She asked me to do it. She wanted you to save Damea. She asked that if it was to be your destiny that I not take that from you."

Cassie seemed stunned. "She really said that?"

"Yes," Andrea said. "She also made me tell her about us. And she told me to tell you she loved you." She saw Cassie's eyes well up with tears again, which nearly made her start crying all over again. She opted to take Cassie into her arms instead and held her. Words didn't always need to be spoken for them to understand each other.

"She saw the bracelet?" Cassie asked, gently moving out of Andrea's hold to take her wrist.

Andrea nodded. "She seemed to approve." She gave her a playful nudge. "I did have to tell her you hadn't actually *asked* me yet."

Cassie rolled her eyes. "I was *going* to. Excuse me if my psychopathic father had to talk to me first before kidnapping me and trying to end the world." She grasped the threads of the bracelet. "So, there."

"Well? I'm here and you're here now and there should be no more talk of the world ending. At least, not today," Andrea said as she tried to get at least *one* teasing remark in.

Cassie snorted. "Damn. You and your 'humor'. Or lack thereof." She inhaled deeply before releasing the bracelet and taking Andrea's hands in her, a somewhat awkward position given how they were lying down.

"Andrea," she said, "to be honest, there have been a lot of times lately when I wanted to give up. And maybe once or twice when I thought you were…well, it seemed like giving up might have been the easy way out at the time."

Andrea noticed Cassie's hands were trembling and frowned. "Don't say that," she scolded. "You held on."

"Because of you," Cassie said. "And when I was close to giving up, I would try to think about what you'd say. And," she let out a breath, "it probably would have been in the form of a lecture, but I knew you would have wanted me to keep going. You make me happier than I ever thought I could be."

Andrea could barely contain the great smile she tried to hide behind pursed lips. "You make me happy, too."

Cassie cleared her throat. "I, uh, I know it hasn't been very long—just a year since I got here—but I know when I'm sure about something. And I'm sure that I want to keep going… together." Her eyes met Andrea's, full of hope, excitement, and perhaps a little fear. "For as long as you'll have me, if you want to, that is!" She shook her head and made a frustrated noise. "I'm not doing this right and now I'm rambling. Will you marry me?"

The next kiss Andrea initiated happened nearly as abruptly as the first though it had just as much intensity but ended much quicker.

Cassie spoke first, her face having gone a slight shade of pink. "I'm going to take a guess and say that means 'yes'? Also, you've been wearing that bracelet for a while so..."

"Yes!" Andrea exclaimed, laughing as she rested her hand on Cassie's cheek. "Of course I will." A thought occurred to her and she froze in horror. "Oh, no! My parents. I never returned after leaving for Gurith. They're probably beside themselves right now. My mother is going to be so angry!"

Cassie didn't seem too concerned. "It's fine. We'll head back there soon and then we can tell them everything."

Andrea tilted her head. "Head back? To Ata?"

"Well, yeah." Cassie gave her a puzzled look. "I thought you wanted to go home."

*Do I?* Ithmeera's offer of a title and a place in Azgadar was still fresh in Andrea's mind. She had wanted to go home to get away from everything that prevented her and Cassie from being left alone but now? She wasn't certain what she wanted anymore.

Her thoughts were interrupted when she felt Cassie's fingers running along the streaks on her arm. "Is this from…?"

The mood quickly sobered. "From when you were taken,"

she said. "They're starting to fade."

"I'm sorry. I…I thought you had died," Cassie murmured. "I thought I had killed you."

"Well, you didn't," Andrea said quickly. "And I'd be lying if I said it wasn't terrible, but it's over now." She closed her eyes. She didn't want to think about the scars right now. While they no longer hurt, the pain they'd caused her, the things they made her do to herself and to others was enough that she was grateful the magic had been taken away from her forever.

A life without being able to touch magic after being so close to it—being *part* of it and it a part of her—was such a strange concept she never thought she'd experience herself. She knew nothing would be the same. *She* would never be the same.

"You hungry?" Cassie asked. "They've been giving you these weird drinks, but it's probably been a while since you ate real food." She pointed to the forgotten tray of food, most of which had now gone cold.

The change of subject, while sudden, was more than welcome as Andrea gave Cassie a small kiss on the cheek. "I could eat for three."

"I'll be right back, then." Cassie rolled off the bed and bowed while waving her hand in a dramatic flourish. "Anything for my *betrothed*," she declared in a rather good impression of some of the Azgadaran nobility they had met.

# Chapter 28

# Rebuilding

The sun set over Azgadar, ushering in yet another evening since the Cataclysm had been stopped and the fate of all enchanters as well as all of Damea had been changed forever. Elisa sat by the window in the empress's quarters, breathing in the cool fall breeze deeply as familiar birds took their final flight of the day over the spire.

Her injured leg, splinted and propped up on a nearby footstool, gave an involuntarily jerk and she grimaced before rubbing light circles over her knee. It was still very stiff and mobility had been an issue since she'd been treated after the battle. A Legionnaire enchanter who, while lacking the ability to control magic had a talent for healing with non-magical means, had treated her in the palace, gifting her a wooden cane to help her get around while her leg healed. Using it felt foreign at best and frustrating at worse and Elisa knew it was very unlikely she would ever be able to walk and move as she had again.

She tried to ignore the leg and focused on the city again. The streetlamps glowed brightly along the streets, which even at this hour were still bustling with people celebrating the victory and the return of their empress. Azgadarans had emerged from their homes the second morning after, making their way to the shops, bakeries, and smithies to resume their work. Merchants in the Market District had begun setting up their stands again. Peddlers from outside the city wheeled their carts through the massive iron gates. At the edge of the city, Legionnaires and Guardians worked side-by-side well into the evening to rebuild the stone wall that had been destroyed in the battle.

Elisa couldn't help but smile at the sight. She never would have hoped this could be her home again. While much of it was indeed familiar, she felt a newness to it all as well. *The view's a bit different, now.*

She glanced briefly at her room, her smile broadening. After all, not many former Legionnaires slept in the empress's private quarters. But then again, not many former Legionnaires courted the empress, either.

As lovely as the scene before her was, the past few days had been difficult, perhaps not like the battle and the events leading up to it had, but in a different way. It had taken time to gather the dead and conduct the appropriate rites. Victor's burial had happened the morning after the battle ended. Alden's body had already been seen to by Petra, but that had not stopped Ithmeera from holding a vigil for him the previous night.

Meredith and Richard had also been cremated, but no one had dared stepped forward to carry out the burial. That was being left up to Andrea and Cassie.

So much had changed in such little time for Elisa. No longer a Legionnaire or an exile, for the first time in years she felt in control of her own life again. Choosing to stay with Ithmeera probably ranked among the most terrifying decisions she'd ever made, but she was certain it was also the best.

"Am I missing anything? Is there juggling happening in the square again?" Ithmeera burst into the room as a young serving girl tailed her closely with a cart carrying two plates filled with cheese, slices of cold meat and fruit, and two cups Elisa presumed were filled with water. Despite having returned to the palace, Ithmeera had insisted the meals remain simple but filling while the rebuilding took place. A celebratory feast was on the horizon, but Elisa was not up to date enough on those sorts of affairs—by choice—to know exactly when.

"Not right now, I'm afraid. They probably went home, as did the fire-breathers most likely. The wall is coming together nicely, though."

"Wonderful," Ithmeera replied, beaming at her before turning to the serving girl. "Thank you. Would you find General Veraun and make sure food makes its way to the wall?"

"Right away, Your Majesty." The girl bowed before leaving Elisa and Ithmeera alone with the cart of food. Ithmeera watched her leave before turning around, her face lit up with an excitement Elisa couldn't figure out.

"What are you so happy about?" she asked.

Ithmeera feigned offense as she presented one of the plates to Elisa, who took it and promptly began to eat. "What? Why does it always have to be some kind of ulterior motive or plot with you? Can I not simply be happy that our land is finally safe and everything is as it should be?"

Elisa stuffed a large slice of melon in her mouth. "Sure," she said, chewing, "but I know there's something else going on."

Unamused disgust flickered on Ithmeera's face before she replied with, "Have we been away from Azgadar so long you've forgotten how to eat properly? Honestly, Elisa, I think you've spent far too much time among the Gurdinfielders."

Elisa nodded and swallowed before helping herself to a slice of cheese from the plate.

Ithmeera just gave her a disbelieving stare before she continued. "All right yes, perhaps this *one* time you happen to be correct. We are in fact, hosting a grand banquet to celebrate our hard-earned victory. Everyone is invited!" She took the chair sitting at her desk and moved it over by where Elisa was situated. "How is your leg feeling today?"

"The same as yesterday. It hurts, but I will live," Elisa said. She saw the guilt on Ithmeera's face and quickly added, "Ithmeera, how many times do I have to tell you not to blame yourself for this?"

Ithmeera wrung her hands. "It's your *leg*, Elisa. And…if you hadn't needed to fight Petra—"

"I did not die and you and Marco are finally safe. That is worth far more than any sword or title." She paused, considering her words. "Though, I would very much like to keep the sword, if that is all right with you."

Ithmeera studied her for a moment, until she finally gave a happy sigh and stood to put her arms around her, making sure not to put any weight on her that might aggravate her injured leg. "I love you so much," she said before kissing Elisa's brow. "And I love being able to say that."

Her eyes burning with new tears—why did it seem like she kept crying lately—Elisa welcomed Ithmeera's comfortable hold. "I love you." Her eyebrows went up when she registered the news about the celebration. "Wait, everyone?"

Ithmeera's radiant smile lit up the room brighter than the carefully placed candles around the suite could and Elisa found it absolutely contagious, once again in disbelief at how she, the daughter of a merchant from Sadford, was now courting the most powerful and beautiful woman in Damea. "Yes! From Gurith to Gurdinfield—I think if we're going to celebrate, we should do it properly. We'll have to set up the ceremony outside the palace of course so all who wish to attend can. Oh, and we must work on the menu for the reception afterwards." She took a cluster of grapes from her plate and plucked one from its stem. "You'll assist with this, yes?"

Elisa grumbled. "I did not give up my career as a soldier to plan parties."

Ithmeera ignored her comment and reached for another grape. "Wonderful."

The rest of their meal was spent with Elisa listening as Ithmeera discussed the reconstruction of the wall and the cleanup of the city after the New Legion's occupation. After a while, though, she reached for Ithmeera's hand, stopping her mid-sentence.

"Hmm? What?"

Elisa used the pad of her thumb to gently stroke Ithmeera's hand. "Just making sure you're well. It's all right to pause and just reflect on what has happened, you know. You haven't really rested since…" She averted her eyes, an unfamiliar but welcome warmth spreading through her as she remembered their night together in the City of Towers.

The chair gave a sudden shift as Ithmeera leaned in and treated her to a long kiss before sitting back again. "I appreciate how concerned you are for me. But I am still empress, Elisa.

We may have defeated the New Legion, but it is my fault they existed in the first place. I will rest when we are done putting the empire back together. But do not think for a moment that I have forgotten about us." She pulled her hand away and went for a slice of meat from her plate. "I went by Andrea's room once more before going to the kitchen."

Her worries for Ithmeera's wellbeing soothed for the moment, Elisa could better focus on her words. "How is she doing?" she asked, watching Ithmeera finish off the slice before placing the plate back on the cart.

"She seems fine for now. They were sleeping so I lit the candles and left."

"For now?"

Ithmeera glanced out the window, where night had finally fallen over Azgadar. Its citizens had finally begun heading back to their homes, the shops closing down for the evening until sunrise. "Master Tobias said it could be some time before she completely heals, if she ever does."

"She will be fine," Elisa insisted. *She has to be.* "Especially with Cassie there to help her. She would be a fool not to recover after all this."

That got a laugh out of Ithmeera. She reached out, placing a light touch on Elisa's arm. "I adore how much you care for them and how poorly you try to pretend that you don't."

"No idea what you are talking about."

"Of course you don't. We shall visit her in the morning. Now, then." Ithmeera procured a piece of parchment and a pen and returned to her seat.

Elisa let out a long-suffering sigh. "Are you truly going to make me sit here and go over color choices with you?"

Ithmeera looked aghast at the notion. "Certainly not, you would just make everything black. We do need to plan the food though." She began scribbling. "Thoughts on the first course?"

# Chapter 29

# Reunion

That night, the nightmares began.

Vivid, terrifying images of their last moments on the spire swirled in Andrea's mind, where she was forced to repeat every harrowing part of the battle. Cassie's screams, the unnatural flare of her eyes, Richard's cold laugh as Cassie's power gripped her and squeezed until the scars on the left side of her body exploded in a blur of blue and white light as she broke apart—it happened over and over again, each time ending with a sickening view of Cassie collapsing just as the portal to Tarrasha opened in a violent spiral of green clouds framed by lightning.

She awoke with a cry, sitting up and clawing at her arm frantically while reaching deep for the magic that refused to surface and alleviate the burning.

"Andrea? Andrea, it's okay—you're okay!" Someone had wrapped their arms around her.

*No.* She used all her strength to rip herself free of her assailant's grip. She had to keep fighting. *Everything* depended on her; she couldn't stop trying. But the magic was not there. It never would be again. "No, no, *no!* Have to find it. Have to… just a bit *more!*" As quickly as she'd been free, she found herself struggling against the tight vice around her arms once more.

"Hey! Hey, it's just me. It's just me, Andrea." *That voice—her voice.*

She opened her eyes and was greeted by darkness, save the faintest of glows creeping under the door from the lit corridor outside the bedroom. The tension in her body began unwinding upon her realizing she was not at the top of the spire but safe in her room with Cassie, who was very much alive and safe. *It's over.* Tears she didn't remember crying rolled down her cheeks. She checked her arm and was relieved to see that the scars were not glowing, that she no longer required magic to keep them from killing her. *Remember that it's over.*

Then why had her nightmare felt so real?

Cassie loosened her hold and kissed the top of her head. "I'm here," she whispered as Andrea let out a shuddering breath. "Do you want to talk about it?"

She sniffed and wiped away the tears. "I thought you were dead and that I had failed you again."

In the low light she could just barely make out Cassie's expression, full of the stubbornness and determination that had become a source of strength for Andrea, before her partner shifted and sat up so they could face each other. "You didn't fail me, Andrea. You saved me, remember?" She opened her arms again. "We're all right and everything is going to be fine, now. I promise, okay?"

Andrea welcomed the invitation as the nightmare began slipping away. As Cassie took her into her arms the two fell back, Cassie's head landing gently on the pillow and Andrea on top of her, making them both laugh quietly. Their laughter was short-lived, though, when Cassie lifted her head up to kiss Andrea hard.

Andrea's worries dissipated as she sunk into their embrace, the intensity of Cassie's kiss igniting feelings she had nearly given up hope of ever experiencing again. "Okay," she whispered as they broke apart. Her heart racing, she ran her fingertips slowly over Cassie's collarbone before dragging them downward. When her hands grazed over the raised skin on Cassie's chest she froze as a knot formed in her throat. She knew what had caused the scar. "Is this…?"

Cassie caught her wrist, her voice breaking as she looked up at Andrea. "Don't. Please, Andrea, I know there's still a lot to work through, but can we just…be us for now? Just for the rest of tonight?" She moved her hands, letting them rest on Andrea's back and holding Andrea even closer. "I promise we can go back to talking about how awful everything was in the morning." She cleared her throat and although Andrea could not really see, she imagined the faintest tinge of pink had risen to Cassie's cheeks. "If you want to, that is."

Andrea thought her heart might burst from her chest. She had missed Cassie's way of talking. She knew of course, that neither would ever forget what happened. But now more than ever she was determined to make every moment they had together count.

Closing the distance between them once more, she decided she would start with tonight. She could do that.

* * *

Reconstruction of the city wall resumed just after dawn the next morning. Legionnaires and Guardians as well as many ordinary citizens of Azgadar ventured out of their barracks, homes, and farms, their tools at the ready, to continue their work. A pleasant coolness hung in the early morning air as the first rays of sunlight illuminated the city, their glow shimmering on the gold embroidery of the iconic swords and shield banners that still hung from the palace walls.

The distant murmurings of Azgadar waking up swept through the open window and into the spacious bedroom, coaxing Andrea out of sleep as her eyes opened. She took a moment to register her surroundings—not having to sleep in so many different places over a short period of time would take some getting used to—and let out a happy sigh when she remembered where she was.

She rolled over slowly, minding her wrist and trying not to disturb the arm that was draped across the small of her back. Her mouth curved upward into a sleepy smile. Facing her was Cassie—still fast asleep, mouth hanging slightly open, her hair loose. Her blondish-brown strands were splayed out, covering the side of her face, which was smushed into the goose-feather pillow.

Resisting the urge to kiss Cassie and risk waking her, Andrea used the extra time to inspect her injuries. Her vision was still clear. Her sprained left wrist was a bit sore but not as much as it had been the previous day. Her right arm was unchanged, still covered in the fading grey scars. But she could move it and that was what mattered, though she discovered while eating that movements like picking up and holding objects proved to be more difficult. Fortunately, Cassie had been there to help her and she was immeasurably grateful her partner had not suffered any long-term physical injuries from her captivity other than the scar on her chest.

She was still a bit tired after having her rest interrupted by the nightmare and considered sleeping in a bit longer, something she rarely did. But just as she was about to close her eyes again, Cassie's fluttered open. Her mouth closed and she blinked a few times before her face lit up, looking about as happy as Andrea had ever seen her. "Hi."

Andrea reached out to stroke the side of Cassie's face. "Hello."

Cassie leaned into the gentle touch, placing her hand over Andrea's to keep it there and making Andrea immediately wish they never had to leave the room again. The bracelet around her wrist reminded her they eventually would have to, but she certainly didn't mind making an exception for that.

"Sleep well?" Cassie asked, the hesitated worry in her voice prompting Andrea to kiss her.

"I did," she reassured her as she pulled away. "No more nightmares." She slowly leaned in for what was to be a longer kiss as Cassie followed suit. Perhaps she would not go back to sleep after all.

Three soft knocks on the door sounded followed by a familiar if muffled voice, causing both of them to freeze in place. *"Andrea? It's Kye, are you awake? Can I come in?"*

If Andrea was not entirely awake before, she certainly was now. Recalling Ithmeera's words that their friends would be stopping by to visit and wish her well, she called out in the direction of the bedroom door, "Erm…just a moment! I'll be right there!" and turned back to Cassie, who seemed startled but did not show signs of the panic Andrea felt. "Clothes!" she hissed—her hands searching under the comforter and pillows and coming up empty. "Where are they?"

"What?" Cassie whispered. "I don't know—around here, I guess? I wasn't exactly keeping track…"

"*Oh, of course,*" Kye answered with his usual politeness. "*Is Cassie with you?*"

Andrea lifted up one of the several decorative cushions before tossing it aside. "I thought I put them—ugh, why does this bed have so many pillows? Who needs *this* many pillows?"

Cassie laughed. "Here, let me look on my side—" She rolled over, hanging off the bed as she began her search on the floor.

Andrea heard another voice, also familiar, mutter just loud enough that she could hear. "*Of course she's in there, boy, why do you think they're taking so long to answer the door?*"

"*Elisa!*" Kye and a *group* of other voices exclaimed followed by loud laughs from Elisa and at least one other.

"Oh, *no,*" Andrea moaned and buried her face in her hands.

"Ah! Here, this is yours. Or is it mine?" Cassie, seemingly unbothered by the entire situation, casually held up a white blouse.

"I…I don't know. Does it come with the ability to make me vanish from here?"

Cassie smirked and threw the shirt at her. "I think it's yours."

It took a few more minutes of fumbling as they searched for their respective clothes, but when both were finally presentable, Andrea sat on the far end of the bed and reluctantly gave Cassie the go ahead to open the door.

Kye practically leapt into the room, his heavy Legionnaire boots giving a loud thump as he went straight for Andrea, shouting her name with glee. "Andrea! I'm so glad you're all right!" he said, throwing strong arms around her and nearly forcing her back onto the mattress.

"Easy there, Kye, she's still recovering," she heard Jacob say before he, too, entered the room followed closely by Diana and then Ithmeera, who assisted Elisa as she shuffled across the threshold—her leg splinted and a crutch under one arm. *Has everyone come?*

She gladly returned Kye's embrace, though. Tears pricked at her eyes as she realized just how much she had missed her best friend. "I'm so happy you're all right too, Kye," she said as they parted. She noticed the leather armor and wrist guards he wore, the Azgadaran crest clear on the center of the chest piece. A sheathed sword topped by a gold hilt hung from his belt. Even his usually unruly hair had been trimmed short. "I don't know that I'll ever get used to you wearing Legionnaire armor!"

Kye rolled his shoulders back, his chest slightly puffing up. "General Veraun had it made for me." His cheeks flushed. "Diana said it was okay because my family is…well, was from here."

Standing a few steps back, Diana chuckled and crossed her arms. "That I did. I'm happy Kye has decided to return to his homeland. I trust he will serve the empire well."

"He had better." Elisa approached her, the crutch creaking under her weight. Bright green eyes looked into Andrea's before she nodded, her expression devoid of humor. "Your actions on the spire were incredibly foolish and dangerous."

Andrea remained silent, uncertain how to respond. The room went quiet—with everyone holding their breath. Ithmeera moved to place a hand on Elisa's shoulder, but Elisa shook her head and shuffled forward one more step so she was within touching distance of Andrea. She extended her hand.

"They were also incredibly brave. I am…proud to call you my friend."

Too stunned for words, Andrea could only clasp Elisa's hand in return. She noted the closeness she and Ithmeera seemed to have—perhaps whatever their relationship had been before had been mended?

"I second that!" Diana announced, beaming at them. "Andrea, we would be honored to have you and Cassie remain in the City of Towers." She nodded to Ithmeera. "Her Majesty has been discussing Azgadar's own plans to learn more about this new way of magic and we would like to use our alliance to give you full access to whatever you would need to research and help us understand how the land has changed."

"You would be granted laboratories both in Azgadar and the City of Towers, of course," Ithmeera added.

With all eyes on her, Andrea had to struggle to tap down the overwhelming urge to say yes to the two most powerful people in Damea. Out of instinct she looked to Cassie, hoping her partner would get a read on her face and redirect the conversation for now.

Fortunately, Jacob saw her anxiety first. "Your Majesties, if I might rudely interrupt, perhaps we might let the girl rest for now?" He flashed her a kind smile.

Andrea tried not to look overly relieved when Diana and Ithmeera relented and agreed to pick up the matter at a later time when she had recovered a bit more. She caught Elisa giving her a curious look as the others wished her well and departed for their duties for the day, with Kye's sword jostling into the doorframe followed by, "Sorry! Sorry," and Diana's laughter after.

"I will make my own way back," Elisa said to Ithmeera, who raised an eyebrow but said nothing as she too left, leaving Elisa alone with Andrea and Cassie.

Nothing was said between them at first. Elisa leaned on her crutch, inspecting the room for a while as the other two watched, waiting for her to say something. Finally, her focus turned to Andrea. She reached out and grasped Andrea's sleeve before pulling it up enough to expose the bracelet she wore around her wrist. "I see congratulations are in order. Unsurprising the others did not notice—they are very much caught up in their own work. Rebuilding takes time I suppose."

"Thank you," Andrea said. "I am sorry about your leg."

Leaning back against the closest wall, Cassie nodded in sympathy.

Elisa looked down at her leg before chuckling. "I suppose I would say it was worth it, but I probably made about twenty unique mistakes in that fight, all of which led to *this*. But I survived. That in itself is something to be thankful for." She pushed herself up in preparation to leave. "I will leave you two in peace. I trust you will let us know when the ceremony will be?"

Andrea and Cassie exchanged barely contained grins. "We will," Andrea told her.

"Good. I will see you both later. Ithmeera has me assisting in preparations for this party of hers." Her tone alone sounded as though she was bothered by the fact, but her face said otherwise.

A thought from earlier came to Andrea and she surprised herself by grabbing Elisa's wrist. "Elisa, wait. You and the empress…?"

Elisa rolled her eyes and jerked her arm away. "The world nearly ends and yet you people still try to poke your noses into my personal life. I think I liked you better when you were too focused on arguing with each other to worry about me."

"But you're going to tell us, right?" Cassie said.

After treating both of them to a scathing look, Elisa pinched the bridge of her nose. "Fine. Yes." She let her hand fall to her side. "Ithmeera was married to my brother. We were best friends. I was her personal guard when Erik, her brother, exiled me and lied to her about it. She and I are together now." She shook her head. "Does that answer satisfy you?"

Andrea laughed. She couldn't say she was entirely surprised, but knowing more of the story behind their relationship certainly made all the tension she had seen between them make more sense. "I am happy for you, truly."

"Knew it." Cassie's smug reply earned her another glare from Elisa.

Pushing her luck, Andrea decided to prod a bit more. "Did this happen recently?"

Elisa made that her cue to leave. "It will take many, *many* drinks before I will share any more details than I already have." She limped back toward the door, grumbling words Andrea could not make out as she left.

# Chapter 30

# Moving On

The next few weeks passed quickly for Cassie as she spent the majority of her days at Andrea's side as much as possible.

Recovery was difficult for them both. Cassie had the occasional bad dream after, but she managed better when she pushed down the memories of her time with Richard. It was when she learned from Kye that Andrea drank the liquid magic she had watched her brew in the City of Towers to stay alive that her guilt really set in. While Andrea no longer required the magic to sustain herself, their first night back together and every night after for the first few weeks had her waking up in a cold sweat either from a nightmare or from an aching need to consume magic. It was heartbreaking for Cassie to see and even though she was no longer under Richard's control, she felt powerless in a different way.

She blamed herself at first, imagining all the scenarios where she could have decided not to follow Richard. Where she could have rejected her mother's necklace when Richard had given it to her. Where she could have just listened to Andrea and not pushed them to return to the Western Hills where they met Richard in the first place. That if she had just been smarter, faster, or remained more vigilant perhaps so many people would not have gotten hurt. Andrea would not have been injured and wouldn't have been driven to consume the potions.

Andrea refused to hear her apologies, though. So did Ithmeera or Diana, despite all of them having lost people and part of their kingdoms damaged as a result of her actions. It wasn't her fault—she had not been in control of herself, they had said and as much as Cassie tried to accept that, it served as a reminder that she had nearly killed people she cared about and had it not been for Meredith intervening when she did, Andrea would be dead.

* * *

The morning of their departure finally came. Andrea packed enough supplies for a few days and they left for the Black Forest, having decided not to attend the grand celebration in Azgadar. People from all across Damea had flocked to the palace steps to hear Ithmeera speak on the land's strength and unity as she, Diana, and Grandmaster Balos had declared a transition to the Third Era.

In a rare offer, Cassie had taken the horse's reins while Andrea sat behind her, their path nearly the reverse of their very first journey together. The trip felt shorter going back than it had when the two had fled to Azgadar while escaping Meredith and her constructs. The low brown hills and dry grass soon gave way to the gnarled trees framing the twisting paths of the Black Forest.

They reached Meredith's mansion a few days later. The sun had cleared the treetops by the time they arrived, with not a single cloud overhead. The days had grown cooler, the warmest days of fall behind them as winter approached.

The mansion looked as Cassie remembered her and Richard leaving it, though much of her memories of being there were fuzzy. The once white siding was stained brown, boards cracked and hanging off in various places. Most of the dark blue shutters were either bent, broken, or had fallen off. A few of the windows were shattered or missing. Thick vines had snaked their way onto the foundation and were slowly creeping up one side of the house.

She exhaled. "Didn't think I'd be back here so soon."

Andrea secured their horse and from the saddlebags grabbed the small burlap sack they had brought along before reaching for Cassie's hand and giving it a light tug. "I didn't think I'd ever be back. Come on, this way."

She led Cassie to a spot in a thicket behind the mansion. A small, clear stream flowed from the edge of the property southward, where it would eventually spill into the westerly river that ran through most of the Black Forest.

"Help me?" She reached into the sack and procured a small, polished wooden box—the three towers and lion crest of Gurdinfield carved into the top and painted blue and gold— before handing it to Cassie. The second box was similar, its entirety painted black. She let the sack fall to the moss-covered ground before switching boxes. "In Gurdinfield, ashes are normally buried," she explained, "but Meredith always liked coming here to think."

"This is what she would have wanted?" Cassie asked. "I mean, he nearly ended the world."

Andrea was quiet at first, a sad smile forming as she opened the box. "She loved him. I think even when she realized who he really was, she still wanted to believe he was the same person she fell in love with twenty years ago. She…" She looked out at the trees ahead. "She taught me so much. And if it hadn't been for her, I wouldn't have met you and Damea wouldn't have been given a second chance." She glanced up at Cassie. "Are you all right with this?"

Cassie made no effort to hide her disdain for Richard, father or not. "I don't think *he* deserves this. But…you're right—maybe she does." She opened her box, exposing Richard's ashes to the cool forest air. "Let's do this."

They knelt down together and poured the contents of both boxes into the stream, the ashes swirling together for a moment before being swept into the current that would take them to the river and beyond the known borders of Damea. Andrea reached for the clasp of her midnight-blue cloak—the same one Meredith had given her in Ata when she became her apprentice—and unfastened it before laying it flat on the ground. She set the empty boxes on top of the dark, now torn fabric, and used a few weighty surrounding rocks to secure them.

As they stood, Cassie noticed a single tear roll down Andrea's face as she watched the last of the ashes float away into the distance, a whisper escaping her lips.

"Thank you."

She threaded her fingers into Andrea's but remained quiet.

She would never understand Meredith's motivations or forgive her for the things she did, but she knew she had played a major role in Andrea's life. The last thing she wanted to do was deny her that closure.

Several minutes had passed when Andrea's voice pierced the daytime calls of the forest. "Thank you for taking me here. And for being so patient and understanding about…everything." She looked up at her. "I know I have to move on, but I'm not entirely sure how."

Cassie gave her hand a tight squeeze. "I don't know either, but not knowing what will happen has never stopped us before, has it?"

Another pause.

"You're right," Andrea said. "It hasn't. Come on." She gave Cassie a playful glance and pulled her arm lightly. "I need to give Ithmeera and Diana my answer…and I believe we have a wedding to plan."

# Chapter 31

# A New Life

**Damea, 1 3rd Era**
**Ata, The Western Hills**

As the sun crossed into the western half of the sky, the people of Ata gathered in the square of their small village where they were finally joined by visitors from the Azgadaran Empire and even as far as Gurdinfield in taking their seats on the numerous wood benches that had been meticulously set up the night before for the long-awaited celebration—Ata's largest in recent memory. Not far from the guest area stood a short platform, the high fencing that surrounded it wrapped in greenery and adorned with white and purple springtime blossoms from the trees that dotted the Western Hills. One of the town's own minstrels played a slow tune on her lute.

Along the left side of the platform stood a small unit of Legionnaires, clad in their black, red, and gold armor and led by Captain Taryn. Wearing the blue and white lion and towers crest on the right was Jacob, with Roe at his side and several armored Guardians standing at attention behind him.

On either side of the three steps leading up to the platform stood Elisa and Diana. Elisa, for once not wearing her old black leather armor, donned the formalwear of the Legionnaire—a red and black tunic with the shield and swords embroidered in gold on her chest and dark pants tucked into boots. Her daggers were gone, replaced by a brand-new Legionnaire's sword with a blazing golden hilt. Diana wore her traditional Gurdinfielder suit, complete with a deep-blue coat over her white, gold-trimmed shirt, the gold lion pendant of House Taylor hanging around her neck. A chair had been offered to Elisa for the duration of the ceremony, but she had vehemently refused it.

Standing atop the center of the platform, trying her very best not to fidget—or faint—was Cassie. She had spent the last few hours with Elisa and Ithmeera, who now stood next to her in a sleeveless red and gold gown, her hair pulled up in a coiled braided bun and looking every bit the regal and dignified empress as the people of Ata had heard she was.

No longer in its usual ponytail, the front of Cassie's hair had been gathered back in an intricate pattern of small braids, while the rest hung loose to her shoulders. She had been given a specially tailored outfit for the occasion, a soft white tunic with fine threads of green, blue, and red Isabel had stitched down the sleeves—a perfect match of the colors of the bracelet she'd picked, and black pants. As she had given the bracelet first, she would be waiting for Andrea.

"She will come to you now. You'll be expected to say the words as soon as she gets here. Then she will give you the bracelet," Ithmeera instructed in a voice just loud enough for her to hear.

Cassie could only exhale a shaky breath and nod in response. The clothes, the ceremony, the crowd—so surreal it was to her that this was really happening.

That's when she saw her. All turned to face the opposite end of the square, where Andrea had just stepped down from her family's horse-drawn wagon with Garrett's help. A woven crown of leaves and more of the white and purple blossoms sat atop dark woven braids, their pattern mirroring Cassie's. She'd opted for a dress, one with sleeves that stopped just above her wrists, the very same threads embroidered into the black garment—designed to contrast her own outfit as was tradition, though to Cassie it seemed even more symbolic. They really were from two different worlds, drawn to each other by the same strands that had brought them together on their journey.

Isabel climbed down from the wagon—drawn by Kira, of course—and was followed by Kye. Cassie grinned when she saw how handsome Kye looked in his Legionnaire formalwear, the great sword no longer swinging as awkwardly at his side as it had when he first received it.

Isabel said a few inaudible words before she embraced Andrea tightly, with Garrett joining in as he placed a kiss on her forehead. They turned to Kye, who bowed his head and offered his arm to Andrea in such a fluid movement that, as they began making their way toward the platform, Cassie wondered how much he had practiced for this.

Seeing each other for the first time in days, as was Damean wedding tradition, Cassie had to remind herself to breathe. The calm young woman before her had none of the frantic fumbling mannerisms or anxiety she remembered Andrea having when they had first met in the Black Forest. Instead, Andrea crooked a half-smile at her, her hazel eyes brighter than ever and filled with a focus Cassie had never seen in them before. Cassie's attention was directed to the small, brown leather pouch Andrea held in her hands as she and Kye came to a stop at the base of the steps. Her own bracelet could be seen hanging from her right wrist, on which, even in the afternoon light, the grey scars had faded to just barely being visible.

She released Kye's arm. He leaned in and kissed her cheek before stepping to the side to take his place next to Elisa as the square became quiet save for the faint chirping of birds and the gentle rustle of the decorative leaves. The fluttering in her chest, which had been manageable earlier, had become full nerves that gripped Cassie as soon as Ithmeera nodded to her. Here goes.

She spoke with the words Ithmeera and Elisa had practiced with her, having to exert considerable effort to be loud enough while also fighting to keep her voice from breaking from the wave of emotions threatening to sweep her away. "Andrea of Ata, you wear the bracelet I have offered." She paused to ensure her next words were said with as much sincerity as she could put into them. "Will you accept me?" When Andrea's eyes began welling up with tears, she nearly lost her own composure.

Somehow Andrea managed to hold the tears back. "I will," she answered with unwavering resolve. She reached into the pouch and gently pulled out a threaded bracelet matching her own, save one particularly bright cord of white that had been woven into the red, green, and blue threads. She presented it to Ithmeera, who took the bracelet and pouch before speaking herself. "You may approach, Andrea."

After a bow of her head, Andrea slowly stepped up and onto the platform, acknowledging Elisa and Diana's encouraging glances with a nod before taking her place in front of Cassie to face her. She offered her hands and Cassie gladly took them in hers, relieved to find that Andrea's were trembling just as much as hers were.

Ithmeera began the rite by speaking briefly of the history of the gifting of bracelets over the Eras across Damea. And while Cassie could still hear the empress, she could not tear her eyes away from the woman in front of her. She nearly laughed when Andrea, who remained silent, playfully scolded her with her eyes for paying more attention to her than to the ceremony.

Cassie never realized she could be *this* happy nor had she ever imagined that her happiness would come to be like this.

They parted hands when Ithmeera finished her part. The empress turned to Andrea and gave her the bracelet. "I speak on behalf of the Azgadaran Empire and hereby bless this union," she announced. Then less formally, "Go ahead, Andrea."

Andrea thanked her and clung to the bracelet as she turned to look up at Cassie before taking a deep breath. "Cassandra of Azgadar," she spoke, the words sounding strange and foreign to Cassie as she rarely used her full name and had never thought of herself from Azgadar but had accepted Ithmeera's insistence and blessing anyway, "I offer you this bracelet, that you might accept me. I am here with you now and," her voice broke just a bit as she continued, "I always will be."

Ithmeera's smile was positively glowing as she directed her next question to Cassie. "Will you accept, Cassie?"

"I will." Cassie answered rather quickly and swore she heard quiet laugher from somewhere in the audience. She remained fixated on Andrea though, who took Cassie's right hand and carefully slipped the bracelet onto it.

She had heard the stories of people feeling a rush of power as they attuned to the magically-imbued bracelets, but she knew that was now a thing of the past and was perfectly happy with a boring, magic-less bracelet if it meant she got to be with Andrea. Still the sense of belonging and home she had grown to feel when she was around Andrea strengthened, and she knew she didn't need magic to know they were bound to each other. She did wonder what the white thread was for but settled on asking Andrea later—the colors people chose for their bracelets were usually kept private.

It was time for Ithmeera to offer her final guidance. "Please, join hands again."

They followed her direction, and Cassie noticed Andrea's hands were no longer shaking as much.

"Let all who witnessed this day go and spread its tale across Damea," Ithmeera declared. "Andrea of Ata and Cassandra of Azgadar, may your days together be long and full of peace." She gave a slight tip of her head, signaling for them to complete the ceremony.

Cassie refused to hold back the overwhelming joy she felt from showing on her face as she pulled Andrea in close and kissed her with everything she had. She stumbled back a bit when Andrea let go of her hands and threw her arms around her neck, returning the kiss with equal vigor, the crowd before them applauding as they cheered and laughed.

She wasn't sure exactly how long they kissed on the platform but at some point, the tears Andrea had been holding back since the start of the ceremony surged forth and she began to laugh and cry at the same time, her arms still wrapped around Cassie as she leaned on her.

She tipped her forehead against Andrea's, speaking at a level she was certain only Andrea could hear. "I love you," she said, which only caused Andrea to cling to her tighter. Then teasingly she added, "These are happy tears, right?"

Andrea's breath hitched before she laughed and treated Cassie to a playful rap on her shoulder. "What do you think?"

# Chapter 32

# Celebration

The celebration began as soon as the ceremony had ended.

As the sun started the final arc of its journey for the day, massive quantities of food of varieties from all over Damea poured out of the bakeries and shops that had been closed earlier. The lone minstrel was joined by her troupe of other musicians and performers who took to the platform to continue their entertaining. High above from the rooftops hung magically-lit stringed lights, their brightness more than enough to illuminate the square. More tables had been set up for the guests, though most of them ate their food while moving about and mingling with others.

Andrea and Cassie sat at the end of the longest table, which also seated Andrea's parents as well as their closest friends. As everyone talked amongst themselves, Andrea was content in merely observing as she caught bits and pieces of the conversations. Ithmeera and Elisa would be returning to Azgadar the following morning with Kye and the Legionnaires. Around the same time, Jacob and Diana would be leaving for the City of Towers with Roe and the other Guardians.

Watching Ithmeera and Elisa, she couldn't help but be

fascinated. Elisa seemed to actually be enjoying herself, exchanging a good-natured verbal spar with Jacob while leaning on Ithmeera's shoulder. The empress let out a loud, melodious laugh at something Jacob said, further cementing to Andrea how odd it was to see the empress drop her usual cool disposition for one that was far more relaxed. But even odder for her was seeing Elisa display physical affection *publicly.*

Evening soon set in, the sun departing in exchange for countless stars and cloudy blue and white wisps that streaked across the sky. The perfect temperatures from earlier dropped slightly, but after a few drinks Andrea couldn't feel the chill. She took another sip of her wine and observed the friendly game of dice Cassie and Roe had started up. Cassie lost within the first few rounds and was melodramatically accusing Roe of cheating when someone tapped Andrea's shoulder, making her stiffen as she turned her head.

"May I have this dance, *Lady* Andrea, Royal Enchanter and *Hero* of the Empire?" Kye was dipped into a bow, knee bent and hand extended as he grinned as her, using the rather lengthy and excessive title Ithmeera had granted her.

Feeling a bit drunk off the wine as well as the utter bliss she'd felt all day, Andrea had no problem being a little silly as she replied with an air of feigned haughtiness. "I would be honored, Legionnaire Kye." Upon taking her hand, he led them out to the cleared grounds near the platform where many of the guests who had finished their meals had taken to dancing, the performers putting on quite a show as they played songs originating from all over Damea.

She was stunned when they started up in a song similar

to the one she and Cassie had danced to in Azgadar and Kye started to lead them. "When did you learn how to dance?"

A blush rose to his cheeks. "Oh! Well, Elisa has been teaching me back at the palace. She's very good, even with a cane." He lowered his voice and winked. "Don't tell her I told you, though. She'll get a big head."

"My lips are sealed," she promised as she struggled to remember the steps Cassie had shown her when they'd had their first dance together earlier. This was not helped by Kye, who suddenly stumbled on his own feet and fell forward. It took both of their combined balance and strength to stay upright before they collapsed in each other's arms laughing.

He pulled away, keeping his hands on her arms. "I've missed you so much. And Cassie, too. And now we're to be apart again!" he moaned.

"You'll be busy, I'm certain of it. Plenty for a Legionnaire to do in Azgadar," she said.

He still seemed disappointed at the thought of being separated, then his face brightened. "Oh! Her Majesty asked if I would perform at some of the events in the palace! She really likes her parties. And Captain Taryn says I've made good progress in my training and she's promoted me to Guardsman! Soon I'll be doing patrols, just like the Legionnaires who chased *us* in Azgadar, only I won't try to arrest innocent people!" he finished excitedly, snark edging into his voice.

They managed to dance through one more song without either of them tripping over themselves. Andrea was more than happy to let Kye tell her about all the adventures he had been on while living in Azgadar.

"I'm really proud of you, Kye," she finally told him, inciting another blush. "You've come so far and now look at you."

"So have you, Andrea."

She hugged him. "Thank you for being here for us today."

They were exchanging promises to visit each other when Diana approached them from the side and extended her hand to Andrea. "Apologies, Kye, but I must intervene. I would be the rudest queen in the history of Gurdinfield if I didn't dance with my royal enchanter at least once before I left."

With another impressive bow, Kye graciously excused himself leaving Andrea and Diana to dance to a slightly more upbeat tune.

"I remember this at our wedding, but I was too drunk to dance to it properly," Diana admitted before beaming at her. "Congratulations to you both again. I've never been to a wedding in the Western Hills before today. It was a beautiful ceremony."

Andrea noticed Elisa and Ithmeera had both gotten up and were now slowly swaying together a few steps away. Despite her bad leg, Elisa was leading them both gracefully. Kye had been right.

She saw Cassie still over at the table conversing with both her parents. She was shocked when she saw her mother burst out laughing at something Cassie had said using rather animated hand movements. Suspicion clouded her mind—she would find out what sort of embarrassing thing about her they were discussing soon enough.

But Diana had been talking to her and she needed to answer.

"I…we both really appreciate you and Jacob and the Guardians being here, Your Majesty," Andrea said. "Thank you…for everything you've done for us."

Diana's brown eyes twinkled, reflecting the glow of the stringed lights above them. "My friend, you helped us reunite Gurdinfield. You helped get us back our home. And you still somehow managed to fit in saving all of Damea while you were at it. Being here is the very least we could do, though I would be remiss to not extend my offer again, just in case you've changed your mind?"

Exhaling a quiet laugh, Andrea shook her head. "I'm afraid not, Your Majesty. But I am grateful for your generosity in letting me leave my post."

Diana stopped dancing and rolled her eyes. "For the last time, it's just 'Diana,' and you were always free to make your own way, Andrea. You know," she said, "Alexander always told me new paths were more terrifying than the well-traveled ones but that the reward was usually worth it."

"He's certainly right about the terrifying part," Andrea muttered.

Diana regarded her for a moment, her tone serious. "Speaking of new paths, there is something I was waiting until after the ceremony to tell you and now is as good a time as any."

Andrea had been about to ask what the matter was when the serious expression vanished from Diana's face. "Jacob and I will be having our first child, Andrea. I'm pregnant."

"What?" Andrea threw her arms around her friend, forgetting formalities and all manners of decorum. "That's wonderful! Congratulations to you both!"

Diana gave a surprised laugh as she returned the aggressive embrace. "Ah! Thank you, Andrea." When they pulled away, the song ended and the lead minstrel announced the performers would be taking a short break.

Andrea bowed her head. "You and Jacob will be wonderful parents."

"I will keep your words in mind. We're both quite nervous," Diana admitted. She glanced around the square. "Speaking of Jacob, I should probably find him before he and Roe try their hand at another drinking contest. The last one ended in quite a mess, as you may recall."

Andrea giggled at the memory of Jacob, who along with an equally-inebriated Roe, had tried to jump atop a table in the dining hall of the palace in the City of Towers to "perform a song for the people of Gurdinfield", as they had announced it. The table had lasted approximately two seconds before it cracked and collapsed under their combined weight. A hint of sadness crept into her reminiscence—it had seemed like so long ago that she was in Gurdinfield. "Hopefully the tables of Ata can be spared from a similar fate." She looked up at the sky, the lateness of the evening and the day's activities beginning to wear on her. "I should find Cassie as well before she and my parents exchange any more embarrassing stories about me."

They hugged once more in farewell before parting, both promising to see each other for their final goodbyes in the morning. Andrea turned and made a beeline to their table where she found Cassie sitting alone, leaning back while taking in the festivities around her and genuinely enjoying herself.

The white thread on her new bracelet—a symbol of the altered strand that had brought them together—gleamed under the light, making Andrea's heart swell with pride.

*We're* married *now.* She felt for her own bracelet, which only continued to fuel the huge smile she'd had on her face all evening.

When Cassie saw her approach, she straightened up. "Hey! You looked great out there. I saw you remembered a lot of the steps."

Heat rushed to Andrea's face as she realized Cassie was being serious. "Oh! No, I was falling all over myself. I think I might have bruised Kye's foot at some point and he was just being too polite to tell me." She glanced around them. "Where are my parents?"

Cassie stood up, her arms extending in a wide stretch. "It was getting late so they went back to the house. They didn't want to interrupt your conversation with Diana so they said they'd see us tomorrow."

Andrea gasped, forgetting about her parents' whereabouts for a moment as she was reminded of Diana's news. "Oh! About Diana...she's with child! She just told me."

"Ah!" Cassie shook her fist in victory. "Called it. Can't wait to see the look on Roe's face when I tell him he owes me."

Andrea narrowed her eyes. "You two...made a *bet* about whether or not our friend—the queen of Gurdinfield, mind you—was pregnant?"

Cassie gave her a blank stare, apparently not seeing the inappropriateness of their actions. "Well, yeah. Roe said Jacob's been super stressed out and anxious half the time lately so I guessed and he disagreed. So, we solved it like true Guardians!"

"Cassie…" Andrea groaned, but if she was being honest with herself, she couldn't really stay upset at anything for long. "This has been wonderful, but I am positively exhausted," she informed her, working the faintest hint of suggestion into her tone as she threaded her fingers with Cassie's. "And if I'm not mistaken, I believe there's been a room arranged at the inn for us."

Cassie looked down at their linked hands and frowned. "Oh. You're tired? I thought maybe we'd dance some more once that lady with the lute gets back."

Andrea tried again. She didn't exactly want to announce her intentions to the entire village. *Surely she'll understand.* "Or… we could go to the inn."

"Yeah, we can do that too, though I'm not really all that tired—"

*Apparently not.* "I'm going to the inn, Cassie." She captured Cassie's lips in a quick kiss and let go of her hand. "Don't make me wait too long." A satisfied smile spread across her face when she saw Cassie's eyes widen just enough that Andrea knew she'd finally understood.

Though it was the polite thing to do, it took far too long in Andrea's mind for them to bid all of their guests their thanks and goodnights. When Cassie finally opened the creaking wooden door for her, Andrea found most of the tables empty save for some of the regulars who seemed content to just be in a quiet space away from the music and noise. She froze when she saw one of the tables closest to the door. It was unoccupied, but she could still hear that clear, confident voice in her head—the woman who had picked up on her abilities the moment she'd walked through the door and invited her to sit and share her stew with her. The same woman who had taken her on what would be the adventure of a lifetime.

Cassie's arm circled around her waist. "You okay?"

Andrea nodded. *Time to move on.* Perhaps she never would entirely.

Their room was larger than the one they'd stayed in at the Legionnaire's Rest in Azgadar or the Lion's Den in the City of Towers, despite Bill's inn being much older than either. A washroom, dressing screen, and a chest of drawers that was probably twice her age surrounded a bed, the mismatched wood of the furniture chipped and scratched in several places.

She closed the door once they were inside, the lock catching a few times before she finally managed to turn it all the way. "You know, in the entire time I've lived in Ata, I've never actually stayed here before. Which makes sense of course, why would I?" *Oh, no.* Of *course* she was rambling. It wasn't the first time they'd been in this situation but that did nothing to quiet Andrea's nerves. Something about tonight was just *different.* "My house is just down the roa—"

Her words caught in a short breath when she spun around and found herself inches away from Cassie. Eyes dark, Cassie hovered just long enough to read Andrea's face for any signs of hesitation—of which Andrea ensured there were none—before pinning her to the door and bringing them together in a dizzying kiss.

Her mind swirling with adrenaline and alcohol, Andrea

let her fingers trace the bottom of Cassie's shirt. Her hands shook as she pulled it up, slipping the soft fabric over Cassie's head before allowing it to fall to the floor. Cassie responded by pushing Andrea back against the door again, running her fingertips up the sides of her dress and tugging on the garment as she left a slow, upward trail of kisses starting from the base of her neck. She rested her head near Andrea's ear, her voice low and rougher than what Andrea was used to hearing from her but the three words she murmured remaining just as powerful as they'd been their first night together. Determined not to collapse on her weakening legs, Andrea guided them to the bed in a stumbling path, echoing Cassie's words as they clung to each other, falling back together.

# Chapter 33

# Farewells

"How about a clue?"

"Nope."

"Not even a small one?"

Cassie grunted with exertion as she and Jacob lifted a large locked trunk and set it down in the back of the family's wagon situated outside the barn. "Andrea," she panted and turned to face her, "the entire point of a surprise is that you don't know what it is. And frankly, the fact that you even know there *is* a surprise is bad enough."

Andrea shook her head. "This is silly. We're obviously going somewhere for a while otherwise we would only be taking a horse and you wouldn't be taking *that* with us." She called out to Jacob. *If Cassie won't tell me, maybe he will.* "Your Highness, do you know what she's planned?"

But Jacob just shrugged. "Apologies, Andrea. I've been sworn to secrecy." He gave her a solemn bow of his head. "Under the most…" With effort, he slung a heavy-looking burlap sack in the back as well. "…sacred tenets of the Guardian code."

Cassie tilted her head. "Wait, there's a tenet about that? I don't remember hearing about it."

"Ha!" Jacob dusted off his hands. "You do yourself no favors, Cassie. Just nod and agree." He pointed to another sack a few steps away. "That one, too?"

*Honestly!* Andrea rolled her eyes and turned away from the pair. Upon returning to her house early in the morning, Cassie had informed her that they'd be leaving Ata around midday but wouldn't say to where. Jacob had shown up not long after to assist with prepping the family's wagon, which they were apparently taking to whatever their destination was.

Cassie had of course been tight-lipped about it all morning and even Garrett and Isabel feigned ignorance when she had interrogated them. To make matters worse, she wasn't even allowed to help with the packing, exiled to assisting Isabel in the kitchen for dinner preparation. Of course her mother would have her peeling carrots right after her wedding day. But then a royal carriage bearing the empire's crest had arrived carrying Ithmeera and Elisa. They were there to visit Isabel about yet another thing Andrea had not been informed about.

She thought up an excuse to find her father as soon as they had stepped inside. She would face an army of one thousand Legionnaires without magic before she suffered through a session of Elisa smirking at her while her mother bossed her around.

The front door swung open and out walked Isabel and Ithmeera with Elisa trailing behind them. The liveliness with which the two were chatting with each other made it seem as though they were old friends paying a house call.

"...before, or you'll overwater them," Isabel finished. She noticed Andrea gaping at her. "There you are, Andrea. I was just telling Ithmeera here about that crop of tomatoes we had that one year…the ones that ended up being the biggest we'd ever had?" She placed a hand on Ithmeera's shoulder. "Thank you so much for your generous offer, Ithmeera."

Andrea wanted to scream at her mother. *Touching* the empress of the Azgadaran Empire without permission? Calling her by her first name? *I simply wore the wrong necklace to Ithmeera's ball and was locked up for it!*

But Ithmeera did not seem offended at all. If anything, she appeared to be enjoying her visit. "Nonsense. It is I who should be grateful to you. It is so refreshing to finally be doing business with the people of the Western Hills and your farm has withstood all that the land has thrown at it. I'm quite confident you and your husband's expertise will be invaluable to the empire's farms."

The heavy crunch of wooden wheels on gravel interrupted the conversation. Andrea glanced out at the road where another horse-drawn wagon approached, driven by Kye with Diana as its other passenger.

"They're here at last," Elisa said, making no effort to hide the pleasure she was taking in observing how scandalized Andrea probably looked right then. She turned to Ithmeera. "I shall ensure the carriage is ready." Then, she bowed to Isabel. "Thank you for your generous hospitality, my lady. I look forward to meeting you and your husband in Azgadar in the fall. Lady Andrea," she finished, extending a polite nod to Andrea before walking away, her steps weighty as her cane came down on the packed dirt.

Isabel observed the wagon as Garrett emerged from the barn holding Kira by the reins as he guided her to the wagon Cassie and Jacob had just finished loading. "Well," she sighed, her tone carrying a sadness Andrea had not noticed earlier. "I suppose it is time then."

*How long are we going to be gone for?* Before today she had figured they would remain in Ata for some time after the wedding, especially since Cassie really seemed to like it there and actually appeared to enjoy the farm life. A few years earlier, Andrea would never have guessed she would return to Ata and certainly would never have planned to settle there permanently. Then again, she hadn't planned for a lot of things.

Soon she, Isabel, and Ithmeera had joined Cassie and her father by the loaded wagon—with Kira properly secured and supplies packed for her as well—along with the rest of their friends. Silence dominated the first moments, save the sounds of the surrounding hills and the distant calls of the village. It was a bit surreal to have her parents and friends all around her as a quiet anticipation hung in the air along with something else that felt…bittersweet?

It was Garrett who spoke first. He patted Kira on the neck before looking at Andrea. "She's a fine horse, as you well know. Take care of her and she'll take care of you."

Andrea blinked. "But…what about you and Mother? You need Kira—I'm certain we can borrow another horse from the stables—"

"Andrea," was all Isabel had to say in a broken voice for Andrea to realize this might not be a few days' trip. Turning back to Garrett, she was stunned to see tears in her father's eyes.

She glanced around, attempting to read the expressions on her friends' faces, growing more frustrated by the second. "Why are you all acting like I'll never see you again? Cassie?" But Cassie only offered a faint smile—definitely not an answer at all.

"There may have been some arrangements made before you left Azgadar." Ithmeera remained her usual cool and collected self, speaking as though she were discussing the weather. Nonetheless, her announcement elicited chuckles from most of the others. She gestured at Cassie. "Your new wife mentioned you had expressed some interest in a certain bit of property along the coast. Onede *is* technically in Gurith's realm but with a bit of diplomacy it was hardly difficult to work something out with Grandmaster Balos."

Andrea thought she'd heard wrong. "W-what?"

Taking Jacob's arm, Diana chimed in. "Consider it our wedding gift to you. It took us some time to get enough Guardians and Legionnaires out there to build it, but you should find it mostly ready when you arrive."

"I helped as well!" Kye added, inciting a laugh from Jacob.

*A...house?* Her *own* house? "I..." No words. She had no words, and wasn't entirely sure how to process the news. The overwhelming gratitude she had for her friends, though—*that* she recognized as soon as it set in. She caught Cassie's gaze. The faint smile on her partner's face had spread into a hopeful one. They would have a home together—their own home. The idea, which had been nothing more than a yearning dream Andrea had made up after the two of them had admitted their feelings for each other, had become reality.

"Of course, we'll expect to see you for the summer festival," Isabel said, though the crack in her voice told Andrea that she did not expect to see them for quite some time.

The words came to her at last. "Thank you. *All* of you." A chorus of nods and "you're welcomes" followed. *A house!*

Cassie cleared her throat. "We should uh, probably get going if we want to make good time."

When Garrett voiced his agreement, Andrea knew it was time to say goodbye. She swallowed, if only to fight back the urge to cry. She felt as though she had done nothing but cry lately and did not want to burst into tears in front of everyone again.

She approached Diana and Jacob first and offered a deep bow, briefly catching the impressed expressions on her parents' faces. "Your Majesty. Your Highness. Thank you again."

Diana just shook her head. "It is always just 'Diana,' Andrea." She released Jacob's arm and wrapped her own around Andrea in a tight embrace. "Be well, both of you," she said. "You will always have a place in Gurdinfield."

"You must visit for the birth!" Jacob insisted as he reached out and placed a hand on her shoulder. "And Cassie." He sent Cassie a commanding look.

Despite not being a Guardian anymore, Cassie stood at attention anyway. "Sir?"

His head tilted at Andrea. "She is still your charge. We clear?"

Cassie gave him a wry smile. "Definitely. I got this."

Andrea had barely pulled away from Diana when she was ambushed by lanky arms being thrown around her, the force of the tall body colliding with hers nearly knocking her off her feet. She yelped in surprise and was answered with laughter from the others.

"I'm going to miss you so much," Kye mumbled into her shirt

and Andrea could feel the fabric growing damp with his tears. He pulled away, the sight of his tear-stained cheeks nearly setting Andrea off as well. "I hope you like your new house."

She yanked him back in and held him tight. "I will *love* it. Thank you, Kye," she whispered and kissed him on the cheek. "For everything."

When they finally released each other, she turned and found Ithmeera and Elisa in front of her. She immediately bowed to Ithmeera.

"Your Majesty. I don't know how I can possibly thank you for all you've done for us."

Ithmeera's regal demeanor did not waver. "I do not hand out gifts flippantly. Rewards are earned in the empire—sometimes at great cost. And…you have earned this, Andrea. This feels odd to say, but I am grateful Elisa was able to break you out of my dungeon." She briefly regarded Cassie before returning her attention to Andrea. "Azgadar is open to you, as is my offer, should you ever wish to return to it."

Repeating her thanks, Andrea bowed once more before facing Elisa, who was ready for her, her expression severe as ever.

"As I have said before, I do not hug," she said. Ithmeera gave a beleaguered sigh. A few steps away, Kye fought to stifle a laugh.

Andrea grinned. "But you will?"

Elisa's response was quick as she handed Ithmeera her cane. "I will." She had barely opened her arms when Andrea leapt at her.

"You…have done many foolish, stupid things." Elisa's voice was strangely muffled as her hands came down on Andrea's back, pulling her in a tight grip. *Is she crying?* She realized that not only was Elisa crying, but now she was too, finally losing her battle with the tears from earlier.

"I know."

Elisa did not let go. "You are an incredible woman, Andrea, and I will miss you. And perhaps Cassie as well."

"Thanks, Elisa, you're not so terrible yourself," Cassie called back, prompting more laughs from everyone.

When Elisa finally withdrew, she along with Ithmeera and Kye bid their farewells to the others before departing in their carriage. Diana and Jacob presented Cassie with a folded piece of parchment.

"The path is marked. Should be just a few days ride from here," Diana said.

"The terrain is not too difficult, either," Jacob added. "Just follow the road." With some final parting advice, they soon climbed aboard their wagon and waved as they embarked on their return journey to the City of Towers.

Joined by Cassie, who put a comforting arm around her waist, Andrea watched as the carriage and wagon rode down the road and wondered when they would see their friends again. When the last dust clouds from the wheels had cleared, she heard Cassie sigh.

"Ready?"

They returned to Isabel and Garrett, both of whom appeared on the brink of tears as well. Andrea's hand went over her mouth when she saw Garrett take Cassie into a crushing hug.

"Thank you, Cassie. Be safe and please do not hesitate to come to us if you need anything," he told her. When he released her, she was taken into a less intense embrace by Isabel.

"You're a good sort, Cassie. I am glad Andrea has you."

With that, Cassie climbed onto the front seat of the wagon and waited, leaving only Andrea facing her parents. She had not been prepared for today, but she knew what she wanted to say.

She hung her head. "Mother, Father. I'm…sorry I left the way I did, running away with Meredith. I…if I had to go back, I would make the same choice. But I never meant to worry you or hurt you."

Isabel's eyebrows arched as Garrett gave Andrea a warm smile and put his hand on her shoulder. "You have followed your own path and changed this land for the better. I could not be prouder, Andrea."

"Nor could I," Isabel said, her cheeks now stained with tears. "We love you so much."

The weight lifted from Andrea's shoulders was so sudden her knees felt as though they'd give. She embraced them both. "Thank you. I love you both." She remembered something she'd heard earlier and pulled away to meet Isabel's eyes. "What did Elisa mean when she said she would see you in Azgadar?"

Her parents exchanged excited looks. "The empress has insisted she support our farm for as long as we need, as thanks for your service to the empire," Garrett explained. "We offered to help the farmers in Azgadar as they adjust to the new state of magic and she accepted."

"They had been using machines all this time, but they don't know if those will eventually stop and they want to be prepared if they do," Isabel added. She squeezed Garrett's arm. "I've never been to Azgadar. It's going to be so exciting!"

Andrea grinned. She had been so amazed at how far she and her friends had come that she had not considered her parents might have grown as well. But they all had.

With their final goodbyes said and one last bone-crushing hug from Garrett, Andrea climbed atop the wagon where she took a seat next to Cassie, who held Kira's reins. With a gentle whip of the cords, Cassie spurred Kira into moving as they slowly took the wagon down the road. Andrea turned and waved at her parents for as long as she could, the wagon groaning as they climbed the first of several low, lush green hills until finally it was just her, Cassie, and the road to the coastal village of Onede ahead of them.

She let out a long exhale as she leaned on Cassie's shoulder. "It's done."

Cassie nodded. "Are you okay?"

"I…I think so. I just didn't expect it to be like this."

"Like what?"

Andrea wasn't certain how to respond. How could she possibly describe everything they'd been through together in a single word?

But she realized, as she let out another long but happy sigh, she *did* know. "Perfect." She sat up to meet Cassie's eyes, the blue in them mirroring the bright, clear skies overlooking the Western Hills.

"Did you really walk up to the two most powerful people in Damea and ask them for a house?"

Cassie shrugged as a smirk played at the corners of her

mouth. "I remember we talked about it right before…well, you know." She averted her eyes, the memory of what happened with Richard clearly still painful for her. "And I guess I thought it might be a nice place to start since we're all about starting new things lately."

Andrea wiped her eyes. "We certainly have been, haven't we?"

Cassie pulled her in close. "I, uh, talked to your parents about it. Told them about…about the nightmares and stuff." She cleared her throat. "They agreed that we both need a bit more time to… to rest."

"I think that's for the best," Andrea said, her voice soft as she reached out and tucked a strand of loose hair behind Cassie's ear.

Cassie suddenly let out a short laugh. "But hey! I think we've been pretty good at saving the world so far, but maybe it might be time for us to just be…us for a while. No civil wars, crazy enchanters, holidays in Rhyad, and *especially* no apocalypses. How does that sound?"

She placed a kiss on Cassie's cheek before looking out at the road ahead. "That sounds like an excellent plan."

# Epilogue

**Onede, Gurith Coast**
**Four years later**

A gentle breeze caught on the rider's deep red cloak, the fine gold-accented fabric rustling behind him as his white mare cantered down the narrow gravel path leading away from the small coastal village of Onede. An experienced messenger who had traveled across the land many times over his career, this was not Alvo's first trip to the region, but it was the first time he had traveled this far out from the main village. His first stop had been at the town square, where he had to ask no less than five people for directions to his destination.

Slowing down, he passed through a small bit of woods that gave way to an open strand of beach that ran north for as far as he could see. Grey and blue waves broke at the shore before receding again—going far out into the Sea of Gurith and beyond to somewhere he'd never heard of. The path continued, however, keeping a good distance from the shore and curving around to reveal a low hill upon which a small house was situated, it's long, narrow sidings a blend of white and sky blue. A modest garden spanning several raised beds of various vegetables had been planted within the low fenced area in the front of the property. To the left of the house stood a small barn, its paint the same color as the house, no doubt a place for the owners' horse and storage.

He spotted no nameplate or post in sight as he reached the front gate. Inside, a long walkway led to a light wooden iron-fitted door. Climbing down from his mount, he heard a heavy thud come from inside the barn. After securing his horse on the gate, he grabbed his pouch from the saddle and adjusted his cloak and clothing before heading to the barn to search for the recipient of the message he had carried halfway across Damea.

Upon poking his head into the barn, he found a blonde woman perhaps in her mid-twenties climbing up a rather precarious-looking shelving unit in the back of the barn. Tools and other small objects fell to the ground as her boots collided with them, though she did not seem to mind or even be alarmed that the entire unit might come crashing down along with her at any moment. Holding on to the shelf nearest to her, she reached up for a small, dark wooden box on the top shelf. On the left, a chocolate brown draft horse quietly observed from inside its stall.

Clearing his throat as to not startle her so much that he might add to her danger, he attempted to get her attention. "Erm, excuse me…my lady?"

Unfortunately, the woman's head jerked up anyway—her foot slipping before she let out a surprised cry and lost her grip on the unit, falling before Alvo could stop her and hitting the straw-covered flooring of the barn with a solid thud.

"*Oof!* Ouch…"

Alvo hurried to her side. A jumble of panicked apologies rushed from his mouth as he helped her sit up. "Forgive me, my lady, are you injured?"

Sitting up, the woman blinked a few times and coughed before seeming to realize he was speaking to her. "What? Oh, uh, it's fine." She chuckled. "Would you believe me if I told you that wasn't the first time that's happened this week?"

Finding her accent a bit strange and not entirely sure how to respond to her, he offered his arm and she took it before climbing to her feet to dust off the stray bits of straw on her loose, grey shirt and dark pants. She took in his appearance for the first time, her bright blue eyes widening slightly when she saw his attire, particularly the notable swords and shield crest embroidered on his tunic. "Oh! You're from Azgadar."

He bowed, composing himself as he reached for his pouch again. "I am, my lady. I have come to deliver a message on behalf of Her Majesty, Ithmeera Cadar, Empress of the Azgadaran Empire."

The woman raised an eyebrow. "Yeah? What's the message?"

Alvo gave her an apologetic look. "I am sorry, but I was instructed to only give the message to the Lady Andrea, Royal Enchanter and Hero of the Empire and no one else."

The woman actually winced a bit when he announced the recipient of his message. "Wow. That title sounds longer every time I hear it. Look, she's not here. I can give her the message when I see her, all right?" She held out her hand, as though to take the contents of his pouch from him, but he shook his head.

"Apologies, but I was informed you might say that and I must insist I deliver this message to Lady Andrea and Lady Andrea only," he said and noted the bracelet around her right wrist. "You are Cassandra of Azgadar, yes?"

She frowned at the name, tensing enough that for the first time Alvo noticed the dagger hanging from her belt, its sheath branded with the towers and lion of Gurdinfield. "I don't want to be rude, but if you're not going to tell me what it's about then I can't help you."

He held up his hand, advising her to give him a moment, before reaching into the leather pouch and pulling out a thick sheet of parchment that had been included with his assignment. "This is actually for you," he said, handing her the parchment.

She cast him a suspicious glance before inspecting the letter. Several seconds went by before her expression softened and she let her hand fall to her side, still holding the parchment. She sighed. "All right. Come on." When his eyes flickered to the mess on the floor, she gave a dismissive wave of her hand. "Don't worry about it. I'll clean it up later."

He followed her out of the barn and by the garden before heading up the walkway to the front door. She pushed down the latch on the iron handle and let the door swing open before welcoming him inside, the entry a little cramped but still inviting. "This way," she said, leading him past a cozy but richly-furnished living room. The house was quite small but Alvo could see that despite the size, it had been built well and was decorated with a fine assortment of items and furniture he knew could only have come from the best crafters in Azgadar.

"Hey, Andrea." She led him down a short corridor, which opened up into a rather impressive study. Nearly as large as the living room and kitchen combined, most of the walls were lined with shelves filled with more books about magic than Alvo had ever seen. Against the far wall under a large window was a long writing desk covered with a few short stacks of even more books. Another woman, her hair dark and reaching just past her shoulders, sat at the desk scribbling in a notebook—her back turned to them.

Cassie called her again, this time with the woman responding by turning around. A long, faded scar crossed her right cheek under hazel eyes that looked back at him curiously in the sunlit room. She placed her pen down, the rolled-up sleeve of her blouse sliding up just enough that he could see the faintest of grey streaks on her wrist under her own bracelet. She tilted her head, waiting for them to speak.

"This guy has a message for you," Cassie said, jerking a casual thumb in Alvo's direction. "Says it's from the empress."

"Oh." Both of Andrea's eyebrows went up and she moved her chair back as though to get a better view of him. "Well? I'm listening."

"Yes, of course, my lady." Alvo reached back into his pouch and procured a wrapped scroll bearing the seal of the empress on it. "With your permission?" he asked, gesturing to the scroll.

Andrea nodded. "Go ahead."

He unrolled the scroll, clearing his throat again in preparation to read the message he traveled halfway across Damea to deliver. With a steady, even tone he began to read aloud. "Her Majesty, Ithmeera Cadar, Empress of the Azgadaran Empire cordially requests your presence in Azgadar to celebrate her marriage to Lady Elisa of Sadford." He closed the scroll before presenting it to Andrea in a stiff bow. "The dates and additional information including required attire are contained in the invitation, my lady," he informed her as she took it. "Shall I deliver your reply?"

He watched Andrea exchange a tentative glance with Cassie before she looked down at the invitation in her hands. "Yes," she said. "Please tell Her Majesty we will be there."

"Thank you, my lady." He offered another bow and one to Cassie as well. "I thank you both for your time. I shall see myself out. Good afternoon."

* * *

When Cassie returned from watching the messenger leave from the front window, Andrea noticed the folded piece of parchment she carried. "What is that?"

A smirk crossed Cassie's features as she tossed the note on the desk. "That is a lovely note from our favorite grumpy Legionnaire friend. I wasn't going to bring that guy inside but then I read it."

Uncertain what was so amusing about the note, Andrea unfolded the paper, being gentle as not to tear it, and peered at the hastily written script. "'Do what this messenger requests or I shall come there and deliver the message myself. Miss you both. Love, Elisa.'" She gave Cassie a doubtful look and placed the note back on the desk. "She did *not* write that last part."

Cassie shrugged. "You're probably right, but I'm pretty sure she meant some kind of physical harm in the rest of it."

"Oh, certainly." Andrea rubbed her eyes and closed her

notebook. "I'm surprised it took this long. I wonder which one of them proposed."

"My money's on Ithmeera," Cassie said as she sat atop the desk with a grin, the force of her weight nearly knocking over the inkwell. "I mean, can you imagine Elisa making a grand, romantic gesture like that?"

Andrea glared at her. "Off the desk! If I have to rewrite my notes again because you got ink splotches all over them, I'm going to be very upset." When Cassie hopped off with a laugh, she rolled her eyes and secured the inkwell by placing the lid over it. "And I don't know—I think Elisa might have been the one to do it. She cares deeply for the empress and she's never been afraid to show it." She reconsidered her words. "Actually, she was just quite poor at hiding it."

They shared a laugh before she felt Cassie's hand in hers. Glancing up, she could see the concern on her wife's face. "What is it?"

Cassie smiled, though Andrea could tell it was strained with worry. "You sure you're ready? We can wait, you know? See them next year or something." She let her eyes circle the room. "You probably still have a book or two you haven't read."

Andrea pushed the chair back and stood up before pulling Cassie in close and kissing her. "I've actually read them all, some more than once even," she said, stealing another kiss. "But yes, I think I'm ready, Cassie. I don't think there is a single book about magic from the old Enchanters' Academy or Azgadar that I haven't read. I need to see it for myself instead of reading about it." Her arms around Cassie's neck, she nodded at the scroll on the desk. "All that did was move up the timeline. Also, I still feel awful about not being there for Diana for the birth."

Cassie responded by pressing her forehead against Andrea's. "She said in her letter it was all right, remember? And…if you're sure, I mean, this was what you wanted wasn't it? The house, the coast, the horse—everything?"

"It is," Andrea said, smiling at the added mention of the horse. "And I've been so happy here. But I'm also…" She trailed off, unsure how to formulate the words she needed to explain how she felt.

Fortunately, Cassie usually knew what she was thinking. "Bored? It's okay to be bored, Andrea. And we already talked about this—you would only go for a few weeks at a time. You don't need to live in Azgadar or the City of Towers to make this happen."

Andrea knew she was right. Over the last few years, she'd had books sent in from all over Damea and had thoroughly read each of them, absorbing everything she could and refreshing her memory on the concepts she already knew. But reading about magic could never match the experience of being around it, and other than a few old farming machines, Onede was not the ideal spot to find magically-powered infrastructure. She needed to travel east to the larger cities for that. "You're not upset?"

The disbelieving look on Cassie's face made her grin. "Why would I be upset? Andrea, I just want you to be *happy*. And yeah, maybe four years ago you weren't ready to do this. And…maybe you're not ready now. But if you want to try, I'll be right there with you."

Andrea placed a hand on the side of Cassie's face, gently stroking her cheek with her thumb. "You're so wonderful.

Sometimes I still can't believe I'm with you." When she saw Cassie's cheeks flush with pink she leaned in for another brief kiss.

As they pulled away, Cassie's eyes flew open before she suddenly cringed. "Oh! I sort of made another mess in the barn. I was trying to reach that stupid box on the top shelf."

Andrea's mouth parted as she treated Cassie to a soft punch in the shoulder. "Cassie, we have a *ladder*. There is absolutely no reason for you to be climbing up there—you could get hurt!"

But Cassie held up her hands in defense. "Listen, part of my Guardian training was learning how to fall down and I am excellent at it. You can ask Jacob—I bet he'd agree with me. And…" Her bravado faded to sheepishness. "I can't remember where I left the ladder." She rubbed the spot on her shoulder where Andrea had hit her. "Also, ow. I'm still sore from falling!"

Andrea shook her head in dismay. "Serves you right, then. Why do you need that box anyway? All it has are the animal figurines from my old room." She recalled finding the box at the bottom of one of the trunks they had brought with them from Ata and, upon seeing its contents and wanting to distance herself from anything enchanting-related for a while, had placed it somewhere she would not think to look. That place being, of course, the top shelf in the barn.

Cassie looked at the ground as guilt lined her voice. "I don't know…I figured since we set up this study for you that you might want them out again. Maybe on a shelf or on your desk or something."

Holding Cassie as close to her as she possibly could, Andrea let out a long, happy sigh. *She's perfect. How did I get so lucky?*

"Tell you what," she began. "You left the ladder behind the house last week. Why don't you get it and I'll meet you in the barn? We'll get the box down together."

Cassie's face lit up. "Great. And then…I guess we should probably start planning for a trip?"

"We should," Andrea agreed, letting her hand slowly brush against Cassie's as they released each other. "It's going to be a long one."

* * *

"Welcome to Azgadar. In accordance with the city law, no visitor is to enter without submitting to an inspection of their cargo. You will also be required to…"

The bored Legionnaire droned on citing numerous rules and the city codes they aligned with before he suddenly stopped and stared, his light brown eyes gravitating to the scar on Andrea's face. "Wait—I know you!" He turned and used his armor-clad elbow to nudge the sleepy Legionnaire slouching behind him. "Eyes up, man! Look who's come."

Sitting at the front of the wagon and dressed in a dark blue, tailored long-sleeved shirt and her favorite black riding pants, Andrea exchanged a confused glance with Cassie before handing the man the rolled up scroll they had carried with them from Onede. "We've come for Her Majesty's wedding. Here is our invitation. You're free to inspect our wagon, but you'll find mostly books and clothes."

Cassie gave a solemn nod. "A *lot* of books, actually."

The guard's mouth split into a grin as he put up his hands to push the scroll back to Andrea. "We certainly know who you are, Lady Andrea. Her Majesty's been looking forward to your arrival and has been sending couriers here twice a day to see if you arrived."

Thoroughly awake now, the Legionnaire standing next to him gave a bow of his head. "Do you need an escort to the palace, my lady?"

"We're good." Cassie held the reins up to demonstrate as she joked, "The palace hasn't moved right?"

He traded a puzzled look with the first guard and eventually gave a slow shake of his head before the two of them stepped away with another bow and allowed the wagon to pass. Cassie urged Kira to move and the wheels crunched against the packed gravel of the street as they crossed under the newer iron gates and into Azgadar's bustling Market District.

"Well, I thought it was funny," Cassie grumbled once they were clear out of earshot of the guards. She shifted to get a better view of the path ahead, her hard leather Guardian armor creaking against the fabric of the seat as they watched the citizens of Azgadar go about their morning routines in the marketplace. "I forgot how stuffy people are here."

Andrea leaned back in her seat, smiling as she shook her head. "You do recall you are in fact, one of these stuffy people?"

"Pfft! Listen, my mother might have been from this town, but that doesn't make me one of them." Cassie slowed them down as to avoid the clusters of people crossing the busy street. "Hey, you think your parents are here already?"

"Knowing how much my mother values punctuality? Probably." Andrea noted the larger brown building as they passed it on the right. A worn sign hung from the awning over the front entrance—The Legionnaire's Rest.

Cassie pointed it out first. "Hey, I know that place. They had the gross ale there."

"Cassie, you say that about every ale."

"What?" Cassie exclaimed. "I can't help that I'm picky!"

Andrea scooted closer to rest her head on Cassie's shoulder as they continued down the street, a playful smile spreading on her face. "I suppose it makes sense to expect such selective tastes from you, given that you *are* royalty yourself."

Rolling her eyes, Cassie let out a dramatic sigh as she pushed Andrea away. "I'm not royalty and that will never be funny."

The Azgadaran Palace, still as imposing and magnificent as it had been when Andrea had first seen it years prior, neared as she persisted to tease Cassie. "Of course…" She let her words trail off, triggering the exact reaction she wanted from Cassie.

"Don't—Andrea, I *swear*, when we get there, I will throw every pillow in the palace at you and—"

"…Your *Majesty*," Andrea finished, inciting a frustrated growl from her wife as the wagon was brought to the front of the palace, where several rather stiff-looking servants wearing the red and gold livery of the empire greeted them.

Taking only what she needed, Andrea allowed one of the servants to help her down from the wagon and thanked them for their offer to take Kira to the royal stables. She waited for Cassie to step down as well before taking her arm and allowing the head servant to escort them to the palace gardens where they were informed the empress and future empress consort would meet them soon.

The gardens were still as expansive as Andrea remembered them. A beautiful and unique blend of trees and plants, some still flowering even in mid-fall, stood next to the hedges lining the rich, dark soil splitting the brick walkways. Along the perimeter sat stone benches bearing the swords and shield crest of the Cadar dynasty. A short flight of long steps hugged the edge of the gardens, leading back into the palace. Andrea had walked between these hedges dozens of times, but she always found herself drawn toward one corner in particular. She recalled the roses being a wide array of colors, her favorites being the yellow ones when she last had been in Azgadar but here she found only white and pink. But the roses were not the only thing to pique her interest.

Cassie nudged her gently, then nodded ahead. Standing in front of the roses, touching one of the white ones with a tiny tan hand, was a small girl, perhaps no more than three years old. Her dark, nearly black hair fell loose in shaggy strands and nearly covered her wide, dark brown eyes. Her lips were drawn back in concentration as she moved to pull the flower from its thorny stem.

Approaching the girl, Andrea kept her footsteps a bit louder than necessary as to not startle her. "I believe it is being stubborn," she said gently once she stood behind the child.

The girl turned her head, her straight-faced expression unwavering as she released the flower. It sprung back into place, the rosebush giving a slight shake as it was left alone.

Andrea leaned past the girl and used her knife to cut the flower off, taking care not to take any of the thorns with it. "Here you are," she said and presented it to the girl, who took it but said nothing. "The thorns can be quite prickly so you must be careful when you pick these."

Cassie stepped beside her. "You sure you're allowed to do that?" she murmured. "Didn't Ithmeera lock you up for messing with her roses last time?"

Andrea giggled. "Well, you know how to break me out if she does." Then, turning to girl she asked, "What's your name?"

Hurried footsteps smacked into the bricks at the entrance of the gardens, startling all three of them. "*Vic!* Vic, there you are!" Marco Cadar emerged breathless from behind a line of hedges, with Amara of Karrea right behind him as both children skidded to a halt. "Oh! L-Lady Andrea!" Marco exclaimed, a single curl of his dark hair falling out of place above his brow from his otherwise short haircut. "Cassie! You're here!"

Amara offered a shy wave. "Hi, Lady Andrea." Her blonde hair was much longer than it had been when Andrea saw her last in Fimen's Hope and had been pulled back in a single thick braid. "We were just looking for Vic. She got away from us and we've been looking *forever.*"

But Marco put up his hands to silence her as a nervous laugh escaped him. "Ahh…Amara, she doesn't want to know that! We definitely knew where she was this entire time, right?"

As Andrea watched this play out in utter amusement, Amara's vacant stare gave way to realization. "Oh…yes. Yes, of course!"

Cassie folded her arms across her chest. "You two aren't fooling anyone, you know."

His eagerness fading, Marco cringed and grabbed Andrea's wrist. "She stepped out of our sight for just a moment, really that's it! Please don't tell my mother…or Elisa!"

"Don't tell your mother what?" Ithmeera's soft, calming voice sounded from the top of the low flight of stairs as she stood, the gold accents on her dark red dress shimmering in the midmorning sunlight.

Elisa stood next to her in a dark tunic and pants, cane in hand as she eyed both Marco and Amara with suspicion. "Dare I ask?" She descended the steps, the low ponytail her copper hair had been gathered in bouncing slightly on her upper back.

Releasing Andrea's wrist, Marco replied immediately with a huge, toothy smile. "We were just welcoming Lady Andrea and Cassie back to the palace!"

From the open doors at the top of the steps stepped out Kye and Diana, followed by Jacob, who took one look at Vic and held out his arms, letting out a loud laugh as the girl raced to him, rose in hand. "Ah! There she is," he announced and scooped her up into his arms much to the delight of Diana, who beamed at them before going to Andrea and wrapping her in a tight hug.

"You're here! You're finally here."

The relief and happiness of finally seeing their friends again after so long nearly brought Andrea to tears as she firmly returned the embrace. "It's good to see you, Your Majesty."

"We worried you might have been held up by the rain that passed through here a few days ago," Ithmeera explained as they congregated at the base of the steps.

Andrea pulled away from Diana and attempted to bow to Ithmeera but was enveloped into another hug just as quickly, leaving her stunned for a moment and vaguely aware of Cassie's light snigger behind her.

"Ah, so good to see both of you again!" With Vic settled in one arm, Jacob extended the other to place a large hand on Cassie's shoulder. "Please, meet our daughter, Vic. She's heard many, many stories about you both."

While Andrea and Cassie introduced themselves to Vic, Ithmeera suggested Marco take Amara to the kitchen for lunch. Both seemed more than happy to be relieved of their babysitting duties and scampered off as Kye stepped forward to greet Andrea. She did a double take when she noticed he had grown again. No longer the scrawny, lanky boy she had met in the dark alleys of Azgadar, his Legionnaire armor fit him quite well—his height almost rivaling Jacob's. The wary, skittish mannerisms he used to carry were long gone, replaced with an air of confidence and pride that made Andrea's heart swell.

He bowed to her before opening his arms and she jumped at him, clinging to him as he lifted her off the ground. "I've missed you," he said, setting her down and turning to Cassie. "And you as well, Cassie!"

"You look good, Kye." Cassie pointed at his armor. "They feeding you in the barracks?"

He laughed. "Just a bit." Light brown eyes lit up and he took Andrea's hand. "I'm so glad you came."

"Me too, Kye. Me, too." Andrea turned her gaze on Ithmeera,

searching the empress's wrist and seeing, to her satisfaction, a multi-colored threaded bracelet hanging from it. *Ha. I was right.* She made a mental note to remind Cassie of her victory later.

A tentative hand came down on her shoulder. Tilting her head, she was surprised to see Elisa standing behind her. The genuine smile on her face left Elisa's green eyes shining brighter than usual and Andrea couldn't help but notice how much happier she seemed since being with Ithmeera.

"I am relieved you could make it, Andrea. You look…rested," she observed, the smile giving way to a smirk. "Interesting, given that you live with Cassie."

"I heard that," Cassie called from a few steps away where she and Kye were catching up.

Andrea took Elisa's hand in hers, relishing the brief surprise that registered in her friend's face. "I am, Elisa. And congratulations to both of you," she said. "We can't wait for the ceremony."

Elisa did not pull away. "Thank you." The smile returned and for a moment, Andrea thought she saw a glimpse of shyness in it. "Even after all these years, well…you probably know."

Andrea squeezed her hand before releasing it. "You deserve to be happy."

"Well, then!" Ithmeera raised her voice above the reunions. "You both must be hungry. Why don't we move inside and I'll have some lunch prepared?" When a chorus of agreements rang out, she waved them along and the group started for the steps.

Catching Cassie's encouraging nod, Andrea took a deep breath and tried to push down the nervousness that had risen up the moment they entered the city. "Actually, I was wondering if I could say something first?"

Her friends stopped—awaiting her question with visible intrigue.

"Cassie and I," she began, "have been nothing but happy these past four years. We love our home, and we are extremely grateful to you all for it. But I was wondering if perhaps either of Your Majesties might need another researcher of magic in your courts?" She swallowed. "I would prefer to visit often, but I could be here for weeks at a time if necessary."

Several sets of eyes stared back at her—to her relief, all of them warm or excited. Ithmeera spoke first, but Diana nodded the entire time she did. "I think it is most generous of you to offer, Andrea. The empire always has need of brilliant minds, especially when it comes to the study of magic."

"As does Gurdinfield," Diana added. "Both of you would be more than welcome."

Ithmeera took Elisa's arm. "Indeed. We can certainly discuss the details of it during your stay, but as Diana said, you are always welcome here, Andrea." She exhaled. "Now, then. I am starving and as Elisa might be a little too willing to share, I tend to get a bit impatient when I do not eat on time."

"'Impatient' is actually not the word I used," Elisa clarified and laughter followed as they moved into the palace, leaving Andrea at the base of the steps next to Cassie, who reached out to take her in her arms.

"See? Easy. Just like I told you." She kissed the top of Andrea's head. "Now you can relax, right?"

Pressing her head into Cassie's chest, Andrea let out a happy sigh. "No promises—this is all still a little frightening for me. But I will try."

"I know. But I'll be there right beside you. Just like with everything else we do." Cassie flashed her a teasing grin. "You're stuck with me, remember?"

Andrea pulled her down to kiss her softly. "I remember." She gazed up into the bright blue eyes of the woman she had come to love more than anything in Damea or any other world she had seen and touched. "I wouldn't have it any other way."

Rhyad
Aegadaran Empire
Western hills
Northland Keep
Darst
City of Towers
Fimen's Hope
Gurdinfield
Hathorn Hold
Karrea
Ata
Onede
Gurith coast
Aegadar
Gurith
Sadford
Black forest
Sea of Gurith
N
S
E
W

# Appendix

## A Brief History of Damea

Although the specifics surrounding how the explorer Dameas and his companions arrived in the land now known as Damea are debatable among the land's historians, it is generally accepted that the first permanent settlements were established roughly one thousand years before the Second Era. The earliest cities and towns were spread across the land, with ruins still being discovered today from the rocky shores of the Gurith Coast in the west to the still mostly uncharted forests in the far reaches of the realm of Gurdinfield in the east. Scholars (particularly in Gurdinfield) mostly agree that Dameas was declared king and ruled over the land until his death. As Dameas had no heirs, the most influential of his companions and their children set out to stake their claim on the land, eventually forming the nations and regions of today—The Azgadaran Empire, Gurdinfield, the Gurith Coast, and the Western Hills—and marking the beginning of the First Era.

Before his death, Dameas encouraged his companions to harness the land's natural energies whenever possible and to share the knowledge of spell casting with the future generations.

While certainly not as prevalent as it was hundreds of years ago, magic is still relied upon to power Damea's way of life—farms, cities, militaries, research, and even its structures— and the great spire that is the Azgadaran Palace was in fact built with magic. The origin of magic is unknown and the explanation as to why magic began to decline is almost as mysterious as its origin. Perhaps more time dedicated to magical research could have been invested by Damea's nations during The Starving and might have provided such answers, but there was no such effort recorded among the many wars and famines that followed that historic and sudden decline of magical energy.

# Climate

Damea plays host to a variety of climates. To the west lies the Sea of Gurith, a cold, deep body of water rarely explored beyond the immediate waters near the Gurith Coast. The fertile Western Hills act as a wall between the coastal villages and the Azgadaran Empire and is called home by many who live in its farming towns and a few wealthy landowners. The Azgadaran Empire stretches across the drier, warmer lands of central Damea, its northern border touching the foot of the treacherous Rhyadan Mountains and its southern border just on the edge of the Black Forest. On the eastern side of the Rhyad River lies Gurdinfield, a colder realm that also shares its borders with Rhyad and the Black Forest, two regions of Damea that few have explored and even fewer have returned from.

# Timeline

**Pre-1st Era** – Damea founded as one nation under the leadership of the explorer, Dameas, and his companions. Exploration continues until his death. His companions and their children established the nations and regions of today.

**1st Era** – Study of enchanting artifacts and harnessing the land's magical energy continued. Magic usage is at an all-time high.

**1st Era** – Crops and infrastructure begin to fail as magic becomes scarcer. Enchanters across Damea grow ill when exposed to unstable levels of magic or when overdrawing on the land's energy. Thousands perish from famine and sickness. The event is dubbed "The Starving" and marks the end of the First Era. It would last over two hundred years.

**200, 2nd Era** – Damea's energy begins to stabilize, although its distribution across the land is inconsistent. Nations enact laws restricting the use of magic. The Starving is declared over.

**200, 2nd Era** – Per King Caleb of Gurdinfield's orders, the Enchanters' Academy in the City of Towers closes. Students and teachers take to the streets in protest, but the school remains closed.

**202, 2nd Era** – House Taylor is attacked at night in their castle in the capital city of Gurdinfield. King Caleb, Queen Helen, and their three children are murdered. Houses Moore and Harrington plunge the nation into a bitter civil war.

**220, 2nd Era** – Events of Enchanters begin.

**223, 2nd Era** – Lydia Diana Taylor is revealed to have survived the attack in the City of Towers and is crowned Queen of Gurdinfield, ending a decades-long civil war.

**223, 2nd Era** – Andrea of Ata, an enchanter's apprentice, leads an expedition into Rhyad where a device designed to siphon Damea's magic is discovered in one of the caves of the Rhyadan Mountains, its origin unknown. The device is destroyed, and the magic is released back into the land. The event is dubbed "The Restoration".

**224, 2nd Era** – Events of Conduit begin.

**224, 2nd Era** – Gurdinfield and the Azgadaran Empire sign a treaty of alliance between the two nations. Azgadar lifts its restrictions on magic usage.

**224, 2nd Era** – A mutiny led by an anti-enchanter cult called the New Legion unseats the Cadar dynasty. The New Legion takes control of the Azgadaran Empire.

**224, 2nd Era** – A massive disturbance outside Azgadar drains Damea of most of its magic and severs the connections between enchanters and the land's natural energy. The event is dubbed "The Cataclysm".

**224, 2nd Era** – Events of Surge begin.

# Regions of Damea

**Azgadaran Empire**

The largest nation in Damea by far with borders touching the frigid wasteland of Rhyad and the northern edge of the Black Forest, the Azgadaran Empire (or just "Azgadar" as it is commonly referred to) has withstood centuries of war and famine while still maintaining the most powerful army in Damea.

While there are divides of rich and poor, particularly in the capital city, the empire's middle class is quite large and growing. Most Azgadarans that are not of the nobility find their calling as craftsmen, farmers, or merchants. The Market District of Azgadar is the center of trade in Damea, with goods imported and sold from all over the land. The nobility, however, is a different story. Citizens born into the upper castes of Azgadaran society enjoy comforts and luxuries that the middle and lower classes can rarely afford. Grand balls and royal parties at least twice a week are typical for an Azgadaran noble, with most families vying for a coveted spot on their ruler's advising council.

The mighty Azgadaran Legion remains the common tie throughout society. Citizens of all social and economic classes often enlist once they are of age, regardless of their social status.

The climate of Azgadar is hot and dry, and its northern region is for the most part desert.

**Black Forest**

Located in southern Damea, the Black Forest is a dark, labyrinthian collection of woods and tributaries. While there are some who take up residence in the forest, it is not a well-traveled region and it is not uncommon for a merchant to take a shortcut through and never come out. The Black Forest does not fall under any nation's rule. For those who can survive its dangers, the forest can be a peaceful retreat—especially for enchanters who wish to perform their research in isolation.

## Gurdinfield

Gurdin, the older of two brothers that served under Dameas took his family and armies east and founded the City of Towers, now the capital of Gurdinfield. Sprawling grasslands and patches of forest of cover most of Gurdinfield, which claims most of eastern Damea up to the Rhyad River and its several farming and fishing villages. The region's summers tend to be hot and humid while its winters see snow most years. The City of Towers was once home to the Enchanters' Academy, and while its doors have long been closed, the nation was one of the last known places to find significant sources of magic in Damea after the Starving.

Most Gurdinfielders enjoy nature and prefer to live closer to it, taking care not to let their villages grow too large. Citizens from Gurith and Azgadar tend to look down on Gurdinfielders for their isolated and slower-paced way of life.

## Gurith Coast

The Gurith Coast starts at the merchant-ruled city of Gurith and spans north along most of the western coastline of Damea. Named after the younger of two brothers that served under Dameas, the Gurith Coast has a milder climate than the rest of

Damea, with wet, rainy winters and dry summers. Temperatures stay consistent throughout the seasons. Smaller towns dot the coast north of Gurith—the largest being the fishing town of Onede. The port city of Gurith itself has no king, but is governed instead by the Merchants' Guild, an exclusive group of tradesmen, craftsmen, and other influential figures in the economy of the city.

Perhaps the most noteworthy thing about the city of Gurith is the infamous Shadow Arena. The annual Grandmaster's Tournament is a highly publicized event where gladiators, usually enchanters, can sign up to duel other challengers in a battle for money, property, and glory. Nobles from other regions are often heard criticizing the event for its violence and the risk it poses to the participants, who are often injured and sometimes killed during the matches. However, the very same nobles have also been seen attending the event when they think no one is watching.

## Rhyad

The northernmost region of Damea as well as the least populous, Rhyad is a cold and mostly mountainous place. Rarely traveled due to its extreme weather conditions and treacherous terrain, Rhyad is not under the banner of any Damean nation. The occasional traveler might use Rhyad's mountain passes to avoid crossing the desert in northern Azgadar, but the risk is so great that most will not risk the journey.

Snowstorms, avalanches, wild animals, and more are what await those who travel to or through Rhyad. The more careful adventurers stick to the foothills of the mountains but are often attacked by the mostly unorganized groups of bandits that plague the region, waiting for an easy opportunity.

## Western Hills

To the east of the Gurith Coast is a barrier of tall, rolling green hills in which several farming villages have sprung up over the last few centuries. Most of the people of the Western Hills are farmers or own shops in their village and it is rare for its citizens to leave the region. They enjoy longer, hot, and dry summers and shorter, wet winters. Several rivers run down the hills on both sides and keep the farmlands irrigated. Most of the villages are settled in the valleys while larger villas belonging to the more secluded nobility rest in the higher altitudes. The Western Hills are not ruled by any government or monarch and most of its residents prefer to think of themselves as from their town as opposed to from the region itself.

# Glossary

**Alden Cadar** – The younger brother of Emperor Nardos Cadar and Ithmeera and Erik Cadars' uncle. Alden served on Azgadar's royal council for most of his life and provided guidance to Ithmeera on all ruling matters. He was slain by Petra in the New Legion coup in 224, 2nd Era.

**Alexander Telman** – A former Guardian, or royal guard, of Gurdinfield's ruling family. Escaped during the assassination of House Taylor in 202, 2nd Era. Adoptive father of Lydia Taylor. Led the Guardians as a militia during the Gurdinfield Civil War.

**Andrea of Ata** – An enchanter from the village of Ata in the Western Hills and the apprentice of Meredith of Darst as well as the Royal Enchanter of Gurdinfield. Known for her role in the defense of the City of Towers during an Azgadaran invasion and for leading an expedition into Rhyad that resulted in the Restoration. Originally a farmer, she is the only child of Isabel and Garrett of Ata. She is romantically involved with Cassie and close friends with Kye of Azgadar.

**Ata** – The largest village in the Western Hills and famous for its festivals which occur in the summer and fall.

**Azgadaran Empire** – The largest nation in Damea, centrally located with its borders touching the southern edge of the wasteland of Rhyad and the northern edge of the Black Forest. Colloquially known as "Azgadar", its climate is hot and dry with its northern region being mostly desert.

**Azgadar (city)** – The capital city of the Azgadaran Empire and home to the ruling family, the Cadars.

**Azgadaran Legion** – The standing army of the Azgadaran Empire as well as the largest and most advanced military force in Damea.

**Balos of Gurith** – The Grandmaster of Gurith's Merchants' Guild and the highest-ranking official on the Gurith Coast.

**Ben Veraun** – The highest-ranking and most decorated general of the Azgadaran Legion. Close friends with the late Erik Cadar and briefly courted Elisa of Sadford.

**Black Forest** – Located in southern Damea, the Black Forest is a dark, labyrinthian collection of woods and tributaries.

**Cassie** – The only child of Richard and Serena, the heir to the Azgadaran Empire during the First Era. Born in the City of Towers, she was taken through a portal to Tarrasha by her mother as an infant, where she was raised until being brought to Damea via an experiment performed by Meredith and Andrea. Known for her ability to absorb and store magic as well as her role in the Restoration. She is a Guardian of Gurdinfield and romantically involved with Andrea of Ata as well as close friends with fellow Guardians Jacob, Victor, and Roe.

**City of Towers** – The capital of Gurdinfield, famous for its three white towers and home to the famed Enchanters' Academy. Notable for also being the site of the start of the Gurdinfield Civil War.

**Darst** – A small town, populated mostly by nobility, in the northeast corner of Gurdinfield at the foot of the Rhyadan Mountains.

**Elisa of Sadford** – A veteran Legionnaire and former Royal Guard of Empress Ithmeera Cadar. The only daughter and youngest child of an Azgadaran merchant and a Gurdinfielder seamstress. Sister of Philip of Sadford and aunt of Marco Cadar. Briefly courted Ben Veraun. Was charged with treason and exiled by Erik Cadar upon refusing to arrest her father for illegal consumption of magic.

**Enchanters' Academy** – Located in the heart of the City of Towers, this prestigious school opened in the First Era to all who possessed the ability to connect with and manipulate magic. Per the orders of King Caleb of Gurdinfield, it was closed after the Starving was declared over to reduce the amount of enchanting done in the city.

**Erik Cadar** – Second child of Nardos Cadar. Younger brother of Ithmeera Cadar and former general of the Azgadaran Legion. Slain by Elisa of Sadford during the Azgadaran invasion of the City of Towers in 223, 2nd Era.

**Fimen's Hope** – A village located on the western border of Gurdinfield. Origin of the famed whiskey-based drink, Fimen's Fire.

**Gurdinfield** – A kingdom spanning most of the eastern side of Damea, covered mostly by grasslands and patches of forest. Gurdinfield was plunged into civil war in 202 2nd Era when its ruling house was assassinated. The war lasted until in 223 2nd Era, when Lydia Taylor reunited the kingdom under her house once more. Gurdinfield's summers tend to be hot and humid and the region typically sees snow most winters.

**Guardians of Gurdinfield** – Once the royal guards of the ruling family of Gurdinfield, the Guardians became a militia after the start of the Gurdinfield Civil War. After the war ended, they returned to serving the Queen of Gurdinfield. Today, all members of Gurdinfield's army are called Guardians.

**Gurith Coast** – The westernmost region of Damea and home to the fishing city of Gurith as well as several coastal villages. Starting in Gurith and spanning north along the western coastline, the Gurith Coast has a milder climate than the rest of Damea, with wet, rainy winters and dry summers.

**Gurith** – The capital of the Gurith Coast and home to the Merchants' Guild, a group of influential figures govern the region and often fund gladiator matches in the city's infamous Shadow Arena.

**Hathorn Hold** – A military fortress built in the First Era and the primary base of House Moore during the Gurdinfield Civil

War.

**Ithmeera Cadar** – The eldest child and only daughter of the late emperor, Nardos Cadar, Ithmeera is the Empress of the Azgadaran Empire. She began participating in meetings with the empire's royal council when she was only fourteen, and quickly impressed her father's advisers with her quick thinking, calm demeanor, and confidence in handling any diplomatic issue thrown at her. Was married to the late Philip of Sadford, she has one son: Marco.

**Jacob of the Southlands** – The son of traders, Jacob was rescued by Alexander Telman and the Guardians during the Gurdinfield Civil War when bandits ambushed his family's caravan. A skilled swordsman and experienced leader, he is married to Queen Lydia Taylor and commands Gurdinfield's army.

**Karrea** – A fishing town located on the border of the Rhyad River in Gurdinfield. Destroyed by House Moore's army during the Gurdinfield Civil War.

**Kye of Azgadar** – The son of the Azgadaran Legion's primary blacksmith. Became aware of his magical abilities when he was seventeen when he accidentally set his family's home on fire, killing them all. Wanted by the Legion for several months, he was pardoned by Ithmeera Cadar the following year. Played a critical role in the battle during Azgadar's invasion of the City of Towers and later joined Andrea's expedition to Rhyad. Is close friends with Andrea and Elisa.

**Lydia Diana Taylor** – Going by "Diana" when among friends, Lydia is the Queen of Gurdinfield. The youngest child of Caleb and Helen Taylor, she was rescued by Alexander Telman during the assassination of House Taylor in 202 2nd Era and raised by him and the militia Guardians of the Gurdinfield Civil War. Married to Jacob of the Southlands.

**Marco Cadar** – The only son of Ithmeera Cadar and Philip of Sadford. Marco is the heir to the Azgadaran Empire.

**Merchants' Guild** – The governing body of Gurith and led by the Grandmaster, the Merchants' Guild is an exclusive group of tradesmen, craftsmen, and other influential figures whose day-to-day dealings have a significant impact on the economy of the city.

**Meredith of Darst** – Born to a noble family in the city of Darst, Meredith was sent to the Enchanters' Academy in the City of Towers as soon as she developed magical abilities. She quickly rose to the top of her class but was forced to leave the academy when the city closed it down due to the magic shortage. Married to Richard. Mentor to Andrea.

**Nardos Cadar** – Late and previous emperor of the Azgadaran Empire. Father of Ithmeera and Erik Cadar. Brother of Alden Cadar.

**New Legion** – A fanatical group who believe that enchanters will bring ruin to the Azgadaran Empire. They have been known to openly assault enchanters and murder them. Responsible for the coup that deposed Ithmeera Cadar in 224 2nd Era.

**Northland Keep** – Located in the Northlands of Gurdinfield. The stronghold of House Harrington, one of the two warring houses during the Gurdinfield Civil War.

**Onede** – A small fishing village located on the west coast of Damea.

**Petra of Azgadar** – Originally from a village in the northern reaches of the Azgadaran Empire, Petra spent most of her life in Azgadar where she eventually became a skilled Legionnaire and was made Marco Cadar's personal royal guard. She served as Ithmeera Cadar's lady-in-waiting as well for several years before revealing herself to be the leader of the New Legion. She currently rules as steward of the empire after deposing Ithmeera in a violent coup in 224 2nd Era.

**Philip of Sadford** – A merchant, Elisa's older brother, and the emperor consort of the Azgadaran Empire. Philip was married to Ithmeera Cadar and is the father of Marco. He was killed by bandits while on a business expedition.

**Rhyad** – The northernmost region of Damea as well as the least populous, Rhyad is a cold and mostly mountainous place. Rarely traveled due to its extreme weather conditions and treacherous terrain, Rhyad is not under the banner of any Damean nation.

**Richard** – Originally from Tarrasha, Richard arrived in Damea via a portal created by a machine he built. He is Cassie's father, an enchanter, and is responsible for building the device in Rhyad that caused the Starving. Was once romantically involved with Serena.

**Roe of the City of Towers** – A veteran Guardian and close friend of Victor, Jacob, Lydia, and Cassie.

**Royal Enchanters of Azgadar** – A small group of enchanters dedicated to researching and understanding magic. The infrastructure of the Azgadaran Empire's farms and cities were designed and built by the royal enchanters.

**Sadford** – Located just south of Azgadar, Sadford is one of the empire's most populous towns and is home to a Legion fort as well as The Dusky Ale, a favored tavern and inn among Legionnaires.

**Serena** – A legendary enchanter who played a significant role in the Azgadaran Empire's expansion during the First Era, Serena was heir to the empire until she met Richard and became romantically involved with him. She was Cassie's mother and took Cassie to Tarrasha via a portal created by Richard's machine, stranding Richard in Damea. She died fifteen years after Cassie was born from an unknown illness.

**Tarrasha** – A continent located across the Sea of Gurith, settled by emigrating Dameans 400 years after Richard built the magic-siphoning device in Rhyad.

**Taryn of Azgadar** – A guardswoman and recruiter for the Azgadaran Legion.

**The Cataclysm** – A catastrophic event that occurred in 224 2nd Era when Richard bound his daughter, Cassie, to an enchanted necklace and forced her to absorb nearly all of Damea's magic. This resulted in a severance of the connection between enchanters and the land's magical energy.

**The Restoration** – The redistribution of magic in Damea after a machine in Rhyad which had been slowly siphoning the land's energy for the last 200 years was destroyed in 223 2nd Era. The Restoration also caused an uptick in the number of potential enchanters across Damea.

**The Starving** – A decline and destabilization in magic in Damea at the end of the First Era, marked by the deterioration and subsequent failure of farms and infrastructure as well as the rise in illness among enchanters who were exposed to unstable magic or overdrew on the land's energy. Lasted until 200 2nd

Era and resulted in nations placing heavy restrictions on magic usage.

**Victor of Fimen's Hope** – A veteran Guardian and close friend of Roe, Jacob, Lydia, and Cassie.

**Western Hills** – A fertile region west of the Azgadaran Empire, populated mostly by farmers who live in the collection of villages dotting the valleys. The Western Hills boasts longer, hot and dry summers and shorter, wet winters.

# To Readers

Thank you for reading Surge! While every effort has been made to edit and find all the typos in the book, it is entirely possible some were missed. If you have found an error and would like to report it, please email it to contact@enchantersnovels.com.

If you enjoyed this book, please consider posting a review on Amazon, Goodreads, Tumblr, Facebook, Bella Books, Kobo, or your own blog if you have one. I often host giveaways and updates about new and upcoming works so be sure to sign up for the newsletter on my website (kfbradshaw.com) where you can also subscribe to my blog.

- K. F. Bradshaw

# About K.F. Bradshaw

K. F. Bradshaw is the author of the Enchanters Trilogy. She loves fantasy, science fiction, and writing epic stories about women who save the world. Growing up, she was often frustrated that there were not enough of these stories that starred realistic female characters, and even less that depicted LGBTQ representation as normalized. While she agrees that "coming out stories" are hugely important, she believes it is just as important to have queer characters in stories where their motivations, desires, and plot arcs have absolutely nothing to do with their orientation or identity.

She lives in California with her wife, who is a lot better at video games than she is, and she would love it if you stopped by her website (kfbradshaw.com) and said hello.

www.ingramcontent.com/pod-product-compliance
Lightning Source LLC
Chambersburg PA
CBHW032159110726
47902CB00003B/766